Tremarnock

Emma Burstall is the author of *Gym and Slimline*, *Never Close Your Eyes* and *The Darling Girls*. After reading English at Cambridge University she was a newspaper journalist in Devon and Cornwall. She now lives in South West London with her husband and three children. *Tremarnock*, the first novel in her new series set in a delightful Cornish village, was published in 2015 and became a top-10 bestseller.

Also by Emma Burstall

Gym and Slimline

Never Close Your Eyes

The Darling Girls

Coming Soon

The Cornish Guest House
(Tremarnock, Book 2)

Emma Burstall

Tremarnock

HEAD of ZEUS

First published in the UK in 2015 by Head of Zeus Ltd.

This paperback edition first published in the UK in 2016
by Head of Zeus Ltd.

This is a work of fiction. All characters, organizations, and events
portrayed in this novel are either products of the author's imagination
or are used fictitiously.

9 7 5 3 1 2 4 6 8

A catalogue record for this book is available
from the British Library.

Paperback ISBN: 9781781857892
Ebook ISBN: 9781781857878

Typesetting: Adrian McLaughlin
Map: Amber Anderson

Printed in the UK by Clay's Ltd, St Ives Plc

Head of Zeus Ltd
Clerkenwell House
45-47 Clerkenwell Green
London, EC1R 0HT

WWW.HEADOFZEUS.COM

For my sister, Sarah Arikian, with love

There are those who have money
and those who are rich

– Coco Chanel

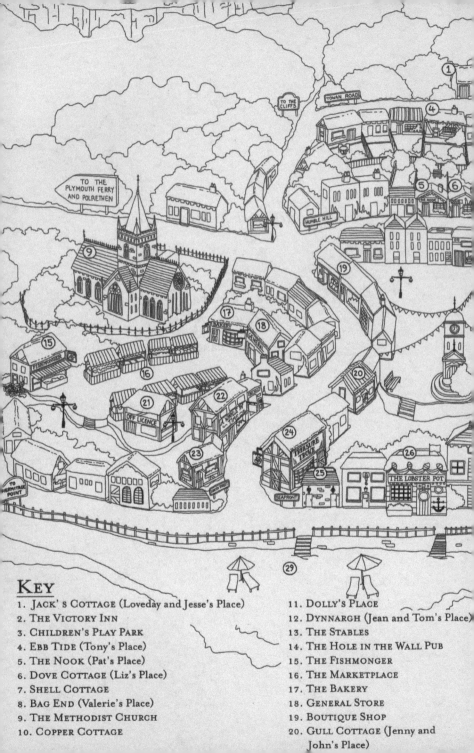

KEY

1. JACK'S COTTAGE (Loveday and Jesse's Place)
2. THE VICTORY INN
3. CHILDREN'S PLAY PARK
4. EBB TIDE (Tony's Place)
5. THE NOOK (Pat's Place)
6. DOVE COTTAGE (Liz's Place)
7. SHELL COTTAGE
8. BAG END (Valerie's Place)
9. THE METHODIST CHURCH
10. COPPER COTTAGE

11. DOLLY'S PLACE
12. DYNNARGH (Jean and Tom's Place)
13. THE STABLES
14. THE HOLE IN THE WALL PUB
15. THE FISHMONGER
16. THE MARKETPLACE
17. THE BAKERY
18. GENERAL STORE
19. BOUTIQUE SHOP
20. GULL COTTAGE (Jenny and John's Place)

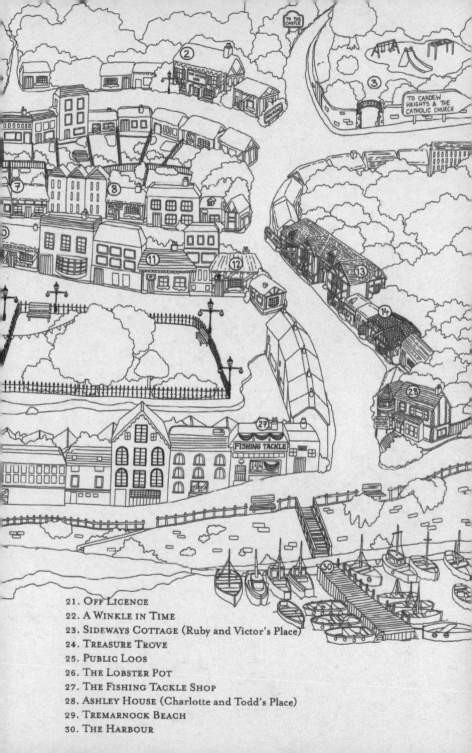

Prologue

'Now it's time to play lotto,' boomed an excited male voice, over a background of crashing music and psychedelic colours: red, purple, black, white and blue. 'Good luck, everyone. And tonight's jackpot is estimated at £2.5 million. Let's release those weekend balls...'

Comfortably settled in her favourite armchair, she nibbled on a biscuit as she watched a young, smiley woman, in a lurid pink dress and red lipstick, press the big square button that made the giant machine flash and whizz.

'Here we go then, here's the first one,' announced the disembodied man as a bright green ball slid down the transparent chute to a volley of clanging, discordant notes. 'And it's number eight!'

She brushed some crumbs off her chest, before a pink ball rolled out to join its neighbour and the male voice piped up again: 'There's the next one, that's number thirty-seven. And next,' he said, as a white ball rattled down, 'how about that one? It's number twenty-six.'

She glanced at the ticket beside her, on the arm of the chair. Three out of seven, she thought, mildly interested. What were the odds of winning the jackpot? About one in fourteen million? Well, someone had to get it.

'Fourth to be drawn is number thirty-two,' chuntered the man, 'drawn last Saturday night and Wednesday last week, been busy.'

Her eyes swivelled back to the ticket and she caught her breath, but there was scarcely time to think before the next ball, royal blue this time, zoomed across the screen in front of her. 'And the fifth one's number seventeen!'

Not quite believing, she picked the ticket up and looked at it more closely. The numbers matched, for sure. This had never happened before but she shouldn't get carried away.

'Sixth one, this for the jackpot, brilliant. Number eleven,' the man said as another green ball trundled out to join the others.

She stared at what she could see was printed and her heart started banging so loudly in her chest that she thought they'd be able to hear it in the street outside. Shuffling forwards, so that she was on the very edge of her seat, she turned the volume up even louder.

'And tonight's bonus is...' the music rose to a manic crescendo, 'number twenty-nine!'

Her mouth dropped open and her head started to swim. Concentrate, she told herself; it would be just like her to make a silly mistake.

'So, Millionaire's Row tonight looks like this in ascending order,' said the man, sounding like a fairground announcer: 'Roll up, roll up for the most exciting ride on earth!'

Now, the ticket was trembling so much that she had to hold it in both hands, checking it against the white numbers as they popped up one by one on the TV in violent red circles: 'Eight, eleven, seventeen, twenty-six, thirty-two, thirty-seven, and the bonus tonight... twenty-nine.'

Did she waver for one moment? Looking back, she'd say that the answer was yes, but if she was honest she'd have to admit that it was only for a few seconds, not even a whole minute.

There was no fanfare, just a slightly muted 'Goodnight' from the glamorous and faintly bored-looking female TV presenter while a folksy band played the programme out. Was that it? She'd have expected a firework display at least, popping champagne corks and dancers in feathery hats and glittering outfits doing the can-can.

In different circumstances she might have jumped up to do the can-can herself, hugged someone or run out into the street screaming at the top of her voice. Instead, she just sat there for a moment, staring at the little pink ticket in front of her, wondering at its significance and waiting for her mind to catch up with the facts.

Weird that one small paper slip, she thought, forcing herself to take a few deep breaths, had the power to change someone's life for ever. She'd never have imagined in a trillion years that she'd meet a winner, let alone hold the winning ticket herself. Suddenly it felt like a red hot coal in her hands and she threw it down and watched it flutter to the floor, almost expecting to smell burning flesh and find that her fingers had been scorched. But no, they were healthy, pink and intact.

She closed her eyes, acutely aware of the ticket still at her feet, savouring what she realised would be her last few moments of normality. Soon, very soon, nothing would ever be the same again.

She'd have liked to talk to someone, to discuss what was happening, but as she knew already what she was going to do, there seemed to be no point in delaying. The TV was still blaring but she didn't notice; she was deaf to anything but the blood swooshing in her ears and the thumping drum-roll in her chest.

Slowly, she rose to pick up the ticket and the phone and dial the relevant number. They answered almost straight away, but whether this was her hotline to heaven or hell, she wasn't sure.

She opened her mouth but at first she couldn't speak, until finally the words came spurting out like scalding water from a kettle: 'I can't quite believe it, I know it sounds mad, but I think I've won the National Lottery!'

Chapter One

LIZ GAZED AT her sleeping daughter and thought that if she loved her one grain more, even just a tiny fraction, her heart might burst, exploding into a thousand pieces.

Rosie was lying on her side, her thick, silky fair hair streaming out behind her like a horse's tail. The duvet was pulled up under her chin so that only her perfect little head was exposed, and Liz noticed the light sprinkling of tan freckles on her daughter's nose, the damp, slightly parted lips, the faint snuffling noises, like a small animal, that accompanied her steady breathing.

Liz sighed, leaning over the bed and running the back of a cool hand against a soft cheek.

'Rosie?' she whispered.

No reply, not even a flicker.

'Rosie darling?'

She spoke louder this time. Rosie's lips moved and a stitch appeared on her pale forehead between the eyes. Liz wanted to smooth it away with her thumb and tiptoe out, closing the door gently behind her. But she mustn't.

'Time to get up,' she said, firmer now and steeling herself for the inevitable protests. There was no point drawing the curtains because it was still dark outside, but she did so anyway, hoping that the harsh sound of metal ring scraping on metal rail would perform the unpleasant task for her.

'Hurry up, sweetie,' she said, sounding far brighter than she felt. 'You need to get dressed.'

Rosie groaned, a hollow sound that seemed to come from deep in an underground cave.

'It can't be morning already. I only just went to sleep.'

At least she was conscious now.

'I'm afraid it is.'

Liz snapped on the desk lamp beside her daughter's bed, wincing in the brutal light that flooded the room.

'Don't!' Rosie grumbled, but her mother threw back the cover of the pink flowery duvet, avoiding glancing at the thin, shivering body against the white sheet. Every instinct told her to cover the little girl up again, to swaddle her like a baby, tucking in the edges tight.

'I'll get breakfast. We have to leave in twenty minutes.'

Across the narrow corridor, Liz could hear Rosie muttering to herself as she reached for her school uniform, which she'd carefully laid across the chair by her desk the night before.

The walls of the old fisherman's cottage were thick and Liz was unable to distinguish the words, but she could guess: 'I don't need to go to Jean's. I'm old enough to look after myself.'

She took a packet of cereal from the pine cupboard to the right of the sink and plonked it on the white melamine table in the corner of the kitchen, along with a bowl and spoon. She knew that Rosie wouldn't be hungry; who was at 5.30 a.m.? And besides, she always had a slice or two of toast at Jean's. But Liz didn't want her daughter to leave the house on an empty stomach; it didn't seem right.

The kettle had already boiled so she poured herself a mug of tea, noticing a chip in the blue and white cup that she could swear hadn't been there yesterday. She swapped hands so that the chip was on the other side and took a sip.

The warm liquid trickled pleasantly down her throat and for a second she closed her eyes, trying to think if there was anything that she'd forgotten.

What day was it? Thursday. Rosie had gym on Thursdays and Liz had already put her sports bag by the door, along with the rucksack containing her reading book, homework and packed lunch. She wouldn't remind her daughter about the PE lesson until the very last minute.

'Be quick,' she called, putting her mug down on the work surface, pouring a few spoonfuls of cereal into the bowl, fetching milk from the fridge and glancing at the round clock on the wall: 5.40 already. Her stomach clenched. 'I'm going to be late!'

'Don't worry, Mum, you won't be.'

Rosie appeared in the doorway, rubbing the sleep from her eyes. She was wearing white trainers that looked too big for her feet, grey trousers, a white blouse beneath her navy V-necked sweater, and a partially done up blue and grey striped tie. Liz felt a rush of gratitude; the tie was always an issue.

'It's so fiddly,' Rosie said apologetically, noticing her mother's look.

'I know,' Liz said, finishing the task and putting the tie straight. 'You've done a beautiful job. I'm just being fussy.'

Rosie smiled her funny, gappy smile and asked hopefully, 'Do I have to have breakfast?'

'You do.'

Liz pulled out the white plastic chair that wobbled, clocking the back of Rosie's head for the first time as she sat down. Her hair knotted easily and there was a tangle that she'd missed. 'I'll do your plaits.'

She took Rosie's good hand as they made their way down the dark, narrow street, their coats zipped up tight in the early morning air. It was April now and it was supposed to be a fine spring day later, warm and sunny, but you couldn't tell at this hour.

Rosie was doing her best to hurry but it wasn't easy.

'I wish I didn't have gym today,' she said in a small voice.

'I know.'

'It wouldn't be so bad if Kyle wasn't there.'

'Let's hope he's gone down with a really nasty bug,' Liz said, trying to make light of it.

'Mu-um!' said Rosie in her schoolmistressy voice. 'You mustn't say that.'

Liz smiled. 'Just a bit of a cold, then, enough to keep him off lessons. Is that allowed?'

Rosie laughed. 'OK, just a sniffle.'

Jean's home was at the bottom of Humble Hill before you turned right towards the harbour. Liz glanced at the names as she passed: Copper Cottage, Shell Cottage, Bag End, Dolly's Place. They all had identities, like real people.

Dynnargh was one of the very few modern buildings and Liz always thought it looked as if it had been tacked on to the row of terraced cottages like a broken chord.

Built of yellowish brick, it seemed quite out of place beside its pretty cream and white, colour-washed neighbours, but it was immaculately maintained, with white lace curtains in the windows, a neat fence round the edge and a front garden bursting with crocuses and daffodils lovingly planted by Jean's husband, Tom. For Rosie, who had been going there since she was three years old, it was a second home.

She was always arguing that, having just turned ten, she didn't need a childminder any more; she was old enough to get herself to school and she'd rather have a lie-in. Even so, Liz noticed gratefully that she half limped, half skipped up the front path to the door and rang the bell, which played the tune of 'Oranges and Lemons'. She loved Jean really; she was like an auntie, or another mum.

A round, smiley woman with sleep-drugged eyes, wearing a large yellow and blue floral quilted dressing gown answered.

'Mornin', chicken! Come on in!'

It was always the same greeting; it would be wrong to change it.

Rosie hopped across the threshold into Jean's arms, disappearing in the folds of her floor-length robe.

Liz checked her watch; she was cutting it fine as usual.

'See you at three twenty,' she said to Rosie, who quickly pulled away from the older woman and went up on tiptoe to plant a kiss on her mother's cheek.

'I forgot to tell you, Granddad phoned last night,' she said, stopping Liz in her tracks.

'Granddad?' She couldn't hide her surprise.

'He's going on holiday to Spain – with Tonya.'

Liz pulled a face; she couldn't help it.

'They're sailing from Plymouth. He says he wants to come and see us first.'

Liz raised her eyebrows. 'Great.'

'Come on in, miss,' Jean said pleasantly, 'or you'll catch your death.'

Liz called goodbye over her shoulder and Rosie shouted 'Bye' back.

A holiday, Liz thought, as she scooted back up the hill towards her waiting car. How nice. With any luck they'd get a postcard.

Liz loved living in Tremarnock. It sounded so Cornish and welcoming, and she felt that the village had, indeed, welcomed her with open arms when she moved here with Rosie seven years ago.

She knew that they must have appeared a forlorn pair, arriving in their battered Ford Focus with little more than a few suitcases and a dusty pot plant or two to their name. The locals would have spotted Rosie with her funny walk and tricky hand and no doubt registered Liz's pale, drawn face, worn out from endless sleepless nights and the pain of her recent breakup with Greg.

But almost as soon as she'd closed the door of Dove Cottage and entered their tiny ground-floor flat, Esme, who lived upstairs, had popped down to introduce herself, then Pat from next door arrived with a bunch of freesias 'to cheer the place up'.

Next it was the turn of Barbara, a widow who ran The Lobster Pot, one of three pubs in the village. The others were The Victory Inn and The Hole in the Wall, so named because there was once a spy hole that enabled smugglers to keep watch for customs men.

Over a cup of tea and a Danish pastry, Barbara had filled Liz in on all the information that she could divulge in one go, including the fact that an excellent childminder, Jean, lived just up the road and happened to have space.

'You'd better see her quickly, mind,' Barbara had warned, writing Jean's address and phone number on a piece of paper in big flowery letters. 'She's that good she fills up fast.'

The following morning, Liz pushed Rosie in her worn-out stroller round the village for a breath of fresh air. They had just turned off the sea front when the little girl spotted a gift shop, Treasure Trove, with enticing display stands of post-cards and brightly coloured spinning windmills spilling on to the pavement, and insisted on going inside.

Rick Kane, the owner, sported an impressive grey beard and sideburns. He sold models of lighthouses and dolphins, clotted cream fudge and Cornish fairing biscuits and cheap toys for kids that provided enormous pleasure for all of about fifteen minutes before being discarded.

Rosie and Liz were his only customers and he soon launched into a surprisingly detailed account of his background and romantic history so that by the end, Liz felt like an old friend.

'The wife went off with a fella from Launceston, see,' Rick explained, while Rosie fiddled with a rail of small wooden hanging signs displaying jaunty messages like: 'A balanced diet is a pasty in each hand!' Liz kept watch out of the corner of an eye.

'She claimed I was too old and boring for her,' Rick went on, shrugging, before explaining that he'd recently joined a dating agency and was enjoying a good deal of success.

'I only go out with ladies my own age or older, mind,' he added. 'Learned my lesson last time.'

'Good decision,' Liz replied, breathing an inward sigh of relief. He was charming, certainly, but she wasn't looking for a boyfriend and besides, those sideburns were awfully thick and bristly.

When it was time to go, Rick popped a few pieces of fudge in a white paper bag and handed them to Rosie.

'On the house,' he insisted, when Liz tried to pay. 'You'll settle in real fast here, it's that friendly.'

Word of their arrival must have travelled quickly because as they left the shop, Ruby Dodd appeared from her cottage almost opposite and introduced herself.

A small, neat woman of sixty-odd, with short, silver-grey hair, she shook Liz's hand and smiled warmly at Rosie.

'I grew up here, moved when I got married, then we came back when Victor, my husband, retired,' she explained. 'Couldn't keep away! We're only a small community but you can feel the love.'

She pointed them in the direction of the market square and the bakery, general store and fishmonger, where Ryan Hales, wielding a hose, was sploshing water across the pavement before swooshing it down the drain.

Rosie wrinkled her nose at the fishy pong and Liz would have passed on, but there was no getting away.

'You new here?' the young man asked, wiping his hands on a bloodstained white overall. He was tall and strapping, with shaggy dark hair and dense black eyebrows that almost met in the middle. When Liz explained that they'd just moved to Dove Cottage, he advised her to arrive early at the shop, which belonged to his older cousin. 'About half eight, when we open. You'll have the pick of the best then. Fresh from the sea.'

'I hate fish,' Rosie piped up, and Liz glared at her. 'Don't be rude!'

Ryan raised his thick brows and laughed. 'That's no good, coming to Tremarnock and not liking fish! We'll have to see if we can convert you.'

Although she'd lived all her life in London – Balham, to be precise – Liz soon ceased to feel like a foreigner and became accustomed to the comings and goings of the tourists, or 'emmets' and 'grockles' as the locals called them, during the holiday season, the tendency of certain neighbours to regard anywhere north of Exeter with suspicion, and the languid, rolling accents with their elongated r's and a's that reminded her of clotted cream. Although her own accent hadn't changed, Rosie had developed a slight Cornish burr like her school-mates, which Liz found enchanting.

She adored the fact that she and Rosie could step out of their front door and within minutes be at the harbour, sniffing the salt and seaweed air, watching the waves crash against granite rocks and harbour wall and the anchored boats bobbing and lurching on the churning water.

On fine days, people would be dragging dinghies and paddleboards down the beach, or getting kitted up in rubbery-smelling wetsuits, aqualungs, fins, masks and snorkels by their feet. There was always something going on.

Alternatively, they'd jump in their grumbling red banger, Eeyore, and soon they'd be gazing far out to sea from high on the rugged, windswept coastline, their only company a handful of seagulls circling way overhead.

She couldn't ever imagine going back to London now. Not in a million years. She thought it would suffocate her.

No, she told herself firmly, as she climbed in Eeyore and buckled up, they didn't need a holiday. They were lucky enough to live in a dream spot. It *would* be good to get away from the treadmill sometimes, though, and Rosie had never been to Scotland or Wales, never mind Spain...

The country lanes, bathed in cold grey light, were deserted at this time, and within twenty minutes she was drawing up at the ferry terminal, watching for the warning signals overhead to turn from red to green. There were only five or six cars lined up in front – early birds like her – and she was able to drive on almost straight away.

She wasn't inclined to leave Eeyore; she was grateful to savour a few moments' rest before the day began for real, opening her window just a sliver to listen to the rattle and steady chug-chug as the chains dragged the vessel from one side of the river to the other.

The ramp lowered noisily and two men in bright orange

fluorescent jackets swung the barriers open. Liz drove slowly up the slip road, past high concrete walls topped with barbed wire that surrounded the dockyard, before she reached the main artery leading towards Plymouth city centre.

Her heart always sank slightly as she sped past row upon row of shabby houses and shopfronts, down-at-heel garages and dingy flats. Everything seemed so crowded and grey after the colour and light of Tremarnock; it was hard to believe that two such different places could exist side by side across a narrow stretch of water, though, thankfully, the scenery improved as you got further in.

Soon she reached the tall, red-brick office block on the edge of the city and parked her car quickly in the staff car park before hurrying up the street to the newsagent. The roads were still quiet so she was glad to see the door wide open and friendly lights blazing in the window of Good Morning News. She wasn't the only one awake at this ungodly hour.

As she approached, a skinny lad of about thirteen left the shop with a red sack of newspapers slung over one shoulder and climbed, wobbling, onto a rather large bicycle propped against the wall.

'Mind how you go,' Liz said, watching him try to gain his balance. 'You've got quite a load there.'

The boy, embarrassed, ducked his head and mumbled 'Bye' before pedalling off down the pavement.

Inside, Jim was stacking cans of drink into the giant, glass-fronted refrigerator while Iris was in her usual spot by the till, leafing through a celebrity magazine.

She looked up when she spotted Liz and smiled: 'Morning love!'

Liz smiled back, noticing that her friend looked different. 'You've had your hair done!'

Iris patted the wavy, shoulder-length hair, of which she was inordinately proud. It was a deeper, richer red than of late, with no hint of grey.

'Saw my stylist yesterday,' she said mock-grandly in her gravelly London accent; she and Jim hailed from Croydon and had moved when the kids were small. 'She comes to the flat. She's called Nadia.'

'Lovely,' Liz replied. 'Very glam.'

'Don't encourage her,' Jim shouted from the back of the shop. 'She costs us a fortune in hairdressing bills already!'

Iris raised her carefully plucked eyebrows and Liz laughed. 'Well, you can't say the same about me. I haven't been to the hairdresser for years!'

'Good girl, that's the spirit!' Jim cried. 'Mine's a tenner at the barber's. Nothing wrong with a short back and sides.'

'You've hardly got any hair anyway,' Iris snapped, then, turning back to Liz: 'I can give you Nadia's number, if you like? She's very good and dead reasonable.'

Liz shook her head. 'I do mine myself. It doesn't need much, that's the beauty of this style.'

Iris looked doubtfully at her friend's perfectly straight, dark, shoulder-length hair pulled back in a ponytail and tied with a red and white spotty scarf. Liz suspected that her fringe might be wonky but the older woman didn't say anything; she was too polite.

'How's lovely Rosie?' she asked, changing the subject. She rarely saw the little girl because Liz usually avoided Plymouth at weekends, preferring to shop in Saltash or Liskeard, which were quieter, but she'd talked enough about her daughter down the years.

'It's gym this morning.'

Iris shuddered. 'Poor lamb. I sympathise.'

'What about you? Good week so far?'

Iris frowned. 'Same old, you know. Mum's knees are playing up and business isn't exactly booming.'

'Children well?' Liz asked hopefully. 'Spencer's getting bigger by the minute, I expect?'

Spencer was Iris's fourteen-month-old grandson. Her frown vanished and her big grey eyes sparkled.

'He's running round all over the place now. You can't turn your back for a second.'

Liz smiled. 'I haven't seen him lately.' He was often in the shop with his mum, Christie, supposedly helping out.

She checked her watch for the umpteenth time that morning. It was definitely time to go.

'Lucky dip?' said Iris, noticing, and walking over to the machine on the far side of the counter.

Liz usually bought her ticket on a Thursday, though sometimes it was another day, ready for Saturday's big draw.

'Always worth a try, eh?' Iris passed her the pink ticket and a ballpoint pen.

'Well, someone's got to win.' Liz quickly wrote her name and address on the back and stuffed the ticket in the purse that she'd fished from her black handbag.

'And your ciggies?'

Liz nodded guiltily. 'I'm giving up – tomorrow.'

'Oh, I wouldn't,' said Iris pleasantly, reaching for a packet of ten from the display behind the counter. 'If you ask me, there's altogether too much abstinence these days. We've got to die sometime; we may as well enjoy ourselves first.'

'Hear, hear,' said Liz, shoving the cigarettes in the pocket of her coat.

She raced up the road, almost bumping into Kasia, her supervisor, at the entrance to Dolphin House. A small wiry woman in her forties with dark skin and thin black hair pulled back in a severe bun, Kasia was fond of pointing out that she and her husband had arrived in the UK from Poland nine years ago with nothing but their passports, his tool kit and a bag of clothes to their names.

Now, he had a thriving electrical business while she was in charge of about twelve women of varying ages at Krystal Klear Office Cleaning Services and ran the company like a military operation.

'You don't get anywhere in this world without hard work,' she was wont to say grimly as she wielded the vacuum and mop, and she was always in a hurry to move on to the next job.

She had a thick accent that was only difficult to understand because her words came out so fast, like bullets from an automatic machine gun. Sometimes listening to her made Liz's head swim.

'Jo is sick,' she fired off. Rat-a-tat-tat. 'We have to work extra fast today.'

Liz's spirits fell. There were only three of them and it was hard when someone, usually Jo, didn't show. She did seem to suffer from an awful lot of ailments.

Kasia produced an enormous set of keys, unset the alarm, opened up and virtually pushed Liz through the glass door and into the main reception area.

'Go to top,' she commanded, as Liz dialled the kwikTracker freephone number and keyed in her pin. An automated voice told her that she was now logged in. 'You do six, five and one, I take two, three, four,' Kasia ordered.

Liz caught the empty lift to the sixth floor, hung her coat on a peg in the cleaning cupboard and buttoned a blue overall over her jeans, sweatshirt and trainers. Four piles of colour-coded cloths were folded neatly on one of the shelves, above two different-coloured mops.

She took a pile of the yellow cloths and a matching mop and placed them on her metal trolley, along with cream cleaner, bleach, furniture polish and yellow rubber gloves.

She always began with the kitchen because it was the worst room. The employees of BB Creative Agency might be whizzes at their jobs but they didn't believe in loading the dishwasher, it seemed, or wiping surfaces smeared with sugar, milk and the remains of takeaway meals. Or throwing out old food from the fridge or removing globs of tomato soup from inside the microwave.

Funny that, she mused, as she hurriedly collected mugs from desks and put them in the dishwasher. You'd think that professionals would have more self-respect.

There again, she thought, eyeing a bowl of glued corn-flakes that would have to be scrubbed off by hand, Greg was a professional of sorts and no one could have behaved more badly than he had. She couldn't understand it and had long since ceased to try.

Chapter Two

BY THE TIME she'd reached the downstairs reception area, which was painted a rather sickly shade of purple, most of the staff were already at their desks, but a few latecomers were still arriving with briefcases and backpacks, folded up bicycles, cycle helmets and polystyrene coffee cups.

There were four different companies within the building and while she vacuumed the carpet and disinfected the make-up-smeared phones at the front desk, Liz liked trying to work out who belonged where.

The graphic design people tended to go casual in jeans and colourful tops and, in the case of the women, short skirts and boots. The recruitment guys were more into chinos, crisp shirts and V-neck sweaters, while the accountants and chartered surveyors wore suits and ties or dark skirts and jackets.

Liz found it amusing to speculate on what would happen if one of the accountants or surveyors decided to break with convention and turn up in a graphic design-style jeans and T-shirt combo, or vice versa. Would the boss have a heart attack and the whole firm grind to a halt?

A few people said hello as they walked past, but to most she was invisible. She didn't mind, she was used to it. Besides, after four hours she was keen to finish the job, go home and put her feet up before collecting Rosie from school; she wasn't in the mood for a chat, though a friendly smile never went amiss.

When at last she'd emptied the final bin, put the rubbish sacks outside in the skip ready for collection and hung the cloths on the pole to dry, all she wanted was her armchair and a mug of tea.

'See you tomorrow,' she called to Kasia, who was standing by her car, knitting her jet-black eyebrows and examining her big red diary.

'Of course,' she said, as if it had been a question. She scarcely took her eye off the book; she was no doubt checking the next appointment, mentally going through what had to be done and working out how quickly she and the next set of girls could complete the task.

She wasn't a bad person, Liz thought as she drove away. She had high standards, certainly, but she didn't leave you to do all the work. She was a Trojan herself, strong as anything. What's more, she'd stick up for you if there was ever a complaint, not that it happened often; they were far too well trained.

She more than deserved her annual week's holiday in Tenerife and her semi-detached bungalow in the Pennycomequick area of Plymouth called 'Mala Polska' or 'Little Poland'. And her miniature poodles called Borys and Cezar whose up-to-date photographs, alongside a rather tatty old one of her husband, she kept in her wallet.

In fact, Liz had come to be almost fond of Kasia and her funny ways after working with her for so long. She did wish, though, that she'd loosen up just a fraction and stop being so *manic*.

*

20

Fortunately, there was a parking space for Eeyore right outside Dove Cottage and as Liz drew up, she could see Pat peering over her china ornament display out of the little front window of her home, The Nook, that looked straight onto the narrow pavement.

Liz gave a wave and Pat's white head bobbed out of view. There was scarcely time to reach in the back for her handbag and the pile of groceries before Pat's canary-yellow front door opened and the old woman herself was on the doorstep, leaning a hand against the wall for support because her legs weren't as good as they used to be.

'All right, my handsum?' she said in her thick Cornish accent and smiled, revealing a startling set of perfectly straight white false teeth.

Pat had lived in and around Tremarnock all her life and married a local fisherman, long since deceased. They'd had no children – 'they never came along' – but she'd grown up with younger brothers and sisters and adored little ones, especially Rosie.

'I've got your shopping,' Liz said, carrying the heavy plastic bag past Pat and into the tiny, neat kitchen at the back of the cottage. She'd stopped off at Lidl before catching the ferry. 'They didn't have the ham you like but I can nip out later before I go for Rosie.'

'What's that?'

Liz repeated herself, raising her voice several decibels. She tended to forget that Pat, a slight, stooped woman with short snowy curls, was rather deaf and wouldn't countenance hearing aids – 'I'd never get on with 'em' – so you had to shout instead.

Pat shuffled over to the sink and turned on the tap. 'No need,' she said, starting to fill up the white plastic kettle. 'I've plenty else to keep me going. Time for a cuppa?'

She turned to Liz, who was starting to unpack the groceries – milk, bread, tomatoes, cheese, eggs, chocolate biscuits, Battenberg cake – and cocked her head on one side.

'Gracious! You look worn out. Busy morning?'

Liz, who suddenly felt as if she had a pile of rocks on her back, nodded. 'Jo was off sick so it was just Kasia and me.'

She opened the door of the small white fridge under the worktop and put the milk, cheese and eggs inside.

Pat clicked her tongue. 'Whatever's the matter with that woman? They should sack her. It's not fair.'

Liz managed a laugh. 'She's not that bad.' She was still shouting. 'Besides, she's got four small children and a useless husband. It must be hard for her.'

Pat folded the now empty white plastic bag and put it neatly in a drawer with the others.

'Well, you've got Rosie – and *no* husband. She should have more consideration.'

She reached up to the top cupboard and produced two pink flowered mugs, which she plonked on the pine table that was just big enough for herself and one other.

'Talking of which, how's my little treasure today?'

Liz leaned on the wooden chair in front. She really was tired and her back was hurting; it was probably hauling those five-litre bottles of floor cleaner that had done it. There was usually a delivery on a Thursday and they had to lug them into the lift and out again at the other end.

'Fine. You're still OK to pop in later?'

Pat said that she was.

Fearing that she might keel over at any minute – her feet were complaining now, too – Liz decided that she'd better skip tea and go home. Her own house felt chilly and unwelcoming after Pat's warm kitchen, but she didn't care.

Pulling the curtains closed in the small, square-shaped front room that she and Rosie had painted in a jolly shade of primrose, she kicked off her shoes and flopped into the squashy blue velvet armchair that she'd picked up in a charity shop in Liskeard, dragged the blanket over her and closed her eyes.

She had a whole blissful two hours before it would be time to shower, get changed, prepare Rosie's tea and psych herself up for work this evening. She fell asleep instantly and even two screeching seagulls, that landed on the rooftop opposite and started a noisy squabble, didn't wake her.

She waited anxiously in the playground for Rosie, not bothering to join in with the chatter of the other mums grouped in huddles on the tarmac, some with toddlers hanging on to their jeans or sweatshirts, others leaning over pushchairs or prams.

Rosie was always one of the last out; it took her a while to gather her things and walk from her classroom at the back of the old Victorian school building through the noisy, crowded corridors to the exit on the right.

Liz could tell immediately what sort of a day it had been; when Rosie had had a tough time her shoulders drooped just that little bit more than usual, her walking was more hesitant and it took just a fraction longer for her face to light up in that gappy smile when she saw her mother.

Today, though, to Liz's relief, her daughter's shoulders were pulled back and her head held high.

'Guess what?' she said as she ran in her funny lopsided way across the playground. Fortunately, she didn't notice the boy of about five or six who was following behind mimicking her, but Liz did. She glared at him and he veered off in the direction of his mum, who slapped him round the back of the head and shouted something before resuming her conversation.

Liz focused on Rosie again, whose thick fair hair had largely escaped from its plaits and was dangling untidily round her face. She smoothed it down and tucked the longest strands behind her daughter's ears.

'What, sweetie?' she said, stooping down to kiss her cheek which was smeared with ink from a leaking pen. Rosie was always nibbling the ends while she thought about what to write.

She thrust her PE bag and rucksack into her mother's arms.

'We're going on a school trip – to London! We're going to see Big Ben and the Tower of London and go on a boat ride and that enormous wheel. We'll stay in a hotel and Mandy says she doesn't mind being in the same room as me. We can choose two friends. I'm going to put Mandy and Rachel.'

Liz felt her stomach clench. 'London?' she said, swallowing. 'We'll have to see about that.'

She took Rosie's good hand and the little girl half limped, half skipped beside her as they walked to the car.

'I can go, can't I?' she pleaded as she clambered in the back seat and buckled up. 'It's for five days and Mrs Springett says we'll see the place where Anne Boleyn had her head chopped off. Do you think there'll still be blood?' She made a shivering noise.

Liz smiled despite herself. 'Maybe. They say her ghost wanders round the battlements, clutching her head under an arm.'

She glanced in the mirror. Rosie's greeny-grey eyes were the size of plates.

'Her ghost? Really? I hope I don't see it. I'd be scared.'

School trips always filled Liz with dismay. Not because she thought they were too much for her daughter. Quite the opposite. Rosie adored going to new places and never seemed daunted by the extra walking involved.

'I'll manage,' she'd say happily when Liz quizzed her about the arrangements. 'If I get tired I'll just tell the teacher I need to sit down.'

No, the problem was that school trips cost money that they didn't have. It was enough of a struggle to save for a day somewhere, let alone four nights and five days away. While Rosie was getting changed, Liz took the opportunity to peek in her bag and take out the A4-sized letter that she knew would be in there.

She quickly scanned the two pages of information: Tower of London, London Eye, Natural History Museum, boat trip on the Thames, staying in a Best Western hotel in Victoria. Breakfast, a packed lunch and evening meal included.

She had to admit that it sounded marvellous and she'd love Rosie to visit the capital; she'd heard Liz talk about it often enough and wondered that she'd grown up in such a huge city miles from the sea. But it was nearly four hundred pounds for four nights away in early October. How on earth were they supposed to afford that?

Liz shoved the letter under a pile of others on the kitchen worktop and turned on the oven. She'd made a shepherd's pie for tea – Rosie's favourite – and hoped that would go some way towards consoling her daughter when she broke the news: Rosie wouldn't be going to London because it was too expensive. She'd have to stay at school, probably being taught in a class with the younger children, because all her friends and her teacher would be on the trip without her.

Liz rarely allowed herself the luxury of self-pity, but right now she wanted to climb into bed and sob her eyes out. She was mentally going through their incomings and outgoings as she chopped up carrots and shoved them in a saucepan: rent, water, gas, electricity, food, TV licence, broadband, Rosie's pay-as-you-go phone, Liz's own mobile, road tax and car insurance, petrol.

Strictly speaking, the broadband and Rosie's mobile weren't essential, but wi-fi was so useful for homework, and Liz wanted her daughter to have her own phone for emergencies.

Liz could shave a little off their grocery bills and ask Robert if she could do a few lunchtime shifts at the restaurant. Rosie was probably old enough to get the bus back from school and wait at home until her mother returned, though she didn't like the idea. What if Rosie slipped and fell or, worse, got pushed and teased by the other children? It didn't bear thinking about.

Anyway, Liz knew that Robert didn't normally need an extra waitress during the day and besides, could she manage three jobs at once? If she fell ill, who would look after her daughter?

The carrots had just started to boil by the time Rosie reappeared, dressed in her favourite fluffy pink sweater and black leggings.

'Can you lay the table?' Liz asked, and Rosie quickly fetched two knives and forks from the cutlery drawer.

'It's shepherd's pie.' Liz reached into a top cupboard and passed two glasses to her daughter who filled them with tap water.

Rosie didn't hear; she had other things on her mind.

'Did you see the letter?' Her cheeks were flushed and her eyes sparkled. 'The one about the school trip to London?'

Liz swallowed.

'I'll go and get it.' Rosie disappeared and Liz waited while she hurried to her bag by the front door. She could hear her rootling around, muttering about how she knew it was in there somewhere.

26

She couldn't put it off any longer; it wasn't fair.

'It's in here,' she called, pulling the letter out from under the pile.

Rosie reappeared looking confused. 'Why didn't you…?'

Liz was leaning against the worktop, the information sheet dangling at her side. The carrots were bubbling furiously and the room was filling with steam but she didn't bother to open a window.

Rosie clocked her mother's expression. 'What is it? What's the matter?'

Her gaze shifted from Liz's face to the letter at her side and back again. She was silent for a moment, processing, then in a small voice, 'We can't afford it, can we?'

Liz shook her head slowly. 'I'm sorry, darling. It's nearly four hundred pounds.'

A shadow passed across Rosie's delicate features before she walked over to her mother and wrapped her arms round her waist.

'Don't worry,' she said, squeezing tight. 'We can go to London another time.'

Liz squeezed her daughter back, burying her face in her thick, soft hair. 'I feel so bad…'

Rosie glanced up and pressed a forefinger to her mother's lips. 'Shh. It'll probably be really boring anyway. I'd rather go just you and me, we'll have more fun.'

Somehow this only seemed to make matters worse. Liz's eyes pricked but she gave herself a mental shake and summoned her best smile.

'I'll take you there one day,' she said, 'I promise. Now, let's tackle that pie before it gets cold.'

*

When Liz said goodbye, Rosie was curled up in front of the TV with the pink fleecy blanket over her knees, while Pat clattered about in the kitchen, making a cup of tea.

Liz was wearing her black skirt and white blouse, one of two outfits that she kept for the restaurant. The other was a plain black dress that she'd picked up in a market. There was just about time to wash and dry one ensemble, ready for the day after next.

She put on her little silver star earrings, tied her hair in a bun of sorts, and stuck in a big flower made of stripy orange felt with a sparkly button in the middle. Rosie had once bought a similar one for her at a church bazaar and they'd got into making them at home, along with other hair accessories. Liz kept a big box of fabric, elastic, wool, ribbons, beads and suchlike in the bottom of the wardrobe in her bedroom.

'Bed by eight thirty,' she told her daughter, whose eyes were glued to the screen.

No acknowledgement.

'Did you hear me?'

Rosie was watching one of her programmes, mesmerised by the teenagers in garish outfits talking in loud American voices.

'Are you listening?' Liz repeated.

Rosie managed to tear her eyes from the programme for a second and give a weary 'Yes'.

'And make sure you read for half an hour before lights out. And don't answer the door unless Pat says you can, or use the cooker on your own—'

'—or go outside. Or play with matches. I can have cereal but not toast. Brush my hair, clean my teeth, any problems and I'm to call you,' Rosie interrupted. 'Stop worrying, Mum, I'll be fine.'

It was always the same drill, of course, but Liz couldn't help herself.

'Right, I'm off,' she said, ignoring Rosie's protests as she pushed in front of the screen, took her daughter's face in her hands and planted a kiss on her forehead.

As soon as she moved away, Rosie's eyes slid back to her programme.

Liz checked in the narrow hallway that her keys were in her handbag, shouted goodbye to Pat and opened the front door, letting in a blast of chilly air.

'I hope it's not too busy and you get lots of tips,' Rosie called out over canned laughter. 'See you later, alligator!'

Liz smiled, more grateful than she could possibly say for the cheery farewell. If her daughter once made a fuss or begged her mother to stay, she knew that she'd spend all night worrying. In fact, she thought that it would probably kill her.

She zipped up her anorak and raised the collar to keep out the chill. If she hesitated for one second more she'd never leave. She took a deep breath and straightened her shoulders, her fingers circling the old brass door knob, ready to pull it shut.

'In a while, crocodile,' she shouted back.

Chapter Three

IT WAS A fine evening as she stepped out once more into the narrow street and headed right up the hill, trying hard to ignore that familiar feeling of guilt nibbling away at her insides. She hated having to leave Rosie to go to her waitressing job but that, and the cleaning, were the only work she'd managed to find when she first arrived in Tremarnock. And although in some ways she'd have preferred a nine-to-five, at least it meant that she could be at the school gates in the afternoon.

She didn't know how she'd manage without Pat, though. Jean the childminder didn't work evenings and besides, with her wages, Liz would have struggled to afford the extra fees.

When Rosie was small, she'd gone to Pat's every evening to watch TV and fall asleep on the sofa until Liz came home. Pat wouldn't take a penny – she said Liz was doing her a favour because she liked the company. Now that Rosie was bigger, the old woman spent the evenings at Dove Cottage instead, insisting that she might just as well sit there as in her own house.

At first Liz assumed that the arrangement was only temporary, but it soon became apparent that it worked for everyone. Pat didn't seem to mind the late nights – 'I've always been an owl, used to drive my husband mad' – though nine times out of ten she'd fall asleep in the chair after Rosie went to bed and Liz would have to wake her.

Rosie adored Pat and called her 'Nan', which seemed to please them both. Liz was eternally thankful.

Before long she took a sharp left down South Street, the winding road that passed two small, smart boutique shops selling beach bags, postcards and colourful women's dresses.

They were closed in the winter months, opening just in time for Easter. Liz had never ventured in, they were far too expensive, but she liked gazing at the mannequins and trying to imagine what wealthy tourists would be sporting round the village come the summer.

Jenny Lambert appeared from Gull Cottage with Sally the Jack Russell and started walking rapidly up the hill towards Liz, who couldn't avoid stopping. It was impossible to go anywhere in the village without bumping into someone who fancied a chat, so she tried to allow an extra five or ten minutes to get anywhere.

'Off to work?' Jenny asked, as Sally sniffed Liz's flat black pumps. Jenny, who was in her forties, came from Sussex originally and her husband, John, ran the fishing tackle shop on the seafront. 'We're coming in Saturday evening – family celebration. Will we see you?'

Liz nodded. 'It's going to be quite busy. We're starting to get booked up at weekends now.'

Jenny frowned. 'Do you ever have a day off?'

'Oh yes,' Liz replied cheerfully. 'Every Sunday – and Mondays in winter.'

'I should think you deserve it,' said Jenny. Sally was pulling at her lead, ready for the off.

She spotted the orange flower in Liz's hair and gave an amused smile. 'Very jolly. I like that big sunflower one you've got, too.'

'I can make one for you if you like?' Liz offered. 'They don't

31

take long and Rosie will help, she loves doing them. We've got them down to a fine art.'

But Jenny wouldn't hear of it. 'You've quite enough to do as it is.'

Liz had only managed a few more steps when Valerie Barrows came out of the small lane leading from the market square. Valerie, a middle-aged divorcee from Surrey originally, had moved to Tremarnock some ten years ago when her marriage broke up, and bought Bag End, a few doors down from Dove Cottage.

Rumour had it that she was unhappy here and had a boyfriend in Bath, which she preferred, and it was true that she seemed to be spending less and less time in the village.

She wasn't particularly warm or friendly but nor did anyone have any real objections to her. Her son Marcus, on the other hand, was a different kettle of fish. Aged about thirty, he'd never appeared to have a job and locals muttered darkly that he'd spent time in jail. He hung around with insalubrious-looking types who'd roll up to stay at weekends and throw litter about, play loud music till three in the morning and swagger around the village as if they owned the place.

There had been frequent complaints until Marcus, too, seemed to have got fed up and, much to everyone's relief, relocated somewhere else, or gone back inside – who knew? Anyway, the house was frequently closed and dark.

Liz hadn't seen Valerie for a while and would have stopped again, but the older woman merely nodded and gave a cool smile. She had bags of shopping in both hands and was clearly in a hurry to be home. Liz, relieved, smiled back and continued her journey.

The restaurant was on the ground floor of what was once a well-to-do sea captain's home almost at the end of the street.

Painted white, with smart bright blue wooden shutters across the windows, its name – A Winkle In Time – was emblazoned in swirly white letters on a matching blue board above the door and there was a two storey flat above.

She was in good time, despite the chat with Jenny, and the door was shut but not locked. Liz stepped inside, noticing that the rough wooden floor needed a sweep. She could hear someone – Robert, probably – clanking bottles in the backyard, and she poked her head in the kitchen to find Jesse, the washer-upper and jack of all trades, peeling potatoes in a black and white checked overall.

He looked up and frowned when she said hello. A handsome lad of eighteen with a mass of blond corkscrew curls, he thought he had better things to do with his time than prepare vegetables and clean dirty pots. Surfing and partying, to be precise. But he needed the cash, having left school with scarcely a GCSE or A-level to his name, much to his mum's dismay.

Liz hung her coat and bag in the cloakroom, washed her hands and checked the number of covers before she set about laying the tables, which were made of stripped, bare wood. Somehow Robert had managed to squeeze eight of varying sizes into the square, low room, which had a welcoming, rough-and-ready feel.

When the restaurant was packed in summer, it was tricky to manoeuvre round the tables but after a couple of unfortunate accidents with soup and suchlike early on, she'd become remarkably nimble.

Tonight, though, they were only half full so she left four tables in the middle bare and laid the ones round the edges; customers, she found, generally preferred sitting by the windows where there was a view of the street.

Loveday was late – no surprises there – so Robert came to give Liz a hand with the glasses, which needed a polish. He didn't speak so they worked in silence; she knew he preferred it like that.

A tall, thin man of indiscernible age with messy brown hair and bitten fingernails, he had a harassed air and a way of fidgeting with his hands and avoiding eye contact that used to put Liz on edge, making her think that he didn't like her.

Once she realised, though, that he didn't say much to anyone, not even his niece, Loveday, she'd ceased to worry, concluding that he was probably just shy. Besides, he seemed to work all hours and was so focused on his business that he didn't have much time for human interaction.

He never spoke of friends, or a girlfriend come to that, but Loveday had revealed that years ago his fiancée, the love of his life, had called off the wedding days before it was due to take place. Since then, Liz had made a special effort to be nice and refused to join in the inevitable anti-boss banter when the kitchen staff got going behind his back.

She also knew, from Loveday of course, that he was born and brought up in Penzance, and that he'd only given his niece the job because her mum was desperate to get her out from under her feet.

Loveday, a big girl of seventeen with long dyed black hair that was shaved up one side and flopped over her face on the other, and an eye-poppingly enormous bust that tended to spill out over her minuscule tops, had enjoyed a passionate fling with Jesse the previous summer when the kitchen had been on fire with suppressed lust.

Now, however, they never spoke and Liz was obliged to pass messages from one to the other when the need arose. She never had discovered why the romance ended, although

Loveday would occasionally mutter darkly about 'That love rat' and Jesse would whisper 'Slag' under his breath when she passed, until Liz warned him about his language.

The first two tables had already ordered their starters and main courses when Loveday finally rolled up, removing her pink coat noisily in front of customers and stalking into the cloakroom without so much as an apology.

Liz glanced at Robert, who was uncorking a bottle of red wine at the bar, and wondered what he was thinking. If he was annoyed, he didn't show it, but she did notice him run a hand several times through his untidy brown hair to push it off his face, only for it flop back again.

'Seems like a nice relaxed crowd tonight,' she whispered encouragingly as she walked past him to the kitchen. 'Shouldn't be any trouble.'

'Mmm,' he said, avoiding her gaze.

Just then, a group of noisy people came through the door. Spoke too soon, Liz thought, as she hovered for a moment to find out which table she was to take them to.

There was always fresh fish on the menu, they were famous for it. Alex, the head chef, went out at 4 a.m. two or three times a week with Meryn, the one bona fide fisherman left in Tremarnock, and they'd come back with lobsters and giant crabs big enough for two. What they couldn't catch themselves they'd buy from the fish markets of Looe and Plymouth: wild mussels, Dover sole, John Dory, king scallops, monkfish and turbot.

Tonight there was a garlicky bouillabaisse that received many compliments but was particularly messy. Liz found herself scurrying backwards and forwards with a damp cloth to wipe bits of shell and the heads and tails of stray prawns off the tables.

Loveday seemed subdued and Liz noticed her slope into the backyard a few times to make calls. The door was open to let out the steam and when she was bringing in some plates, she heard the girl shout, 'That's crap and you know it.'

There were sniggers from Alex and Josh, the sous-chef, while Jesse, up to his elbows in grease and soapy water, pretended that he hadn't heard.

Later, when she popped in for table two's desserts, she caught Loveday asking Robert if she could leave early because she was 'having a bad evening'.

He cleared his throat in that nervous way he had and rocked back and forth on his heels. 'It's not fair on everyone else, Loveday.'

Alex handed Liz two white plates with an upturned, cup-shaped melting chocolate pudding on each, a drizzle of cream and a handful of raspberries.

Loveday stuck out her bottom lip and Liz detected tears in the kohl-rimmed eyes. 'Please, Uncle Robert. I really need to sort this out.'

Robert's left eye twitched. A lock of hair was sticking up at right angles to his head.

'All right,' he sighed as Liz headed out again, a plate in each hand. 'Just this once.' His voice tailed off to nothing.

That girl runs rings around him, Liz thought, as she returned for more desserts. She never had mastered the art of balancing two plates on each arm. What Loveday really needed was a stiff talking-to but there was no way Robert would do it; he wouldn't say boo to a goose.

It was almost midnight by the time she arrived home. She roused Pat, who'd nodded off in front of the TV as usual, and saw her safely to her front door before tiptoeing in to Rosie.

She was fast asleep on her back, her hands beside her on the pillow, and Liz pulled the duvet up a little higher round her shoulders. Then she went around the small flat, turning off lights which she always left on when she was out so that Pat and Rosie wouldn't get spooked.

She knew that she should go straight to bed but she was almost beyond the point of exhaustion so she decided to make a cup of tea instead. While the kettle was boiling, she unlocked the door beside the bathroom, which opened on to a small concrete yard overlooked by the back of a terrace of white, higgledy-piggledy cottages.

There was just room for a washing line and two plastic garden chairs, but as it didn't get much sun the chairs were somewhat redundant. Taking a cigarette out of the new packet in her handbag and lighting it with a match, she closed her eyes and inhaled.

There was a light on in Tony Cutt's study, but the blinds were drawn and she guessed that he was working late. He was in PR and divided his time between London and here. Tony, in his forties, would occasionally have boyfriends to stay but for some reason they never lasted long. Perhaps he got on their nerves – he could be rather loud and boisterous – but he was kind to Liz and she liked him.

There was no way Tony or anyone else was watching, but still she felt guilty. She took a few puffs before stubbing the cigarette out half finished. She'd give up soon. She must. It was all her friend's fault that she'd started in the first place. Jackie, her best mate at secondary school, once stole a packet off her older brother and they went back to her house and smoked the lot in secret in the garden before her mum returned from work.

Liz smiled, remembering Jackie's cheeky grin and the way that she'd hold the cigarette up, puffing skywards, which she thought made her look more sophisticated. They'd both felt sick afterwards, of course, but it hadn't stopped them nicking more fags next time the brother's back was turned. Liz wondered where Jackie was now; she'd been such a laugh. They'd lost touch around the time that Liz had started her first job.

She walked over to the plastic bin in the corner and dropped the half-finished cigarette inside. It was easier to blame the other girl, particularly as she wasn't around to defend herself. They'd raided her parents' drinks cabinet once, too, and got a bit tipsy on Martini.

It was all so long ago; Liz couldn't imagine herself then, so giddy and reckless. She thought that she must have been a different person entirely.

She carried a mug of tea into the sitting room, shutting the door quietly behind. Settling back into the comfy blue velvet chair where Rosie had been earlier, she could almost feel the presence of her small, warm body in the folds of the material.

As she put her mug on the floor beside her, ready to turn on the TV, she noticed some crumpled sheets of white paper covered in black type and stapled at the top to keep them together. Her stomach lurched. Picking them up, she glanced at the words 'London Eye' and 'Best Western'.

Liz dropped the paper on the floor again and sat back in her chair, remembering that she'd scrunched up the information about the school trip and shoved it in the bin under the kitchen sink after telling Rosie that she couldn't go.

Liz pictured her daughter searching for the letter among the pile of other rubbish and smoothing out the wrinkles before padding back into the sitting room to read intently on her own. She'd have absorbed every detail, pausing every now and again to try to imagine each site in turn. She'd never stayed in a hotel before so she'd have difficulty visualising the rooms, but she'd no doubt have lots of ideas of what she and her friends would chat about after lights out.

Liz knew that Rosie wouldn't have shown the letter to Pat; she wouldn't want the old woman to feel sorry for her or, worse still, blame Liz for not letting her go. She'd have kept it to herself.

She leaned over to pick up her mug of tea and took a sip. One of Rosie's grey fluffy cat slippers was lying on its side in the corner of the room, the soles almost worn through. Liz had given them to her one Christmas and she loved them with a passion. They had silly little poking up ears and a cat's face with big green eyes, a pink nose and whiskers. Rosie longed for a kitten but Liz said pets needed special food, not to mention the vet's bills.

Rosie had settled for the slippers, which she sometimes cuddled and stroked rather than wore. She wasn't a greedy or demanding child. She never pestered for the latest fashions or begged to go to the cinema with the other girls.

It would be so hard when the coach left for London without her.

Something snapped. Liz rose and grabbed the phone and her address book from the shelf behind the TV, checked the number and punched it in.

It wasn't long before a familiar yet distant voice answered in a puzzled, sleep-soaked voice: 'Hello?' Liz felt sick and almost pressed the off button.

She had no idea what sort of place Greg lived in now, but she pictured him beside his sleeping wife or girlfriend or whatever, surrounded by bits of the stupid motorbikes that he was always pulling apart and putting back together.

In fact, it was unlikely that the girlfriend would put up with greasy motorbike parts in the bedroom. Only Liz had been foolish enough to do that. He used to leave oily footprints on the carpet, too, which had been a devil of a job to remove.

'Who's this?' the voice asked, sounding more together now.

Liz pulled herself back to the present. She'd better reply quick or he'd put the phone down. 'It's me.'

There was a pause when she thought that she heard a woman's voice complaining.

'Just a moment,' Greg whispered then, to Liz, 'One second, I need to get some clothes on.'

Time was, Liz reflected, when the mere thought of Greg without clothes would have sent shivers of excitement up and down her spine. Now, she just wished he'd hurry up and get on with it.

She was still standing by the TV and realised that she was shaking. In all the years since he'd left she'd never asked for anything. He was always broke and, more to the point, she didn't want anything from him anyway. She took a deep breath or two, reminding herself of the task in hand.

Courage, Liz. Stick to the point.

Finally, he came on the line again. 'Do you know what time it is?' He sounded wide awake now.

She swallowed, feeling young and stupid despite herself. The millstone round his neck, preventing him from scaling the great heights of... she didn't know what. Then she remembered her daughter.

'Rosie really wants to go on a school trip to London but it's four hundred pounds and I can't afford it,' she blurted. It was out now.

Greg was silent but she could imagine his expression – an ugly mixture of anger and self-pity. The only man whose exgirlfriend had ever made such an unreasonable demand.

He made a whistling sound like the air being squeezed from a Lilo.

'Money's very tight at the moment.' No surprises there. 'I lost my job back in January, you know?'

Why would she know that? There was scarcely any communication between them. Only the odd card for Rosie if he happened to remember her birthday and stuck it with a tenner in the post.

'I've just got a new job. It'll take a while to get back on my feet.' Excuse Number Three. She'd been counting. She kept schtum.

'I'd love to be able to help but—'

'She's never been on holiday,' Liz interrupted. 'Please – just this once?'

Greg sighed, the weight of the world on his shoulders.

She crossed her fingers.

'All right, I'll pay half. It won't be easy...'

Already Liz was going through the figures in her mind: fifty pound deposit by the end of next week, another one hundred and fifty due in the middle of June. His two hundred pounds would cover that. A further one hundred was payable by the end of July and the balance in September, the start of the school year. Would that give her enough time to save? Only if she could get extra work from Kasia, or Robert had some lunchtime shifts for her.

'How do you want it?' He sounded exasperated – she was bleeding him dry.

'A cheque's fine,' Liz replied, amazed at her boldness. 'As soon as possible.' She gave him the address because she was certain that he wouldn't be able to lay his hands on it straight away.

He couldn't wait to get off the phone and now that she'd

achieved half her aim, at least, she wasn't keen to hang about either.

It was only after they'd said their formal goodbyes that she realised he hadn't asked a single question about his daughter.

Chapter Four

LIZ LOVED SATURDAY mornings. It was sheer luxury to be able to lie in bed listening to the seagulls, the footsteps passing by her window, the odd voice. Allowing the natural light that seeped through the thin blue curtains gradually to bring her to her senses. She wiggled her fingers and toes and moved her legs across the cool sheet. Her body felt delicious, wickedly relaxed and heavy. She breathed in and out deeply, savouring the sense of well-being flooding through her.

She and Rosie had the whole day ahead – right up until five thirty. Heaven! They'd have breakfast in their pyjamas then decide what to do. It would depend on the weather, of course, but the options seemed infinite: an amble along the coast or just round the village if Rosie preferred; a picnic in the country park; tea and scones at Peggy's Parlour in nearby Polrethen. That was one of their treats. Or, if it was raining, they might stay in their nightclothes and play cards and watch a film snuggled up together in the old armchair which could still just about fit them both.

She opened her eyes, got up slowly and padded to the window. As she peered over the top of the blue and white checked café curtain, which was necessary because the room looked directly on to the pavement, she could see bright blue sky overhead. Better and better.

The clock by her bed told her that it was still only 8.10 and she was tempted to jump back in for a while, but then she spotted Nathan the young postman coming up the hill wheeling his bicycle.

Short and fair, with a snub nose and ruddy complexion, Liz had watched him turn from a skinny boy into a strapping youth whose upper body seemed oddly out of proportion with the rest of him. This was owing, no doubt, to the protein shakes and strenuous workouts that he put himself through each evening. He'd once told Liz that he had his own personal gym at home, complete with rowing machine and weight bench.

At first glance you'd think that he wasn't someone to mess with, but it was all show. He was a pussycat, really, who'd chat with anyone.

He stopped whistling outside her house, took something out of his bag and slipped it in her letter box, before glancing up to give Liz a cheery wave.

Her heart pitter-pattered and she ticked herself off; she mustn't get excited, it was probably a bill.

She opened her bedroom door and Rosie was already in the hallway in her white and yellow spotted pyjamas and cat slippers, brandishing a brown envelope.

'It's for me,' she said with a puzzled expression. 'What is it?'

Liz ruffled her daughter's thick fair hair and noticed there were dark red stains round her mouth. Blackcurrant juice. She could hear the TV on next door.

'Let's find out, shall we?'

They jumped into Liz's still warm bed and Rosie started to rip the envelope with eager fingers, her good hand doing the work while the tricky one held the envelope in place.

'Careful,' said Liz. 'Don't tear.'

Rosie tipped the envelope up and a cheque fluttered onto the duvet between them.

Liz watched intently as Rosie turned it over and read the familiar, small black writing.

At last she handed the cheque to her mother and looked at her with wide open eyes.

'I think it's from my dad,' she said uncertainly. 'It says two hundred pounds.'

Liz examined the cheque which was payable to herself and was, indeed, for that sum.

'What's it for?' Rosie asked, sitting up very straight. 'Why's he sent it?'

Liz paused a second, hardly daring to believe.

'It's for your school trip,' she replied hesitantly, rereading the figures, the date and the signature. There could be no mistake. He really had sent the money. Somehow or other she'd scrabble together the extra; there was time.

At last reality sank in and she broke into a grin.

'You're going to London!' she shouted, giving Rosie a hug. 'You're going to see the Tower and the London Eye and stay in a hotel and have a wonderful time!'

Rosie squeezed Liz so tight that she could scarcely breathe. Then she got up and started bouncing on the bed and Liz had to tell her to stop or she'd be sick and the springs would break.

'But why's Dad given it to us?' Rosie asked, when she finally settled down again and looked once more at the cheque. She'd spent all yesterday at school assuming that the trip was off.

Liz peeked inside the envelope to see if there was something else. No note. Nothing. So what? Somehow she'd managed to prick his conscience and he'd decided to be generous for once in his life. Well, she wasn't going to complain!

'Because he cares about you and wants you to have a nice time,' she replied, regretting it immediately. She'd always tried to be honest with her daughter, or as honest as possible. She wished that she could swallow the words back whole.

Rosie bit her lip and frowned. 'He doesn't care about me, you know he doesn't.'

Liz took the cheque from her daughter's hand and put it on the table out of sight.

'Who gives a monkey's?' she replied, tickling Rosie's ribs and making her laugh. 'He's come up with the goods!'

Rosie couldn't stop chattering about the trip while they ate breakfast and washed up. What would it be like? Would the queen really die if the ravens disappeared from the Tower? Was the food different in London?

Liz laughed. 'You're not going to Timbuktu!'

They agreed they'd shelve all other plans and drive into Plymouth to pay the cheque in straight away. Liz hated the city at weekends but didn't want to tempt fate and leave the job till Monday. Who knew? He might have spent the cash by then and the cheque would bounce, a thought too hideous to contemplate.

The day felt even more full of possibilities as they zoomed in rickety old Eeyore through the country lanes so narrow in places that the brambly hedges brushed the sides of the car. As they passed by patchwork fields, grazing cows, bed and breakfast signs, logs for sale, villages that consisted of nothing more than a few houses and a general store, they sang old Edwardian music hall songs at the tops of their voices that Liz's mother had taught her when she was a child: 'Daisy Daisy' and 'My Old Man', 'Where Did You Get That Hat?' and 'I Do Like To Be Beside the Seaside'.

They found a parking space in the multi-storey in the heart of the city and headed straight for the main bank, which was open on Saturdays. Liz let Rosie operate the paying in machine, then tucked the acknowledgement slip carefully in her purse. The cash wouldn't show in her account for a few days but there was still time before the deposit was due. It was all working out rather well.

Afterwards, they decided to stroll around the part-cobbled streets of the historic Barbican harbour area, pausing to gaze at the giant, peeling Elizabethan mural painted by a local artist, now faded and covered in wooden batons.

'He was a bit weird, wasn't he?' Rosie asked, squinting at the grotesque, strangely modern faces that seemed at odds with their white ruffs and old-fashioned Tudor hairstyles.

'He was,' Liz agreed. 'But he was a very good painter.'

They stopped at a little, old-fashioned confectionery shop and Rosie chose a small bag of toffees, which they ate sitting on a bench in front of the Mayflower steps where the Pilgrim Fathers had supposedly sailed from in 1620. They were jarringly sweet and Liz said they'd have to give their teeth a good brush when they got home.

It was bright and sunny and they enjoyed swivelling round to watch the bobbing boats on the marina behind them and people going in and out of shops and galleries. Two small children, a boy and his older sister, were chasing seagulls – and each other – on the path in front, their cheeks pink with exertion, eyes flashing with naughtiness and amusement. Round and round they went until the girl, puffing, came to a halt beside her young mother, who was chatting with a man – her husband? He cupped the girl's small chin in a big hand and looked at her. They couldn't hear what he said but you could tell that it was affectionate.

Rosie was still sucking on a toffee but Liz knew what she was thinking: she wanted to run in endless circles just for the sheer fun of having two good strong legs; she wanted a dad to cup her chin in his hand and call her things like 'princess' and 'little lady' and 'sugarpuff' and whatever other silly nicknames fathers had for their daughters.

Liz found her mind drifting back to when Rosie was born. Her waters had broken at thirty-one weeks and after two days they'd rushed her in for an emergency Caesarean. The baby, a tiny, fragile 3 lbs 13 oz, wasn't breathing and Liz thought that she'd lost her. But they managed to resuscitate her, only for her to pick up an infection.

She was in an incubator and for a rollercoaster two weeks her life hung in the balance. But she was a fighter and when, after six weeks, they were finally allowed to bring her home, Liz thought that she was the luckiest woman in the world.

How proud Greg had seemed when they handed him the small bundle with masses of thick black hair wrapped in a white blanket, ready to pop her in the car! It was as if all his reservations about the pregnancy were wiped away in a second. He was a father – and the baby even looked like him.

They took her back to the flat and everything seemed fine at first. True, he never showed much interest in Rosie after that, or either of them to be fair, but he seemed to like referring to 'my daughter'. 'My daughter's very alert,' he'd say proudly to friends who visited. And: 'You can tell she's bright the way her eyes follow you round the room.'

But as Rosie grew, Liz noticed how it was always her chubby right hand that reached for the rattle or ball, never her left. And when she began to walk, then try to run, she didn't look like the other kids in the toddler group. Her left foot insisted on going up on tiptoes and didn't seem as strong as the right, and she leaned over to one side in an odd, drunken fashion.

The other mums pretended that they hadn't noticed but Liz had. Greg insisted there was nothing wrong until it became so obvious that even his dozy brother commented and he had to agree to see a specialist. When Liz heard the diagnosis she thought she might faint, or be sick, and had to put her head between her knees. Greg, however, was impassive.

Rosie, it seemed, had cerebral palsy, hemiplegia, to be precise. The left side of her brain had been damaged, probably during the difficult birth or just after, and it was impossible to tell at this stage what sort of quality of life she'd have. Words like 'wheelchair' and 'epilepsy' and 'learning difficulties' were bandied about and for Liz, it was like a bereavement. She wept and shouted alone and hated other mothers for having healthy children and told herself that she couldn't cope.

But gradually she realised that nothing about Rosie had changed. All they had was a diagnosis, a label – and what did that really mean? She was still the same little girl with now fair hair, chubby wrists, greeny-grey eyes and a dimple in her cheek.

'She can't be disabled,' she said to Greg as she built a brick tower with Rosie on the carpet one evening. 'Look, she's clever as anything.' But Greg remained silent.

Liz thought it was the ankle brace that finally did it. They said that Rosie needed one on her left leg to stretch the Achilles tendon and bring her foot to a neutral position. Rosie hated the brace because it rubbed and gave her blisters and she'd do her best to pull it off. Sometimes, when she refused to walk with it and crawled instead, Greg would shout at her and make her cry.

Finally, he shouted once too often and Liz screamed back, surprising herself as much as him. She rarely raised her voice

49

but now she was furious, spitting venom. She hadn't even realised that she could make so much noise.

She expected Greg to yell back but when she'd finished at last, he gave her a shifty look.

'We can't go on like this,' he said. He seemed almost pleased – or was she imagining it? 'You can stay here until you find something else. I'll sleep at a friend's.'

Off he went on his motorbike with a large suitcase and she was so shocked that she didn't even think to ask which friend's he was going to.

'It's just you and me now, Rosie,' she found herself saying as she sat at the kitchen table, spooning yoghurt into the little girl's mouth and wiping away her own hot tears, all her fight gone.

'Mummy and Wosie,' the little girl replied gaily.

She was an early talker and, as it turned out, not nearly as badly affected as doctors had first suggested. Her symptoms were mild and she could do most everyday tasks, though they required a lot more effort and took longer.

Not long after they moved to Cornwall she'd had corrective orthopaedic surgery to lengthen the muscles and ligaments in her left foot and leg. She'd needed a good deal of physiotherapy but soon it went down to once a week, then once a month until they devised a programme of exercises that she could do at home.

Now, bar yearly check-ups, she led a pretty normal life, all things considered. She'd even been able to abandon the hated ankle brace and wear insoles instead. Greg should have waited, he should have had more faith...

Liz came back to the present when the small girl's brother yelled sharply as the dad buckled him into his buggy. She glanced at her daughter, who was swinging her legs back and forth on the wooden bench, still staring.

'I fancy a coffee,' Liz said briskly, keen to get away. 'Coming?'

They rose, leaving the family behind, and popped into a café to pick up a cappuccino and some orange juice, a rare treat, before nosing around some of the stores selling strange wood craft ornaments and funky jewellery, past pubs, expensive restaurants and the gin distillery and back towards the peeling painting.

Rosie wanted her fortune told by a palm reader but Liz shuddered. 'Best not. It's all a load of nonsense anyway.'

It occurred to her that Rosie might need new clothes for the trip; her jeans were too short though they still fitted round the waist. She was very thin, despite Liz's best efforts to feed her up, and she only had one decent sweatshirt; the other girls would have a choice, for sure.

Liz could feel her heart start to race and gave herself a shake. Greg was paying half. There was time to save for the other portion, plus a few garments and bit of spending money. Today of all days they should be happy.

'Do you want to walk a bit further or shall we go home and play games and watch a film?'

'Home,' Rosie said firmly. 'You need to rest before work.'

Sometimes, Liz thought as they headed back to the car, Rosie was like the mother and she the child, rather than vice versa. She didn't know if this was good or bad, it's just the way things were.

There was no space for Eeyore outside the cottage and they had to park up the hill on the corner of South Street, near the boutiques.

As Liz was opening the door she heard a loud 'Hello!' and turned to see Charlotte Pennyfeather and her husband, Todd, dressed in bright waterproof jackets and serious-looking brown leather walking boots.

The Pennyfeathers were weekenders who owned a big house overlooking the harbour, as well as two nearby cottages which they rented out. Liz always found Charlotte, in her late forties, quite extraordinarily efficient because as well as working part-time and running several homes, she'd raised four children virtually single-handed, it seemed, while Todd made his fortune in the City. For years she'd looked worn out. Now that the children were almost grown-up, however, she was more relaxed, and the couple often sauntered through the village hand in hand.

They told Liz that they'd been for a hike along the coast and were looking forward to hot showers.

'I love it so much here,' Charlotte sighed. 'If we were in London there'd be eight or ten of Todd's work colleagues coming to dinner and I'd be spending the entire day in the kitchen.'

They said their goodbyes, and Liz was just thinking that she had more than two whole glorious hours before it would be time to leave for work, when Robert came down the hill towards her, carrying a large brown cardboard box.

He was walking fast and seemed lost in his own thoughts so she wasn't sure if he'd even spot her and Rosie, but he gave a look of recognition so she smiled. To her surprise, he stopped and put the box down by his feet.

'Is this your daughter?' he asked. His eyes were darting this way and that and she noticed a nasty cold sore on his upper lip that hadn't been there yesterday.

Rosie, who wasn't so shy in her mother's company, took a step forwards and announced formally, 'I'm Rosanna Broome but everyone calls me Rosie.'

Robert seemed taken aback. Liz saw him glance Rosie up and down and notice her tricky arm, which was pulled up to her chest and held at an unnatural, flexed angle. Liz was always telling her off about it – the arm would only get stiffer if she didn't stretch it.

Feeling protective, she was about to make their excuses and leave. Rosie had enough to deal with; she didn't need to go bumping into strange adults who had no idea how to speak to her.

'I like your hairband!'

Liz blinked. Robert was pointing at the deep pink velvet band that Rosie had chosen this morning. It had a big flower in the centre, the same colour as the rest.

Rosie smiled her funny gappy smile. 'We're fond of our hair accessories, aren't we, Mum? We make them ourselves.'

She looked at Liz, whose hand instinctively went to the canary-yellow chiffon scarf that she'd tied around her pony-tail this morning. It had seemed the right option on such a sunny, happy day and it was still in place.

'We are,' she replied, trying not to focus on Robert because it made him uncomfortable. He cleared his throat loudly and shifted from one foot to another.

'I bought a thousand kitchen cloths for six quid from the discount store,' he said, nodding at the cardboard box which was sealed with sticky tape. Then, for no apparent reason, 'They're blue.'

'Handy,' Liz replied, because she couldn't think of anything else.

Rosie came to her rescue. 'It's a big box,' she said brightly. 'You could decorate it and put things in – like...' She frowned. 'Like cufflinks and ties and stuff.'

There was a pause then Robert laughed, a deep infectious

laugh that Liz didn't think she'd heard before. In fact, she wasn't sure that she'd heard him laugh at all.

'Good idea!' he said, examining the box, his head on one side, as a sculptor would a slab of virgin marble. 'I haven't got enough cupboards and drawers. I could do with some more storage.'

Rosie, pleased, offered to paint it and he said he'd like that very much.

'Delighted to make your acquaintance,' he said mock-grandly, shaking Rosie's good hand when they finally parted. To Liz, he merely nodded.

So, she thought, as she watched him head off briskly in the direction of his restaurant, the box in his arms, he's all right with kids. It's just adults that he can't deal with.

'He's nice,' said Rosie, as they walked hand in hand down the hill.

'Mm,' Liz replied, thinking that people could be very eccentric – some rather more so than others.

She was opening the front door of Dove Cottage when Esme, from upstairs, came down to enquire if she'd smelled gas.

The cottage, which had been built in 1790, was divided into two small flats and Esme had a separate entrance up some iron steps at the side. She was a potter in her sixties with a kiln and shared studio in the neighbouring village. She sometimes held exhibitions in the local gallery and Liz liked her work, though it was rather expensive.

She was another oddity, in Liz's book: a bit of a loner with a funny, old-fashioned way of talking; they weren't friends, but rubbed along perfectly well as neighbours. Esme tended to complain a lot; her latest gripe was the fresh graffiti in the public loos and the fact that someone had broken a plant container outside The Lobster Pot, which she took as evidence of a crime epidemic.

Esme, who was wearing her trademark navy cotton fisherman's smock over a droopy floor-length purple and black swirly cheesecloth skirt, came into the flat while Liz checked that her gas rings were turned off. They both agreed there was no odour and Esme said that she'd probably imagined it.

'I have an overdeveloped sense of smell,' she explained, scrunching up her thin pointed nose. Her long grey hair was tied up in a wispy bun. 'It's a curse, you know. Even the slightest whiff sets off my olfactory nerves.'

Liz didn't know what olfactory nerves were but could guess and she quickly opened the kitchen window to get rid of the pong of burned toast left over from this morning.

After lunch, she and Rosie played a few games of cards – blackjack was their favourite – then Rosie fished out her collection of coloured rubber bands that she balanced on her lap. She'd learned to make intricate bracelets and necklaces, looping the bands together one by one until they formed a chain which she'd then join end to end. Liz marvelled as the work of art gradually took shape, Rosie's good fingers doing the plaiting and weaving while her tricky hand held the lengthening bracelet in place.

They watched *Frozen* while she worked. They must have seen it five times already but she never seemed to get bored. Liz found her eyelids drooping as she leaned back against the armchair, wrapped in the pink blanket. Yellow sunlight was seeping through the window, warming her shoulders and the left side of her face, and she rested her head on the back of the seat, her hand on Rosie's knee.

She was woken with a start by the piercing ring of the phone on the shelf behind the TV.

'I'll get it,' Rosie said, scattering rubber bands everywhere as she jumped up. Liz started to keel over before righting herself. Her mouth was dry and for a moment she couldn't remember where she was.

She could tell from Rosie's formal response that it wasn't someone she knew well: 'Yes', 'No', 'Fine, thank you', and, eager to bring the conversation to a close: 'Would you like to speak to my mum?' She passed the phone across.

'Eliza?'

She knew immediately who it was; only her father called her Eliza. With her mother it had always been Liz or, more often, Lizzie.

He was on the mobile and the signal was poor so she had difficulty catching what he was saying, but understood that he and his wife, Tonya, were on their way to Plymouth tomorrow, from where they were planning to catch the overnight ferry to Santander.

'We'll drop by before we sail,' he said hesitantly. 'Around midday. Will you be in?'

It occurred to her that it would be rather odd if they were to drop by when she and Rosie weren't in, but she didn't say so. She gave him the address and instructions on how to find them.

'Knock on the door and I'll give you a permit. It's residents only round here. If you can't find a space outside keep on going up the hill. There's usually one at the top.'

After hanging up, she stood for a moment in stunned silence. In all the years that she and Rosie had lived here, her father hadn't visited once. In fact, the only times they'd seen him was when Tonya's now twenty-year-old daughter, Davina, had been taking part in a gymkhana somewhere in Devon, and Liz and Rosie had driven down to join them for the day.

She realised that she hadn't asked if they'd stay for lunch and decided she'd better get something in. She recalled that Tonya was a fussy eater but couldn't for the life of her think what it was that she disliked.

Rosie was plugged back into *Frozen*, her nimble right hand working again at the rubber bands.

'Can you remember what Tonya doesn't eat?' Liz asked, thinking that she'd have to be quick at the shops as it was nearly time to prepare supper and get ready for work. Rosie had a remarkable memory for random facts.

'Cow's milk, shellfish, anything with wheat, cheap meat...' She was mentally ticking the items off. 'Oh, and things like ham and salami. She says they're bad for you.'

Liz sighed. 'Is there anything she does like? What on earth can I cook?'

Rosie brightened. 'Smoked salmon. She put loads of it on her plate when we went into that posh tent to have lunch.'

Smoked salmon, Liz thought uneasily, as she grabbed a pile of plastic bags and headed out again, leaving Rosie to watch the end of the film. It was so costly, and she wasn't sure they'd have it at the convenience store. If only they'd told her earlier then she'd have been able to go to the supermarket.

What did you have with smoked salmon? Alex would know, but she didn't have his number and needed to shop now. She knew about smoked salmon sandwiches but that was no good because of the wheat thing. Unless they stocked wheat-free bread, which was doubtful. Besides, they might want something more substantial than sandwiches before a long journey...

She could do smoked salmon and rice; she'd heard they went well together. And a big salad. Her dad wasn't a salad fan but Tonya watched her weight so she'd be pleased. And if she bought some cooking apples she could make an apple pie in the morning to have with cream or ice cream.

She'd have to tidy the house, of course, and she wished she'd had time to wash the curtains and cushion covers, but it was too late now. Truth told, she'd have liked to give the sitting room a lick of paint, too. After all, it was a special occasion and she didn't think Tonya would approve of faded walls.

As she walked swiftly back up the hill, she realised that she was nervous about seeing them both after so long. She and Rosie weren't used to visitors, especially not *family* visitors.

Was it normal to feel nervous about seeing your dad? Probably not. There again, he wasn't exactly your typical dad, if such a person even existed.

Only in storybooks, Liz decided, quickening her pace. Not real life. Best to dwell on the good bits rather than shine a torch into the dark corners. That way they could all relax – or try to, anyway.

Chapter Five

Rosie was in her bedroom putting on her pyjamas when Liz went to say goodbye. They were cute, old-fashioned pink and white checked ones that used to have mother-of-pearl buttons up the front. Barbara from The Lobster Pot had kindly passed them on when her granddaughter outgrew them as they were pure cotton and expensive, rather special.

Rosie didn't get on with buttons, though she was so good with other fiddly tasks when she wanted to be, and as they were always in a rush in the mornings, Liz had sewn poppers on instead. It was the same with her school shirts and trousers.

It was a tiresome job but she was used to it. She tried never to grumble, reminding herself that it was much harder for Rosie who'd rather have buttons anyway. What she wanted more than anything in the world was to be just like the other girls, right down to the socks and shoes. But that was never going to happen so they just had to get on with it.

Rosie seemed to be struggling with the top popper because the material kept buckling and Liz had to force herself not to help, knowing that she must learn to be independent; physiotherapists always said that the more she used her tricky hand, the more dextrous she'd become.

It was hard, though, to watch her frowning in concentration, the tip of her tongue poking out as she battled to push

59

one side of the stud into the other until it snapped shut. Liz would have done it in a second.

'Don't forget to watch the lottery at seven thirty,' she said, zipping up her navy anorak. 'And text me if we've won!'

Rosie took the pink ticket off her bedside table, tucked it in her breast pocket and patted it.

'Don't worry,' she said gravely. 'I will. I've got a funny feeling about tonight.'

Liz laughed. 'You have a funny feeling every week!'

Pat was already settled in the blue armchair, mug of tea in hand. She and Rosie looked forward to their Saturday nights together. They both loved *Britain's Got Talent* and *Come Dine with Me*, and Rosie would occasionally agree to tune in to one of what she called Pat's 'old granny programmes'. These were repeats of slow-moving detective shows, many of which they'd seen already, hopefully with at least two or three killings thrown in.

'I say,' said Pat, turning to face Liz, who was in the doorway, ready for the off. 'Seems Rick's got another new girlfriend. He was in the pub with her last night. All lovey-dovey they were.'

'That's nice,' said Liz. Normally she'd have relished news of Rick's latest conquest; he'd switched to Internet dating recently and was enjoying a flurry of new liaisons with mature ladies from all over the region. Tonight, though, she hadn't time. 'Sorry, got to dash.'

'Apparently, the last one gave him an ultimatum,' Pat went on, regardless. 'Said unless he married her she was on her way. Well, Rick told her he had no intention of marrying her, or anyone else for that matter, so she packed her bags.' She chuckled. 'He's having too much fun!'

It had gone very dark and was spitting with rain as Liz stepped out and when she was halfway up the hill she saw a flash of lightning, quickly followed by a low rumble of thunder, so she started to run. She was only wearing black plastic pumps and didn't fancy wet feet all evening.

She managed to get through the door just before the heavens opened – with the kind of thick, heavy, relentless rain that soaks you through in seconds. She hoped that it wouldn't deter customers; a busy restaurant meant job security and with Rosie's school trip looming, she needed that now more than ever.

Jesse was in the kitchen prepping the vegetables while Alex and Josh were hovering in the porch having a fag. They weren't allowed, so Robert mustn't be around. You could smell the smoke from a hundred paces.

'It's absolutely pouring,' Liz said, tying the white apron that she'd taken home to wash and iron round her middle and smoothing out the creases.

Jesse mumbled something that she couldn't catch. His skin was an unhealthy grey and there were dark circles under his eyes. Even his blond corkscrew curls seemed to have lost their bounce and lustre.

'You OK?' she asked sympathetically.

'Heavy night.'

'Ah,' said Liz. 'Party?'

This wasn't unusual. There was generally something going on after the restaurant closed.

Jesse transferred a pile of carrot batons from the chopping board onto a large roasting tray and started on the courgettes.

'It was the whisky that done it,' he sighed. 'If I hadn't of started on that I'd have been all right. We were doing the conga at four a.m.' He shook his head. 'Been chucking up all day.'

Liz winced. 'Early night tonight?'

'Nah. It's my mate's eighteenth.'

She sloped off to lay the tables, marvelling at his stamina. She could no more conga till 4 a.m. then go to a party that same evening than fly to the moon.

Loveday was late, of course, and the first customers were due in twenty minutes. Liz would need Robert to do the drinks and asked Alex when he'd be coming back. Alex was divorced and in his thirties, though it was hard to believe because he looked much younger. He'd trained at a top London restaurant and was a very good chef, though rather slow and methodical.

'He went up to the flat for something,' he said in reply to Liz's question, nodding ceilingwards. 'He's been ages.'

Liz frowned. 'I wonder what he's up to. I'd better go and check.'

The flat was owned by a wealthy couple from Truro. It was normally rented out but had been vacated recently by the previous tenants and the new ones weren't due to move in for several weeks.

Robert, who knew the landlords, had a key to the flat and kept an eye on it for them. They paid him something for it, which must have helped tide him over during the winter months when business was slow. He owned his own place in Polrethen, though he never spoke about it; as far as Liz knew, Loveday was the only member of staff who'd been there.

Although the flat had a separate entrance to the side of the restaurant, there was an interconnecting door, usually locked, which led from the far corner of A Winkle In Time straight into the hallway. It was through this that Liz gained access.

'Robert?' she called.

Hearing what she thought was a muffled reply, she padded on the thin beige carpet up the narrow stairs to the first floor and peeked in the small kitchen and the good-sized front room which overlooked the street. The flat was furnished but felt bare and empty with no one in and smelled of damp. There was no sign of Robert so she ascended the next, steeper flight to the converted attic.

She found Robert in one of the two bedrooms, standing beside an aluminium stepladder and staring intently at an open skylight in the roof through which heavy rain was splashing on to the carpet below. Outside it was dark and glowering.

'Filthy evening,' she said, assuming that he was about to shut the window.

He swivelled round to check who it was before resuming his watch. So still and focused was he that he resembled a priest waiting for a sign from Heaven.

She was puzzled. 'Can I help?'

'What?' Robert scratched his head and shifted from one foot to another. She hoped that he wasn't irritated but the dark wet stain on the carpet was getting bigger. Soon it might leak through to the room below.

'No. I'll do it. I can, you know.'

Stung by his tone she paused, watching him put one foot on the bottom of the ladder and grip the sides tightly as if he were about to climb. He seemed to stand there thinking about it for an age, like an old man just out of bed, willing his stiff, recalcitrant legs to do as they're told.

Finally, he took his foot off the step and swung round, his eyes fixed firmly on her black ballet pumps. His face was putty-coloured and she wondered if he were unwell.

'The thing is...' he said, nibbling the corner of a nail and still refusing to catch her gaze.

She couldn't imagine what was coming next.

'You see...' He cleared his throat again.

'Yes?' Had she done something wrong?

'The fact of the matter is...'

He was clearly in some distress; should she call for help?

'... I can't stand heights.'

Liz nearly burst out laughing but he looked so sheepish that she felt sorry for him and bit her cheek instead.

'Here,' she said, pushing past him and shinning up the ladder quickly before he could protest. 'Let me do it.'

The ceiling was high and she had to climb almost to the top to reach the window while Robert stood at the bottom, steadying the creaking ladder below.

Soon her fingers were gripping the metal handle that pulled the window down. She turned it and the mechanism slipped tightly into place. She was only a little wet herself.

'Well done,' Robert said, relieved when she was back on solid ground. 'Thank you.'

He looked so pleased that she thought for one wild moment he might be about to kiss her.

She quickly moved the ladder away from the damp patch on the carpet. 'No problem. Good job you thought to check or there might have been a lot of damage.'

She was about to head back downstairs when he cleared his throat loudly.

'Um, Liz?'

She waited, examining the frill on the bottom of her apron to try to put him at his ease. It was quite hard forcing yourself not to look at someone; she'd never be able to keep it up.

'I'm afraid I've always had this thing about heights,' he went on humbly. 'I think it started when my father made me climb to the top of a tree when I was a boy and I fell off.'

'That wasn't very nice of him,' she blurted, thinking suddenly of Greg. It was just the sort of thing that he'd make Rosie do, if he ever saw her.

'He wasn't a very nice man,' Robert replied darkly.

Liz was curious but he didn't like questions and besides, there were customers to think of. 'They'll be here in a minute...'

He followed her to the stairs.

'How's your daughter?' he asked, just like that.

Such a non sequitur. He never asked her anything personal.

'Well, thanks. She's very excited about a school trip to London in October. We're busy saving up.'

She was on the point of descending when he touched her lightly on the upper arm, making her start.

'I'd be grateful if you wouldn't mention this – the height thing, I mean – to anyone.' He swallowed. 'The boys, you know, Jesse and Josh, they might—'

'Of course,' Liz said briskly, thinking they'd have a field day if they knew. He'd never live it down. 'Just between you and me.'

She sneaked a glance and saw that Robert's frown had disappeared. She might even have detected the faint trace of a smile.

'Thanks again for closing the window.'

'Any time,' she replied, thinking that he might almost be handsome if he wasn't such a bundle of nerves. He could do with gaining a few extra pounds, too; she'd noticed how tightly he had to fasten the belt of his dark blue jeans to stop them slipping down.

'It's funny, I don't mind heights myself,' she said reassuringly, 'but I'm not at all keen on beetles. Beatles music, yes, Beetle cars, lovely, I even like beetling along, but the black

65

insect variety? Not at all.' She shuddered. 'If we find one any-where near our house or even worse, inside, I go all wobbly and have to get Rosie to deal with it.'

It was a jolly crowd, thanks to the entire Lambert clan cele-brating old Mrs Lambert's seventieth birthday, so the evening went quickly. John Lambert ordered a bottle of champagne and lots of wine, too, which Liz knew would please Robert.

He and Alex were very creative with the menus, always coming up with new ideas for dishes which they'd test out before launching them on customers. Being knowledgeable about wine, too, Robert liked nothing more than to advise folk on what to order with which particular course.

At one point she caught his eye as she brushed past him to reach the kitchen and, instead of looking at his feet, she thought that she detected that faint smile of his again. It was as if in those few short moments upstairs they'd formed a slight connection, his little secret binding them together in some invisible way.

His fear of heights seemed to her to be a trivial and, if anything, rather endearing phobia, but he was embarrassed and she'd never spill the beans. She hoped that he trusted her. She thought he did. Perhaps she was imagining the connec-tion, though.

Sometime before eight she felt her mobile vibrate in her apron pocket. Knowing what it would be, she sneaked out to the backyard to check.

Hi Mum. We're not millionaires yet!! Luv u. Rosie xxx

Liz smiled at the thought of Rosie and Pat peering excit-edly at the TV as the winning lottery numbers were called, checking their own tickets and shrugging off the disappoint-ment.

'Let's have a nice cup of tea and a chocolate biscuit to celebrate not being rich,' Pat might have said afterwards. 'We're perfectly happy as we are, aren't we, lambkin?'

They were both great believers in looking on the bright side.

She noticed a portion of crème brulée sitting on its own on the kitchen counter when she carried in the final tray of coffee cups and plates. Loveday spotted it, too, so Liz picked it up quickly and took it to the bar, where Robert was wiping down bottles.

'For you,' she said, placing a clean spoon on a white linen napkin beside the dish.

He eyed it uneasily but he must have eaten it because she saw that the same dish had been put back on the worktop a little later, scraped clean.

When she arrived home at around 1 a.m., Rosie was tucked up in bed and Pat had fallen asleep with the old encyclopedia on her lap, open on the page about London.

Rosie had told her all about it, then. The excitement was building. Liz thought of the generous tip she'd received this evening from the Lamberts, and resolved to put it straight in an empty jam jar labelled 'Rosie's Trip'.

Thankfully, with the summer coming, she could expect a few more of those and what's more, Robert had offered her next Saturday lunchtime as well. She was a little surprised because it was Rita's shift and she couldn't imagine that he'd need more than one waitress at this time of year. Still, she could manage one Saturday and she wasn't about to turn it down. Things were definitely on the up.

The rain cleared overnight and the following morning was bright and sunny again. Liz had set her alarm and got up early to make the salmon and rice dish, along with the salad and apple pie. That done, she cleaned the flat, starting with the front room and moving on to the kitchen. She decided to leave the bathroom till last as she and Rosie would need a shower later.

The table was only for two, so she decided to put the knives, forks and plates on it and they'd have to carry their food into the front room and eat on their laps. There were only two chairs in there – the blue one and another yellow chair that had a hole in the seat, so she threw a cream blanket over to cheer it up. Then she carried in the two kitchen chairs, reminding herself to nab the wobbly one, and put a small bunch of daffodils that she'd bought at the convenience store on the window sill.

By the time Rosie had finished breakfast – Liz was too nervous to eat – and they'd both had showers and spruced the bathroom, it was half eleven. Where had the morning gone?

'Get dressed, quick,' Liz commanded. 'They might be early.'

Rosie's face fell and she looked close to tears. 'What shall I wear?'

Liz cursed herself for putting her daughter on edge.

'You look lovely in anything,' she said, taking a deep breath and kissing the top of her head. 'How about your stripy sailor top and leggings?'

Rosie never wore skirts or dresses because she hated the trainers that were a size too big to accommodate her special insoles.

Liz flung open a few windows to air the place before hurrying into her bedroom. She didn't have much to choose from other than jeans, but she put on a clean pair with a loose white cheesecloth top that she rather liked, and attached a silky fuchsia flower to her dark hair, just above the ear.

'You look pretty!' Rosie commented, when Liz popped in

to smooth her duvet once more and do her plaits. 'I hope they hurry up cos I'm practically pooing my pants just thinking about it.'

For once, Liz let it pass.

Half past twelve went, then one. Rosie wasn't allowed to turn on the TV so she tried to read her book instead, sitting on the floor of her room as she was forbidden from messing up the bedclothes.

Meanwhile, Liz paced around, trying to see the flat through fresh eyes, as Tonya would, checking for dirty fingermarks round light switches and stray socks or pencils, anything that might give a clue to their real, haphazard lives. Normally, Liz didn't bother about a bit of dust, or evidence of Rosie's ongoing art projects, or fluff under the bed. Today, though, she wanted everything just so.

By the time two o'clock had come and gone, Rosie was in such a state that she had to head to the back garden to do breathing exercises.

'Mrs Springett says we should do them before a test,' she explained, when Liz went to check on her. Mrs Springett was the class teacher.

'You have to inhale deeply...' Rosie closed her eyes and took a long breath to demonstrate, puffing out her chest exaggeratedly, 'and exhale slowly, counting to at least four or five. Ahhhh,' she said loudly, opening her eyes to make sure that Liz was copying correctly. 'More slowly,' she instructed.

'Ahhh,' Liz repeated obediently, before plonking down on the step, her head swirling. 'I feel dizzy now.'

At last the doorbell rang and they both froze.

'You go,' Liz said, unable to conceal the panic in her voice.

'No,' Rosie snapped. 'He's your dad.'

'Well he's your—'

She could hear herself, just like a big kid.

'All right then,' she muttered, rising quickly. 'I'll do it.'

It was Tonya who swept into the tiny hall first in a halo of long, honey-coloured hair, followed by Liz's father, Paul, who was shorter than his wife by a good couple of inches.

'We had to wait in for Davina's Waitrose delivery,' Tonya said, by way of apology. Well, Liz assumed it was an apology. 'She was out last night and didn't get back in time. We can only stay an hour.'

Paul had to go outside to put the parking permit in the car window.

'How was your journey?' Liz asked when at last she'd ushered them both into the two comfy chairs while she perched cautiously on the wobbly one.

'A nightmare,' said Tonya, adjusting a pair of big black sunglasses that were on top of her head and turning to Paul, who nodded.

She brushed an invisible speck of something off the leg of her tight white jeans and cast an eye around the room.

'But Liz,' she said, with a cry of surprise, 'this is absolutely charming!'

Liz glowed with pleasure, thinking that all that polishing and dusting this morning had been worthwhile.

Her father seemed older than before, she thought, and plumper. He'd always been a short, stocky man, prematurely balding, but now what little hair he had left was quite white, and his face, loose, damp and pouchy, reminded her of the clay bust she'd once made at school. She'd added too much water the first time and its features had begun to slip, so she'd been obliged to start all over again.

He had a little white moustache on his upper lip that hadn't been there when she last saw him, what, two years ago? And his breathing sounded heavy and laboured, as if he'd just been for a vigorous walk rather than sitting in the car for hours.

They all turned when Rosie appeared at the door and Liz felt a surge of pride. She knew that Rosie was shy of them but masked it well as she walked, in her slightly lopsided way, over to her step-grandmother and extended her good hand, just as Liz had taught her.

'Gracious!' Tonya said. 'How formal! Come over here and give me a kiss.'

Rosie glanced at her mother who smiled encouragingly, before leaning forwards to be enveloped in a cloud of heavy perfume, powder and hairspray.

'That's better,' said Tonya, patting Rosie on the back. She had long red nails. 'Much more friendly.'

They'd eaten, it seemed, at a service station and didn't want anything more.

'We'll have dinner onboard,' Tonya explained when Rosie extricated herself. 'The restaurant sounds perfectly adequate, doesn't it, Paul?'

Liz's father, who had sunk so far into the cream blanket-covered armchair that it was difficult to tell where it ended and he began, murmured in assent.

'I've reserved a table for nine o'clock,' Tonya went on. 'And no red wine for you.'

Noticing Liz's look of surprise, she cupped a hand round her mouth and whispered loudly, 'Makes him snore.'

Liz was about to ask about the trip when Tonya fixed her gaze on Rosie again, who was now sitting on the other plastic chair beside her mother, her knees clamped tightly together. 'So tell me, how's school?'

It was such a general question and Liz could see that Rosie didn't know where to begin.

Thankfully, Paul butted in: 'She doesn't want to talk about school, Ton. It's the weekend. What are your hobbies? What do you like doing?'

Rosie told them a bit about her art and Paul said that he'd like to see some of her work. While she sat on the floor beside him and his wife, flicking through her sketch pad, Liz found her mind wandering back to the time before Tonya, to the period soon after her mother died when neither she nor her father knew what to do and he was scarcely able to put one foot in front of another.

She saw her mother everywhere back then – in the swish of the silvery-gold curtains that she'd sewn for their living room in Balham, in the crocheted blanket that she'd made for their spaniel, Basil, that Liz had washed and taken for herself after he died. In that strange interlude between evening and night-time, when it was too early to put on the lights but the house was swathed in shadows. That was when they'd often pulled on coats, if they needed them, and headed out for a walk on the common. Her mother always said a breath of fresh air was good before bedtime; it would help them sleep.

Once she knew that her mum really wasn't coming back, Liz's biggest fear had been that her father would die, too, leaving her quite alone. After that, she'd made it her mission to look after him, to cook him his favourite meals and make him happy, so that the worst catastrophe in the world would never come to pass. It had worked, up to a point. He went back to his job and began smiling again, though she quickly realised that she could only ever be a poor substitute for the real thing.

She assumed that he'd spend the rest of his days in a state of mild depression, whiling away his spare time watching football on TV or doing crosswords that he never finished.

Then he'd met Tonya through a dating agency and everything had changed.

Tonya burst into their lives like a tornado. Younger than he was by more than thirteen years, she had a five-year-old daughter, Davina, and very firm ideas on just about everything.

Before agreeing to move in, she'd insisted they redecorate the house from top to bottom in her bold, contemporary style. All the curtains had to go, of course, and a good deal of the furniture, too.

'You're nearly eighteen and you'll soon be off to college or university or whatever,' she told Liz briskly. 'So it's only fair that Davina should have your bedroom. The other one's far too small.'

In truth, Liz hadn't decided about college or university because she'd thought that perhaps she wouldn't be able to leave her dad. So when she received disappointing grades at A-level, it made sense to look for a job straight away and find a room to rent.

'You'll be far happier being independent,' Tonya agreed when Liz broached the subject. 'I mean, who wants to live with boring old parents when you can be footloose and fancy-free?'

It was lucky that she managed to find a job so quickly. She was only the receptionist in a small firm of accountants in Clapham, but it was a start. The phones didn't go that often so she made a lot of tea and coffee and ran errands for the boss, like picking up his dry cleaning and buying flowers for his wife. She didn't mind; she preferred to be useful.

It was on one such errand, when she was ordering sandwiches for the team from the deli up the road, that she'd met Greg, waiting in line for a tuna and cucumber baguette. Funny that she still remembered what he'd asked for.

At twenty-three, Greg was only five years older but seemed more. He told her he was 'in recruitment' and he had a motorbike and a mortgage on a tiny flat just off Balham High Road, thanks to some money left to him by his grandmother in her will.

He was very easy to talk to and they arranged to meet for a drink later in the week. Soon, Liz was spending more time at his place than in her own bedsit and he asked her to move in.

'You can put the money that you would've been paying in rent towards the mortgage,' he explained reasonably, and it did seem like a good idea. Especially since her landlord was planning to do up her place shortly and sell it.

They muddled along happily enough for a few years. He seemed to like the fact that she'd been used to looking after her dad and knew how to cook and keep a place clean.

'You're low maintenance,' he'd sometimes tell her in an affectionate moment, ruffling her dark hair. 'Not like some of the harpies I know.'

She was a little surprised when he quit his job after a row with the managing director and set up on his own.

'It's a fool's game working for someone else,' he informed her. 'You slave away while they keep all the profits for themselves.'

Privately, she couldn't help thinking that she'd never seen Greg slave away; he seemed to have plenty of free time for his friends, riding his bike and going to the gym, but she didn't say so. It couldn't have been easy for him trying to run a business from their one bedroom flat but he said he preferred the freedom. They did miss his monthly pay checks, though, and of course when Liz fell pregnant, he was understandably concerned.

'We need this like a hole in the head,' he'd told her gravely. 'Can't you have an abortion?'

But Liz had already begun to feel different; her breasts had swollen, she felt sick and kept imagining this tiny person growing inside her that seemed, to her, like a symbol of hope rising from the ashes of her mother's death. She couldn't get rid of it.

'Shall I make you a bracelet?'

Liz was brought back to the present by Rosie's high-pitched voice.

'No, cherub,' Tonya replied. 'We must go or we'll miss our sailing.'

Liz jumped up, almost knocking over the plastic chair. 'But you haven't even had a cup of tea!'

Tonya had risen herself and was smoothing down her turquoise top, which was cut quite low at the front and showed a fair amount of brown, freckled cleavage.

'Another time,' she said, flashing Liz a dazzling smile. Her eyes, though, were focused on the slim gold watch on her left wrist. 'Come on, Paul, we're cutting it fine.'

Liz's father rose slowly from the chair, pushing himself up with his burly arms. It seemed to require some effort.

'I'm sorry it's been so brief,' he told Liz when they were finally facing each other, just a foot or two apart. She could smell his familiar odour; dried sweat through washing powder. 'Everything all right though?'

'Oh yes,' she replied brightly, glancing down at Rosie who'd snuggled into her side, one stockinged foot resting on another. 'We're doing great, aren't we?'

'Good,' said her father, 'I'm glad you're both well.'

He reached into the pocket of his navy trousers and pulled out a brown wallet. Liz could sense Tonya's eyes on him as he fished out a crumpled note from the back of a pile and handed it to his daughter. 'Buy something nice for yourself and Rosie.'

Liz was about to protest but Tonya was already hustling him towards the door. 'Hurry up! We'll be late!'

There was just time to kiss his clammy cheek – he ruffled Rosie's hair – before they were climbing in the car and motoring up the hill.

Mother and daughter stood on the narrow pavement outside and watched. It was only when the black saloon had disappeared from view that Liz looked at the pink note she was still clutching in her left hand and saw that he'd given her fifty pounds.

'Look,' she said to Rosie, holding up the gift. She wasn't sure that she'd ever possessed a fifty pound note before. 'We'll put it straight in your "Rosie's Trip" jar!'

The little girl flashed a quick smile before exclaiming with a frown, 'They didn't eat any of the food!'

'Never mind,' said Liz, closing the door behind them and squeezing her daughter's good hand. 'All the more for us, eh?'

Chapter Six

FOR SOME REASON she woke up feeling unusually glum and it was several days before the fog began to lift. It was a relief when she popped into Good Morning News before work to see Iris's friendly face smiling at her over the top of *Hello!* magazine; she needed cheering up.

'You all right, darlin'?' Iris said in her gravelly London accent. 'You look like a wet Wednesday morning.'

'It *is* a wet Wednesday morning,' Liz said gloomily.

'So it is!' Iris replied, glancing at the rain drizzling down the window pane leaving dirty streaks before splattering on the concrete pavement below. 'I was that caught up in Wills and Kate I'd forgotten about the filthy weather.'

A young man in white overalls and steel-capped boots was waiting to buy a copy of the *Daily Mirror* and a can of Coke. Liz stepped back while he paid.

When he left, Iris returned to Liz and asked what the trouble was and she found herself telling the older woman a little about her father's visit.

'They were only with us an hour – more like fifty minutes,' she explained. 'Dad and I hardly spoke and I've no idea when I'll see him again. I know Tonya doesn't mean any harm but she can't help dominating the conversation. And he didn't look well...'

Iris clucked sympathetically and passed her a clean white tissue from an open packet on the counter.

'Can you and Rosie go and visit – when they're back from their holidays, I mean?'

Liz blew into the hankie and shook her head. 'We can't afford it and anyway, there's no room for us in their house. It's too small.'

Iris knitted her carefully plucked brows. 'I thought you said there were three bedrooms? Your dad's in one and that daughter—'

'Davina,' Liz said helpfully.

'Davina,' Iris repeated, looking as if she had a bad taste in her mouth, 'is in the other. So that leaves one spare.'

Liz pulled off the pink chiffon scarf with hand-stitched sequins from her ponytail that was dangling damply round her neck and wrapped it through her fingers.

'Yes, but it's only a boxroom, really. There's just a single bed in there.'

Iris seemed to rise a few inches from her seat, puffing out her sizeable chest that was encased in a tight, leopard print sweater.

'Well, she can have the single bed and you and Rosie can use her room. It'd only be for a few nights, for goodness sake!'

Liz frowned, thinking there was no way that she'd ask Davina to vacate her bedroom. Iris didn't understand. Davina liked to have her things around her and she'd probably worry that Rosie would fiddle with her make-up and stuff.

'Sorry to moan,' Liz said, feeling guilty for having raised the subject. Everyone had bad weeks, after all. She wasn't the only one.

She was writing her name and address on the back of her lottery ticket when Iris asked what she was up to at Easter. Liz had almost forgotten that it was coming up.

'I haven't thought,' she said truthfully. 'I guess Rosie and I will go for a walk along the coast. Maybe I'll take her to a farm to see some chicks.'

'Come to ours for lunch on Easter Sunday,' Iris cried, delighted with her own suggestion. 'Christie will be there with Spencer, and Darren and his new girlfriend, Kelly. And my mum, of course. She loves chocolate. She'll be quite happy sitting there munching her way through an egg.'

Liz was grateful, she really was, but there was no way that she was going to gatecrash someone else's family get-together.

'No, honestly...' she started to say, but Iris was having none of it.

'I always do a big roast lamb,' she said cheerfully, 'and Jim does the veg for me, and the gravy. He makes lovely gravy.' She smacked her lips in anticipation. 'It won't be any trouble. I'll get Christie to organise the Easter egg hunt – nothing special, you know, but the kiddies like it, don't they? – and Spencer will enjoy having Rosie to play with. Otherwise it's just boring old adults.'

Liz hesitated. Rosie did love little children – she played with them at Jean's house – and she supposed that Christie might be quite glad to have someone to entertain her son. It would be good not to spend the holiday on their own for a change, and it would certainly take her mind off her dad's visit.

'All right,' she said at last. 'If you're sure?'

'Course I am!' Iris replied, clapping her hands, which made her gold bracelets jangle. 'Jim likes company and Christie and Darren will be pleased. We'll have a jolly old time, I promise you.'

As she left the shop with her ticket and pack of ten cigarettes, Liz hoped that she'd done the right thing and that Iris wasn't just being kind. There again, they could stay just for a little while if they felt they were getting in the way, and Rosie rarely spent time with a *real* family. It would be an experience for her.

She was cleaning soap off the mirror in the third floor toilets – how did they manage to get the soap up there? she could never understand – when she felt her mobile vibrating. She kept it in the pocket of her blue overall and only answered in emergencies. Her heart pitter-pattered when she saw that it was Rosie's school but she told herself not to be silly; it was probably nothing. Even so, she dried her hands quickly on a paper towel and picked up.

'Mrs Broome?' They always called her 'Mrs' even though she wasn't married. An old-fashioned formality, she supposed. Greg had wanted his surname, Wilder, on Rosie's birth certificate but Liz had included Broome, too, and dropped the Wilder when they'd moved to Cornwall.

The school secretary explained that there'd been an incident in the playground: 'Nothing serious – she's not hurt – but Rosie's a bit upset and wants to go home.'

Liz frowned. She knew that it must be bad because her daughter was usually pretty resilient and wouldn't have wanted to bother Liz unless absolutely necessary.

'What sort of incident?' she asked warily.

The school secretary was suspiciously guarded. 'The head's talking to the other children now. She wants to see you when you get here. Rosie's waiting for you.' Her voice softened. 'I think she needs a big hug from her mum.'

Liz's mind was racing. 'The other children?' She'd bet Kyle had something to do with it. She'd like to strangle him with her bare hands, she really would.

She glanced in the mirror and saw that her cheeks were flushed red. This sort of thing had happened quite a lot when Rosie was younger but she'd toughened up.

She finished the mirror in double-quick time and mopped the floor – she hated to leave a job undone – before putting her overall and cleaning equipment back in the cupboard and calling Kasia.

'I've had a call from school – I have to leave,' she told her boss, who was somewhere in the building with Jo.

'Oh my God,' Kasia exclaimed in her thick Polish accent, ever one to make a crisis out of a drama. 'What happened?'

Liz gave her the outline and Kasia said she must go immediately; for all her faults, she knew that family came first. She'd be sure to knock the hours off Liz's end-of-week pay packet though.

Liz could imagine Jo's face when Kasia informed her that she'd have to finish the third floor and do reception, too. She'd probably need the rest of the week off to recover from the shock.

Rosie was sitting on a red leather chair outside the head's office when Liz arrived; she'd clearly been crying. Her face was pale and there were dirty streaks along her cheeks and her nose was damp. Her class teacher, Mrs Springett, was hovering alongside but Liz didn't acknowledge her.

'What is it?' she cried, scooping Rosie out of the seat and enfolding her in her navy anorak. She could feel the bones through her uniform; she was light as a feather. 'What's happened?'

For a moment Rosie didn't speak then, when Liz released her, squatting down to her level and looking her in the eyes, she said, 'They were calling me names, saying I couldn't walk properly and I had big ugly feet.'

Liz dug a hankie out of her pocket and wiped her daughter's eyes, noticing that she had mud on her jumper and the knees of her trousers. The palms of her hands were dirty, too.

She wanted to shout at someone – anyone. She wanted to whisk Rosie away to a desert island and never see a soul again.

'They told Rachel and Mandy not to play with me because I was disabled,' Rosie stumbled on, 'and Mandy said she didn't want to share a room with me in London because I've got a claw not a hand. Then they pushed me and I fell down and everyone laughed.'

Liz reeled, as if she'd been slapped.

'How dare they?' she said through gritted teeth. 'The little—'

'Mrs Broome?' The voice seemed to come from nowhere and Liz glanced up to see the class teacher still hovering. 'The head would like a word with you now.'

Liz held Rosie's hand tightly as they entered the head's office, a light room just off the main corridor with a pale wooden desk in the middle and a large computer on top.

Mrs Cox – a tall, grey-haired woman in a dark jacket – rose swiftly and shook Liz's hand. They knew each other of old, she and Liz. Many a time Liz had had to demand meetings when Rosie was younger, usually to discuss some incident or other or complain about the way teachers had a tendency to baby her. They weren't alone in assuming that just because her body wasn't perfect, her mind was affected, too. But as she'd moved up the school and the staff had got to know her better and understand her capabilities, she'd seemed so much happier and more settled.

Mrs Cox had always appeared helpful, but Liz had learned the hard way that she had to fight her corner. There was only so much that Mrs Cox was prepared to do and the reputation of the school came first. Always the reputation. She didn't want people saying there was bullying at Mere Primary; really she just wanted Liz to shut up and go away.

'I'm shocked—' Liz began to say. She rarely raised her voice but when it came to Rosie, she was a tigress. The head held up a hand as if to fend off the verbal blows.

'Please sit.' Her steadiness was calming and Liz did as she was told. Rosie climbed on her lap, something she rarely did now as she considered herself far too grown-up.

The incident, it seemed, had occurred at morning play and staff had identified the children involved. They'd been in to see Mrs Cox en masse and letters would be sent home with them for their parents at the end of the day.

'I've told them that this sort of behaviour won't be tolerated,' she said in clipped, professional tones. 'I underlined how thoughtless and hurtful their comments were and they have apologised to Rosie.'

Liz glanced sideways at her daughter, whose head was lowered. She'd hate being the centre of attention; all she ever wanted was to blend in.

'They seemed genuinely contrite,' Mrs Cox went on. 'I'm sure the message sank in. Some of them were in tears...'

She eyed Liz, whose mouth set in a hard line; she could hardly feel sorry for her daughter's tormentors. They'd soon forget the whole thing but it would be with Rosie for a long, long time.

'I also had an individual word with the boy who pushed her...' Mrs Cox continued, looking faintly self-satisfied.

Liz glanced again at Rosie, whose mouth drooped a little further at the corners. Kyle. Of course.

'He said he was very sorry and assured me that it won't happen again.'

Liz felt the blood rise to her cheeks and her heart started pumping furiously. It was all she could do not to stand up and hit something – or someone.

'That boy – Kyle – has done his best to make my daughter's life a misery since the moment she arrived at your school,' she blurted, her voice shaking with emotion. 'I'm sick and tired of his bullying and I want to see him properly punished. Either that or I'll complain to the governors and ask them to take charge.'

She was a little shocked by her vehemence but it seemed to have the desired effect. Mrs Cox's eyes widened and she visibly paled.

'That won't be necessary,' she said hastily. 'I can assure you that we have a very rigorous disciplinary procedure in place...' She cleared her throat. 'But you're right, I think that perhaps this does require a firmer line.'

Liz waited, ears pricked.

'Kyle will be suspended for a week,' the head went on rapidly. 'And his parents will of course receive a letter detailing the reasons. I hope you find this satisfactory?'

Liz nodded, grateful for this small victory, and gave Rosie, who had been sitting quiet as a mouse on her lap, a consoling squeeze; they both knew what Kyle was like, but at least this would silence him for a while. She just hoped that his parents wouldn't kick up. She knew what they were like, too.

They drove home along the narrow lanes bordered on either side with fields dotted with glossy brown cows. It was still drizzling and the animals were mostly lying down. Rosie was quiet, lost in her own thoughts.

'I'm sorry they disturbed you at work,' she said at last in a small voice.

'That's all right,' Liz replied gently. 'You know you can call me anytime.'

They drew up at a crossroads and waited for a tractor carting bales of hay to reach the other side. The farmer leaned out of his cab and waved cheerily as he went by.

'Do you think Mandy meant it when she said she didn't want to share a room with me in London?'

Liz felt her face heat up again. She was overwhelmed by the injustice of it, the cruelty. Mandy was supposed to be Rosie's *friend*, one of the few who saw past her wonky leg and tricky arm.

'I'm sure she didn't,' she replied, doing her best to soothe. 'She was just too scared to stand up to Kyle. I'm afraid bullies are like that. They force other children to join in even when they don't want to. I expect her mum'll have a word with her tonight. She'll be very upset when she gets the letter.'

There was a pregnant pause and Liz wondered what was coming next.

'Why am I disabled?'

Liz swallowed hard. 'Because there were complications when you were born and you picked up an infection. You were very poorly for a while, but you're a real fighter and you pulled through. You're special, you see. You're my very special girl and I wouldn't swap you for the world.'

They had to stop again while a man in wellies and a big green mac, accompanied by two barking collies, crossed over and headed through a wooden gate leading to a field of sheep.

'I wish I didn't have a limp,' Rosie went on. 'Or a tricky hand. I wish I could wear nice shoes like my friends.'

Liz took a deep breath. 'I know, but then you wouldn't be special, would you? You'd be like everyone else. Boring and normal.'

Rosie fell silent again, digesting the information. Liz fancied that she could hear the cogs in her brain whirring.

They were almost back at the cottage now and she spotted Esme, long purple skirt flapping damply in the wind, walking down the side of the building towards her door. Liz paused

– there were no cars behind – waiting for her to go inside. She didn't feel like chatting today.

They drew to a halt beside the cottage and she noticed that she'd forgotten to draw the curtains in her little bedroom window when they'd left soon after five this morning. It seemed like a lifetime ago.

'I think I'd rather be boring and normal,' Rosie added quietly.

It was extra hard having to leave for work that night, not least because Rosie was complaining of a headache and Liz gave her some medicine to clear it.

'Try to get a good sleep,' she told her daughter, kissing her nose as she sat under the pink blanket, hugging one of her cat slippers with the TV on. Pat had pulled the other chair up close. 'You'll feel better in the morning.'

'Do I have to go to school tomorrow?' Rosie asked, knowing full well what her mother's reply would be.

'You do. They won't be mean after what Mrs Cox said.'

'A day off won't hurt, will it?' muttered Pat, who always took Rosie's side. 'I can mind her for you.'

But Liz shook her head. She hoped that Rosie wouldn't remember it was the dreaded PE lesson. She hated being given special exercises because she couldn't do the same as the other children. Getting dressed and undressed was a problem, too; she was always last.

Liz was quite relieved when she arrived at A Winkle In Time to find that there weren't many bookings, though she always worried that Robert might decide to lay her off. It hadn't happened yet; he said it was important to stay open even in the quiet months. People might make the journey from Plymouth, he reasoned, they sometimes did; it really wasn't far – and he

86

didn't want to gain a reputation for being a seasonal place only. She wasn't complaining; she needed the work.

Loveday, unusually prompt, was already laying tables when Liz entered the room, dripping on the wooden floor.

'Hi!'

Loveday scowled back. Her chestnut brown eyes were circled with thick black smudgy kohl and her long black hair, shaved on one side, was pulled up on the top of her head in a fat bun. It reminded Liz of a cottage loaf.

'Oh dear,' Liz said, without meaning to.

'Yeah, well you'd be in a bad mood if you'd had my day.'

It seemed that she and Nathan the postman, her latest squeeze, had been intending to go clothes shopping in the city. Nathan had hurried through his round so that they could leave promptly to look at trainers for him and jeans and tops for her, but his car had run out of petrol some way out of Tremarnock.

'We were in the middle of bloody nowhere!' Loveday grumbled. 'He walked to the garage because he didn't have any spare petrol and it was miles away, so I had to sit in the car for hours watching the bleeding rain.'

Liz felt a little sorry for Nathan.

'By the time he got back I was cold and starving and it was only a couple of hours before I needed to get back to the hellhole...'

Her eyes swept around the room so that no one could be in any doubt which particular hellhole she was referring to.

'It would've been all right – we could've still gone – if Uncle Robert wasn't such an old woman. I don't know why he makes me get here at five thirty. It's like a flipping morgue tonight, there's no one coming.'

'Bad luck,' Liz said, hanging her coat on the peg and tying up her apron. She thought it wise not to point out that Loveday rarely arrived at five thirty anyway. 'Can you go shopping tomorrow?'

'No, because there's a party at Spike's tonight,' the younger girl grumbled, 'and I've got nothing to wear.'

'You can borrow something of mine,' Liz said doubtfully, 'if there's anything you'd like?'

'Nah,' said Loveday ungraciously. 'It's Nathan's fault. He should've filled up the tank before we left.' She flung down the white napkins and stomped out to the backyard for a break.

Liz straightened the napkins before popping into the kitchen to see how Jesse was doing.

'She's in a worse mood than usual,' he said, wiping his eye with the corner of a sleeve. He was peeling shallots.

Liz explained what had happened.

'She's going out with that muppet, is she?' Jesse threw the onion peelings in the bin beside his feet. 'More fool her.' He was trying desperately to sound nonchalant, and failing.

Liz leaned forward so that no one else could hear. 'I think she's going off him.'

Loveday appeared to be working her way methodically through the younger members of the village's male population so this wasn't a great revelation.

'I shouldn't imagine he'll last much longer.' She ran an imaginary knife across her throat with a finger and nodded.

'I'm not surprised,' said Jesse, perking up instantly. 'Have you *seen* him? He looks like a parsnip.'

Towards the end of the evening, Liz offered Robert a dish of leftover pavlova while he was checking through the diary at one of the far tables.

He took it gratefully, popping a heaped spoonful in his mouth.

She'd been mulling over a problem all night and now seemed as good a time as any to broach the subject. She wasn't looking forward to it, though.

'I wondered,' she said hesitantly. He was wolfing down the dessert like he hadn't had a meal in years. 'I was just thinking...'

She straightened up. Courage, Liz, he won't bite.

'Would it be all right if I bring Rosie with me on Saturday lunchtime?' she blurted. 'She'll be no trouble, I promise. She can sit in a corner and read.'

Robert put his spoon down and looked up at her, fixing his eyes somewhere in the region of her left cheek. Was there a smear? Instinctively she put a hand up to wipe it away before returning it quickly to her side.

She knew that it was an untoward request and couldn't tell what he was thinking. She could feel herself shrink.

'I feel bad about leaving her,' she rattled on. 'You see, Pat usually pops in but she's going to see her niece on Saturday. Ruby said Rosie could go to hers but she doesn't know Ruby quite so well and I—'

'Is something wrong?'

Robert's question floored her and for a moment she didn't know how to reply. The last thing she wanted was to alert him to her difficulties, but the thought of leaving Rosie even for a few hours after what had happened at school seemed worse than posing the question.

'No,' she fibbed. 'Everything's fine.'

She felt him examining her, which was unnerving. There was a candle on the table and she caught sight of the amber flecks in his hazel eyes – she'd never noticed before.

'Liz, if something's the matter...'

His eyes slid from her but his expression was so earnest

that she felt she couldn't fob him off; she was hopeless at lying anyway.

'Something happened at school today,' she began, before giving him a brief outline.

When she'd finished he frowned and for a moment she thought that he was going to say no. There'd be all sorts of legitimate reasons why: health and safety, other customers wouldn't like it, taking up a table, etc, etc. She wouldn't blame him.

'She can come,' he said at last, 'and she doesn't need to sit in the corner, she can go upstairs.'

Liz exhaled rapidly; she hadn't realised that she'd been holding her breath.

'Thank you so much,' she gushed, feeling her lungs deflate, her shoulders relax. 'I really am grateful...'

Robert, embarrassed, looked down at the diary again and picked up a pen. He seemed to have forgotten about the pavlova.

'See you tomorrow,' she said, assuming that she'd been dismissed, but instead of resuming his work he ruffled his thick brown hair and sighed.

'Human beings,' he said with feeling, 'can be so cruel.'

She was surprised. He spoke, she thought, as someone who'd been at the receiving end of some great unkindness himself. Perhaps he was referring to his father, who'd made him climb that tree. Or maybe it was the ex-fiancée? She remembered what Loveday had told her, about how she'd pulled out just before the wedding, leaving him shattered. You could tell that he was still raw.

She must have been quite a woman because it was a long time ago and there was no way that he'd moved on. Perhaps he wouldn't get over it; some people never did.

Chapter Seven

ROSIE WAS RELUCTANT to go to school the next day and complained that her headache hadn't gone. Liz would have liked to keep her at home but knew that it was important to face the other children as soon as possible. Besides, she couldn't afford to miss a cleaning shift. She did feel guilty, though, as they trudged up the road to Jean's as usual in the early hours. She tried not to show it.

She was relieved at pick-up time to discover that the day had passed almost without incident. Mandy and Rachel, it seemed, had been extra friendly and Kyle, of course, wasn't there.

'Another boy, Charlie, was staring at me when we were on the bench talking,' Rosie said as they were driving home. 'I shouted: "D'you want a photograph?" and he ran away.'

'That's my girl,' Liz replied, doing a thumbs-up in the mirror. 'You've got to stick up for yourself.'

Privately, she feared that it wasn't over and Kyle would try to get his own back somehow once he returned to class. But he wouldn't dare for a while and in the meantime, Liz was building up a new arsenal of put-downs for Rosie to use when necessary.

She was delighted when Liz told her that they'd be going together to A Winkle In Time on Saturday.

'Can I help serve the customers?'

When Liz said no, Rosie came up with another plan: 'I can bring my paints and decorate the box that nice man was carrying. He asked me to, remember?'

Liz smiled. 'I don't think you can paint in the flat, it'd be too messy. Anyway, he'll probably have forgotten about the box. He's very busy, you know.'

Robert was in the backyard when they arrived, unloading a crate of white wine and stacking it in the floor-to-ceiling wooden rack in the white painted shed.

'Is it OK if I take Rosie up to the flat?' Liz asked, hoping that he hadn't forgotten.

He was bent double and rose suddenly when she spoke, as if she'd given him a fright. He was wearing faded jeans and a creased pale blue linen shirt, rolled up beyond his elbows. He looked so surprised to see them that she feared he *had* forgotten.

'What? Oh yes, of course.'

He stood up straight and ran a hand through his hair, pushing it off his face; he really was very tall and slim, like one of those long-distance runners, Liz thought. Lean and nervy. She couldn't help noticing that he had nice broad shoulders, though, and his arms were surprisingly muscly. Must have been lifting all those heavy crates that did it.

She found the key to the flat hanging on its usual peg in the kitchen and led Rosie up to the first floor sitting room.

One of the windows was slightly ajar and the place smelled fresher and sweeter than before. To her surprise, there was a little vase of blue hyacinths on the coffee table that was like a ship's chest, complete with a big key in a bronze keyhole. There was also a carton of orange juice and a packet of crisps on a silver tray.

'Look,' said Rosie, making herself comfortable on the olive green sofa. 'That man's box.'

Liz followed Rosie's pointed finger and the big brown cardboard box with 'DiscountLand' on the side was, indeed, behind the table.

'Robert,' Liz said, wondering. 'His name's Robert. You've got to stop calling him "that man".'

'Oh, I don't mind.'

Liz spun round to see Robert himself in the doorway; he had to bend his head slightly to enter as the frame was low. There was a faint smile on his lips and she found herself reddening; she wished that she didn't do that.

'Hello again, Rosie,' he said, still hovering at the door. 'I hope you'll be comfortable up here?'

Rosie was now kneeling on the sofa facing him. Liz told her to get down but Robert insisted that she wouldn't do any damage.

'I thought while your mum's working you might like to do an art project,' he went on, nodding at the box. His arms were crossed defensively but he sounded relaxed, more so than when he spoke to Liz. 'That one we talked about?'

Rosie jumped up. 'I'll paint it for you. What's your favourite colour?'

Liz frowned. 'I told her not to bring her paints. They'd make too much—'

Before she could finish, Rosie had produced a box of watercolours from the black rucksack she'd brought with her and was waving it aloft.

'I've got glitter, too – and some stencils and luminous pens. Do you like flowers? I'm good at flowers.' She hesitated, thinking of something. 'Or is that girly? I can do boats or cars if you prefer, only I'm not as good at them.'

'Hmm,' he said, stroking his square jaw, which had a faint trace of stubble. 'What about a seascape? Could you do some fish, maybe?'

Rosie was pleased. 'I love doing fish! I'll paint an octopus on one side.'

'Are you sure this is a good idea?' Liz asked, worried. 'She'll make a mess. Especially the glitter—'

'I'll put newspaper down,' Robert interrupted, carrying the box over to the wooden dining table pushed against the left-hand wall at right angles to a window. 'Look, you can sit here. The light's better.'

He went to fetch some old newspaper while Liz showed Rosie where the bathroom was.

'Don't move anything,' she said sternly. 'And don't touch the walls or furniture with painty hands.'

When she came downstairs she became aware of quite a kerfuffle going on in the kitchen. Josh was shouting at Jesse because he hadn't chopped the carrots into small enough batons and Alex was looking desperately at Robert, who whispered something in his ear and his face visibly paled.

She was just about to ask what was up when Robert crooked a finger and they all gathered round.

'We've got a food critic here from London,' he said, clearing his throat. 'Rita recognised her from her picture byline in the *Daily Post*. It's got a huge readership so everything must be tip-top.'

Liz's heart fluttered because she knew how important this was for him – for everyone. Visitors from all over the country could read the review which would either bring them here in their droves or persuade them to give the restaurant a wide berth.

'She's only just arrived,' Robert continued. 'Liz, I'd like you to look after her because Rita's already doing tables one and two. Try to steer her on to the scallops or chilli crab and roast turbot if you can, but obviously be subtle about it.'

He turned to Alex. 'Which dessert, d'you reckon?'

Alex scratched his head. 'Probably the walnut tart with crème fraîche or the mandarin soufflé.'

Robert nodded, then, noticing Liz's frown: 'Don't worry if she picks something else. It's only if she asks for a recommendation.'

Liz hurried to the loo to check her appearance, wishing that she'd known because she'd have made more of an effort and put on some make-up. Too late now. She redid her ponytail, straightened the red, white and grey crocheted scrunchie tying it together, and gave her fringe a quick comb before grabbing the wine list.

Keep calm, she was telling herself, aware that her palms were sweaty and her pulse was racing. On this of all days she needed to exude cool, and for Robert's sake most of all, she mustn't slip up.

The critic, a pretty woman in her early thirties, probably, with a neat shiny dark brown bob streaked with red, was sitting at a window table opposite a female friend. Both looked relaxed and well groomed. You could guess that they weren't local by their clothes. The critic was wearing a white shirt under a navy blazer while her friend was in a tailored plum jacket, not the sort of garment that your average Cornish person would sport on a windy Saturday afternoon, even in a smartish restaurant. Chunky sweaters and cagoules were more usual.

Liz put on her most charming smile as she took their order for aperitifs – both wanted a gin and tonic – and she tried not to flinch when, on returning with the menu, neither wanted scallops or turbot. The critic ordered oysters and Robert's and Alex's somewhat experimental Indonesian seafood curry, while her friend opted for squid with cucumber and watercress salad, followed by local cod and chips.

She was relieved, however, when Robert came to advise them on drinks, that they settled for his recommendation – a white wine from the Languedoc region of France. After a couple of glasses, their voices rose, the laughter increased and Liz was pretty certain that, turbot or no turbot, they were having a good time.

Once she'd served the main courses, she asked Rita to cover for her for a few minutes and popped upstairs to check on Rosie. Brush in hand, she was painting scales on what looked like a silvery-green mackerel. It was long and sinuous, gliding through dark reeds that cast a shadow on its head; it really was rather lovely.

Liz noticed that she was leaning in close, focusing intently on her work.

'Do you need to be so near?' she asked, frowning. 'You'll get paint on your nose!'

Rosie ignored her.

There was glitter on the floor but Liz could easily vacuum it up later.

'Where did you get that from?' she asked, spotting a glass of fizzy orange on the table.

'He brought it – Robert,' Rosie replied, still not looking up. 'He said he's going to put sweaters in my box; he said it's too nice for socks.'

Liz was enormously grateful; his kindness made it so much more comfortable for her daughter, who might have felt like a nuisance otherwise, getting in everyone's way.

Back in the restaurant, the women had finished their main

courses leaving scarcely a crumb on their plates. After clearing away and refreshing their glasses, Liz passed them the menu again.

She overheard the critic – whose name was Gretel – talking about a man that she was clearly keen on.

'He's bloody gorgeous,' she grinned, then, leaning across the table to whisper to her companion, 'Shame he's married. All the best ones are taken.'

The friend nodded and whispered back, 'I say, the guy who owns this place is rather cute, too. Have you noticed him?'

'Yeah,' said Gretel. 'Nice eyes and hair. Wouldn't mind him in my super kingsize tonight.' She sighed. 'Best not mix business with pleasure, though. There again, if we were down here for a bit longer...'

For some unaccountable reason, Liz found herself bristling.

'Are you ready to order?' she asked crisply. Then she remembered herself and smiled sweetly. 'The walnut tart with crème fraîche is really good, and the mandarin soufflé.'

She was secretly delighted when they took her advice and went for one of each, washed down with an expensive dessert wine. This time, though, she didn't call Robert to advise them, she did it herself.

By the time they'd eaten their last mouthful, the women's cheeks were flushed, they'd removed their jackets and rolled up their sleeves and were giggling uproariously.

'That was totally scrummy,' Gretel said to Liz with a satisfied sigh. She wiped her mouth on a crumpled linen napkin and dropped it theatrically on the table. 'I couldn't eat another thing.'

Liz gave an inward cheer and was about to offer coffee on the house, rather hoping that they'd refuse, when the critic added, 'I say, we'd love to meet the chef and give him our compliments. And the boss, too. It's such an unusual and inventive menu.'

Liz, forgetting her earlier annoyance, hurried off to find Robert and Alex who she knew would be thrilled. However, as she reached the entrance to the kitchen her heart missed a beat.

To her astonishment, standing there in the middle of the room was a half-naked Jesse, who'd stripped off his black and white checked overall and the T-shirt underneath, dropped them on the floor and was flexing his biceps like a contestant for Mr Universe, admiring his reflection in the industrial oven's stainless steel splashback as he did so. The other men, meanwhile, were nowhere to be seen.

'What on earth—' she started to say, but before Jesse could explain, she heard a loud gasp behind her.

Spinning round, she realised that far from waiting for her return, the women had, in fact, followed hot on her heels and were standing open-mouthed just a few feet away by the door.

Liz was aghast, wondering what they'd make of it, but Jesse, completely unfazed, simply shrugged.

'Gets a bit warm in here,' he explained in his broad West Country accent, doing one more quick bicep flex before dropping his arms to his side.

His blond hair curled like a halo round his head and his well-toned surfer's torso, already lightly tanned, glistened with sweat.

'Always bring a change of shirt,' he went on, bending down to pick the clothes off the floor and wiping under his arms with the white tee. 'It's in my bag. I was just about to get it. Wasn't expecting visitors.'

At that moment Robert appeared from the backyard and gazed with horror first on his semi-nude employee, then on the restaurant critic and her friend gawping at him.

'What the—' he spluttered and Liz clenched her teeth, waiting for the fireworks.

They never came, however, because before he could finish Gretel interrupted with a cry. 'Oh, please don't!'

Liz glanced at her in surprise.

'Put your shirt on, I mean,' Gretel continued, smiling naughtily when she realised that everyone was staring.

'You look rather good as you are,' she added, lowering her eyes and fluttering her lashes coquettishly. Her friend giggled and chipped in, mock-shocked: '*Gretel!*'

Realising that he was being admired, Jesse's bright blue eyes twinkled and he broke into a wide, lazy grin, revealing perfectly white teeth.

'You can see a bit more if you want, girls,' he joked flirtatiously, waggling his slim hips and starting to undo the thick brown leather belt on his jeans.

Robert shot him a thunderous look that soon stopped him in his tracks.

'On second thoughts,' Jesse said, sounding somewhat disappointed, 'I'd best get my clothes on.' He nodded obediently at Robert but managed a quick, sly wink at the ladies before sloping off.

Robert ran a hand through his brown hair, his forehead a mass of wrinkles.

'I'm so sorry—' he began, but Gretel raised a hand.

'Stop,' she said. 'We've just had the best meal in ages and quite frankly, this was the icing on the cake.' She smiled cheekily. 'I guarantee you'll be getting a five star review in my newspaper, especially now I've met the eye candy behind the scenes!'

When the women had departed, the staff breathed a collective sigh of relief, all except Jesse who was sulking after what, under the circumstances, had turned out to be a very minor telling-off from Robert.

'Never again,' Liz had heard Robert say. 'If you want to change you do it in the cloakroom with the door shut.'

Catching his eye by mistake, she couldn't help noticing, though, that he had the faint trace of a smile on his lips which Jesse failed to pick up.

'Phew!' she mouthed, raising her eyebrows, and he gave her a furtive thumbs-up.

With all the excitement she'd almost forgotten about Rosie but as soon as the last customers left, she bounded upstairs to find her.

The little girl seemed very content, putting the finishing touches to her creation. There was a tremendous mess of paint pots, brushes and paper all around but once Liz had vacuumed the carpet, thrown the newspaper in the bin outside and brought down the silver tray, the room looked perfect again; you wouldn't have known that anyone had been in there.

'Thank you,' she said to Robert as she and Rosie put on their coats in the backyard where he was stacking empty bottles into a crate ready for recycling. 'I didn't want to leave her alone for such a long time.'

'No problem,' he replied, formal again and directing his reply at Rosie, not her. He'd changed before the customers arrived into a loose white cotton shirt and darker jeans and she noticed that there was a dirty smudge on the end of his nose, probably from one of the bottles. Apart from that you'd never know that the afternoon had been quite so eventful.

'Actually, I wanted to have a word with you.' He glanced at Liz now before focusing quickly on a point behind her; she almost turned to see what he was looking at before remembering that it was just one of his habits.

'It was very useful having an extra pair of hands,' he went on, chewing the corner of a nail. 'Not just because of the unexpected visitors. Business is beginning to pick up and I wondered if you could come every week, at least until the end of summer?'

Liz's mind was racing. The money would be so handy with the London trip looming; she still wasn't quite sure how she'd pay for it, even with that fifty pounds her father had given her. But could she really leave Rosie for four whole hours in the middle of the day – and, what's more, could she ask Pat to mind her? She relied on her so much already and besides, Saturday was her day for seeing family.

She was about to ask if she could think about it when Robert cleared his throat noisily.

'You can come whenever you like.' He was addressing Rosie again. 'It's better while the flat's empty, of course, but when the new tenants arrive I could put a table in the corner of the restaurant out of everyone's way.' He was speaking more to himself now than her. 'You might get bored but if you bring something to do… Unless you'd rather go and play with a friend, of course.'

Liz thought privately that there was no way she'd impose on Robert unless absolutely necessary; she'd never make it regular. Rosie's friends didn't seem to invite her to play much, not even Mandy or Rachel. Robert wouldn't understand that, but it was very kind of him to think of these things anyway.

'All right, I'll do it,' she said suddenly, before stopping herself and looking at Rosie. 'That is, if it's OK with you?'

Rosie's face fell. 'But what about our walks – and tea at Peggy's Parlour? It means we'll only have Sundays.'

Liz swallowed. 'Just until the end of September?' She had to steel herself; she'd miss the outings with her daughter, too. 'It'll be such a help.'

'All right, just until September,' Rosie repeated uncertainly.

Liz suddenly became aware of Robert, listening intently. He was looking at her feet, now, rather than the wall, and taking in everything that they were saying.

'Sorry—' Liz began, wishing that she and Rosie had kept the conversation between themselves. He didn't need to know about their problems.

'On second thoughts,' he said suddenly, shaking his head. 'Silly of me. I only need you for two hours, not four. From half eleven till half one.'

She opened her eyes wide. It sounded like the perfect compromise as there'd still be time for a walk or tea at Peggy's, and two hours wasn't such a long time to be away. She was sure that Jean or Ruby, Jenny or Tony Cutt, for that matter, would step in if Pat was busy. Rosie wouldn't mind too much, surely? Even Esme or Rick Kane would lend a hand if asked; Rosie could help Rick in the shop.

'It's double pay in summer,' Robert went on rapidly.

Liz was about to say something but he shushed her.

'I have to get these bottles to the bank before it shuts.' He bent down to put two more into the crate, bringing the conversation to a close.

As she and Rosie walked back up the hill, Liz was thinking that she couldn't quite believe her luck. Fourteen pounds an hour. That meant twenty-eight pounds for two hours work, instead of four. It would boost their budget and she'd still have the mornings and most of the afternoons with her daughter.

She remembered she'd mentioned to Robert that she was saving for Rosie's school trip when they were up in the flat, dealing with the open skylight. A nasty thought wormed its way into her head. He couldn't have remembered that, could he? Maybe he didn't really need her to do the extra hours? Maybe he felt sorry for her.

But he was a businessman, for goodness sake, and even the nice ones didn't pay people out of the kindness of their hearts. If he said he needed an additional waitress for the busy season, then he did. Perhaps he was anticipating a particularly successful year, thanks to Gretel's promise of a five star review.

Chapter Eight

Soon it was Easter Sunday and Liz found that she was looking forward to lunch with Iris more than she'd realised. She and Rosie loved their times together, but sometimes she did find herself wondering what other, normal families got up to on public holidays.

They always received invitations from neighbours. In the past, Liz had accepted some of them, especially when they first moved to the village and were getting to know people. But, in truth, she'd found it strangely lonely piggybacking on others' special occasions and had decided it was better to try to make their own fun.

Occasionally, though, when they went for walks around the village, she'd find herself looking into windows. Sometimes she'd see six, eight or ten people sitting round a laden table and hurry quickly on, hoping that Rosie hadn't noticed, too.

Christmas Day was the most difficult; during the lead-up the whole community would get together to string coloured lights around the village and they'd wander in and out of each other's houses to eat mince pies and drink glasses of mulled wine. And on 25 December, brave souls would gather to swim at 10 a.m. while the others would buy drinks from The Lobster Pot and watch from the comfort and safety of the sea wall.

But at around midday, when everyone peeled off with their extended families, Liz and Rosie would be left alone. She tried to create a sense of occasion, but unwrapping their presents seemed to take no time at all and then there was the whole afternoon and evening ahead with just each other for company. Rosie didn't seem to mind, though. She was always happy at home; it was only school that made her upset.

Iris had invited them for twelve so they got ready slowly then Liz helped Rosie with her stretching exercises, which they often rushed due to lack of time and also because she hated doing them.

Rosie lay on her back on the floor while Liz placed a can of beans first to the left of her, then to her right, and she had to reach across the middle of her body a set number of times to pick the can up, groaning as she did so because it was so hard for her.

When she'd finished, Liz held her feet while she practised the 'wheelbarrow walk', walking on her hands across the room to strengthen the shoulder muscles and encourage her to bear weight on both arms. Then she had to roll a ball with her good hand to increase the weight even further on the tricky one.

'Enough!' Rosie insisted, when they'd completed six different routines. Liz could see that she was exhausted and she always felt like a monster, but it was for Rosie's own good.

'Well done,' she said, giving her daughter a hug. 'Now the hard work's over, let's have some fun!'

Rosie chose to wear jeans and her favourite pink fluffy jumper with a white T-shirt underneath in case it was hot in Iris's house. Liz opted for jeans, too, and a loose yellow smock top with tiny blue flowers on. She didn't wear it often because Rosie said it was too big for her, but it seemed Eastery.

Rosie wanted to keep her hair loose, so Liz gave it a good brush. It was so thick, straight and shiny, a mass of hair for one so small. Her crowning glory.

'Shall I trim the ends?' she asked, thinking that she hadn't done it for a while; it was down below her shoulder blades now. Rosie said no; she wanted to grow it long enough to sit on.

Liz riffled through the box of hair accessories that she kept in the bottom of her wardrobe, and found a yellow and white spotted, 1950's-style dolly bow to match her top.

Looking at herself in the mirror above her small chest of drawers, she decided that her fringe, which now obscured her eyebrows, was too long; soon she wouldn't be able to see out.

She took a pair of kitchen scissors and sliced off the ends. Snip snip snip. The whiskery bits went up her nose, making her sneeze. She brushed the remaining hairs on top of the chest into her hand and put them in the wastepaper basket.

It was odd being able to see her eyebrows again. They were dark brown and slim, arching in the middle and tapering into a narrow line at the sides. Her eyes stared back at her, very dark also, and for a moment she thought that she could detect the girl who'd once attracted Greg's attention.

She glanced away; it was a long time ago. She held the yellow and white spotty fabric round her head and twisted twice to secure it on top like a flower. She was ready.

She and Rosie walked, hand in hand, to the local shop, choosing the longer route down cobbled Fore Street towards the harbour and along the sea front. They stopped briefly to say hello to Esme, on her way via Ruby's to the clifftop Catholic church at Cardew Heights, and Barbara, who was watering the flowers outside The Lobster Pot.

It was a fine day – cool and windy but sunny – and there was a different feel in the air. Liz couldn't decide if this had more to do with the weather, the fact that it was holiday time or the sense that spring had finally arrived, decking the trees with pale green leaves and putting blooms in window boxes.

There were a lot more people about, too, folk that she didn't recognise from the rented cottages. A cheerful family – mum, dad and two boys of about Rosie's age – was going in the direction of the bay, carrying buckets and crab nets.

Dressed in brightly coloured cagoules, shorts and flip-flops, you could tell that they had money. The mother, in her thirties, had expensive-looking blonde hair, bold red shorts and big black sunglasses perched on top of her head while the dad, tanned, looked as if he'd just come back from a skiing trip. But most of all, Liz decided, it was their faces: relaxed and unlined. Perhaps you always looked like that when you were on holiday.

They were optimistic, she thought, to be braving the beach today; the wind was deceptively cold and she suspected that they wouldn't last long.

Tony Cutt was just leaving the grocery store as they arrived, with a handsome young man in tow. They were wearing matching sky-blue scarves and, Liz noticed, bright red Converse shoes.

'Meet Felipe,' Tony said loudly. 'He's Brazilian and hardly speaks a word of English.' Felipe, who had dark hair and smooth, olive skin, shrugged and smiled at Liz, who extended a hand.

'Does he speak Spanish?' Rosie piped up, eyeing the stranger curiously.

'Portuguese,' Tony replied cheerfully. 'Impossible language. I've got him a private English tutor, but I'm afraid he's a very lazy student.'

He gazed at Felipe adoringly and the young man grinned back. They seemed very loved up.

The store was busy and there weren't many Easter eggs left. Liz and Rosie chose a milk chocolate one shaped like a bunny for Spencer, some truffles in a gold and silver box for Iris and Jim and the same for Iris's mum.

'Shame we didn't win the lottery last night, we could have bought that one,' said Rosie, pointing to an enormous egg surrounded by smaller gold ones in a box on the top shelf.

'You'd be sick if you ate all that,' Liz laughed.

'No I wouldn't,' said Rosie.

They parked in Liz's usual spot in the office car park. It was strange to see it so empty at this time, the windows of the building dark and faceless with no sign of activity inside. It would be a different story on Tuesday when it reopened.

Rosie hadn't been in Good Morning News for some years and was interested to see Iris again and remind herself where it was that her mother bought their weekly ticket.

'Is Iris *always* in that same place?' she asked, spotting her through the window at the counter. 'Is it always empty?'

It occurred to Liz that there were only ever one or two customers, if that. Sometimes no one came in when she was there, even when she bought her ticket after work. She supposed it must be hard trying to make a living as a newsagent these days. Maybe they needed to be right in the centre of town.

'Here's our Rosie!'

Iris jumped up when they entered and hurried around the counter to greet them, enveloping Rosie in a big hug.

She was looking particularly glamorous. She must have straightened her wavy, rich-red hair, which was now smooth around her face so that you could see the carefully cut layers, and she had on lots of bright purple eyeshadow and thick mascara. She smelled of flowery perfume and the gold bracelets on her arms flashed and jangled like Gypsy Rose Lee.

Rosie, pulling back, looked a little shy and Iris tutted.

'Sorry, love, I'm overwhelming you. It's just, your mum tells me so much about you. It doesn't seem like yesterday since you were this size!' She signalled to about knee height to demonstrate.

She called to Jim, 'They're here!' and he appeared from a room at the back of the shop. He, too, had smartened up and Liz commented on his blue and white checked shirt – 'Very smart!'

He was short and grey-haired, balding, with a round beer belly straining at the buttons of his top. He reminded her slightly of her dad, although Jim was a good few years younger than Paul.

'Come on in,' he said jovially, putting an arm round Liz's back to guide her. 'Iris is going to close up. No point staying open. The place has been dead as a doornail all morning.'

Liz had never seen the flat and she was slightly concerned, as they climbed the dark, narrow stairway to the top, that Rosie's spirits would be failing. But once they reached the landing, it opened out into a small but light three bedroom apartment with a kitchen at one end and a reasonably sized sitting-cum-dining room in the middle.

There was scarcely time to take it all in, though, because before they knew it people were emerging from different doors, smiling and embracing them. It was difficult to imagine, in such a small space, where they all fitted in. Only Iris's mum was nowhere to be seen.

'The old girl's watching *EastEnders*,' Jim explained, as if reading Liz's mind. 'She'll be out later, soon as she smells the grub.'

It was hard to manoeuvre her way into the sitting room as Spencer's toys were all over the burgundy carpet. He was a sweet, chubby toddler, still uncertain on his feet, with fair hair and enormous blue eyes.

Rosie lasted all of about two minutes beside Liz on the brown velvet sofa before she was down on her hands and knees, vrooming toy cars in and out of the plastic garage, much to Spencer's fascination and delight. The garage had a lift that you could wind up and down but it didn't work very well and the toy people kept falling out.

'Whoops!' Rosie said when another one took a tumble, and Spencer squealed with laughter.

'She's good with little ones, isn't she?' Christie commented. Liz had met her before, of course, but had never found her particularly easy to talk to. At twenty-one, there was the same age gap – twelve years – between her and Liz as there was between Liz and Iris. But for some reason she felt that she had far more in common with the older woman.

Although Christie was a single mum too, she lived at home still and Iris would be the first to admit that she spoiled her rotten.

'I can't help it,' she'd say to Liz, usually after explaining that she'd cancelled some engagement of her own to babysit Spencer so that Christie could go out. 'She looks at me with those big blue eyes – just like her dad's – and I melt. Still, I can't complain. Spencer's no trouble.'

Liz thought back to when Rosie was a baby and couldn't remember a single occasion when she'd gone out on her own or with Greg. They had no family to help and couldn't afford babysitters. He, of course, had hardly altered his routine at all; he was still out every night while she'd kissed her old life goodbye and grown up fast.

'What's your tipple?' Jim shouted; he was standing right in front of her and had a very loud voice.

Liz hesitated. She rarely drank these days and wasn't sure what to say. 'Um, what do you have? I'll have the same as everyone else.'

Jim laughed. 'We've got the full works here, it's like a bloody off-licence. Beer, lager, wine, G and T? Her mother likes a drop of whisky.' He nodded in the direction of the door and raised his eyebrows.

'No thanks,' Liz said quickly, thinking of the drive home. 'I'll have wine, please.'

'Get me a lager, will you, Dad?'

Darren, their nineteen-year-old son, was opposite Liz, a heavily tattooed arm wrapped around his slim blonde girl-friend, Kelly.

Darren occasionally wandered into the shop but rarely helped out, as far as Liz could tell. He was doing a plumbing course at college but Iris was always complaining that he wasn't putting his back into it and missed too many classes.

A handsome lad with closely cropped dyed blond hair, a small gold loop in his left ear and a ready smile, he was more outgoing than his sister.

'Whereabouts d'you live then, Liz?' he asked politely, and when she told him: 'Bit quiet there, isn't it?'

She explained that she liked the quiet but that it was a different place in summer, packed with tourists.

'Not much in the way of nightlife, though?' He looked puzzled, as if no one could possibly choose to settle in such a deadbeat location.

'I don't go to nightclubs much – at all, actually,' she added truthfully, 'so it doesn't really bother me. The young ones always seem to be going to parties, though. I guess they hang out at each other's houses when the pubs shut.'

Darren made a sound, like a small explosion.

'You don't go clubbing? You haven't lived!'

He glanced at Kelly, who nodded. She looked very happy tucked under his arm and seemed like the sort of girl who'd agree with whatever he said.

'We'll have to take you down the Anglers one night. We'll get a crowd together. It'll be a laugh.'

He leaned over to Christie, who was watching Spencer and Rosie on the floor.

'That's right, isn't it, Chris? We'll take Liz clubbing one night?'

Christie looked up and nodded. 'Yeah. Not the Anglers though.' She didn't seem very enthusiastic. 'Options is better.'

Darren huffed. 'Nah, that's for tarts and nancy boys.'

'I beg your pardon.'

Iris, who'd been clattering pans in the kitchen, walked into the room in a floral apron and cuffed him playfully on the head. 'You mind your language, young man, or I'll wash your mouth out with soap.'

Jim reappeared with glasses of wine for Liz, Christie and Kelly, a bottle of lager for Darren and a beer for himself. Iris was already clutching a gin and tonic, which she raised ceilingwards: 'Chin-chin!'

'Cheers!' they chorused.

It wasn't long before delicious smells were wafting from the kitchen and Liz felt her tummy rumble.

She offered to help Iris, who refused. 'You just sit down and relax. It's all under control.'

112

'Famous last words,' Jim joked, giving his wife a squeeze.

He winked at Liz. 'Need to keep an eye on her. She gets a bit happy-go-lucky when she's had a few.'

'Cheeky!' Iris laughed. 'I'm a better cook than you, that's for sure.'

'Too true,' Jim nodded. 'I only married you for your roast dinners.' He paused for effect. 'Actually, it was for your body. Erm, your mind.'

Rosie had found a pile of books and Spencer was now sitting on her knee, entranced as she read to him. It was a funny sight because he was chubby and she was so slight that it seemed he might crush her, but they looked content.

'Moo went the cow, baa went the sheep,' Rosie said dramatically, before turning the page.

Liz noticed that she was holding the book rather close to her face, before lowering it to show Spencer the picture. Was she short-sighted? She must ask Rosie about it later; perhaps she needed an eye test.

Darren and Kelly got up to lay the table in the far corner of the room while Iris and Jim disappeared into the kitchen again and Liz found herself chatting with Christie. She didn't have a job. 'I can't,' she explained. 'Spencer's dad useless and there's no one else who can look after him when Mum's in the shop.'

She seemed a little listless until she got on the subject of nail polish. Liz had complimented her on her beautifully manicured nails, coloured an unusual shade of lilac with a tiny hand-painted flower on each surface.

'There's this brilliant girl – she's Korean – who used to work in New York,' Christie said animatedly. 'She can do all these different designs. Sometimes she uses foil strips, which work great. She did me lush gold glitter ones last week.'

'Has your mum ever been to her?' Liz asked, thinking of Iris's purple eyeshadow and gold bangles. 'I bet she'd love it.'

Christie shook her head. 'Nah. Says she can't afford it. I can't either.' She shrugged. 'But I do it anyway.'

By now Liz was really hungry and she was sure Rosie must be, too; it was hours since they'd eaten breakfast.

Iris's mum clearly felt the same way because she emerged from her bedroom and poked her head round the door asking if lunch was ready.

'Not yet, Gran,' Christie told her. 'Won't be long.'

Doris, as she was called, shuffled into the room and sat down with some effort beside her granddaughter.

'Would you like your whisky, Gran?' Darren called and Doris nodded: 'Thank you dear.'

She looked at Liz, who hadn't yet been introduced.

'You must be Iris's friend. She told me about you.' She shifted slightly, wincing. 'Arthritis,' she explained, rubbing knobbly hands along tan-coloured tights. 'My knees are playing up something shocking. The doctors say I need two replacements but there's a long wait.' She shook her head. 'Don't know what's happened to the NHS. It's gone to the dogs.'

'It's not that bad, Gran.' Darren handed her a big tumbler of whisky which seemed to perk her up. 'Once you've got your new knees you won't know yourself.'

Rosie was now building a tower with different sized plastic rings which Spencer kept knocking down, making them both laugh.

Doris, noticing, smiled and her face lit up, making her appear years younger. 'Look at the pair of them. Bless 'em.'

She turned back to Liz. 'I know I'm lucky. Iris is so good to me. And Darren and Christie.' She glanced at them affectionately. 'And Jim,' she added hastily. 'Is your mum close by?'

Liz said that her mother was dead and steered the subject quickly on to Croydon where Doris, too, had grown up. She didn't fancy discussing Paul – or Tonya for that matter. It was too difficult to explain.

At last lunch was ready and they all moved to the table, which now had a white cloth on and a bunch of pink carnations in the middle. Someone had also put a mini Easter egg, wrapped in red foil, beside each glass.

It was too much for Spencer. Strapped into a white plastic highchair, he leaned across the tray in front of him, straining to reach his egg and failing. When no one came to his aid he kicked his feet against the table and screamed.

'Hush,' said Iris, putting down an oval plate with a big leg of piping hot lamb on top surrounded by sprigs of rosemary and roasted garlic cloves. 'Give him it, Chris, or we won't be able to hear ourselves think.'

Rosie, sitting between Spencer and her mother, was delighted to be allowed to peel the egg for him and watch while he squished it between podgy fingers and smeared it round his mouth and nose.

'More's gone on his face than down his trap,' Iris laughed comfortably, sitting beside Jim who was at the head of the table, sharpening his carving knives.

'He won't eat his dinner now,' Christie complained, making a dive towards her son with a paper napkin which he pushed crossly away.

'Leave him alone,' Doris cried. She was in place of honour at the other end of the table. 'He's having a fine old time.' She leaned towards her great-grandson. 'If you can't eat chocolate on Easter Sunday, when can you have it, eh?'

There was a magnificent spread of crispy roast potatoes, broccoli, parsnips, peas, carrots and Jim's famous gravy.

'Tuck in,' Iris cried, taking a sip of the red wine that Darren had poured. 'Don't let it go cold.'

She rose to put a pile of vegetables on Doris's plate along with several slices of lamb, which were cooked perfectly: dark brown on the outside and pink within.

'Here, I'll cut it for you,' she said, slicing the lamb into bite-sized pieces and pouring a generous helping of gravy on top while Doris nodded appreciatively.

Liz, who'd noticed Rosie eyeing her lamb, swiftly did the same for her before she could object. She didn't usually want help, but tough meat could be a problem and Liz knew that she'd be mortified if she made a mess.

'Aren't we the lucky ones?' Doris exclaimed, picking up on Rosie's unease. 'Bet you wish you could have your food cut up for you, don't you, Jim?'

'Sure I do,' he replied. 'Wouldn't mind being like Spencer in that chair of his either, waited on hand on foot.'

He winked at Rosie who broke into her gappy smile and said, 'You'd look funny in that chair.'

'Don't reckon my belly would fit,' replied Jim, patting his gut.

'No way,' Doris chipped in, taking a slurp of wine. 'You'd break the bloody thing to pieces.'

The conversation flowed and the room filled with laughter as Darren recounted the tale of how one of his mates on a lads' trip to Prague got stuck on a fire escape wearing nothing but his underpants and clutching a bottle of vodka.

'The door shut and there was no way back in, see,' he said, his eyes filling with tears of amusement. 'He was hammering away but we didn't hear, the telly was on too loud. It was only when this massive landlady – she was huge...'

He opened his arms wide to demonstrate.

'... it was only when she was doing her rounds and heard him bashing on the door that she let him in. She was furious – he said he thought she was going to lay into him, she was that mad – and she confiscated the vodka.

'When he got back to the room he was shivering and we didn't know what he was on about. We hadn't even noticed he was missing.'

Liz found herself laughing so much that her stomach hurt; it was partly Darren's facial expressions that did it.

She could see that Rosie was enchanted, too. She kept looking, wide-eyed, from one adult to another, soaking it all up. Every now and then she'd stop to pop a mouthful of mashed potato or a bit of carrot in Spencer's mouth with her good hand. He, too, seemed to be enjoying the occasion because for once he was quiet, only drawing attention to himself now and again when he whacked his spoon on the plastic tray and sent bits of food flying.

Almost everyone wanted seconds – it was so good. Only Christie said little but Liz noticed that she was gentle with Doris, chopping up her new serving of lamb and reminding Darren to refill her glasses with water and wine. And she was clearly taken with Rosie, allowing her to play mummy.

'A bit less,' Liz heard her say softly when Rosie tried to pop a large chunk of lamb in his mouth. 'That's it. He hasn't got all his teeth yet.'

Liz wasn't sure if she could manage dessert, but when Iris produced a bowl of home-made trifle and a chocolate cheese-cake, she couldn't resist.

'I won't be able to eat for a week,' she said, fiddling with the waistband of her jeans which suddenly felt tight.

'Ach, you could do with fattening up,' Jim said jovially,

helping himself to another slice of cheesecake. 'There's nothing of you.'

Later, after they'd all helped with the clearing away, Doris repaired to her bedroom with the truffles that Liz and Rosie had given her, to watch an old episode of *Downton Abbey*. Christie, Darren and Kelly, meanwhile, said they'd organise an Easter egg hunt for the children round the flat. It wasn't going to be easy in that small space with Rosie's beady eyes on them, though she promised not to peek.

Jim settled down to read the paper and Liz found herself chatting with Iris in the kitchen.

They were perched on two wooden stools, sipping mugs of tea, and Liz said how grateful she was to have been invited.

'We've had such a lovely time,' she said, meaning every word. 'You've got a wonderful family. You must be very proud.'

'I'm glad you could come,' Iris replied. 'Your Rosie's a little star.'

They got onto the subject of work and Liz mentioned that she'd been offered an extra shift at the restaurant on Saturdays.

'You should come sometime,' she said brightly. 'The food's really good. All freshly cooked.'

Iris's grey eyes clouded and she took a sip of tea. She looked tired, suddenly, and Liz hoped that catering for so many hadn't been too much.

'Don't s'pose we could afford it. We don't go to restaurants these days, to be honest with you. Business has been so bad and then there's Jim's—'

She stopped herself but Liz could see that there was something she wanted to share.

'What is it?' she said, concerned. 'He's all right, isn't he?'

Her mind had scattered in all directions.

118

'Lord yes,' said Iris, placing one plump knee over another. She was wearing a tight white top, black trousers and black high heels. 'He's fit as a fiddle, my Jim. He'll outlive us all. No the thing is...'

She got up to close the kitchen door before leaning closer to Liz and resuming in a lowered voice: 'The thing is, we had a bit of savings. Not much, you know, but it was a nest egg. Put by for a rainy day, sort of thing. Well, Jim met this bloke down the pub one evening, Simon, he said he was called, Simon Reeves, and they got chatting and he persuaded Jim to put some money into this bar he was going to open.'

Liz had a nasty feeling that she knew what was coming but kept quiet, allowing Iris to continue.

'Well, it was supposed to have a theme. The last days of the Raj or something, I don't know.' She raised her eyes heavenwards. 'Anyway, he was very plausible, this Simon, and when Jim came home he was buzzing, telling me all about how it was a brand new concept, there was plenty of demand round here, he'd shown him the business plan and it was all kosher, blah blah blah.

'I said we didn't know anything about this Simon and we shouldn't go putting all our savings into some crazy venture but Jim wasn't having any of it. "We'll be rich," he said. "I'll buy you that Porsche you always wanted. And a house on the seafront and a retirement place in the sun." Those were his exact words.'

Iris looked tearful now and Liz fetched her a piece of kitchen towel, for want of anything else to hand.

'Anyway,' said Iris, composing herself. 'You can imagine how it ends, can't you?'

Liz winced.

'He took our money and the next thing we knew, he'd buggered off, left the country most like, and no one knows where he is. He's not even called Simon Reeves, founder of Spectrum Enterprises. There's no such person, no such company. So it's goodbye to our savings, hello skid row, cos the shop's losing money, too, and I don't know how long we can keep it going.'

She blew into the kitchen roll.

'I never imagined I'd be in this position in my mid-forties, you know. I thought we'd be, well, not exactly living in the lap of luxury but at least comfortable. We've always worked hard – and now we've got nothing to show for it.'

Liz was speechless for a moment, until anger kicked in and outrage on her friend's behalf. She couldn't quite believe it.

'Surely the police can do something?' she cried. 'Surely they can trace him somehow?'

Iris patted her friend's knee, as if she were the one who needed comforting.

'They don't even know who they're looking for, that's the problem. He's very clever and he covered his tracks well. I'm afraid we were had, good and proper.'

Chapter Nine

As THEY DROVE home that evening, Liz felt an overwhelming sense of sadness. Rosie was chattering away about Spencer and all the experiences she'd had that day, but Liz found that she couldn't join in. She just 'mmmed' every now and then to keep her daughter happy.

She was shocked by the injustice of what she'd heard. Here they were, this kind, hardworking couple, trying their best for their children and grandchild, not to mention Iris's mum, when along comes a fraudster who spots an opportunity to fleece them of their savings and seizes it.

Of course it was silly of Jim to tell him about the money – and even stupider not to be suspicious – but it just showed how trusting he was and how much he wanted to help his loved ones and find a way out of their financial difficulties.

You could tell how much they all adored one another, Jim, Iris, Darren, Christie, Spencer and Doris; they were such a close-knit bunch. There was a lot wrong with society today, she thought, noticing a traffic jam ahead and shifting gear. Families were far too fractured. She wished more people were like them.

'Mum, you're not listening,' Rosie called crossly from the back seat.

'Sorry, I'm concentrating on the road,' Liz replied. 'I think there's been an accident.'

She worried that Iris and Jim had spent too much on lunch that day and found herself pondering what she could do in return. There wasn't room in the cottage to entertain them all and she couldn't afford to take them out. Perhaps she'd treat Iris to something. A pizza in town one Sunday evening, maybe, if Pat would mind Rosie. It wasn't much but it would be a thank you of sorts.

The next time Liz popped into Good Morning News to buy a lottery ticket, Iris didn't mention their conversation and seemed her normal, chirpy self again. Liz couldn't help noticing how bare the shelves beyond her counter were, though. How long had they been like that? She hadn't looked properly before.

Cans of soup and beans sat forlornly beside dusty-looking bottles of shampoo and boxes of cat food, while the small chilled food section on the other side contained little more than a few packets of ham, some cartons of milk and the odd lump of cheese. She couldn't imagine anyone stopping by for last-minute groceries here. The problem was, she supposed, that they never did.

She was so busy that the next few months whizzed and before she knew it, the summer holidays were on them. Instead of going to school, Rosie spent the mornings with Jean, who had a big paddling pool in her garden and sometimes took her charges on outings to the beach or park.

She whinged a bit because there was no one her age to play with, but she liked helping Jean with the little ones and besides, Liz was normally back to pick her up by twelve.

Tremarnock, of course, was heaving with holidaymakers and Liz couldn't find a parking space for love nor money near the cottage and had to park way up the hill or round the corner. In truth, it felt like a different village entirely. The air was filled with strange voices, the pavements, pubs, harbour and shops packed with folk who seemed to forget that they were visitors and behaved as if the place belonged to them.

She didn't complain, though, because she knew that the locals depended on the money they brought in. Without them, the village would die. So she smiled when they walked two, three or four abreast, stepping onto the road and circling round instead of asking them to make way. And if they looked lost, she was the first to stop and offer help with directions or recommend the best places to drink or eat.

Certainly, Robert was having a good summer. Gretel had indeed written a fantastic review about the restaurant in her paper, applauding the breadth of the menu with its foreign influences, as well as the classic, locally caught fish and shellfish dishes. She'd also added that the service was 'attentive and personal' and the staff 'enchanting', which Liz couldn't help suspecting was a sly reference to Jesse's impressive torso. Whatever, it seemed to do the trick.

A Winkle In Time was full every evening during the latter part of July and all of August and Robert even had to turn people away. Liz and the others were virtually run off their feet, though Loveday still seemed to manage to slip out for regular phone breaks to arrange her social life or dump another hapless boyfriend.

As Liz had predicted, Nathan the poor postman was history and Loveday was now stepping out with Barbara's youngest son, Aidan, who helped run The Lobster Pot. At thirty-three he was rather old for her, plus he had a couple of kids from a former relationship over in Launceston. Seemed he was a good dad who tried to see them as much as possible and Loveday was already complaining. Liz suspected that his days would be numbered, too.

She was exhausted by the end of each shift but it was worth it, making up for the quiet times in winter when she guessed that Robert might make a loss. What's more, she was raking in the tips.

She'd count them every evening when she got home, putting aside what she'd need to pay Jean for the extra hours of childminding and popping as much as she could of the remainder in the 'Rosie's Trip' jar, which she kept on a shelf in the kitchen cupboard.

It was coming along nicely now, in fact she'd almost scraped together the full amount; the rest would be for new clothes for Rosie and spending money. She was determined that her daughter wouldn't go short.

There was a mini heatwave in the latter part of August when the temperature gauge swung briefly into the early thirties, which was fine if you were holidaying but not so great for the workers.

Dolphin House, a 1970s-built office block, was badly insulated – too cold in winter, too hot in summer – and felt stuffy even in the morning. Kasia seemed to feel it the most.

'It's like a sauna,' she said grumpily, when they were putting on their overalls at the start of the day. Her face was damp with sweat already. 'Too much glass… air conditioning doesn't work.' She was talking so fast that Liz couldn't catch every word but the gist was clear enough.

She was loading her trolley so quickly that a bottle of cleaning fluid toppled off and landed on her foot, which put her in an even worse rage.

'How they expect us to do our jobs in these conditions?' she rattled, before stomping off down the corridor. 'Is inhuman.'

'Sheesh,' said Jo, who was watching the proceedings with some trepidation, fearing, no doubt, that Kasia would take it out on them. 'She don't like the heat, do she?'

A large young woman with a greyish complexion and greasy blonde hair pulled back off her round face, she was having some difficulty doing up the buttons on her blue overall. When at last the job was done she bent forwards and clutched her stomach, as if something were hurting.

'You OK?' Liz asked, concerned.

'Time of the month,' Jo replied darkly.

'D'you want a painkiller? I think I've got one in my bag.'

Jo shook her head. 'They don't do no good. There's so much blood, great big clots. Danny says I should have a... what's it called?'

'A hysterectomy?' Liz said helpfully, wishing that she could be spared the medical details.

'That's it, one of them. Well, he says I should have it but I want another baby.'

'Another one?' said Liz, aghast. Jo was only twenty-eight and already had four children, which always seemed like four too many the way she talked about them.

Jo shrugged. 'I know, I'm bonkers, aren't I? My mum says it's my hormoynes.'

'You mean hormones?' Liz asked, puzzled.

Jo nodded gravely. 'They're the ones. Little buggers they are. Mum says they've a lot to answer for.'

Liz had visions of Jo's mother wagging a finger at her daughter's troublesome hormones to no avail. It seemed that they might be deaf to all reason.

Having finished the sixth floor, she took the lift down to the flight below and after cleaning the kitchen, made her way to the office. There'd obviously been a celebration of sorts the night before because there were the dry remains of a cake on the central island, along with plastic cups, some half filled with stale-smelling wine, and a few empty bottles.

She plonked the cake in a black bin bag and was sweeping up the crumbs with a cloth when she heard a strange noise, half yawn half groan, coming from behind.

Spinning round, she was astonished to see a dishevelled-looking woman emerge from underneath one of the desks and attempt to smooth down her creased black pinstriped skirt.

'Oh!' said Liz, lost for words.

The woman, bleary-eyed, was barefoot and clutching a crumpled jacket that matched the skirt.

'Sorry for scaring you.'

She was about the same age as herself, Liz thought. Tall and attractive, were it not for the smeared black mascara and hair that suggested she'd been out in a gale force wind.

'I was out last night and couldn't get home,' the woman explained, bending down to put on her high-heeled shoes which had clearly been kicked off in a hurry.

So that's why the alarm was off when they entered the building. Kasia had gone on about burglars though Liz suspected that security had simply forgotten to set the overnight switch.

'Had quite a good kip, actually.' The woman grinned sheepishly. 'Better have a shower before the others arrive. I must look like a dog's dinner.'

Liz couldn't help laughing. 'Good night, was it?'

The woman winced, rubbing her forehead as if it hurt.

'Got a bit carried away with some clients. I had a drink here first and I was supposed to have just one more and drive home. Unfortunately it didn't work out like that.'

'Let me get you some coffee.'

The women chatted for a few moments in the kitchen

while the kettle was boiling. Liz gleaned that her new friend was called Hannah, an accountant, and she'd only been in the job three weeks.

She asked Liz a little about her situation and she found herself mentioning Rosie and the restaurant job.

'Gosh, you've got your hands full.'

Hannah revealed that she'd been to boarding school in Hampshire, which explained the cut-glass accent, and that she was single.

'Haven't met Mr Right yet, but that's not for want of trying,' she smiled, swigging back a whole glass of water in one go before starting on the coffee. 'That's better. Bloody hell, it's boiling again today, isn't it?' She was wearing a less than pristine white shirt and raised an arm, sniffing her armpit and pulling a face.

'Pooh! Thank God I've got a clean shirt. Always keep one in case I slop something down the front. It's my forte. And a spare pair of knickers for other eventualities.' She winked at Liz.

'There's some cereal in the cupboard if you're hungry?' Liz replied, changing the subject quickly. She wasn't sure that they were quite well enough acquainted yet to discuss Hannah's sex life. 'I don't know whose it is but I'm sure they won't mind.'

Hannah grimaced. 'Ta, but I'm not hungry. Coffee's hitting the spot, though. I'll go for a fry-up later. That usually does the trick.'

Liz was so hot and sticky by the time she picked up Rosie from Jean's that she suggested going straight to the beach for a swim. Rosie fancied driving to the sandy one three miles away but it was half twelve once they'd changed into their bathing suits and picked up towels and a picnic and Liz was anxious about getting back for the restaurant.

'Parking will be a nightmare,' she pointed out. 'Let's walk to Tremarnock beach. It'll be more relaxing.'

The small beach, a mix of sand and shingle sheltered on both sides by rocky promontories, was heaving and it was quite hard to find a space to lay their towels. It was low tide and the warm pools, exposed when the sea retreated, were full of small children searching for shells, crabs and other interesting creatures. Meanwhile, mums, dads and grandparents were spreadeagled on the ground, soaking up the rays or huddling under parasols.

Behind them was the sea wall and beyond that, gaily painted houses, shops and pub in white, yellow and pink. The bright seemed to sun bounce right off them so that Liz was grateful for her sunglasses and straw hat.

Rosie complained while Liz smothered her in suntan cream which masked the scent of salt and seaweed, but she wasn't going to take any risks; her daughter's skin was so pale that she'd burn in a second.

'Let's swim,' Rosie said when Liz had finished.

'I have to do myself first. You go ahead. I'll join you in a second.'

Her heart ached as she watched her daughter in a red and white stripy costume make her way down the beach towards the water. Her limp was more pronounced without her shoes on and although she no longer tiptoed on her bad foot, you could tell that one leg wasn't quite right and the foot turned in at an odd angle.

Liz was aware of other people watching and could imagine what they were thinking: 'Poor little girl.' Some were probably thanking their lucky stars that their children weren't thus afflicted.

If only they knew, she thought. Rosie was so much more

128

than a funny leg and a tricky arm. She was a hero, so brave and grown-up; she was Liz's inspiration.

She was about to jump up and follow her daughter when the shingle scrunched beside her and someone sat down.

'Hi.'

She turned to see Robert, wearing a khaki wide-brimmed hat loosely tied at the chin, a long-sleeved white shirt and jeans. She noticed because he seemed so out of place with only his feet bare; everyone else was in bathing suits.

'Hello,' she replied, thinking that he might want to ask her to come to work earlier and fervently hoping this wasn't the case. She was careful not to look him in the eye.

'I was passing by and saw you down here.' He was fiddling with the button on his white cuff. 'How's Rosie?'

Liz said she was in the water and that she was about to go and join her.

'Fancy a swim?' she asked, thinking even as she spoke that it was a stupid question; he wasn't exactly dressed for it.

He shook his head. 'To tell you the truth, I'm not that keen on swimming. Never liked the water.'

'Oh.'

Heights, water. How could you not love the sea, she thought, when you lived in Cornwall? And whatever else wasn't he keen on? She didn't ask, though.

He cleared his throat noisily. 'I'll keep an eye on your stuff.'

'You don't need to, there's nothing valuable,' she said quickly, not wishing to detain.

'I'd like to sit down for a bit,' he replied, pulling his hat down further and resting back on his elbows. 'Not too long, though. Can't take a lot of sun.'

She felt self-conscious as she walked towards the water's edge in her sensible navy swimsuit, hoping that he wasn't watching. She was very white – not like the beach babes showing off nut-brown limbs in teeny bikinis. Some were little more than sandwich-sized triangles of material tied together with a bit of string.

Rosie was sitting on the water's edge, swishing her legs, scissor-style, in the lapping waves.

'It's cold,' she said as Liz dipped a toe in. It was, indeed, icy. She'd been so hot on the beach but now the prospect of full submersion was somehow less appealing.

'Come on, let's run.' She pulled Rosie up by her good arm and hand in hand they jumped over the waves until a big one knocked Rosie under and she resurfaced, spluttering and laughing.

'You get in.'

Liz, who was still standing, held up a hand. 'Wait.' She was building up to it. 'Don't you dare splash.'

Once she'd done a few strokes and grown used to the temperature, she had to admit that the water was lovely: cool, crystal-clear and deliciously refreshing after the office. They went out a little way, just beyond the crowds but not so far as to be out of their depths, and floated on their backs, gazing up at the cornflower-blue sky.

'This is the life, isn't it, Mum?' Rosie said, lapping the water gently with her hands and feet to stay afloat.

'It sure is.' Liz sighed, thinking that just for a moment she was completely happy. She wouldn't be anywhere but here, right now in the moment. If she could bottle the feeling up and keep it on her bedside table to release on gloomy days, she would.

'Where would we get to, if we carried on swimming far out, in that direction?' said Rosie, flipping round and pointing at the horizon.

'Ooh, I don't know, America maybe, if we kept going long enough.'

'I'd like to go to America one day. With you.'

They swam some of the way back underwater. Liz didn't like opening her eyes because the salt made them sting, but she could feel the ripples made by Rosie close beside her and imagined that she was a mother dolphin, guiding her calf.

When at least they reached the shore, she was almost reluctant to get out but she was hungry now and Rosie would be, too.

'Let's have our picnic,' she said, heaving herself up from sitting.

Remembering Robert, she scanned the beach and he was still sitting beside their pink and yellow towels.

'Look, there's "that man",' she joked. 'Robert.'

'Where?' said Rosie, squinting.

Liz pointed up the sand. 'Beside the lady in the turquoise bikini with the blue and white striped parasol. Just in front of The Lobster Pot.'

He was quite a long way off but she could easily pick him out because of his khaki hat and white shirt. The only clothed person.

'I can't see him,' said Rosie crossly, turning away.

Liz frowned. 'Do you think we should see the optician? Maybe you need glasses.'

'There's nothing wrong with my eyes,' Rosie huffed. '*You* go to the optician.'

Robert rose as they approached and handed them their towels, which they took gratefully. It was surprisingly chilly out of the water.

He hovered for a moment, looking hot and uncomfortable and fiddling with the button on his other cuff.

'I've made some sandwiches,' Liz said, fully expecting him to bolt at any moment. 'Would you like one?'

She thought that his face brightened a little – he seemed to be very good at feeding everyone but himself – but then he muttered about not wanting to impose.

'There's plenty, honestly.'

'Mum always makes too many,' Rosie chipped in, 'and we end up throwing them to the seagulls.'

She was shivering slightly and Liz helped her into a sweat-shirt. 'You can take it off when you've warmed up.'

At last Robert sat down again, eyeing with interest the square package wrapped in silver foil that Liz had produced from a red canvas bag.

'They're all cheese and tomato,' she explained, passing the opened package round. 'A bit dull, I know. I hope that's all right.'

Of course Rosie's fingers were gritty and she got some on her sandwiches and Liz had to rinse her hands with water.

'Here,' she said, passing the half-eaten food back to her daughter. 'A few specks won't do you any harm.'

It was only when she'd settled down again that she noticed a little pile of tomato slices neatly stacked by Robert's knee.

'I've got a bit of a thing about them,' he explained sheep-ishly. 'I think it's the texture.'

'You own a gourmet restaurant and you don't like toma-toes?' Liz teased. 'I won't tell the customers. Anything else you won't eat?'

Robert scratched his head. He was gazing out to sea. 'Um. Well I've never been fond of grapes – or rice. That's about it.'

Liz laughed. 'You like fish, I hope?'

'Oh yes, I like fish.'

'And puddings,' she added, thinking of the way he gobbled down the leftovers of dessert that she brought him.

'Definitely puddings.'

When they'd finished their sandwiches, Liz produced a brown paper bag filled with dark red cherries which they munched companionably side by side.

Three children of differing ages nearby, who'd been playing with a ball, were now demolishing ice lollies.

'I'm all sticky,' the smallest one cried to the eldest, waving a hand in the air.

The bigger girl inspected the little one's hand before taking another lick.

'We'll go in the sea and wash it off,' she announced gravely. 'When we've finished.'

'Do you have a brother or sister, Robert?' Rosie asked, putting a cherry stone on the leftover foil which had become the wastepaper bin.

Robert cleared his throat. 'I've got a younger sister who lives in Penzance. Her daughter Loveday works at the restaurant with your mum.'

'Do your parents live in Penzance, too?'

'No,' he replied. 'They're both dead.'

There was a pause while Liz tried to think of something less personal to talk about. She didn't want Rosie putting her foot in it. But she was too late.

'Are you married?' Rosie asked fake-innocently. She understood perfectly well that she was being nosy; Liz knew her of old.

'Rosie, I—'

'No,' Robert replied rather fast, and Liz feared that he was offended.

'Why not?'

Liz put a hand on her daughter's arm to stop her but he was frowning, poised to answer.

133

'I was going to get married once, but she changed her mind and it never happened.'

He looked sad and Liz wished that Rosie hadn't raised the subject. The last thing she wanted was to dredge up painful memories for him, especially on such a beautiful day.

'I'm sorry,' she said, scowling at her daughter who could be in no doubt now that she'd overstepped the mark. 'Rosie shouldn't have asked.'

'Oh it's all right,' Robert replied, folding his arms around his knees. 'It was a long time ago.'

He didn't look as if he'd got over it, though.

Having finished all the cherries and wrapped the stones up, Rosie wanted Robert to make a sandcastle.

He produced a phone for the first time from his breast pocket and sighed.

'I need to get back to work. We'll build one another time, if you like?'

'At the sandy beach?' Rosie suggested. 'It's better for castles; there aren't so many stones.'

'OK.' Robert pushed himself up to his full height. 'We'll get there just before high tide and build an enormous fortress and watch the waves come and knock it down.' He seemed to have recovered from the cross-examination and was waving his long arms round to demonstrate.

Liz had risen now as well, and felt naked suddenly in her swimming costume. She would have reached for her towel, except that would only have made it more obvious.

'Thanks for the picnic,' he said, formal again. Perhaps he'd noticed her unease. He was staring at her feet and she couldn't help glancing down to make sure that he hadn't spotted a nipping crab or a wasp or something. There was nothing there, of course.

'It's a pleasure,' she smiled, meaning it. 'Excuse the tomatoes, though. I'll remember next time.'

She realised as she watched him scrunch gingerly up the stony beach carrying his shoes that she was sorry to see him go. He was peculiar and awkward, no doubt about it, but there was something charming about him, too, in a funny sort of way. A vulnerability that touched her.

She took a deep breath and turned to Rosie. 'Last swim before we pack up? First one under wins a prize!'

Chapter Ten

IT WAS STILL hot by the time they left the beach and Rosie had to stop at the sea wall to drink the remaining water.

'Yeeuch! It's boiling,' she said, wiping her mouth with the back of her good hand.

'You can have a big glass of water with ice when we get home,' Liz said reasonably.

Rosie was reluctant to move and Liz had to hurry her. 'I've got to get showered and changed before work.'

Rosie nudged her. 'Look.'

Liz turned to see what she was staring at and clocked a young couple, sitting on the wall a few feet away with their arms wrapped around each other, locked in a steamy embrace.

She couldn't make out their faces properly but guessed from their general appearance that it was Darren and Kelly. She hadn't seen either of them since Easter Sunday.

Rosie giggled. 'That's disgusting.' She was thrilled.

Kelly spotted them with one eye and said something to Darren, who turned and gave a cheeky wave.

Liz thought it best not to disturb them but before she knew it, he'd jumped up and was loping in their direction. He looked very handsome, tanned and muscular, in a white vest top that showed off his biceps and tattooed forearms, denim shorts and flip-flops.

'Hi,' he said, unembarrassed. 'Been jostling with the emmets?' He had a pronounced West Country accent.

Liz nodded. 'It's so hot, isn't it?'

Darren stretched lazily. 'Yeah. I love it.'

He looked down at Rosie. 'How are you, young lady?

She flashed her gappy smile, delighted with the compliment.

Kelly strolled towards them, slim, blonde and very brown, in a fluorescent pink bikini, one of the smallest Liz had ever seen.

'All right?' she said, taking Darren's hand in hers as if she couldn't bear to be separated from him for a second.

Liz asked after Iris, whom she hadn't seen since last week, and said she'd be popping in to buy her lottery ticket.

'We live in hope, don't we, Liz?' Darren commented.

She smiled. 'Chance would be a fine thing. What news of Doris – has she got a date for her knee operation?'

'She had one but it got cancelled so we're back to square one.' He brightened. 'It's her birthday on Saturday. Seventy-five. Mum's organised a picnic.' He laughed, as if picnics were amusing; not the sort of thing he'd normally get up to anyway. 'She said she was going to invite you so I'm doing it instead. Fancy coming?'

Liz felt herself redden. It was sweet of him but she wouldn't accept even if she could. 'Oh no, I'm—'

'We're going out Tintagel way, I think. Gran likes a drive.'

He was so easygoing; there couldn't be many young men as friendly and relaxed as him.

'You been to Tintagel, Rosie?' Darren continued. 'Where King Arthur lived?'

Rosie hadn't. It was fifty miles away on the other coast, and somehow they'd never made the journey. Liz had always wanted to take her, though.

'I work Saturdays,' she said apologetically. 'Unfortunately.'

'Rosie can come then? She doesn't work Saturdays, does she?'

He winked at her and she smiled shyly back.

'I'll talk to Iris about it,' Liz said, thinking that an extra child was the last thing her friend would need.

'You do that,' Darren replied, putting an arm round Kelly, who snuggled into his side. 'See you Saturday then, Rosie, eh?'

They picked up two iced buns at the bakery on the way home for Pat and Rosie to eat later, but when Rosie sat down on the end of her bed in the cool, she said that she had another headache.

Liz frowned. 'I expect you've had too much sun. You should have worn that baseball cap like I told you.'

'I hate baseball caps.'

Liz went to fetch some medicine and noticed that the bottle was almost empty.

'You've been getting a lot of headaches lately. We should see an optician, just in case.'

Rosie looked tearful. 'Stop going on about opticians. I'm not going to wear glasses. Then they'll tease me about those as well as my big feet and claw hand.'

The penny dropped. So it was the thought of glasses that bothered her. Liz sat down beside her and gave her a hug. 'I'm sorry for bringing it up again.'

She made a mental note not to reintroduce the subject until Rosie was feeling better.

She popped into Pat's before work, ostensibly to accompany her to Dove Cottage. Really, though, Liz wanted a quiet word, away from Rosie, to warn the old woman about the headache.

'She's been getting them a lot recently,' Liz shouted.

They were standing in Pat's hall. The front and back doors were open and a welcome through breeze was fanning their hot legs and faces.

'What's that you said?' Pat was flapping her skirt around her like a flamenco dancer. She seemed to be getting deafer.

Liz repeated herself more loudly this time: 'I'm wondering if she might need glasses.'

Pat wiped her hands on her floral apron. She'd been dead-heading roses in her small back garden and the secateurs were sticking out of a pocket.

'I 'spect she's just hot and bothered like the rest of us, poor lamb.' She wiped a few strands of snow-white hair off her sticky forehead. 'We're not used to heat like this; it doesn't agree with us.'

Robert had opened all the doors and windows at A Winkle In Time but it still felt oppressive. There was a small fan whirring noisily on top of the bar but unless you were standing right alongside, you couldn't feel the benefit.

'I hope the heat doesn't put everyone off,' he muttered, staring disconsolately at Liz's feet. 'I tried to buy more but they only had two small ones left.'

'It's a pity they won't let you put tables outside,' Liz observed. 'I suppose there wouldn't be room for people to pass.'

In the kitchen Jesse was assembling the other fan, which was much bigger and stood on the floor.

His skin was burned to a deep golden brown and his hair, blond at the best of times, was now bleached almost white. He could be in an advert for the Cornish Tourist Board.

'Been at the beach again today?' Liz asked. She knew that he usually hung out at the sandy one that Rosie liked, which was a surfer's paradise.

He looked up and grinned and his teeth gleamed like pearls against his tanned face.

'Yeah. No waves but the crumpet weren't half bad.'

'That's sexist!'

Liz spun round to see Loveday glowering at the door in an eye-wateringly tight white vest top and a black miniskirt that could barely cover her backside.

Her hair, still shaved on the left, with one large hooped silver earring visible, was tied in a loose ponytail that hung down the right side of her face coquettishly.

'I apologise, your ladyship,' said Jesse, bowing sarcastically.

'You shouldn't talk about girls like that,' Loveday replied, stomping towards the backyard, wiggling her bum. 'It's disgusting,' she added for good measure.

They were fully booked all evening and Liz scarcely paused for breath. Before she'd had time to clear the tables, new customers were already arriving to take their seats, hovering while she laid clean knives, forks and glasses and asking for the drinks menu.

She got off to a bad start with an imperious customer in his early sixties, probably, out with his mousy-looking wife. You could tell that he was in a foul mood from the get-go due to his sour expression and the way he hustled his wife rudely through the entrance. Unless he always treated her like that, Liz thought, feeling a twinge of sympathy.

She asked them to wait a moment while she finished preparing the table and the man announced that he wanted the one by the far window. He was clearly used to getting his own way. When Liz said that it was already reserved, he went red in the face and claimed that as no one was there, he and his wife should have it.

'If they turn up late that's their lookout,' he stormed. The room had gone silent.

Liz tried to explain that they weren't in fact late; they'd booked for 9 p.m. and it was still only five to. And they'd specified on the phone that it was this particular table that they required whereas, as far as she could see, he'd stated no preference.

'It's outrageous,' the man said, grabbing one of the four chairs from the desired table for no apparent reason and plonking it in front of his own. 'Never known such poor service,' he bellowed at his wife, who nodded lamely.

'Can I get you the wine list?' Liz asked sweetly when they finally settled down. She was hoping that a stiff drink, perhaps, would improve his mood.

When he ordered a specific brand of gin – 'with plenty of ice and lemon. Don't give me the wrong one' – she noticed Robert hand some cash from the till to Jesse who raced out the back way to the off-licence, which was fortunately just round the corner and didn't close till half eleven in summer.

Naturally there was something wrong with every course, which had to be returned to the kitchen for modifications.

The wife, who'd looked rather pretty when she arrived in a pale blue frock and pearl necklace and earrings, seemed to diminish in size as time wore on and acquire extra years, so that by the end of the meal she seemed positively ancient.

The man wanted brandy to finish and insisted that his wife have something too even though she clearly didn't want it. By now, his cheeks were flushed, his eyes glazed and he was talking very loudly. Every now and again he'd glance round, smiling, to see if anyone was listening, pleased with his own joke or observation. The wife nodded and smiled back but said very little.

When Liz finally handed him the bill in a black wallet, he took an inordinately long time to check the figures against the menu. She stood with her hands behind her back, pretending to look out of the window and wishing that he'd hurry up.

All the other customers had left and he could tell that it was closing time. Liz could hear Jesse clanking dishes extra loudly in the kitchen and Alex walked past in civvy clothes to say a pointed, 'Night, Liz.'

At last the man looked up, frowning.

'You've charged me extra for spinach and peas.'

'You altered the order, if you remember, sir,' Liz said coolly. 'Your wife changed her mind about the rocket and parmesan salad so we took it back to the kitchen and the chef did spring vegetables instead.'

The man's eyes narrowed. 'So why are the vegetables more expensive? Does it cost more to cook a bit of spinach and a few peas than prepare a salad, hm?'

Liz took a deep breath. 'I'm not sure about that, sir. I don't decide on the menu or buy the ingredients, but those are our prices.'

The man set his elbows on the table and wrapped one hand over a fist, as if preparing for a fight. He was clearly in no hurry to go home. Liz's shoulders sagged and she could feel the sweat pricking under her armpits. She was dying to get out of her uniform.

'I'm not prepared to pay two pounds extra for a few vegetables when we only ordered them because the salad was mouldy. And my wife said there was too much salt in the spinach.'

Liz gritted her teeth. There was no way the salad was mouldy; she'd seen Jesse washing the rocket and lettuce leaves and they'd looked perfectly good to her; Robert wouldn't allow anything but the freshest ingredients.

But she needed to get shot of the man. 'If you'd like a refund I can talk to the manager—'

'Of course I want a refund, you stupid woman.'

Liz's mouth dropped open; she was so taken aback that she couldn't speak.

'People like you shouldn't be let loose on customers; you've got no idea about service,' he blustered. Spit had formed at the sides of his mouth which turned her stomach and she had to look away. 'You should be washing dishes, not waitressing. You need a brain to be a waitress, you know. It's quite clear you haven't got two brain cells to rub together.'

The last remark hit particularly hard. Tears of anger and outrage sprang to her eyes and every instinct screamed at her to defend herself. However, a small voice reminded her that this was Robert's restaurant and she should let him deal with it; she didn't want to say the wrong thing and make the situation worse.

Biting her tongue, she ran out back as quickly as possible where she found her boss locking the wine store. When she told him about the dispute, he actually growled. It sounded more like a lion cub than a lion but it was a growl nonetheless.

'I knew that man was trouble the moment he walked in. I can't stand people like that. He's a stuck up, arrogant...'

He stopped himself before the air turned blue and shook his head instead.

Liz hovered just out of sight by the kitchen door while he spoke to the man because she wanted to witness the fireworks. Jesse was right beside her, twitching with excitement and willing Robert on.

'D'you think he's going to let rip?' he whispered happily. 'The others'll be sorry they missed it. I've never seen him so hopping mad. In fact I don't reckon I've ever seen him mad at all.'

Robert had his back to her and the man raised his voice a few times. She caught the words 'totally unprofessional' and 'appalling service' and he waved his arms around but Robert, whose thin frame was silhouetted in the candlelight, appeared to take the verbal blows without a murmur.

Liz kept hoping that she'd hear him defend himself and the restaurant but he was bending forwards, nodding submissively, and in the end the man's posture relaxed and he was quiet.

When she asked afterwards what had happened, Robert shrugged. 'I knocked off the drinks and the wife's meal.'

'What, three whole courses?' Liz asked, aghast.

'Yes.'

'But why? There was nothing wrong with it. He was up for a fight. He was just making a fuss.'

Robert sighed and ran a hand through his hair.

'Not worth having an argument. Wanted to see the back of him. The customer's always right.'

Liz had to swallow her anger yet again. Maybe that was a good way to run a restaurant but if she were Robert, she'd have sent the man packing with a flea in his ear. It wasn't as if they wanted him back, after all. With luck he'd never darken their doors again.

Robert noticed her silence and bit the corner of a nail.

'I'm sorry he was rude to you, Liz.'

He shifted from one foot to another.

'He shouldn't have upset you.'

She paused, hoping for something more.

When nothing came she pulled on her cardigan and slung her bag over her shoulder.

'Good job I've got a thick skin,' she replied airily. 'See you.'

She didn't go back to the kitchen to fetch the portion of

lemon syllabub that she'd put aside for him, though; he'd have to find it himself.

Her pulse was still racing as she walked swiftly home through the dark streets and she had a peculiar urge to cry. 'Upset' was an understatement: that man had insulted her big time and it was the injustice that hurt more than the words themselves. She hoped that he had really bad indigestion and woke up with a crashing headache in the morning; he deserved it.

She realised that she was hurt, too, about Robert. She should have known that he'd wimp out of an argument but for some reason she'd expected more support.

She couldn't help thinking, as she put the key in the lock and tiptoed into Dove Cottage, that if war broke out Robert was the last person you'd want on your side. He'd probably team up with the enemy because he couldn't bear to offend them.

Pat was fast asleep in the chair, as usual, and all was quiet, but Liz was surprised to see the light on in Rosie's room. Her heart sank because she was so tired that she could barely move. She'd been hoping for a few quick puffs of a cigarette to calm her down, followed by a wash and bed, then she felt guilty for thinking of herself not her daughter and gave herself a mental ticking off.

She roused Pat gently and helped her on with her coat. She seemed a little dazed, so Liz held her by the arm as they went into her house and up the stairs.

'Thank you,' Liz whisper-shouted gratefully, as Pat sat on the end of her bed and slipped off her shoes. 'Was Rosie all right?'

'Seemed a bit quiet, to be honest with you,' the old woman replied, turning back the bedcovers and smoothing down the pink undersheet. 'Not her usual chatty self. 'Spect she was tired, poor lamb.'

Back home, Liz walked softly into her daughter's room to find her propped up against the pillow, a book on her lap.

'What's up, sweet pea?'

'I don't feel well,' Rosie replied tearfully. 'I've tried to get to sleep but I can't.'

Liz came and sat on the bed beside her and felt her brow which was warm, but that could have been the heat.

'What's the matter? Is it your head still?'

Rosie nodded.

Liz went to fetch the medicine bottle again and poured the last drops into a plastic spoon. 'This should do the trick.'

But a few hours later, Rosie appeared in Liz's room wearing pants and a T-shirt. It was too hot for anything else.

'C'mon then, hop in,' Liz said, shifting over and pulling back the sheet. If it was going to be a sleepless night, they might as well be insomniacs together.

Rosie climbed in and Liz snaked an arm round her daughter's slim back.

'Will you sing the bubbles song?' Rosie mumbled, slightly embarrassed because she knew that she was too old, really.

'I'm forever blowing bubbles...' Liz began. It was a wistful sort of tune; Liz had no idea where it came from but her mother had sung it to her at bedtime and she'd continued the tradition.

'Pretty bubbles everywhere,' she finished. 'Shall I do "Dream a Little Dream of Me" now?'

Rosie said yes.

Liz then worked her way through *Joseph and the Amazing Technicolor Dreamcoat*, which her mother had taken her to one birthday. So delighted was she that she'd gone home and learned all the lyrics.

As she sang, she found her mind drifting back to that

evening. Her tenth birthday, it was, so she'd have been the same age as Rosie now. Her mother, Katharine, had loved musicals, not that they went often because it was too expensive.

Katharine had learned tap and ballet as a little girl; she'd had singing lessons too and she was always humming tunes from some show or other. She'd probably have liked to go on the stage except that her parents weren't keen and anyway, she met Paul and had Liz and that was that.

But her enthusiasm for music and drama never waned and being a young mum, she seemed always full of fun, energy and ideas. She'd help Liz put on little plays with her friends which they'd show to the other parents. In truth, Liz was rather shy and had none of her mother's theatricality, so she'd usually choose a small part and assign herself to wardrobe or prop duties. But she enjoyed it all the same.

On her tenth birthday, they'd set off hand in hand for the theatre in central London. They'd caught the bus there and her mother had bought ice creams for them both at the interval; it was a tremendous treat.

Paul hadn't shared his wife's passion so it was something that she and Liz had just between the two of them, a special bond. Rosie, too, liked singing and plays, though she was too self-conscious to perform, and Liz thought how much she'd have enjoyed Katharine's ebullience and how dearly grandmother and granddaughter would have loved each other. If only... It was a heart attack that killed her. There'd been no warning, it had taken everyone by surprise.

She could hear Rosie's breath becoming slow and heavy at last.

'Shall we have "Close Every Door" again?' she whispered, knowing that it was her daughter's favourite. She seemed to prefer the ones with the haunting melodies.

'Rosie? Rosie?' she repeated softly.

But Rosie didn't answer; she was fast asleep.

When Liz popped in to buy her lottery ticket later that week, Iris immediately raised the subject of Doris's seventy-fifth birthday and the picnic in Tintagel.

'Is Rosie coming?' she asked matter-of-factly. 'I do hope so. She'll enjoy herself and it'll be company for Spencer.'

Liz hadn't checked with Rosie because she'd assumed that Darren was only being kind and there wouldn't be room for her in the car, anyway. But it seemed that they were taking two cars – the family Ford and Darren's Punto. Quite how he had the money to run it was a mystery as he was at college and didn't seem to have a part-time job. She suspected that it was probably poor Iris and Jim who forked out – when it came to their kids, they seemed unable to say no – but it was none of her business.

Rosie leapt at the idea, which pleased Liz because she wanted her daughter to be independent. Plus it would be a lot more fun than staying home on her own. Pat was seeing family, and Liz didn't want to have to ask Robert if she could bring Rosie to the restaurant again. She was probably old enough now to spend a few hours alone during the day which wasn't ideal, but if there was a problem she could always call on Esme, Jean or Tony Cutt, and Liz was only round the corner, after all. Even so, she was happy that, in the event, Rosie had better things to do.

They got up early that Saturday and drove to the flat, after picking up some biscuits and crisps for the picnic from the general stores. When they arrived, Iris was already outside loading baskets, colourful rugs and bottles of fizzy drink into the boot of the white car.

'There's enough to feed an army,' she laughed. 'I hope you're hungry, Rosie?'

She said that she was.

It felt strange saying goodbye but Liz knew that Rosie would be well looked after; she trusted Iris totally. She felt a twinge of envy when she saw the older woman take her daughter's hand and lead her into the shop because Liz would have liked to go herself, of course. As she drove away, she wound down the window because it was getting hot and sticky already, and turned up the radio, telling herself to be glad that her daughter was going to have a lovely day.

She and Robert had scarcely spoken since the debacle with the bad-tempered customer and she had the feeling that he was avoiding her. The lemon syllabub that she'd saved for him that night was still in the fridge and she wondered when, if ever, it would get thrown out. Perhaps it would still be there in a year's time with green mould growing on top, a nasty reminder of the customer's breathtaking rudeness towards her and the galling fact that he'd been allowed to get away with it.

She had a call from Rosie in the afternoon when she returned from the lunchtime shift. The signal was poor, but she could hear laughter in the background and Rosie passed the phone to Spencer, who gurgled something unintelligible and heavy-breathed a few times, unsure what to do with this strange new toy. Eventually, Rosie grabbed the phone back and the little boy shrieked.

'We'll be home around seven,' she shouted gaily. Liz could just about make out the words. 'Jim's going back with Darren, Kelly and Gran, and Iris is staying with me till you get home.'

'What about Christie and Spencer?' Liz wanted to know, thinking it would be an awful squash in the Punto with all six of them. 'Is Iris OK about waiting?' But the line had already gone dead.

Liz imagined that this was how it would feel when Rosie was in London; she'd have to brace herself: she was going to miss her dreadfully.

Iris was curled up in the armchair watching TV when Liz arrived home soon after midnight, and the two women embraced warmly.

'Rosie's such a character,' Iris said, rising. 'We love her to bits. Spencer follows her round like a puppy.'

Liz offered to put the kettle on but Iris refused, saying she was tired and was sure that Liz was ready for bed, too.

'We'll have another jaunt soon,' Iris promised, 'maybe one Sunday when you're not working. Bring your diary next time you come to the shop.'

Rosie's light was off, but she called out when Liz tiptoed past. It seemed that she couldn't sleep again but not, this time, because of a headache.

'It was brilliant,' she said, sounding excited and horribly wide awake.

Liz knew that she was itching to recount the day's events so she sat beside her in the dark, stroking her long fair hair and breathing in her daughter's particular scent, which reminded her of apples and orange blossom. Liz often found herself marvelling at how she always smelled sweet, even when she hadn't showered, and wondered how long it would last.

'The drive took ages and Gran kept needing to pee so we had to stop while she went in a field,' Rosie chattered. 'It was so funny.'

It seemed that they'd pitched camp in view of the castle

remains and Darren and Kelly had taken Rosie across the bridge and up a dizzying set of cliff steps to the island; Gran couldn't manage the walk, Spencer was too little and Jim was 'too lazy' so the others had stayed behind and watched them go.

'Darren says it's where King Arthur was born. You could really imagine him there. Darren, Kelly and I pretended we were knights and we had a sword fight with sticks and then Kelly said she didn't like fighting so he killed her and she pretended to die. She was so bad, we couldn't stop laughing.'

They'd played football with Spencer, but he kept picking the ball up and running off with it. Then they'd eaten a big picnic with sausage rolls and chicken legs and sandwiches and crisps and fizzy orange, which Rosie was never allowed at home.

'Iris made a massive chocolate cake for Gran but the candles kept blowing out. Gran said it was just as well because she didn't have enough puff for seventy-five candles anyway.'

On the way home they'd stopped for a swim – Spencer paddled and got his nappy all wet and had to be changed 'for the millionth time,' said Rosie, sighing dramatically. Then they'd bought fish and chips and eaten them on the beach and Gran had nodded off in the car and started snoring so they'd had to poke her.

'It was really fun,' Rosie said, slowing down at last. Liz had begun to think that she'd never stop.

'I'm so glad,' she replied, kissing her daughter's cheek. 'You must get some sleep now or you'll be shattered tomorrow.'

As she crept out of the room, Rosie whispered, 'Mum?'

Liz paused, wondering what was coming next. 'Yes?'

'I wish I'd met your mum. I wish she hadn't died – don't you?'

Liz swallowed. It was hard to talk about, even now. 'I do. You'd have loved each other so much.'

She hoped that was it but Rosie wasn't done yet.

'I wish we had a big family like them,' she went on, 'with a gran and a brother and a sister and cousins and a baby, maybe.' Her voice sounded very small in the darkness.

Liz took a deep breath. Rosie had never said that she was lonely but it was bound to crop up one day. She'd picked a bad time, when Liz was tired and unprepared. It was difficult to think straight.

'I know, but we've got each other, haven't we?' she said at last. It was hard to sound bright but she managed it somehow.

'It's not the same, though, is it?' Rosie persisted, pushing deeper. 'There aren't so many people to do things with.'

Liz racked her brains for the right words. Something comforting. She could do with being comforted herself right now. 'Well no, it's not the same, but we still have fun, don't we?'

Rosie was silent for a moment. You could tell that she was ruminating. 'Ye-es,' she said finally, 'but sometimes I feel sad when I see mums and dads and grandparents out with their children. Do you feel sad, too?'

A painful lump lodged in Liz's throat but she was determined not to give herself away. 'Sometimes, but not often.'

Please let this be the end of it. She was hovering anxiously in the shadows.

'Do you wish you and my dad were still together?'

This was easy. 'Me and your dad? No.'

'But don't you wish you had a husband? Not my dad, then – someone else?'

Another stab. Liz felt herself sway slightly. Sometimes it was OK to tell a white lie, wasn't it?

'I don't want a husband, I've got you. That's enough.'

At last Rosie seemed satisfied, or perhaps it was just exhaustion. 'Night, Mum.'

'Night,' Liz replied, closing the door softly behind her. 'Sweet dreams.'

But she knew that she wouldn't be dreaming sweetly that night. As she lay in bed her mind was like a carnival ride, swooping up and down and round and round, making her giddy. For one moment she'd rest, then before she knew it she was hurtling off again, turning the conversation over and over until she felt sick.

Was Rosie deprived? Had she, Liz, made a mistake thinking that she could bring her up alone? Perhaps they should never have moved to Cornwall; they could have stayed in Balham, close to Greg. At least then Rosie might have had some sort of relationship with her dad.

Maybe, in time, he'd have had her to stay with him for the odd weekend. She'd have met his girlfriend or wife or whatever, got to know his drippy brother and chilly parents. Become part of that family, for good or ill. Perhaps any family was better than no family at all?

Then Liz remembered the way that he'd shouted at Rosie for crawling instead of walking on her sore foot, bruised and blistered by the hated ankle brace. The way he'd changed and grown colder towards her after her disability was diagnosed, as if she were somehow to blame.

She bit her lip, feeling wounded and outraged all over again on her daughter's behalf. He'd never have accepted her. The day that he heard the words 'cerebral palsy' she'd all but died for him.

He'd been glad when Liz had confronted him, she recognised that now. He'd been searching for a way to leave and she'd given him the perfect excuse. He'd made the choice to go, not her.

The twitter of birds outside the window, soft at first then

louder, told Liz that she'd been awake all night. She was relieved, hoping that the dawn light would flood through the room, sweeping her dark thoughts away.

She crept up to draw the curtains a little so that she could watch the sky turn from inky black to cement grey. Someone walked by and their dog barked, drowning the birdsong, and she was pleased to think of folk getting up early, even on a Sunday. Going about their normal business.

Rosie was better off here by the sea, she told herself, jumping back into bed and pulling the covers up under her chin, where the pace was slower and she was hundreds of miles from London and Greg's toxic presence. She, Liz, was right about that, surely. Her instincts all those years ago hadn't been wrong.

Had they?

Chapter Eleven

THE HEATWAVE DIDN'T last and come September, they were all out of shorts and sundresses and into jeans, sweatshirts and waterproofs because it wouldn't stop raining.

'Good for the garden,' Pat said, relieved that she'd no longer have to traipse outside twice a day to water her roses. In truth, Liz was also quite relieved to see the back of the very high temperatures though she wouldn't have minded a slightly more gradual transition into autumn.

Thanks to her extra Saturday shifts at A Winkle In Time, which had finished now, and a spate of very generous tips – the restaurant had been a roaring success all summer – she'd managed to pay the final amount owing for Rosie's trip and there was even some left over.

She and Rosie spent a happy weekend shopping for new jeans and leggings, a couple of tops, socks, pants and pyjamas. Rosie, who wasn't used to having money spent on her, was in ecstasy among the girly outfits and accessories and Liz splashed out on a silver headband with three little hearts on for her, and two pale blue butterfly hairpins with a dusting of silver glitter on top for herself. She hadn't seen anything quite like them before and thought that she could maybe copy them in different coloured fabric at home.

They also needed a sponge bag and toiletries, plus a purse

for Rosie who'd never had one of her own. She gazed longingly in a shoe shop window at a pair of quilted leather black ballet pumps with a bow on top, but Liz hustled her on.

'There's no point torturing yourself,' she said firmly. 'A lot of the other girls will be wearing trainers, too.'

Rosie was all packed days before she was due to leave, right down to the toothbrush which Liz then pointed out that she'd need in the interim, so it had to come out of the yellow sponge bag again. The night before, Liz tried to get her to bed early but it was no use because she was a bundle of nervous excitement. In fact Liz was too, though in her case excitement was seasoned with a generous dollop of anxiety. Would Rosie cope with all the walking? Would they look after her properly, and most of all, would the other children be kind?

The coach was leaving the school at six o'clock on Monday morning and Liz had warned Kasia in advance that she'd be late. Some mothers and children, plus a few dads, were already waiting by the long white vehicle when they arrived in Eeyore and parked a few yards up the road.

Dressed casually in jeans and sweatshirts, mostly, with brightly coloured backpacks at their feet, you could sense the children's eagerness and butterflies. Some were laughing and pushing each other playfully while others hovered at their parents' sides, wanting reassurance.

Mrs Meakin, the new class teacher, was standing with a clipboard, ready to tick off names, wrapped in a white quilted jacket against the early morning chill. Liz noticed a thermos at her side – coffee to wake her up? She'd need plenty of energy to cope with this lot.

It was a good half-hour before everyone had mustered and Liz was relieved that Mandy and Rachel, who were to be Rosie's roommates after all, stood with her the entire time, chatting mostly about what they'd brought with them. Mandy admired Rosie's silver headband with the hearts on.

'Where did you get it?' she asked, and when Rosie named the shop, she danced off to point it out to her mother, who nodded and smiled. Rosie's pleasure was palpable.

At last it was time for the off and Liz scarcely managed to kiss her daughter before she was clambering up the steps.

'Don't forget to write,' Liz cried, a cold, clammy hand suddenly gripping her heart. They weren't allowed phones; the letter said very clearly that it was important for the children to learn independence and speaking to their parents might only make them homesick.

'I won't,' Rosie cried, before disappearing into the gloomy bowels of the coach while Liz searched frantically for her daughter's face among the jostling bodies. Silly, she told herself as she waited. It wasn't as if Rosie was to be swallowed up never to be seen again, but it felt like it.

As the coach pulled away she spotted her through the window, peering round Mandy's shoulder and wearing a brave smile. Was she anxious? Only a little – and she wasn't going to show it.

'Peace at last,' one of the mums joked as the vehicle disappeared round the corner of the country lane.

Liz smiled but a painful knot had lodged deep in her intestines and it was all she could do not to cry, so she hurried to Eeyore, leaving the other parents chatting at the roadside. Work was what she needed, she thought, as the old engine spluttered into life. Motion and distraction. And after all, it was only four little days...

She was glad to find Hannah at her desk already, mug of coffee by her side. Hannah had taken to arriving early and they often had a chat – she said she got more work done in the hour or so before the others turned up than during the entire day. They still laughed about the time when Liz had startled her napping under the desk but so far there hadn't been a repeat performance.

'Good weekend?' Hannah called cheerily, not looking up from the computer, while Liz trundled her trolley as quietly as she could towards the back row of desks and set about cleaning the phones.

Hannah was looking very neat and professional in a crisp pale pink blouse rolled up at the sleeves. Her dark hair was pulled back in a bun with little wispy bits falling round her face, and her small, rectangular, black-framed glasses were perched halfway up her nose.

'Fine, thanks. You?'

'Bit riotous,' said Hannah, peering at something on the screen. Her weekends were always riotous but somehow she still managed to turn up at work on a Monday morning looking like Miss Moneypenny. Liz was full of admiration. 'Friend from Exeter uni had a house party.'

'Nice,' Liz replied.

'How's Rosie?' Though she led a single girl's lifestyle, Hannah was always asking after Rosie, which Liz thought very sweet and kind.

'I just dropped her off at school. She's gone on her trip – to London.' Was her voice cracking? She hoped not. She must pull herself together.

Hannah laid her glasses on the desk and swivelled round, cocking her head on one side.

'Hey, you OK?'

Liz took a hankie out of her overall pocket and blew her nose. It was better not to talk about it, really. It would only set her off.

'Come here.' Hannah rose and walked, open armed, towards Liz, who'd reached for the furniture spray and was polishing furiously, intent, it seemed, on rubbing the top layer of varnish off the desk.

Liz took a step back and raised a hand – 'I'm all right, really' – but Hannah was already wrapping her in an embrace. She was tall, much taller than Liz, and smelled of expensive perfume and starch.

'She's going to have a great time and she'll be home before you know it,' Hannah said gently. Liz tried to nod but she was being hugged so tightly that she couldn't.

'Think of it like this – you've got, how long is it? Four days? You should make the most of it.'

Liz pulled away and wiped her eyes. 'I'm sorry, I've made you all wet.'

Hannah laughed a tinkling, naughty sort of laugh and it was so infectious that Liz joined in. 'I'm being silly, I know.'

'You need distractions,' Hannah said firmly, returning to her previous point. 'What have you got planned? I hope you're going to have some fun?'

Liz frowned. She'd planned to clean Rosie's room from top to bottom and sort out the clothes that were getting too small. And sleep. A lot. With no school run she could catch up properly. Fun certainly wasn't on her agenda.

'Why don't we go out one night?' Hannah said suddenly. 'Girls' night. We could go for a drink somewhere, or for something to eat maybe. Whatever you fancy. On me.'

Liz blushed, touched and embarrassed at the same time.

'That's really kind but tonight's my only night off. I'm at the restaurant the rest of the week.'

'Dammit. I'm meeting bloody clients.' Hannah frowned. 'Can't we make it another evening?'

Liz shook her head. 'Boss wouldn't allow it.' Which wasn't strictly true; with notice Robert could find someone else. Rita, who normally only did Saturday lunchtimes, would probably step in. He wouldn't mind, either. He was so soft and it wasn't as if Liz was unreliable; she never missed a shift.

But the truth was, she needed every penny. Her earnings barely covered outgoings as it was and the landlord had been making noises about putting up the rent. There was no point trying to explain all this to Hannah, though. Lovely as she was, she had no idea about being poor. She'd grown up with a pony in the paddock and a silver spoon in her mouth.

There was much talk, as Liz, Jo and Kasia left the building, of the black knickers that Jo had found in one of the toilets.

'Didn't know what it was at first,' Jo sniggered. 'Thought it might be a rat.'

'I wonder who they belong to,' Liz joined in. 'D'you think there was a party after work or someone broke in later? Good job security didn't catch them. How embarrassing!'

Kasia clicked her tongue. 'Young people don't know how to behave these days.' She sounded at least eighty.

'Maybe they weren't young, maybe they were your age,' Jo said cheekily.

Kasia knitted her jet-black eyebrows and muttered something about the next job.

'I never would behave like that, I have more self-respect,' she said through thin lips, without stopping to say goodbye before slamming her car door shut.

Jo sniggered again. 'Bet her old man doesn't get much; she'd snap his balls off and eat them for breakfast!'

Liz felt marginally better as she drove back to the village. The rain had ceased at last and the streets and gardens looked dewy fresh. She wound down her window to savour the scent of newly washed pavement. A few remaining holidaymakers had ventured out and were making their way towards harbour or beach, wearing cagoules and deck shoes. It was an older more sedate crowd now because the children were back at school, but soon the stragglers would be gone, too, and they'd have Tremarnock to themselves again.

She stopped at Pat's to drop off some shopping but declined tea on the grounds that her flat was a mess and needed a good clean.

'I hope you're not going to overdo it now,' Pat said disapprovingly. 'I should think you deserve a bit of a rest while the littl'un's away.' She unpeeled a packet of biscuits and started putting them in an ancient-looking red tin with a faded Christmas tree on the lid. 'Ooh, but we're going to miss her, aren't we?'

Once inside the cottage, Liz kicked off her trainers gratefully and plonked down in the blue armchair. It was extraordinary to think that as she didn't work Mondays at the restaurant, she had all afternoon and evening to do nothing. Well, not nothing, but no school run, no tea to make, no deadlines. The last time she'd experienced freedom like this was before Rosie was born, before her first job, before her mum died, really, when she was still living with both parents and enjoying weekends with her friend Jackie and school holidays of her own.

She felt suddenly panicked, as if, cut free from her chains, or her anchor, rather – she couldn't bear to think of Rosie as a shackle – she might drift away and find herself unable to swim back to shore.

Her life was so bound by routine that she'd forgotten what it was to wonder what to do next. Even on Sundays, hers and

Rosie's special, work-free day, the schedule shifted but it was still there in another form: breakfast, lunch, tea, fresh air for Rosie, something different to entertain and amuse her. Homework, perhaps. Housework. Catching up on jobs that couldn't be done during the week. There was always a time-table of sorts.

Now, she didn't even need to eat if she didn't fancy it. She could leave her bed unmade, keep the curtains closed, not bother to wash up. She felt like a naughty teenager home alone and finding herself missing the very things against which she'd once imagined that she'd like to rebel.

She was about to rise and put the kettle on, because it seemed comforting and normal, when the doorbell rang, making her jump. So lost had she been in her own thoughts that she'd forgotten about the outside world.

She realised that she was almost glad – even Nathan the postman would have lifted her spirits. She could ask how the exercise regime was going, and his new relationship. He still went on about Loveday rather a lot but had started dating a girl called Annie, from Torpoint. She sounded far more suitable because she was a fitness trainer while Loveday, Liz suspected, didn't know one end of a rowing machine from another.

She wondered if she could persuade Nathan to stay for a quick drink; he'd occasionally pop in for a cuppa on Saturday mornings if the weather was cold. Then she chided herself for being weak. As Hannah said, she must make the most of her freedom and see this as an opportunity; it mightn't come again for a very long time.

The last person that she'd have expected to find on her doorstep was Robert. He looked so anxious, running a hand nervously through his hair and rocking from side to side, that at first she thought something terrible had happened.

162

'What is it?' she cried, her mind racing hither and thither. Was the restaurant on fire? Had there been an outbreak of food poisoning? Had Loveday and Jesse had a screaming row and resigned simultaneously?

Robert cleared his throat noisily.

'Nothing,' he said, chewing on the corner of a nail. She relaxed a bit. 'Everything's fine. Um, may I come in?'

He had to stoop to get through the entrance and into the little sitting room at the front and when Liz gestured to the blue armchair and he sat down, it looked too small for him, like something from a child's nursery.

'I gather your daughter's away,' Robert began, before Liz had time to ask if he'd like a drink or how she could help. He must want something, after all, to have called on her like this.

She might have thought that he'd need her to work tonight but the restaurant was closed, so it couldn't be that. Lunchtime tomorrow and the rest of the week? She wouldn't say no if he asked; Rosie's room could wait.

'I wondered if I could take you out – for supper? To apologise,' he said quickly.

She was so taken aback that she didn't answer. She wasn't sure which part of his statement was more surprising – the supper invitation or the apology. Nor was she certain what, exactly, he was apologising for.

'I shouldn't have allowed that man – that customer – to insult you,' he went on, as if reading her mind. 'No one should have to put up with that, it was totally out of order.'

One long spindly leg was sticking out in front of him, while the other was bent and jiggling up and down as if a wasp had flown up his trousers and he was trying to shake it out.

Liz *was* still annoyed with him about the obnoxious customer; she knew that it was wrong to hold grudges but the fact that Robert had behaved coolly with her ever since hadn't helped. There again, she supposed that she hadn't exactly been friendliness itself either. He must have noticed that she no longer saved him a dessert from the kitchen, though he'd never mentioned it.

They hadn't been rude to each other – Liz wouldn't dream of rubbing him up the wrong way, she valued her job too much – and she didn't think he had it in him to be unkind to anyone. The truth was that they'd probably gone back to how they were before she'd found him hovering anxiously at the foot of the ladder in the flat above the restaurant: polite but distant.

He looked so stricken that she wanted to say something conciliatory to calm him down. After all, it was only words the customer had used; it wasn't as if he'd struck her.

'It's all right, honestly—' she started to say, but Robert butted in.

'It's not all right. I was desperate to shoo him out, to shut him up, you see, because he was drunk and I thought he might start throwing punches. But as soon as he'd gone I knew I'd done the wrong thing. I shouldn't have let him get away with it. I should have stuck up for you – as a valued member of staff,' he added quickly. 'I've been cursing myself ever since.'

'Well I *was* angry,' she admitted, taking care not to catch his eye. He was rubbing the side of his face with the back of his hand, now. 'I wanted you to defend yourself and the restaurant – and me a little, I guess.'

She glanced at him for a second but he seemed to be examining a particular book on the shelf behind her. 'It's over now,' she said. 'Forget it.'

He leaned forward, resting his elbows on his knees, and kneaded his head a few times with both hands as if shampooing his hair.

'Thank you,' he said in a low voice, staring at his black trainers. 'What about supper?'

Liz got up to open the window; the room felt stuffy suddenly.

'You don't need to take me out, honestly.' She sensed his eyes on her now that her back was turned – or was she imagining it? 'It's kind of you to come here, but you don't need to do anything more.'

Robert rose too and stretched, wincing as if his joints hurt, but it was probably embarrassment.

'Please,' he implored. 'I'd like to – that is, if you don't mind?'

His brow was deeply furrowed and he looked so wretched that really she couldn't refuse.

'All right then. Thank you.'

Straight away a smile spread across his face and his brow lifted so that she could once more glimpse his rather lovely hazel eyes.

'Good,' he said. 'I'll pick you up at half seven. Oh, and wear something smart.'

She was about to ask what, exactly, he meant by smart but she was too late; he was already striding up the road on long legs and she'd have had to run to catch up.

Chapter Twelve

As SOON AS he'd gone Liz went into her bedroom and threw open her wardrobe doors, eyeing the rail of clothing with suspicion. She couldn't think of one single item that would fit the description 'smart'. As she never went out in the evenings other than to work, she didn't need to dress up and lived in jeans or leggings, mostly, and an assortment of what she realised now, flicking quickly through the metal hangers, were distinctly shabby tops.

Probably dreadfully old-fashioned, too, not that she knew much about fashion other than what she'd observed on smart tourists or, indeed, Loveday. She supposed that Loveday must be trendy but it was a highly individual style that Liz felt she couldn't possibly emulate. Besides, she didn't have the boobs, the shaved hair or the cultivated bum-wiggle, come to think of it.

Despondent, she turned to the mirror above her chest of drawers and noticed the pale blue butterfly hairpins with a dusting of silver glitter that she'd bought with Rosie and hadn't yet worn. They'd have to be the focus of her ensemble.

Heartened, she brushed her hair and slid the pins in on either side, leaving some loose strands to dangle softly round her face. They certainly made a difference, giving her a slightly magical, other-worldly air, especially when coupled with her silver earrings with stars on the end.

But what to do about the rest of the outfit? A T-shirt and sweater simply wouldn't be right and she hadn't the time or money to go shopping. She wished that she'd known earlier, then perhaps she could have borrowed something from Iris who seemed to have loads of jazzy clothes, and Christie had worn a lovely floaty pale blue top on Easter Sunday.

Suddenly she remembered a length of pale grey satin that she'd had for months. It had been on sale and she'd bought it dirt cheap, thinking that it might do for cushion covers, though she'd never got round to making any.

The colour seemed suitable for evening and it was very pretty, soft, shimmery material. She'd hand-sewn a few little loose, A-shaped tunic tops with spaghetti straps for Rosie for the summer and it occurred to her that she could do the same for herself. Why not? It shouldn't take too long.

Quickly, she pulled the material from under her bed and cut it to size. As it was such a simple design it wouldn't need much stitching, then she could use some of the lace, ribbons, sequins and jewels that she kept for making hair accessories to decorate it.

Conscious of the time, she set to work with the radio on in the background and found herself humming along to some old favourites on Mellow Magic, her favourite station, though Rosie always scoffed, claiming it was old-fashioned. She wouldn't have been too sniffy, though, to join in with a few Motown hits or Harry Nilsson's 'Without You', which they both knew off by heart.

Liz used to enjoy dressmaking when she was young and would have loved to have her mother's old sewing machine, but unfortunately Tonya had thrown it out before she'd had the chance to stop her. She'd manage to rescue Katharine's flowery sewing box, however, complete with thimbles, pins and needles, a vast assortment of buttons and different-coloured threads.

Battered it may have been, but it was one of her most treasured possessions because it reminded her powerfully of old times. She could almost picture her mum stitching by the window of their front room in Balham, looking up and smiling when Liz entered and holding up whatever it was that she was making for her daughter to admire. She'd been very pretty, slim and dark-haired, with a laugh like gurgling water. She was always happy, telling jokes and keeping everyone entertained, or that's how Liz remembered her, anyway.

After she'd completed the main garment, she chose some antique cream lace for the neckline and hem, an assortment of glass pearls, vintage-looking sequinned flowers, silk ribbon roses, mother-of-pearl buttons and charcoal ribbon for the front and tops of her shoulders.

When she'd finished, she slipped the garment on with some slim-fitting, cropped black trousers, the only smart pair that she possessed, along with the black pumps that were her waitressing shoes, and stood back to check herself in the mirror. The top, she decided, wasn't bad at all, quite boho chic with a hint of Victorian romance against her pale, almost white skin. She felt quite pleased with herself, especially as the whole endeavour had only taken three hours.

Having resolved the panic of what to wear, Liz could relax a little. She decided that the cleaning could wait and instead went for a long, hot shower, thinking again how strange it was not to be rushing, one eye always on the clock, anxious not to be late.

'I hope you're going to have some fun.'

With Hannah's words ringing in her ears, she set about putting the finishing touches to her evening out. She wasn't convinced that Robert would be the most entertaining company but as no one else was likely to be inviting her for supper, she might as well make the best of it.

Wrapped in a towel, she padded back to her bedroom to dress and blow dry her hair. She wasn't really into make-up but dabbed a touch of grey-blue eyeshadow on her lids and found an old black mascara that, when she added a few drops of water, still seemed to have enough left in it to do her lashes. As to whether they were now 'long and luscious' as promised on the side of the tube was another matter.

Robert arrived punctually, and she must have looked a little different from usual because she noticed his eyes widen when she opened the door, before he glanced over her shoulder, apparently distracted by something of great interest at the end of her hallway.

'I've booked for eight,' he said, transfixed now by a point on the pavement. A crack, perhaps? 'My car's just up the road.'

It was rather a nice car actually, Liz thought, as she settled into the white Audi beside him. New, or newish, anyway, with comfy tan leather seats and electric windows that worked; Eeyore's tended to shudder up and down and occasionally stop altogether so that you needed two hands to persuade them into position. Liz always worried that one day they'd get stuck halfway and refuse to budge.

Robert hadn't told her where they were going but as they whizzed along the country lanes leading out of Tremarnock, she found that she really didn't care. It was getting dark – the evenings were rapidly drawing in – and she was enjoying watching the fields speed by and listening to softly playing jazz music (she'd said she didn't mind what he chose) against the background purr of the engine.

At first he didn't say anything and she was happy not to speak. He was driving quite fast but she didn't feel unsafe.

'How was your daughter when she left?' he asked at last, and she wondered why he was still so formal; he knew Rosie's name perfectly well.

Liz explained that Rosie had been fine, *she* was the one who was worried. 'I just hope the other kids are nice to her.' She almost wished that he hadn't raised the subject, because she could feel the heat rising through her body, up to her neck and face.

Robert pulled into a verge to allow an oncoming car to pass – it was a windy road, too narrow for more than one vehicle – and said the teachers would look after her. Liz, thinking of the thirty-odd children on the trip, all with their own needs and demands, wished that she could be so sure.

They chatted a little about the restaurant and he laughed when she told him that she thought Jesse still had a soft spot for Loveday, despite the fact that they were both so horrible to each other.

'I didn't realise they'd been an item,' he commented, and Liz secretly marvelled at his lack of observational skills. You'd have to be blind not to have noticed, she thought, which only confirmed her view that he had his head in the clouds, or his menus, wine store and accounts books, anyway. He didn't seem much interested in people when it came down to it.

They'd been going for over half an hour now and she had no idea where they were as there were no lamps, save their own, and she couldn't see any signs; they seemed to be in the middle of nowhere.

She was just beginning to wonder if they'd ever arrive when Robert veered sharply right and they pulled into what appeared to be a long drive with candle flares on either side and glowing lights at the end indicating a large, imposing building.

As they drew closer, she wondered if she was in a dream for it seemed that he'd brought her to a stately home or palace, with a grand covered entrance supported by ivy-clad pillars, and a man in tails who signalled to Robert to wind down his window.

'You can leave your car, sir,' the man commanded. 'We'll park it for you.'

Liz, gripped with dismay, gasped out loud; she couldn't help it. 'We're not going here, are we? I'm only wearing trousers and a home-made top.'

'You look perfect,' said Robert, and there was no time to protest further because the gentleman in tails was already opening her door.

Once inside, they were met by a woman in black who checked the reservation. Liz glanced up at the heavy twinkling chandelier and down at the gleaming wood floors before taking in the jardinières, overflowing with blue and pink hydrangea blooms, and the curved staircase ahead covered in a thick, peacock-blue carpet.

A young woman wafted by in a red, off-the-shoulder gown and high black heels and eyed her disdainfully, she thought. Her insides curdled. She'd never been anywhere like this before and felt like a foreigner, an alien, who'd pitched up in the wrong country with no idea of local customs or even how to speak the language.

Dumbly, she followed the woman in black into a giant room to the right with floor-to-ceiling shelves groaning with leather-bound books, and sat gingerly on a plush crimson sofa by the stone fireplace, which was glowing red and orange.

Robert, still standing, ordered the drinks menu before

taking an armchair beside her. He was wearing a dark blue jacket – why hadn't she noticed? It was a bit of a clue – white shirt (no tie) and dark trousers. She should have insisted that she didn't have the right clothes for a place like this; she should have refused his invitation.

'D'you like it?' he asked, oblivious to her discomfort and scanning the room with approval. 'I thought we'd come to a hotel as Rosie's staying in one. It's very good food.'

He settled back in his chair, one long leg over another, but Liz couldn't relax. A middle-aged couple wandered in, laughing, and she noticed with dismay the woman's dark green, low-cut silk dress and expensive-looking necklace against alabaster smooth skin.

They must wonder what on earth she was doing in her cheap earrings and stupid butterfly hair clips and her boho camisole that hadn't seemed so daft back home in Tremarnock; she felt as if she had 'cleaner and waitress' and 'handmade outfit' branded on her forehead. Any moment they'd probably expect her to scurry upstairs to check the bathrooms and turn back their bedcovers.

When she didn't reply to Robert's question, he tried again: 'I've only been here once.' He ran a hand several times through his wavy brown hair and continued to inspect the bookshelves. 'I heard they'd hired an excellent new chef – French, apparently, from Marseille. I'll be interested to see what's on the menu tonight.'

He scratched his cheek. 'I quite often eat out on Monday nights. All sorts of places. Keeping an eye on the competition sort of thing.'

A waitress arrived to take their drinks order and Liz could feel sweat under her arms and was sure that her face had turned blotchy and red. She wanted to cry.

'What would you like?' Robert asked, still not noticing.

Should she ask for wine? Or was that gauche? Maybe they expected her to have some fancy-sounding cocktail, but she'd been so busy worrying about everything else that the menu was still beside her on the sofa, unopened. And then she probably wouldn't be able to pronounce the name properly. They didn't serve cocktails in A Winkle In Time; it wasn't their thing.

'I'll have port. Um. Brandy. Wine. Anything,' she said desperately. Her mind had gone fuzzy and she couldn't think straight. You only had port after dinner. She must sound like a complete fool, a dimwit. She blew a few strands of hair off her face to try to cool herself down; she was burning.

'Liz, are you all right?'

He must have said something to the waitress that Liz didn't catch because the young woman backed away discreetly.

'Yes,' Liz said desperately. A painful lump had lodged in her throat that she couldn't swallow down. 'No, I mean...'

If she said anything more she'd give herself away.

Robert leaned forward, resting his elbows on his knees, so that he was quite close to her.

'What is it?' he whispered urgently.

Liz shook her head, staring hard at the red and gold rug beneath her feet. Tears were welling and she poked the corners of her eyes with her fingertips, hard. She was furious with herself for making a scene; she'd never be able to forgive herself.

Suddenly he rose, pulling her gently but firmly by the wrist. 'C'mon, we're going.'

Mortified, she stumbled after him, head down, not looking left or right because she was certain that the other guests were staring.

'My friend's not feeling well,' he said to the lady in black at the reception desk.

Liz didn't see her expression but could imagine the look of disapproval. She probably thought that he'd dragged a right nutcase in with him, not at all the sort of guest that they were accustomed to.

They didn't speak while the car was fetched and brought to the entrance for them. Liz clambered inside and Robert accelerated down the drive, but as soon as they'd turned the corner, he pulled over and stopped the engine, reaching up to flick on an interior light. She'd already decided during the few moments that it had taken to leave the grounds that she was going to lie; she'd say that she really was feeling ill. Maybe she had some sort of bug; she hadn't been quite right all day.

But when he touched her arm with his hand, she found that she couldn't fib.

'I'm sorry,' she spluttered. 'That place, the man in tails, the chandeliers. All the women in glamorous evening dresses. I felt so stupid and shabby, like a joke...'

She tore the clips out of her hair and threw them on the floor by her feet. 'I hate places like that.' She sounded angry now; she *was* angry. With herself for feeling ugly and inferior and with Robert for taking her there.

He groaned loudly, a deep, low sound that startled her so that she had to look up.

'I'm such an idiot.' He slapped the driving wheel hard, halting her tears mid-flow. 'I should have thought...' He stopped and shook his head. 'I thought you'd like it. You looked so lovely...'

His voice was hollow and so unhappy that Liz almost forgot her own misery. 'It doesn't matter,' she said, small and strained.

It was pitch black outside and they could have been anywhere. Robert turned to face her and their eyes met in the yellow glow of the interior light. It was so unusual that she had to pay attention.

'Yes it does,' he said sadly. 'I wanted to apologise for what happened the other day. I wanted to treat you. Well, I suppose I was being selfish, too. It wasn't just about you. I wanted to spend time with you – away from work, I mean. I thought it would be quiet there, somewhere we could talk, where I could really get to know you…'

His eyes slid from hers and he stared out of the windscreen at the darkness that enveloped them. 'But instead I've made you cry,' he went on. 'I feel like a monster. I've ruined everything.'

Liz could hardly breathe. Had she heard correctly?

'I really like you, Liz.' His words, though quietly spoken, seemed to fill the entire car.

Her ears pricked. It couldn't have been easy for him to say that.

'I like you too.'

Her voice came out more strongly than she'd expected, catching her by surprise. She'd stopped crying completely. Suddenly the air around them seemed fresher and alive with meaning. The events of the last half-hour had acquired a whole new significance.

'Can we go somewhere else?' she asked timidly. 'A pub or something. Anywhere, so long as there aren't any men in tails?'

Robert let out a long breath and then laughed, a low, throaty sound. 'Of course. Wherever you want.'

He started up the engine and she expected him to pull away but instead he paused. 'Will you put those butterfly clips back in your hair? They're pretty and they go so well with your top.'

Startled and smiling a little to herself, she bent down obediently to retrieve them from the footwell and replace them carefully on her head.

Wouldn't Rosie be surprised if she knew? she found herself thinking as they sped back along the country lanes. Wouldn't Pat raise her eyebrows, and Iris and Hannah in the office, even Kasia and Jo? Wasn't *she herself* surprised?

Robert leaned forward to put the music back on and she sat back, deciding that for the rest of the evening she'd try her best to relax, go with the flow and take Hannah's advice to *have some fun*.

Now that they'd cleared the air, that shouldn't be too difficult, should it?

Chapter Thirteen

THIS TIME SHE chose an old inn with a thatched roof, flagstone floors and low-beamed ceilings on the edge of a creek that had lovely views in the daytime. Liz had been there once after a walk with Rosie. They'd sat on a bench in the garden overlooking the water and sipped lemonade and munched crisps and watched the other customers with assorted children, dogs, lovers, grandparents and friends chit-chatting in the sunshine. She remembered thinking that it was a perfect spot.

She followed him through a series of irregular-sized rooms into a little one at the back with an anchor on the wall and glass display cases containing different sailors' knots with an explanation of each underneath.

'How's this?' he said, pointing to a dumpy, L-shaped brown leather sofa in the corner. In front was a low-lying, rough-hewn table that looked as if it had been fashioned from a ship's hull.

'Perfect,' said Liz, settling down happily.

'What'll you have to drink?'

While Robert went to the bar, Liz perused the menu and was relieved to find plenty of things that she liked. Alex sometimes persuaded her to taste some of the adventurous dishes at A Winkle In Time, but she wasn't keen on fancy sauces called 'jus' of this or 'coulis' of that; she was used to plainer food.

When he came back with a pint of bitter for himself and a glass of white wine for her, she felt her stomach flutter. In the car she'd almost managed to forget about her mortifying behaviour earlier, so busy had she been mulling over Robert's words.

But now, beside him in the dimly lit pub, she felt suddenly shy and stupid again. It was a good thing that they were at right angles to one another rather than face to face because it meant that he didn't run the risk of catching her eye.

He asked her a little about Rosie's trip, what she'd be doing and so on, and Liz explained that they weren't allowed to talk on the phone unless there was an emergency. 'They're supposed to write letters so I hope I'll get one before she's back, but it might arrive after.'

'She's a very special little girl,' he said, 'you're doing a great job.'

Grateful and embarrassed at the same time, she switched the focus from herself and asked how he'd got into the restaurant business. It seemed that he'd started from the bottom.

'My parents ran a café in Penzance,' he explained. 'Nothing fancy, it just served teas and coffees, cakes, soup, pasta, salads and sandwiches at lunchtime, that sort of thing. But my mother was a good cook and it did quite well and my sister and I used to help out in the school holidays. When my father died and my mother became ill, I more or less took over. Then when she passed away, I decided to sell up and open a fish restaurant in Tremarnock. I'd always wanted to try something more ambitious and creative.'

Liz couldn't imagine Robert as a child, serving tables in a café; it seemed to her that he'd always run A Winkle In Time. He was part of the furniture, the fabric of the place. He'd been there for ever, surely?

178

'What were they like, your parents?' she asked. She was curious and hoped that she wasn't prying.

Robert took a swig of beer and frowned. 'My mother was a remarkable woman, very kind and smart and loving, but my father, well, he was a bit of a tyrant.' He swilled the cloudy drink around his glass and stared into it, as if searching for something at the bottom.

Liz cocked her head on one side. 'In what way?'

He cleared his throat. 'He was a brutish man, prone to violent mood swings and I'm afraid he took it out on us. He used to hit my sister and me, and my mother. We were all scared of him. Being the only other male I tried to stand up to him but he was physically strong. To be honest, it was a relief when he died.'

Liz shuddered, thinking it was no wonder that he'd chosen to sell the café and move. Like her, he must have wanted to escape the unhappy memories. And she supposed that having a violent parent could make you develop in one of two ways – either into a bully yourself, or reluctant to confront anyone. Clearly with Robert it was the latter.

She was aware of her perception shifting, in the way that a different camera angle can reveal something fresh in someone's face that suggests quite a different person from the one you thought you knew. Here were new facets to explore, a deeper perspective.

'How old were you when your parents died?' she asked. He seemed reasonably relaxed and unfazed by her questioning.

'Sixteen with Dad and twenty when Mum died.'

'And your sister's how much younger than you?'

Robert took another swig of beer and wiped his mouth with the back of a hand. 'Five years.'

So she would have been only fifteen when they were orphaned.

'Did you look after her? That can't have been easy.'

Robert smiled grimly. 'She wasn't an easy teenager, that's for sure. I laid down plenty of rules – all of which she broke. But she finished school, anyway. Then she met her husband – that's Andy – and they had Loveday. It was a bit of a shock because my sister was only just eighteen, but we managed somehow until we sold the café and they could buy their own place. He's a nice lad, Andy – well, man now – but he's not much good with money...'

His voice tailed off and Liz found herself doing a quick mental calculation. Loveday was seventeen, she knew, which meant that Robert's sister must be thirty-five. So that made Robert forty, slightly older than she thought.

'You had a lot of responsibility early on,' she observed, trying and failing to picture what it must have been like for a young man of twenty to be saddled with a naughty teenage sister and then her baby, too. Not to mention Andy. She'd bet Robert still helped them out. It sounded like it.

He didn't seem to hear her comment. 'Wasn't easy for my sister,' he mused, 'losing her mum like that then having a kid so young. Loveday's a bit of a handful, of course, but Sarah – that's my sister – she did a good job, the best she could. Like you,' he said, bringing the conversation full circle. 'Can't be easy for you either, being on your own.'

Liz guessed that he'd like to ask about Rosie's father but she didn't want to sully the evening by bringing Greg into it.

'She's no trouble,' she replied. 'I can't complain.'

He rose to order more drinks. Liz was already feeling slightly light-headed so she was relieved when the waitress finally arrived with their food.

The presentation was a little strange. Her Cumberland sausages had been stuck at right angles into the buttery mashed potato while his burger had been spiked with a cocktail stick with a pink parasol on the end. They laughed, deciding that the chef was in an eccentric mood, but it all tasted good so they didn't complain.

'It's a relief to have something basic for once,' Robert commented. 'I love experimenting with the menu but to tell you the truth, sometimes all I want is good old-fashioned grub – even with a parasol stuck on top!'

Liz couldn't help agreeing.

While they ate, she told him a little about her and he was surprised to hear that her father saw so little of Rosie.

'His only grandchild?' he mused, shaking his head. 'You'd think he wouldn't be able to keep away.'

She gave a brief description of Tonya, trying to be fair and balanced, but still his eyebrows shot up. 'She sounds terrifying! She'd better not come in the restaurant. She'd complain about everything!'

Liz giggled despite herself. 'She's not that bad, honestly. She just knows her own mind.'

'Scary,' he repeated, shaking his head. 'I feel sorry for your dad.'

She chose chocolate mousse for pudding while he had banoffee pie and cream. She was amused by how quickly he wolfed it down, scraping every last crumb off the dish.

'Told you I had a sweet tooth,' he said when he realised that she'd been watching. 'It wasn't as good as Alex's.'

'Well, you still made short work of it,' she smiled.

She noticed him eyeing her leftover mousse. She'd only been able to manage half, it was so rich.

'Would you like it? I haven't touched this side.' She pushed

181

the plate towards him and he polished that off, too, wiping his mouth contentedly with the napkin when he'd finished.

After two large glasses of wine and a big meal, she felt satisfied and at peace with the world. She leaned back in the sofa, crossing one leg over another.

'Has there been anyone special since, you know, since your ex-fiancée?' She was loose-tongued now; it must be the alcohol.

If he was offended, he didn't show it: 'Not really, no.'

'Why not?' She was brazenness itself!

He shrugged. 'I guess I just never met anyone I liked enough.'

Or as much, she thought, deciding again that the ex must have been quite something and resolving not to probe further.

'What about you? Have you been out with anyone since Greg?'

Liz was taken aback to hear the name on his lips; she'd forgotten that she'd ever mentioned it. Then the idea of her having a boyfriend seemed so absurd that she almost laughed. 'I think he put me off men for life.'

Robert chewed the corner of a nail; he hadn't done that all evening, or not that she'd noticed, anyway. She was sorry that she'd replied so hastily.

'I'm just so busy,' she added quickly, 'what with Rosie and work. You know how it is?'

'I do,' said Robert gravely.

They left it at that.

She talked about a walk that she and Rosie had done recently round the bay, passing some old coastguard houses and two Napoleonic forts and ending up in a clifftop café with breathtaking views of the headland.

'It was about two miles which was an awful lot for Rosie,

but we took our time and she managed OK. The promise of an ice cream at the end helped.'

Robert asked if they'd ever been to a farm which sold dreamy organic ice cream made from the farm's pedigree cows. When Liz said they hadn't, he offered to take them there sometime when the weather was fine. 'Half term, maybe. when Rosie's off school.'

Liz said they'd enjoy it.

He wanted to buy more drinks but it was already gone eleven and she had to be up at five. He seemed reluctant to leave, as she was, but ordered the bill and insisted on paying, despite her protests.

'You didn't need to take me out to apologise for anything. It's all water under the bridge.'

But he'd have none of it.

By the time they reached Dove Cottage it was past midnight and there wasn't a soul around. Even the old-fashioned gas streetlamps had been switched off because the local council wanted to save money. It was only a few paces to her door but he left the car and waited while she searched for her keys. They were hidden in the bottom of her cavernous bag, of course, and it seemed to take an age to find them.

At last she produced them: 'Ta da!' and opened up. 'I'd ask you in for coffee but I've got such an early start—'

'It's OK. Maybe another time.'

His voice sounded deep and mysterious and she could scarcely make out his features.

'Thanks again for a lovely evening.'

She turned, ready to enter. Her hand was on the open door, one foot on the step. She felt awkward suddenly, she didn't know why.

'Liz?'

It seemed urgent. She spun round again, leaving the key in the lock.

In one quick movement he bent down and brushed her lips with his, a butterfly kiss, soft and tentative, surprisingly sweet. She would have pulled back but realised that she didn't want to so she closed her eyes and lingered. Just a few moments more...

In the end he was the one who drew back. 'You'd better get some sleep,' he whispered, stroking her hair with a hand. 'See you tomorrow.'

Once she'd recovered enough to say anything he was already climbing in the car, starting the engine and turning on the lights.

She stood and watched as he drove away. He glanced back at her just the one time and smiled briefly but tenderly, she thought. A promising smile. Perhaps a little playful, too.

Anyway, her heart skipped and she couldn't stop smiling to herself as she undressed, washed and brushed her teeth and climbed gratefully into bed.

Lying there hugging herself in the dark, she was filled with a sense of wonder, of possibility. Robert, she was thinking to herself. Peculiar, awkward, antisocial, funny old Robert. A man who was scared of heights and hated the sun, sea and tomatoes, and loved puddings and loathed eye contact. Who looked out for his sister and was kind to Rosie and the people who worked for him, and who even put up with his wayward niece, possibly the worst waitress known to man.

Robert, who'd kissed her! And what's more – she'd liked it. Rather a lot, in fact. Much to her amazement, she found herself thinking that she'd be counting the hours tomorrow before it would be time to go the restaurant. They'd be sure to drag. She needed to see him again immediately. To make sure that she hadn't imagined it all...

She hadn't. She knew. She wanted to share her secret, to tell someone what had happened and how delicious it had been. She was being silly. It was only a kiss, after all.

But he'd said he really liked her; he wasn't pretending, she could tell. He wasn't pushy or selfish like Greg. He was gentle and sensitive, considerate, handsome, even. A bit vulnerable. Sexy. That was the biggest revelation of all but it was true. And my! That kiss!

She could hardly wait to see him again.

She couldn't get to sleep for ages, of course, then when the alarm went she'd finally fallen into such a deep slumber that at first she didn't hear the shrill, persistent ringing. She felt so groggy as she staggered to the shower and turned on the water that she wondered if she were ill. Then she remembered the night before and her spirits lifted so that even the prospect of four hours of hard cleaning couldn't dampen them.

Nevertheless, she found it almost impossible to hurry and mislaid her trainers which were lurking under the bed. And then she couldn't find her keys which she'd thrown on the blue armchair for some reason when she got in. She decided that she must have been floating on a cloud or something, out of her mind, because she never put them there; they always went back in her bag.

All this meant that she missed her usual ferry and felt thoroughly out of sorts as she waited for the next one. She hadn't had time for breakfast and probably looked a right mess, having dressed and brushed her hair in a last minute flurry.

Still, there was nothing she could do to speed her passage so she sat back as they chugged across the water and allowed herself the luxury of musing again on the previous night's events. What would Robert be doing now? Had he been thinking about her constantly as she had him?

She hadn't heard from Rosie, of course, but as the saying went, no news was good news. She couldn't quite believe that her daughter had only been away for twenty-four hours because so much had happened already. Was it really only yesterday morning that they'd stood shivering by the coach waiting for the other children to arrive? She hoped that Rosie had slept well and was enjoying herself. She'd certainly have a lot of tales to recount, like Liz, though she'd have to censor hers.

After parking, she couldn't resist dashing up the road to see Iris. She knew she shouldn't but she'd always been punctual till now – Kasia couldn't fault her on her timekeeping – and today everything felt strange. She was allowed one slip, surely? Jo was always taking whole days off, never mind a few measly minutes.

'Morning, love!'

Iris put down her magazine and smiled. She was wearing glossy lipstick in a rather startling shade of purple. 'This is a nice surprise! I don't normally have the pleasure of seeing you on a Tuesday morning, do I?'

Liz paused, waiting for something more. She couldn't quite believe that Iris hadn't noticed. Didn't she, Liz, look different? Couldn't her friend tell that something had changed, that she was hiding a big secret? Surely it was obvious to the whole world that she'd been *kissed*!

'How's my lovely Rosie? Have you heard from her?'

Liz was deflated; she couldn't help it. 'Well, the coach left OK but I haven't heard a squeak. They're going on the London Eye today. Hope they have decent weather for it.'

Iris glanced out of the window at the overcast sky. 'Looks like rain,' she said gloomily. 'But maybe it's better in London.'

She leaned forwards and examined Liz anxiously. 'How are you doing? Missing her dreadfully I'll bet, but she's not gone long.'

Liz wanted to laugh – or shout: Look at me. Really look. Something *big* has happened!

'I went out last night,' she said shyly, itching to spill the beans.

'Oh yes?' Iris eyed her enquiringly.

'With my boss from work.'

Iris crossed her arms over her ample chest and cocked her head on one side. 'That strange fella who's all of a twitch?'

Liz nodded. She'd told her friend about him.

'What was that like then?' At last her curiosity was piqued, Liz could tell.

'Lovely, actually.' She glanced down at her closely cut fingernails, embarrassed.

'Lovely?' Iris burst out. 'It wasn't a date, was it? You never went on a date with him?'

Liz grinned. 'Well sort of, I suppose. Yes. He's really rather nice.' It sounded so peculiar, as if she were talking about a different person, not the same Robert that she'd thought she knew.

'Is he now?' Iris looked intrigued. 'Tell me more. Will you be seeing him again then?'

Liz paused, realising that he hadn't mentioned another date. Well, only to the farm for ice cream with Rosie sometime. Maybe last night was it. Maybe there wouldn't be another occasion with just the two of them. It would be difficult when Rosie returned and anyway, he'd had his heart broken by the ex. She felt her spirits plummet, a bird falling from the sky.

'Don't look so glum. You'll see him later, won't you?'

Liz nodded.

'Well, I expect you'll fix something up then.'

The bird's wings fluttered. It wasn't dead after all, just stunned.

Iris clapped her hands, making Liz jump. 'How exciting! You've got a suitor!'

Liz laughed. 'I wouldn't exactly describe him as that. We've only been out once.' She glanced at her watch and yelped: 'I'm really late.'

Iris reached for her pack of ten cigarettes and lottery ticket while Liz fished out her purse and handed over the correct money.

Grabbing the cigarettes, she flung them in her bag and made for the door.

'Wait!' called Iris, waving something in the air. 'You haven't got your lucky dip!'

Liz paused for just a second and frowned, imagining Kasia's big black eyebrows knitting with displeasure: 'You have made us all behind schedule.' Rat-a-tat-tat. 'You must work double quick fast or there will be complaints.'

'Keep it for me, will you?' Liz cried to her friend. 'I'll pick it up later.'

Iris nodded and swivelled round, putting the ticket in a secure place under a red cigarette lighter on a shelf behind her.

'It'll be quite safe there,' she promised. 'I'll keep an eye on it. I'm not going anywhere.'

An elderly man walked past Liz into the shop with a mongrel on a lead.

'Morning,' she said hurriedly, pleased to see another customer.

She remembered something and swung back to face Iris, who had returned to her celebrity magazine, already absorbed in the gossip about Cheryl or Jordan, Paris or Posh 'n' Becks.

'Oh,' Liz called over the man's shoulder, thinking that she shouldn't really take chances. After all, if Iris wasn't looking and the ticket fluttered off the shelf on to the floor, anyone could pick it up.

The older woman glanced up, so Liz knew that she must have heard. The man with the mongrel was inspecting chocolate bars on the display in front of the counter.

'Don't forget to write my name and address on the back!'

Chapter Fourteen

SHE HAD HER head down the loo and was scrubbing something nasty off the side of the pan when her mobile went. It was almost the end of the shift and she was looking forward to finishing. She peeled off her rubber gloves quickly and dug into her overall pocket to find her phone, hoping that she wouldn't miss it.

She hadn't time to check the number and was instantly on the alert when she recognised the tinny voice of Rosie's class teacher. Not Kyle again, surely?

'I'm afraid something's happened,' the teacher was saying. She sounded anxious, like she'd rather be anywhere than on the phone to Liz right now. 'Don't worry, she's all right. She had a funny turn at breakfast... took her straight to hospital... in an ambulance now.'

Liz's head started to swim. She could scarcely process the words. 'What do you mean, a funny turn?' It didn't sound that bad – so how come they'd taken her to hospital? It must be bad. Mrs Meakin wasn't telling her everything.

'What happened? Where are they taking her?' The questions gushed like water from an overflowing bathtub but she was unable properly to focus and nothing made sense.

'Went floppy,' Mrs Meakin said. 'Stable now but they want to do some tests.'

What was she talking about, floppy? Wasn't Rosie always a bit floppy on the left side? She was overreacting, surely. She'd got the wrong end of the stick.

'At first they thought it was to do with her bad arm and leg, a trapped nerve maybe, but her face had dropped on the left side and her eye looked strange.'

Liz was aware of her heart hammering in her chest and she could hear her breath, sharp and rapid. Peculiar sounds were coming from the back of her throat, something between a moan and a whimper.

She sank down on the cold hard tiles, clutching the phone to her ear like a lifeline. It was her worst nightmare, the one that every parent dreads when their kids are away from home. It *was* a nightmare, wasn't it? Any moment she'd wake up.

She was being hysterical; she needed to compose herself. If she'd been there she'd have known what to do.

Rosie. She must go to her. 'Where is she?' she said, determined to concentrate this time.

At last the other woman's words came together to form a proper sentence. She was on her way back from London to the hospital here, in Plymouth, where they were going to do some tests. She was with the ambulance crew and another member of staff. They'd just left and should arrive at about 2 p.m. Liz was to go to main reception and they'd tell her where she was.

She managed to rise, abandoning her mop and bucket, her trolley and rubber gloves, and flew out of the building into the grey October morning, past the girls in front answering calls and queries, past office workers arriving late with folded up bicycles and cups of coffee.

She knew that she must speak to Kasia but didn't know where to find her. Blindly, her fingers fumbled again for the mobile that she'd chucked in her overall pocket and scrolled for the number.

'Wait,' the older woman commanded when Liz told her what had happened. 'Do you have bag, keys?'

Liz realised with a pang that she'd left them in the top floor cleaning cupboard.

'I bring them to you. Stay there. Don't move.'

She couldn't go anywhere without them anyway.

She paced up and down the car park, unable to rest for a moment. Her mind was working overtime, her head pounding so that she thought it might explode, splattering her brains across the concrete.

Why hadn't they called her the minute Rosie was taken ill? Why hadn't they rung from the London hospital? She couldn't believe that while she'd been going about her work as usual, this frightening drama that she knew nothing about had been unfolding.

At last Kasia came running out, clutching the bag and overcoat, her jet-black eyebrows knitted together and mouth set in a determined line.

'I drive you,' she commanded and when Liz started to protest: 'You can't drive yourself. Is dangerous. Look at the state of you.'

Liz realised then that she was shaking and understood in a vague way that Kasia was right, that she shouldn't get behind the wheel.

'I told girls at reception to put note on your car,' Kasia went on. Rat-a-tat-tat. 'You can leave here. You won't get ticket.'

The journey passed in a blur; Liz was only half aware of Kasia, muttering beside her every now and then about some driver or other and beeping her horn impatiently. In any other circumstances she would have felt guilty for the inconvenience she was causing; as it was, all she could think of was her daughter.

She, Liz, had always been there for her. If she cut her knee or felt sick or there was a problem with the other children at school, Rosie always knew her mother would come at the drop of a hat if she asked her to.

Except that today, when she needed her most, Liz had been miles away, not just physically but mentally, too, because she'd had no idea what was going on. And now it was four whole hours before she'd see her and there was nothing in the world that she could do about it. She felt powerless and desperate, too panicky even to cry.

'Don't worry, is probably false alarm.' Kasia's words cut through the fog and Liz almost laughed.

Of course! Rosie was probably exhausted, hadn't had any sleep being in the same room as the other girls. Her tricky arm and leg were probably worse than usual. Everyone was just being super-cautious.

But then Mrs Meakin's words took hold again: 'Her face had dropped on the left side... her eye looked strange.'

Were they hiding something from her, waiting to tell her face to face? She felt her heart start to pound again and wanted to scream.

Calm down, Liz, you'll be no good to anyone. You've got to hold it together.

At last they drew up at the main entrance to the hospital. Kasia offered to stay but Liz refused: 'You go to work. I don't need you now, honestly.'

'Call me when you know something,' Kasia commanded and Liz promised that she would.

She raced into the building, oblivious to the stares from

folk hanging around just inside the entrance and hospital porters trundling patients in wheelchairs towards different departments or the lifts.

'Something's happened to my daughter,' she told the woman behind the desk. Was it really her speaking? 'They're bringing her here in an ambulance – from London.'

It seemed to take an age for them to make sense of Liz's story, to gather who exactly it was that she was talking about and then locate where Rosie would be taken. At last, however, she was led into a waiting room in the children's accident and emergency department where a female nurse in a light blue uniform offered her a cup of tea.

'Here,' she said kindly, passing a plastic cup. 'I put some sugar in. I should think you need it.'

There were other parents in the room, children at little tables with colouring pens and pads of paper, or sitting on the floor in front of boxes of toys. Everyone was waiting, it seemed, even the kids, while the adults stared blankly at the cream walls, talked quietly with each other or flicked disinterestedly through magazines.

'I need to know how she is,' Liz said desperately, conscious of enquiring eyes. 'No one's told me anything.'

The nurse sat patiently beside her, putting a comforting arm round her shoulder.

'Please don't worry,' she said kindly. 'I know you *are* worried but Rosie's fine. They wouldn't have put her in an ambulance if she was in any danger, they'd have kept her in London. They're going to bring her here to do some tests and you'll be able to see her soon.'

'But what could be the matter?' Liz asked, desperate for the smallest grain of information. It was the not knowing that was the worst. 'She was fine when I put her on the coach yesterday.'

The nurse gave her a squeeze. 'I don't know, but I gather she's been chatting to the paramedics in the ambulance, keeping them entertained, so she must be all right.'

Liz's spirits rose at this and she managed a small smile. It was the first heartening news that she'd received. If Rosie was chatting then she must be OK.

'The tests will show what's going on,' the nurse went on. 'She's in the best hands, I promise.'

Liz nodded gratefully. Rosie wasn't dying and the nurse didn't know anything more. They'd be here before long and then, at last, there'd be some answers. In the meantime, all she could do was while away the time as best she could.

The sweet tea calmed her a little more and it crossed her mind that she should text Robert to tell him that she wouldn't be turning up for work; she had his number in her address book. She didn't give many details, only that Rosie had been taken ill in London and was being brought back here.

She didn't mention last night, it was insignificant now. She could hardly believe that only this morning she'd been behaving like a silly lovesick schoolgirl. She was angry with herself, wanting to forget.

He replied almost immediately: *Very sorry to hear the news. Please don't give work a thought. All fingers crossed for Rosie and let me know how you get on. Robert x*

Only a couple of hours ago, Liz would have dwelled on that kiss, analysing its significance, trying to fathom if it was serious or casual, something that he did at the end of every text or that was meant for her alone.

Not now. She deleted the message and stared out of the window, looking for signs of hope in the heavy sky but there were none. Breathing in that stuffy smell, peculiar to all hospitals, of disinfectant and old meals, of hot bodies packed together, of sickness, anxiety and resignation. Of waiting. Always waiting. It was a different world, cut off from anywhere else. Once in there you felt as if you might never escape.

Good luck dont forget text me, came the message from Kasia. Liz could imagine her pausing, just for a second, from bashing the hoover across the carpet to jab the keypad with a finger before shoving the phone back in her pocket. Rush rush. But she was grateful; she needn't have done that.

She reached for a magazine from a tattered pile beside her and leafed through. Health advice: 'What to do if you've got a verruca.' She turned over quickly. Property advertisements: 'Luxury four bed house in quiet location.' She flicked again. 'I think my hubby's having an affair.' She tossed the magazine back on the table and glanced at the woman opposite with a sleeping baby in a pushchair and a little boy, playing with a plastic figure at her feet.

Was one of her children ill? They must be, to be here. But they seemed all right and the mother didn't look anxious. She rootled in an orange carrier bag and produced a packet of sweets. The small boy glanced up and she passed him one, which he unwrapped greedily and stuck in his mouth. Then she opened one for herself and sucked on it contentedly, staring into space.

Perhaps it was just a minor thing with whichever child; a routine check-up or signing off. Liz felt a stab of envy before telling herself not to be stupid. She had no idea what to expect for Rosie and shouldn't allow herself to imagine the worst.

A different nurse came over to ask if she was hungry. 'There's a canteen on the third floor where you can get sandwiches and cakes, that sort of thing.'

Liz realised that she hadn't eaten since last night, all she'd had was two cups of tea. But she wasn't hungry. In fact the thought of food made her feel sick.

'I'm all right,' she said and the nurse wandered off.

At long last she heard her name called and jumped up.

'She's arrived and they're checking her in.' It was the first nurse again. 'The doctor will be with her soon. Come with me and we'll go and find her.'

Liz's heart leaped. Rosie! Everything would be all right once she could see her and hold her in her arms.

She followed the nurse down in the lift and along a maze of corridors before reaching their destination. The nurse pushed open a heavy set of white doors and Liz blinked in the bright lights before her eyes adjusted and she could pick out the small fair head.

She was strapped against a white sheet, a thin little arm resting by her side. Tears trickled down Liz's cheeks as she took in the stretcher surrounded by strange people: a tall female paramedic in a green suit and yellow fluorescent jacket, walkie-talkie crackling, nurses walking to and fro, a receptionist behind a desk taking details from another paramedic, an anxious female member of staff from Mere Primary whom Liz vaguely recognised. And there, in the centre of it all, her daughter.

'Rosie, oh!'

The little girl barely had time to turn her head before Liz had rushed over, flinging her arms around her while Rosie burst into tears.

'Are you OK?' Liz asked at last, pulling back, a hand on each of her daughter's cheeks. She needed to examine every feature: her eyes, nose, mouth, the small, flat, cappuccino-coloured mole on her jawline below the ear, to make sure that they were all there. To stare into her eyes and be certain that it was her own precious girl.

Rosie made a hiccupping noise. 'I felt all funny at breakfast. Everything went fuzzy and I couldn't move my tricky arm or leg. Everyone was talking to me and I could hear but I couldn't say anything. It was horrible.'

She started to cry again and Liz shushed her, bending over the trolley and cradling her like a baby. 'It's all right darling, it's all right. Mummy's here,' she was saying, not caring that she was being watched. Relieved, in spite of her daughter's distress, in spite of the fact that she could see her face was drooping on the left as if someone were tugging at it with an invisible thread, that she sounded like old Rosie, *real* Rosie. They could deal with anything, she thought, now that they were together again.

They wheeled her into a little room just off the reception area and transferred her to a proper bed. In a low voice the teacher told Liz what had happened during and since breakfast and Rosie filled in the details.

'It all happened so fast,' the teacher said. 'I barely had time to call Mrs Meakin before they were bundling us in the ambulance.'

She looked exhausted; she'd been through a terrible ordeal, too. Liz thanked her and told her to get back to her family. Her husband, apparently, was already waiting outside to collect her.

Out of the ambulance and back with her mother, Rosie was sitting up now and beginning to sound more like herself.

'Can I go back to London when they've done the tests?' she asked hopefully, unaware, it seemed, that she looked different. 'The hotel's really nice, Mum. You should see it, it's so posh. You even get free shampoo and soap. I don't want to miss the dinosaurs at the Natural History Museum. I can go back, can't I?'

Liz, not wanting to disappoint, said that they'd have to wait and see.

When the female doctor arrived in a white coat and sat at the end of the bed, Liz half expected to be told that it was all a mistake and they could go home. Rosie's face would right itself in a day or two and they'd forget that this had ever happened.

The doctor, who was tall, attractive and young, far too young to have such a responsible job, smiled and chatted, asking Rosie about the ambulance ride.

'Did they put on the flashing lights?'

Rosie nodded.

'You'll have a few tales to tell when you go back to school.'

Rosie smiled her funny gappy smile, only the left side of her mouth wouldn't go up like the right. Liz felt the panic start to rise and couldn't bear it any longer. 'So what is it? What's wrong?'

'Well,' said the doctor, glancing at her notes, 'we think she may have had a stroke but we can't be sure until we've done the tests.'

It sounded like such a normal, matter-of-fact occurrence. Liz felt a buzzing in her ears and her mouth went dry. Stroke? Only old people had those, not little girls.

'That's not possible. Why would she have that? There's no reason.'

The doctor smiled reassuringly at Rosie before turning back to Liz.

'No,' she said gently, accustomed to dealing with worried parents. 'We're not sure. We need to find out what's going on.'

The next few hours passed in a daze of blood tests, heart tests, bleeping monitors, strange meals that Rosie disliked and casual conversations with other parents and children on the ward to which they were finally taken.

'The doctor will come and see you as soon we've got the results,' the nurse promised, but gave no indication of timescale or whether they'd be going home that night. More waiting.

It was now after seven and Liz was pretty certain that they'd be in for the night. She called Pat, because she was the only one who had a key to the flat, asking her to pop in and pick up her pyjamas and toothbrush, a change of clothes and the book beside her bed, as well as a few things for Rosie.

'Stick them in a cab – I'll pay at this end,' she said but Pat, sounding anxious, wouldn't hear of it.

'I'll ask Jean to take me – or Barbara or Aiden will do it.'

'It's too late,' said Liz.

'Oh no it's not.'

An hour or so later, Pat appeared at the door of the ward in a beige anorak and dark skirt clutching a plastic carrier bag and a packet of chocolate biscuits. Behind her was Jean, in a pale blue sweater and brown trousers, her face creased with worry. She must have left in a hurry because she didn't even have a coat.

So relieved was Liz to see them that she would have burst into tears, except that she knew she needed to hold it together for Rosie's sake, so she hugged them instead.

Pat smelled of salty sea air and overblown roses. Her soft, slack cheek felt familiar and slightly prickly.

'My oh my,' she said, patting Liz's back with a knobbly, arthritic hand, 'what a to-do.'

Jean, who was stout and strong as anything, probably from all those years of lifting babies and heavy toddlers, squeezed Liz so tightly that she could hardly breathe.

'One of my mums was late or we'd have got here sooner,' she said. 'You must be worried sick.'

When Liz pulled back, the two women went to Rosie's side.

'Hello, chicken,' Jean said softly, settling on the bed next to Rosie and taking her hand, while Pat hovered anxiously nearby.

Liz could tell that they'd clocked the lopsided smile – you couldn't miss it – but they didn't comment. 'You've given us all a right old fright,' Pat commented. 'I brought a packet of choccy bickies – our favourite, eh?'

She winked at Rosie who glanced at her mother slyly. 'We only ever have one though, don't we, Nan?'

'We do,' Pat laughed. 'Just the one then we *always* put the packet away.'

She sat on a plastic chair beside the bed while Liz perched on the end. Jean kept hold of Rosie's hand, patting and stroking it every now and then as you would a pet, and they chatted for half an hour or so. The colour had returned to Rosie's face and apart from the droop on her left side, she didn't look ill. In fact it seemed strange that she was here at all.

Liz found herself thinking again that they must have made a mistake; Rosie hadn't had a stroke, of course not. It was just that they weren't familiar with her condition and had misinterpreted the signs.

In any case, the droopiness seemed to be improving; it was definitely less pronounced than when she'd arrived. It was probably a trapped nerve or something; she just needed a good night's sleep.

When at last the young woman consultant returned and started to pull the yellow curtain round the bed, Liz was feeling quietly confident that the news would be positive.

'We'll be off,' Jean said, rising. 'Keep us posted, won't you?'

'Are you sure you can find the way?' Liz wanted to know. The hospital was such a maze of corridors and staircases.

'Course we can,' Pat replied chirpily. 'We're not senile yet.'

Liz moved to the chair while the consultant settled at Rosie's feet, clipboard in hand. She appeared neither grave nor cheery, making it impossible to read her. After asking Rosie how she felt, she turned to Liz, whose stomach lurched and she found herself wrapping her arms tightly round her body like a shield.

'Rosie's had what we call a mini-stroke.'

There was a whooshing in Liz's ears and she struggled to concentrate.

'We need to do an MRI scan... stay here tonight... transfer her to Bristol tomorrow...'

She sounded so calm and reassuring that Rosie was untroubled; her only concern being that she wouldn't now be able to re-join her school friends.

'You'll have to get your mum to take you to London another time,' the consultant said pleasantly. 'I don't think it's all it's cracked up to be anyway – too many crowds and too much pollution. It's much nicer down here.'

Rosie was tired and more than ready to sleep when they dimmed the lights at nine thirty and the other children on the ward settled down. There was a foldaway bed for Liz alongside her daughter, and the nurse provided a sheet, pillow and blanket, but it was narrow and uncomfortable and anyway, her mind was racing.

She crept along the corridor in semi-darkness to the parents' kitchen to make herself a cup of tea and two slices of buttered toast. The bread tasted like cardboard in her mouth but she forced it down, knowing that she'd need all the strength she could muster for what lay ahead.

After she'd washed up, she sat by herself on a red plastic chair in the parents' lounge beneath stark overhead lighting.

She had her book but was unable to read. Instead, she curled up in a ball, resting her head on the back of the seat and closing her burning eyes.

It seemed impossible to process what was happening and she longed to be able to reverse the clocks and go back to how things were. Her life seemed so simple then. Money was a problem, true, and she had to work very hard. Maybe sometimes she was a little lonely. Rosie had her problems but she was basically happy and that meant that Liz was happy, too.

Now everything had changed, the landscape before her was dark and frightening, and Liz found herself wondering if she could cope.

She'd been strong for so long, ever since her mother died when she was just sixteen, leaving her with a heartbroken father when her own heart seemed as if it would never mend; since the moment that she'd taken Rosie back from hospital after her condition was diagnosed, and realised that it was her job now to make her disabled daughter's life as full and obstacle-free as possible. Since Greg had told her that he was leaving. She'd felt utterly defeated, paralysed with fear and unable to imagine how she'd manage. But somehow she'd picked herself up, kept going and made a new life for them both. It was a good life, mostly. They were happy. And now this.

Sitting alone in the middle of the night in the white, friendless room, for the first time that day she allowed the hot salty tears to pour down her cheeks and her body heaved with sobs. A mini-stroke. What did that mean? Was Rosie's life in danger? She put her head on her knees and rocked herself to and fro, repeating over and over again like a mantra: 'Please don't take her away from me, please let my daughter be all right.'

Chapter Fifteen

SHE BARELY SLEPT so that remembering to call Kasia at 5 a.m. wasn't a problem.

'Don't worry,' Kasia said breathlessly. Liz imagined her rushing round her house, banging mug and plate on the table and swallowing chunks of toast before she'd chewed them. 'I have temporary girl. I guessed you won't be back for few days.'

Liz's mind strayed to financial matters. She'd get two weeks' sick pay with Krystal Klear and the same, she thought, at the restaurant. Rosie would surely be back at school by next week so that was one thing at least that she didn't need to worry about, though they'd miss the restaurant tips.

She decided to text Robert again; she couldn't face talking to him. The evening in the pub seemed unreal, a moment of madness. He was no doubt thinking the same. From now on she'd be totally professional; it would be easier for them both.

Rosie being transferred to Bristol, she wrote. *Having MRI later. I won't be in work today or tomorrow. Apologies for inconvenience.*

His reply was equally brief: *Hope scan goes well. Let me know. Robert.* There was no kiss this time. In a way she was relieved.

Already she'd started to feel peculiarly institutionalised, almost accustomed to the comings and goings of nurses, the toing and froing to the loo with Rosie, the dull, heavy hours of waiting so that even the arrival of the tea trolley lifted her spirits slightly, providing temporary relief from the boredom. Never mind that she didn't want a drink, or biscuits for that matter. She'd have them anyway.

When they finally said that Rosie was to be transferred at midday, she felt her heart skip because something was happening at last. Until she remembered what it was that they were going for.

'How are you feeling?' she asked Rosie anxiously, examining her daughter's face yet again for signs of improvement. She was almost back to normal now, surely? There was nothing wrong.

'OK,' Rosie said bravely. She hadn't caught sight of herself in a mirror, Liz had been very careful, and she said that she could see better now; the fuzziness had lessened. 'I wish I was still in London, though.'

It took a couple of hours to reach Bristol and when they arrived this time, everyone seemed to know exactly who they were and where they were going. They were hustled through registration and before long, Liz found herself waiting again while they performed the scan, watching her daughter anxiously through a screen.

They'd explained what would happen to Rosie and how she'd have to keep very still. There'd be strange noises and it might seem frightening, but it was important to do exactly as she was told. She made no fuss and was good as gold, listening to Radio 1 through the headphones. Her body was encased in the machine, but occasionally Liz could see a small foot tapping in time to the music, and she resolved never again to be frightened of beetles or the dentist's drill.

Afterwards, they were taken to another children's ward

where Rosie sat up in bed and drew pictures of the other patients with the pad and colouring pens that Pat had packed for her. She was bored; she wasn't used to sitting around.

'Can't we go outside?' she asked. 'It's so hot in here.'

Liz glanced out of the window. It was already getting dark and she imagined other, lucky children letting off steam in the dusky garden before bed, watching what they wanted on TV or playing with their toys.

It was no use wallowing in self-pity.

She shook her head and Rosie's face fell. 'I want to go home.'

'I know,' Liz replied, sympathetic but firm. 'But we have to wait for the results. It won't be long now, I'm sure.'

In truth she had no idea how long it would take. Perhaps they wouldn't hear anything for hours, or until tomorrow or the next day, even. There were so many patients to treat and doctors had to prioritise. However, when at around 5 p.m. a nurse told Liz that the consultant would see her now, she was surprised because it was only an hour and a half since the scan.

'Should Rosie come too?' she asked but was told no, they wanted to see Liz on her own.

Liz tried to argue; she couldn't bear to leave her daughter for a second. After what had happened she thought that she might never be able to leave her side again.

'She won't be any trouble, honestly. She'll just sit there quietly; she's very good.'

But the nurse was insistent and Liz had to kiss Rosie goodbye. 'I'll be back soon.'

It was a terrible wrench. She turned at the door of the ward to wave and Rosie waved bravely back. As Liz followed the nurse to the neurology department, down endless identical corridors that smelled of stale air and disinfectant, she was telling herself that lightning rarely struck twice. Rosie had cerebral palsy and that was enough for any child to cope with. The scan would be clear and they'd be going home soon.

The sign on the door said 'DO NOT DISTURB' but still her conscious thoughts were of false alarms and smiles of relief all round. It was just bad luck that it had happened when Rosie was on a school trip. Perhaps the excitement had been too much for her – she wasn't physically strong – and she should take it easy for a while.

Her legs felt wobbly and her teeth were chattering, though, as she sat opposite a middle-aged man in glasses with a pale blue shirt rolled up at the sleeves and a name tag on a cord round his neck. Alongside him was a woman in a white tunic, and the nurse who had brought her here sat beside Liz.

'I'm really sorry but it's not good news,' the man said, looking her straight in the eye. 'Your daughter has a large brain tumour.'

Liz's mind took off like a light aircraft, swooping out of control in ever widening circles until she thought that she'd surely hit the ground with a thump and black out.

'It's in the frontal lobe, pressing against her optic nerves and the fibres that operate the left side of her body...'

She bent forwards, engulfed in a blizzard that came without warning, white lights, buzzing and overwhelming nausea. An arm around her back. 'I think I'm going to be sick.' A cardboard bowl in her hands, retching, but nothing much came out.

'Steroids to try to shrink the tumour. We'll operate next Tuesday.'

An image flashed before her. Another hospital, a different doctor, another time. The moment when they'd told her that

207

Rosie had cerebral palsy. It had seemed like the end of the world then, only it wasn't: this was so much worse.

'Is she going to die?'

She searched the man's face but couldn't tell what he was thinking. There was sympathy, sure, but also guarded professionalism. This can't have been pleasant for him, either, however often he had to go through it.

'We'll do everything we can to make sure that doesn't happen.'

She believed him; he was telling the truth. But did she trust him enough to save her daughter's life?

He produced the black and white scan and pointed to a large mass invading the healthy tissue, the enemy intent on annihilation. Terrifying. She had no choice but to trust him.

She returned to the ward and summoned her best acting skills to give Rosie a sanitised and optimistic version of the facts.

'You're very poorly at the moment,' she began, 'but everyone is going to do all they can to get you better.'

She didn't think that Rosie had noticed the crack in her voice, but she had.

'Don't cry, Mum,' she said, reaching forwards to give her a hug. 'It's going to be all right.'

Her little hand was patting her mother's back, there there, trying to comfort and protect. She could never bear to see Liz unhappy.

It was too much and despite her best intentions, Liz broke down, her body racked with sobs.

'I didn't mean to, I'm sorry,' she was saying, wiping her nose and eyes with the back of her hand, her sleeve. 'It *is* going to be all right, you're going to be fine.'

But Rosie was no fool; she read books and watched TV. She knew that brain tumours were serious. In that moment

Liz resolved to be as honest and concrete as she could from now on, she owed her daughter this much. But it was going to be so hard – and was she strong enough? She'd have to be.

In the event, they didn't make it till Tuesday because the steroids weren't working and they said that Rosie was deteriorating. The left side of her body was getting weaker and she might suffer permanent damage.

They operated on the Sunday morning and Liz tried not to visualise what they were doing. If she dwelled on the image of her daughter's precious skull, the surgeon picking through the contents of her very essence, her brain, she'd pass out for sure. Instead, she paced the hospital corridors and tried to do crosswords in newspapers left lying around, forcing down cups of weak tea. The nurses suggested sedatives but she wouldn't take them. Rosie had been braver than she thought possible, so she would be, too.

She didn't want anyone with her, either. They'd offered, of course. Iris, Pat, Barbara, Jean, Ruby, Rick, even the riotous Hannah with her cut-glass accent rang – she'd missed Liz at the office and got the news from Kasia. And Robert.

Greg asked if she needed any cash, which was unusually generous of him, and her father promised to send a Get Well Soon card to the ward, which seemed a little premature. He said he'd have come to join Liz if it weren't for the fact that he had to take Davina's car in for a service. The car was likely to be out of action for a few days so she'd be using his.

In any case, Liz turned everybody down. It had always been just them. Liz and Rosie, Rosie and Liz. She'd known that virtually from the moment that Rosie was born, really, and no one other than the medical team could help them now; if they were going to get through this they'd do it on their own.

The operation took nearly eight hours. When at last they took Liz to the recovery room to see Rosie, she was trembling so much that two nurses had to hold her by each arm and ask if she needed to sit down. Their voices sounded strange and far away, but she was determined not to faint. Rosie needed her. Willing herself forwards, she straightened up and approached the bed, tentatively taking the small, limp hand in hers.

She didn't look like Rosie. Her head had been shaved, all her beautiful long hair gone, and was wrapped in thick bandages, her eyes were bruised and swollen and tubes seemed to spring from everywhere, including her thin, frail neck. And there was dried and fresh blood, so much of it. Liz let out a sob and her hand flew to her mouth to stop it.

'It went well,' said the surgeon, the same man who'd spoken to her about the scan. He was pale and weary-looking, but smiling in his blue hat and overalls, seeking to reassure, relieved himself, no doubt, that his day's work had been a success.

'We managed to remove ninety-five per cent of the tumour. We've given her morphine. She won't come round properly for a couple of days.'

As Liz sat beside her daughter in the high dependency unit, stroking her cheek, watching the machines that monitored every precious breath, waiting, waiting for Rosie to emerge from whatever deep, unconscious place they'd put her in, she allowed herself for the first time in six days to think about the future.

If Rosie survived, which they'd assured Liz that she would, she knew with certainty that their lives would never be the same. No one could say yet whether her daughter would be further disabled after such complicated surgery, or in what way. Plus the fact, of course, that five per cent of the tumour remained, too dangerous to remove. The hope was that it would stay dormant but if it started to grow, further treatment might be needed. They'd have to face that battle if it came.

Would Liz be able to return to work? It was doubtful. It would be months before Rosie could go back to school full-time and then there'd still be hospital check-ups and, perhaps, chemotherapy and radiotherapy. They'd need cash from somewhere.

She'd never claimed benefits. No way. After Greg left, she'd wallowed in misery for a few weeks before realising that no one was going to help her and Rosie out of this mess except herself. Somehow she'd managed to give herself a stiff talking-to, pick herself up and make the decision to leave London.

And she'd been proud of their achievements. They might be hard up, but at least they were standing on their own two feet. She thought she'd rather have two, three or four jobs than rely on state handouts. Now, though, it seemed that she'd have no option.

Eeyore, of course, was still parked outside Dolphin House and Hannah was kind enough to drive it to Bristol for Liz one evening, three days after the surgery. They met in the reception area downstairs at around 7 p.m. and Liz felt as if her glamorous friend had been beamed in from a planet called Normal. She'd forgotten that it even existed.

Slim and elegant, Hannah was wearing a dark pencil skirt, high red heels and a white shirt rolled up at the sleeves, her jacket slung over a shoulder. She had a healthy glow and easy, confident smile and everyone turned to look at her, they couldn't help it. You could tell that she was going places.

She hesitated a moment before hugging Liz. 'Darling, you look exhausted.'

Liz shrugged. 'Hospital pallor. Everyone goes the same colour after a while.'

They sat for a moment on a squeaky red sofa by the coffee machine, their knees almost touching, so close together yet divided, Liz thought, by an invisible glass barrier. Like a flower planted in the perfect position, Hannah was on the bright, well-watered side, while Liz and Rosie dwelled in the murky shadows.

'No worries, hun,' Hannah said breezily when Liz thanked her for the umpteenth time. 'It's a good excuse to meet up with my old school chums here and I enjoyed the spin.' She raised her eyebrows. 'I say, that Eeyore's seen better days though, hasn't she? She's almost vintage!'

She invited Liz to go for a meal with her and her friends, but she wouldn't leave Rosie.

'I'll give you a call in a few days,' Hannah said, handing over the keys. 'Look after yourself, won't you – and try to get some sleep.'

After Rosie had come round and been moved to a normal ward, it was Pat who arrived by coach to sit with her while Liz drove back to Cornwall for the day for interviews to claim the various benefits to which she was entitled. She answered the questions as best she could but felt numb inside, as if the very thing that she'd treasured most since she and Greg split – her ability to support herself and Rosie – had been stripped from her.

They were kind, of course, and understanding, helping her to fill in the forms for everything that she was entitled to, but that wasn't the point. She was dependent now on the generosity of others and thus beholden. Greg was the last person who'd done that to her, pointing out that it was his flat that she lived in, his benevolence that she and Rosie lived off. She'd

212

almost come to believe that she relied on him for her very existence and she'd never wanted to feel that way again.

'You shouldn't feel bad,' said Pat when she returned from her trip, trying to comfort. 'You've paid your tax and national insurance contributions and you need that money now, it's your right.'

But it didn't help.

A week after the operation, Rosie had her first bath. The bandages had been removed and Liz was allowed to wash her daughter's poor, shaven head, which was matted with so much blood that the water turned crimson.

As she gently massaged shampoo into her scalp, careful not to catch the staples that held the deep incision together, she breathed in and out slowly to control her rising nausea. What they'd done was horrific, brutal, and she trembled with anger, furious that she'd been powerless to protect her daughter from such inhumanity, telling herself that the alternative to surgery was far worse.

Rosie lay quietly in the bath, trusting her mother to be gentle, not to hurt.

'All shiny and new,' Liz said brightly as she helped Rosie from the warm water, wrapping her in a big white towel.

Her scarred head, misshapen still and sore, was like something out of a horror film. Liz thought that she'd never be able to watch one again.

Seven days after that, they removed the seventy staples from her scalp and, at last, she was allowed to go home. When Liz received a text from Robert asking if he could come and visit she said no, Rosie wasn't well enough.

Can I call you in a few days? he replied, but she didn't answer back. What would she say to him anyway? That she couldn't trust herself to speak rationally to him and she didn't know him well enough to share her fears? It was hard enough holding herself together for her daughter; she couldn't put on a brave face for him, too.

She carried Rosie, light as a feather, from the car into her bedroom which smelled of closed windows and unwashed sheets.

'Just a moment while I lock Eeyore,' she said, settling her daughter carefully against the pillows.

As she passed her own bedroom she noticed that it was unmade and realised, with a start, that she hadn't been in it since the night over two weeks ago when she'd gone out with Robert. She hadn't been able to sleep for stupid excitement and had woken late for work and rushed from the flat in a panic.

How long ago that seemed now, a flash in time like a spark that had briefly illuminated the room before dying. But then wasn't all of memory like that – a few isolated moments that stood out, like the blips on a heart monitor, then quickly faded, their intensity soon forgotten?

Rosie called her: 'Mum?' and she hurried to the car to bring in the bags and plonk them on the hall carpet, before closing the front door tightly and double locking. Cocooned in their own little world with no one to interfere or upset them, she and Rosie had everything they needed. She felt half inclined never to see a soul, apart from hospital staff – and Pat and Jean, perhaps – ever again.

It didn't last, that sense of loneliness, anger and isolation. The local nurse came to check on Rosie every day for two weeks and as she started to get better, Liz felt better, too. Visitors began to arrive with gifts – toys and teddies for Rosie, boxes of chocolates and flowers for Liz. Soon the flat looked like a florist's, bursting with sweet-smelling blooms and overflowing with greeting cards.

Tony and Felipe dropped by with a delicious assortment of expensive bath oils and body lotions, soaps and scented candles because Rosie and Liz 'needed pampering'. Liz was incredibly touched.

There were even home-cooked, hearty meals of lasagne, chilli con carne and stew for her to put in the freezer to eat when they fancied, and Jean made her special chicken and ham pie, topped with the flaky puff pastry that Rosie adored. The three small children that Jean looked after had done a finger painting of a smiley girl in a pink top and blue trousers, standing in a field of yellow daffodils.

'You can put it on your bedroom wall – if Mum says that's OK,' Jean added quickly.

Esme, who frequently went to her pottery studio first thing and came back mid-morning, called in with home-made cakes from the bakery. She was the least maternal person, but she made Liz and Rosie a matching ceramic mug and breakfast plate each with 'Mummy' and 'Rosie' written in swirly letters, and also offered to keep an eye on Rosie if Liz wanted.

One evening, Esme came and sat with the girl for a good hour while Liz had a shower, and spoke to her like a grown-up, recounting stories from her childhood. It transpired that she'd spent the first years of her life in Africa and run around barefoot until she was eight, before the family located to the Middle East. Rosie was enchanted.

The arrival of Mandy from school a month after the operation gave her a welcome boost, too. Mandy's mother dropped her off for a couple of hours and the girls sat in the primrose-painted front room, chatting and making jewellery from a special kit that Rosie had been given.

Her vision would never recover fully, because of the tumour that had been pressing on her optic nerves. She would forever need to hold things up close to see them properly and, in time, get used to glasses and go for books with large print. It pained Liz to think of her daughter's poor, precious eyes, but in the end it was a small enough price to pay for her life.

Rosie, embarrassed by her shaved hair that was just starting to grow back, soft and downy like a baby bird, was wearing one of Liz's scarves, but Mandy wanted to see the scar.

'Did you really have staples in?' she wanted to know. 'It must have really hurt.'

Liz was pleased to hear Rosie describing the operation in some detail, proud, it seemed, of her battle wound.

'My doctor, Dr Amin, said my hair's going to grow back just the same as before and he thinks that horrible tumour thingy's dead.' She made a sound, like someone being choked, to demonstrate.

Liz smiled. Hair first, tumour second. Rosie had her priorities, like everyone else.

She made peanut butter sandwiches for lunch and was glad when Rosie ate almost everything apart from the crusts, which she'd always nibbled around. When Mandy left, Barbara from The Lobster Pot stopped by with a new navy jumper with a cat on the front and a pair of bright pink leggings 'for the patient'.

'I couldn't resist them,' she said, sipping a mug of tea that Liz had made. They were in the kitchen, leaving Rosie to watch TV next door. 'When I saw the top I thought of our Rosie immediately.'

She chatted a little about the pub and mentioned Loveday, who'd dumped her son Aidan when he refused to take her shopping because he'd arranged to see his kids.

'She was far too young for him,' Barbara sighed. 'I did warn him but he wouldn't listen. I said it would end in tears.'

Apparently Robert had been having trouble with the new waitress, a flighty madam from Torpoint who made faces at the customers behind their backs.

'I should think he misses you,' Barbara said, eyeing Liz curiously.

She felt a pang – poor Robert, the last thing he needed was another member of staff running rings around him. And she did miss the hustle and bustle of the restaurant and even the cleaning job, oddly, but that was then. Rosie was all that mattered now.

'Can I have a biscuit?' Rosie demanded from the other room. Liz rose wordlessly to fetch the tin.

She'd allowed her daughter to get away with murder these past few weeks, happy to fetch her anything she wanted, especially food. There was plenty of time to re-establish rules when she was fully recovered.

'I should think you could do with a break,' Barbara said when Liz returned. 'Let me look after Rosie for you one afternoon. Aidan can mind the pub. We can make cupcakes, I'll bring the ingredients. She likes those, doesn't she?'

At first Liz refused as she'd done with Pat and everyone else who'd offered: 'I don't want to leave her yet, it's too soon...'

Rosie called again, this time for a drink.

'You must be absolutely exhausted,' Barbara commented. 'A change of scenery will perk you up. Go for a walk or see a friend. I expect it'll be good for Rosie to see a new face, too.'

Liz thought about it. Was Rosie bored with her mother's company? She certainly missed her old life and friends and had enjoyed spending time with Esme, and Mandy earlier. Perhaps Barbara was right and they should have a little break from each other. Plus, Liz needed to go to the bank and there was something else on her mind, too.

Weirdly, Iris hadn't been in touch since the operation. She'd sent frequent messages when she'd first heard about Rosie and after they were transferred to Bristol. She'd wanted to know all about the MRI scan and Liz had endeavoured to keep her as up to date as possible, but since just before the surgery that Sunday, nothing.

Liz was hurt, she couldn't help it, but then she'd told herself that there must be a reason. Was it the business, or had something happened to one of the children or Spencer? Was Gran in hospital or was Iris herself unwell?

Still, she'd been so busy with Rosie that she hadn't had the time – or indeed energy – to pick up the phone to find out. She was up to her ears in problems of her own. Now, though, with Barbara's offer, it seemed like the ideal opportunity to re-establish contact.

There was another thing as well. The other night she'd caught the tail end of the lottery programme on TV. It wasn't so interesting to watch when you hadn't bought a ticket, but it had jogged her memory and she realised that she'd forgotten to pick up the lucky dip that she'd asked Iris to look after for her, just before she'd received the dreaded phone call from London about Rosie.

Her oversight wasn't exactly surprising under the circumstances, Liz thought, but she should check it out just in case and find out what Iris had done with it. She'd ask her about it when they met.

'All right,' she said. 'I'll pop over on the ferry to see my friend.'

'Great,' said Barbara. 'I'll buy some food colouring for the icing. It makes things more fun.'

And so it was arranged. Barbara would come the day after tomorrow and sit with Rosie for a few hours, or as long as Liz needed. If there was the slightest problem, if Rosie was even just the tiniest bit sad or unwell, she'd call Liz immediately. And that was a promise.

Chapter Sixteen

IT WAS A cold, blustery day in mid-November when Liz left the cottage, blinking in the light as she'd been spending so much time indoors. She had ventured out, but only for short trips to the shops for bread or milk, tinned custard and sponge pudding, biscuits and chocolate, anything that Rosie fancied, really. The prospect of a few hours away from her seemed strange and unsettling.

Eeyore was reluctant to start and at first Liz wondered if the battery had gone flat, but at last the old engine growled and spluttered into life and she headed for the ferry, as she'd done so many times before in quite different circumstances.

She decided to go to the bank first as she had a cheque to pay in from her father. 'Use this to buy a treat for Rosie,' he'd written. Little did he realise that treats of the sort he meant weren't exactly on their agenda. Their benefits had come through and they'd get by, but there was nothing left over for luxuries. Her father's gift would go towards food and petrol, which were more important. In any case, he meant well and she was grateful.

It was a busy Wednesday afternoon and Liz had to queue for a parking space in the ugly concrete multi-storey. Everywhere her eyes fell, strained-looking folk were scurrying this way and that, heads down against the wind, clutching

220

carrier bags and small children, dogs and parcels. She thought that she'd never seen so many people until she reminded herself that it was always like this. It's just that she'd been isolated for so many weeks that she'd forgotten what the city felt like.

When at last she'd paid in her cheque and stopped at the chemist to buy a few items for Rosie – more queuing – she couldn't wait for the peace and quiet of Tremarnock again. She'd thought that she might have a cappuccino in a café, but didn't fancy jostling for a seat and changed her mind.

She left the multi-storey and headed out of the city centre with relief. Passing by the office she wondered if Hannah was there, tapping away at her computer, using a phone cleaned not by her, Liz, but by some other girl who was probably just as efficient when it came down to it. No one was indispensable, after all, and she supposed that the gap she'd left would have closed over by now, leaving little or no trace. After all, it didn't take a genius to polish desks and stick dirty coffee cups in the dishwasher. It was no doubt the same story at the restaurant, too.

As she pulled up outside Good Morning News she was dismayed to see a giant yellow skip filled with rubbish on the pavement and a workman up a ladder, boarding up the window with planks of thick wood, bashing nails into the frame with a heavy metal hammer.

Her immediate thought was that the worst had happened and they'd had to wind up the business, which would explain her friend's silence. Poor Iris, she thought. Poor Jim. She felt guilty for having doubted them for a second. No wonder they hadn't been in touch.

She rootled for change in her purse and stuck some in the parking metre before walking uneasily towards the door.

There were lights on inside but she couldn't see Iris's auburn head at the counter and it crossed her mind that they might have left already. But where would they go? The business was their livelihood and they lived above the shop, all of them, including Gran and Spencer. How would they get by? What would become of them?

Her eyes widened as she scanned the interior, looking left and right, taking everything in. The counter was bare, no till, no Iris, no lottery machine or cigarette packets stacked neatly behind, row by row, so that she scarcely had to move from her position to reach for them.

Her thoughts wandered back to the days when she was still working at Dolphin House and she'd stop by every week for her ticket. It was always the same; she and Iris would put the world to rights, then she'd check her watch and her friend would quickly pass her a packet of ten cigarettes and a lucky dip, open the till to put Liz's money inside and give her the change.

Without fail, Liz would then write her name and address on the back before stuffing it in her purse and racing up the road to begin her cleaning shift. The routine never changed, except for that one day when she'd forgotten to go back for the ticket. It seemed like an age ago now.

The shelves were mostly empty, barely a chocolate bar, bag of sweets, newspaper or magazine in sight, and the dust that hung thickly in the air chased up Liz's nose and made her sneeze. Even the giant drinks cabinet at the far end of the room was wide open and pulled away from the wall, its cord trailing sad and lifeless across the floor like a dead snake. No diet Cokes or flavoured waters on offer today. Nothing for sale.

A tall, fair-haired young man in white overalls had his back to her and was throwing items from the unlit food chiller into a black plastic bag: cheese, cartons of milk, packets of ham that no one had ever wanted to buy.

'What's happened?' she asked, conscious of a quiver in her voice. It seemed that in the weeks she'd been gone, everything here had changed, too.

The young man turned abruptly but when he saw Liz's face he shrugged and smiled in a friendly sort of way.

'Closing down,' he said in a thick local accent. 'They told us not to keep anything.'

He held up a tub of butter and peered at the lid. 'It's in date – d'you want it? Might as well, it'll only go to waste.'

Liz shook her head and swallowed. 'Are they here?'

He dropped the butter in the open rubbish bag and picked up a box of eggs: 'Two days late.' Then: 'Reckon someone's upstairs. Friends of yours, are they?'

Liz nodded. 'I haven't seen them for a while. My daughter's been ill. I didn't know.'

'Ah,' he replied. 'Going Looe way, they said. House on the seafront. All right for some, eh?'

He laughed easily and she was thrown. Didn't he realise? Maybe they hadn't told him the circumstances, so she bit her tongue.

Four other men arrived, big burly types in rolled up overalls with tattoos on their arms. The older one in a red beanie, the end of a fag hanging out of his mouth, nodded at Liz and growled a greeting.

'You come to take the heavy items, Mick?' the young man asked. 'I'd start with that fridge there, mate. She's a monster.'

Mick eyed the empty drinks cabinet suspiciously. 'For the dump, you said? Don't nobody want to buy it?'

The young man tied a knot in the bulging black rubbish bag and slung it over his shoulder.

'Nah. Everything to go. The whole lot.'

'You'd think they'd get a few bob for it,' Mick commented, then, 'C'mon lads. Let's get moving.'

While the workmen stood round the fridge, debating the best way to lift it, Liz scuttled upstairs. The door to the flat was open and she noticed that the pictures she'd seen on her visit here at Easter – scenes of Cornwall, mostly, plus a few family photos – were gone, leaving dirty outlines and holes in the cream walls where nails had once been.

From the landing she could see into the sitting room, now devoid of furniture. The burgundy carpet, once covered in Spencer's toys, was pitted with deep furniture marks and stains that hadn't been visible when there were so many bodies.

Along the corridor, the small kitchen where she and Iris sat had been emptied, too, and without her friend's jolly mugs, pots, pans and pictures on every surface, it looked cheap and shabby. The washing machine and cooker had been pulled out and taken away and the brown linoleum underneath was torn and dirty.

She swung round, thinking that she could hear noises in one of the bedrooms.

'Iris?' she called. 'Jim?'

When no one answered she padded down the landing, trying each door in turn. Small bathroom, bedroom one, bedroom two. All vacant. When she reached the third bedroom at the end she knocked and opened.

Darren and Jim were bent over an exercise bike, a toolbox between them, but they looked up when she entered. She was so glad to see them that she cried out, 'Thank God! I thought you'd gone!'

Jim took a step back, his eyes wide open as if he'd seen a ghost, and Darren stood motionless, staring too.

'Liz!' said Jim at last, as if speaking her name would somehow fix her to the floor, transforming her into a living breathing human being. 'What are you doing here?'

Liz, ignoring his question, walked over to him, arms opened wide.

'I'm so sorry,' she said, feeling his stiff, stocky body relax a little in her embrace. 'I had no idea.'

Pulling away, she hugged Darren too, who felt like a piece of furniture, knobbly shoulders, wooden, inflexible limbs. His shirt was slightly damp and he smelled of sweat. They must be devastated about what had happened to the business.

'How's Rosie?' he asked, stepping away as soon as she'd let him, and Liz gave a quick update of the past four weeks.

'That's good,' said Darren, not meeting her gaze. 'I'm glad she's on the mend.'

He sounded odd and detached, but Liz put it down to trauma.

'Tell me everything,' she said, having wrapped up her own story. 'How's Iris? And Gran?'

There were no chairs though she wouldn't have minded sitting on the floor. Neither of the men suggested it, though, so they stood around the half-dismantled bike.

Jim cleared his throat before explaining that they'd decided to call it a day.

'Had enough of it,' he said, scratching his head and examining his dirty white trainers. 'We're moving up the coast. Iris always fancied a sea view. She's there now. We're just...'

His voice trailed off as he glanced at the bike and Liz nodded back; it was clear what they were doing. 'We're off ourselves in a minute,' he went on. 'We were going to chuck this out then Iris decided she wanted to keep it after all.'

He shifted from one foot to another and Liz wondered

why they were discussing an old exercise bike. Reminded of Robert's awkwardness, she was confused by her friend's discomfort, until she told herself that Jim had his pride like everyone else and probably loathed admitting his failure to anyone.

Not wishing to rub salt in a fresh wound, she cast around for something positive.

'A sea view?' she said, imagining that they'd probably found a bungalow to rent, perhaps, or one of the holiday chalets. There were quite a few along the coast in the numerous holiday parks. They were pretty bleak in winter but no doubt cheap and that, presumably, was the essence. 'Iris will love that.'

Neither of the men picked her up on it and she had a sense that they wanted her to go, but told herself that she must be mistaken.

'Is Iris OK?' she asked again. 'I haven't heard from her. I had a nasty feeling something was up. I would've called only I've been so busy with Rosie.'

Darren crossed his arms over his chest. 'She's all right, isn't she, Dad?' He eyed his father, who nodded in agreement. 'It was a shock but—'

'We came into a bit of money, see,' Jim interrupted, suddenly straightening. 'Just in the nick of time. Decided to get out while we can.'

'That's fabulous!' Liz said, feeling her spirits lift. 'I'm so pleased!'

Jim gave a small smile. 'Yeah, well, Iris is happy not to be stuck in here all day. It was doing her head in – and mine.'

'So what are you going to do?' Liz asked, thinking that maybe they'd found work in the holiday park, managing it, even. They'd be good at that.

Jim took a deep breath. 'Dunno yet, do we, Darren?'

He put an arm round his son, who grinned for the first time, showing his teeth. 'Little as possible, I reckon.'

Liz frowned, thinking that Iris would need Jim and Darren to bring in money, Christie too, but she wasn't going to pry; she just wanted to know that they'd manage.

'Can I have the address?' she asked, not wishing to delay them further. 'Rosie and I will come and visit. She'll enjoy that. She's hardly been out since the operation. She'll love seeing your new place and getting some fresh air.'

Jim's gaze slid from her and he patted the pockets of his jeans, his shirt, looking for something.

'Don't have it on me,' he said at last. 'Can't remember it offhand, can you, Darren?'

He turned to his son who shook his head vigorously. 'No clue.'

'What about the removal men? Would they know?'

Jim frowned. 'Don't think so. I haven't given it to them. They're just clearing this place out, y'see. They're not taking anything up to the house.'

Liz paused. She was on the point of asking if he'd drop Iris a text but stopped herself, as the realisation sank in – he didn't want her to have it. Of course he must know where he was moving; he could describe it to her, anyway, give her the name of the holiday park or whatever and she could look it up.

She reddened, feeling suddenly awkward and foolish, then told herself that perhaps he was ashamed of the new place.

'I'll give Iris a ring,' she said uncertainly, convinced that a chat with her friend would soon smooth out the wrinkles. As if she, Liz, cared where they lived; her own home wasn't exactly luxurious. The main thing was to let her friend know that she was thinking of her and wanted to see her.

Jim tucked his red and blue checked shirt into his trousers, which he'd pulled down well below his waist to accommodate the paunch. 'She's not got much time to talk at the moment, to be honest with you. She's very busy, what with the move and that.'

Liz stared at him, confused, but there was no eye contact and his face was blank and expressionless.

She felt a hollow forming in the pit of her stomach. This was going too far; anyone would think they were strangers, the way he was talking to her.

'Give it a few weeks,' Darren added more kindly. 'She's in one of her manic moods, sorting everything out. You know what she's like. She'll be fine once she's got things how she wants.'

Liz couldn't help thinking that it would hardly take weeks to rearrange the contents of the small flat in a new place, but nodded obediently.

'Well, tell her I called, won't you?' she asked hesitantly, keen to get away suddenly and breathe in some fresh air. It was claustrophobic in here with just the three of them and she was beginning to feel like the kid who hadn't been invited to the party.

Jim bent over again, took a large spanner from the toolbox and set about unscrewing the handlebars of the bike.

'Excuse us,' he said, 'best get this finished.'

'Of course,' Liz replied, curling up inside like paper over a flame. 'Sorry to have interrupted you.'

She looked at Darren, hoping for some crumb of comfort, evidence of warm, welcoming, caring Darren, but he was watching his father at work, helping to steady the bike.

'I'm going,' she said unnecessarily, her arms dangling aimlessly at her sides. Neither made a move to kiss her goodbye. 'Good luck with it all.'

'Thanks, Liz,' said Jim, pulling on the handlebars to loosen them. 'You take care of yourself – and Rosie,' he added almost as an afterthought. He didn't look up once.

Liz stumbled from the flat, down the stairs and out into the shop, her mind racing and close to tears. She'd been looking forward to seeing Iris; she'd missed her. Had she, Liz, done something to upset them all? But if so, what? She couldn't imagine. And if Jim was cut up about the business, why take it out on her?

The giant fridge had gone now and Mick and his mates were heaving the food chiller through the door, grunting and muttering instructions to each other: 'Left a bit, right a bit. Easy does it.'

'All right?' said the young man, who'd been throwing things into the rubbish bag when she first arrived. He was leaning against the counter languidly smoking a cigarette and looking at her curiously.

'Fine,' said Liz, trying to disguise the catch in her voice and not wishing to be drawn into a conversation. 'I'm in a rush. My car—'

'S'pect you'll be visiting the big house, then?' he carried on, ignoring her. 'They're only renting though, is that right? While they find a place to buy?'

His bright eyes were fixed on her and he couldn't hide his interest.

'Bet they're after a stonking big mansion,' he went on, still gazing. 'With a swimming pool and that. Maybe they want to buy a plot of land and build one themselves? I would.'

Bewildered, she shook her head. 'I don't know anything.'

She looked desperately at the exit and saw that the men were outside now, loading the chiller into the back of a giant green lorry on the forecourt.

Seizing her chance, she hurried from the building, aware of the young man staring after her, his words still ringing in her ears.

'Big house', she was thinking, as she climbed into Eeyore. 'Place to buy.' 'Mansion.' What was he talking about? And if they'd come into that much money, why wouldn't Jim have told her about it when surely he'd know that she'd be delighted for them?

She was aware that she was driving badly as she headed back to the ferry and several cars beeped at her impatiently. She couldn't quite believe that Jim and Darren had been so cold, especially once she'd told them about Rosie's life-saving operation and the hell that she herself had been going through.

Images of the Easter Sunday lunch danced and flickered through her mind; Jim's warmth towards Rosie, Darren's ready jokes and welcoming smile. The wine, abundant food and laughter. Iris's insistence that they should come in the first place, her confidences as they sipped tea in the kitchen on their own.

She, Liz, must call her to sort everything out. Not tonight or tomorrow, but when she was feeling stronger. Iris would explain the situation, she was salt of the earth, was Iris. A pearl among women. She'd looked after Rosie like one of her own when they went on that picnic to Tintagel.

There was no side to her, no airs and graces. What you saw was what you got. In fact, Liz would go so far as to say she was among only a tiny group of people that she felt she could really rely on.

She was still smarting from the encounter with Jim and Darren as she pulled up outside the cottage, chewing over the conversation and trying to work out why they'd behaved so oddly.

It was almost five thirty – she'd been gone more than three

hours – and she was surprised as she left the car to see Loveday walking towards her in the gloom. She was heading down the hill in the opposite direction from the restaurant carrying an enormous plastic bag. Late again, Liz thought wryly.

The pair hadn't met since Rosie had been taken ill, though Loveday had signed a Get Well card from Robert and the other staff, wishing her a speedy recovery. She was wearing a dark, knee-length coat and walking quite fast in the middle of the road in high platform shoes that made her appear much taller than she really was. Her head was still shaved on one side, while the rest of her long hair cascaded over her shoulder like black lava.

Liz waved, fully expecting Loveday to say that she was in a hurry and couldn't stop, but the girl came to a halt in front of her and flung her arms around Liz's neck.

'I've missed you sooooo much,' she said, pressing Liz's face into scratchy wool and a hard plastic button on her coat because the younger girl towered over her. Something inside the carrier bag was digging into Liz's side. 'When are you coming back? Please say you're coming back?'

Liz pulled away, laughing, surprised, really, that Loveday had noticed her absence at all. She was normally so busy juggling boyfriends and organising her social life that there didn't seem to be much room for anything else.

'I don't know,' Liz replied truthfully. 'It all depends on Rosie. What's happening then? What's the new waitress like?'

Loveday pulled a face. 'She's a cow, I hate her. She calls me Lovebite behind my back and refuses to serve any meat dishes because she says she's vegetarian. And she's always late so I have to lay the tables. I've told Uncle Robert he should sack her for being lazy, but he says she's still new and we should give her a chance.'

'She sounds like a nightmare,' Liz said sympathetically.

'She is. And she likes Celine Dion songs. Can you imagine? Who the hell under forty likes Celine Dion? And she flirts with everyone and she's always checking herself in the mirror and thinks she's really pretty but she's not.' Loveday shuddered. 'She looks like a ferret with these horrible weasel eyes.'

'Oh dear.' Liz didn't like to think of the behind-the-scenes atmosphere; she'd bet there were fireworks.

'How are the boys?' she asked, changing the subject.

Loveday shrugged. 'Same as ever. Jesse's always going on about some stupid girl or other and Alex and Josh just moan.'

'And Robert?'

Loveday sighed. 'Even more of an old misery than usual.'

'Why's that then?'

'No idea. You know him. You'd think the world was coming to an end, the way he behaves.'

Liz felt sorry for him. No one saw beyond the strange, awkward exterior and recognised how kind he was and how lucky they were to have him as their boss, least of all his niece.

'He's not that bad,' she said gently. 'I can think of far worse people to work for. He's just shy, that's all. You should try being nicer to him.'

Loveday pouted. 'There's no FUN any more, everyone's so serious.' She tugged on Liz's coat sleeve. 'You've got to come back, you really have.'

Liz explained that Rosie was getting better by the day but that it was a long slow process.

'They think she'll be able to go back to school in a couple of weeks but only for an hour or two at first. She mustn't get tired. It was major surgery and she's still weak. I can't even think of work until she's one hundred per cent, d'you see?'

Loveday nodded dumbly. 'I s'pose so.'

There was a pause while Liz tried to think of something to cheer the girl up.

'So how's the love life?' she asked at last.

Loveday brightened immediately. 'I'm going out with Ryan now, he's gorgeous.' Her kohl-rimmed eyes went dreamy and faraway. 'He's really fit. He and Nathan are sworn enemies because of me. Can you imagine that?' She looked thrilled. 'We were at this party and Ryan didn't like the way Nathan was looking at my chest, so he had a right go at him and there would've been a fight if Spike hadn't of separated them.'

'But I thought Nathan was going out with Annie-the-fitness-trainer?' Liz said, puzzled.

Loveday grinned. 'He is, but he prefers me.'

'Poor Annie, does she know?'

'Everyone does,' Loveday scoffed, 'but Annie doesn't care because she knows I love Ryan now.' She sighed longingly. 'He's got this tattoo of a shark on his—'

'Anyway, where are you off to in such a hurry?' Liz interrupted, thinking that it was high time to relieve Barbara; she'd be wondering where she was.

'To see you, silly!' Loveday thrust the giant carrier bag at her. 'I almost forgot. Uncle Robert asked me to give this to you. I think it's a present for Rosie.'

'Oh!' Liz was touched. 'He shouldn't have.'

He still texted her periodically asking for updates and she always replied, keeping strictly to the facts.

'I think he misses you too,' Loveday observed. 'Whenever I mention you he looks sad.'

Liz frowned. 'I doubt it.' She remembered their evening together and shivered. Somehow, in the weeks that had passed, Rosie's stroke and that kiss had become so intertwined in her mind that the former couldn't exist without the latter.

233

She knew that Robert – and her own silly infatuation – were hardly responsible for the tumour, but couldn't erase the feeling that because of them, mentally she'd been a million miles away from Rosie just when she needed her most. Never again.

'Send him my regards anyway, won't you? I'll get Rosie to write a thank you.'

She found Barbara and her daughter sitting on her bed, looking through old comics with pictures of teen heart-throbs and cute fluffy animals. Rosie wasn't overly pleased to see her mother, which she took as a good sign.

'We've had a lovely afternoon,' said Barbara, rising. 'She never stops talking, does she?'

Liz smiled.

'There's plenty of cupcakes left over if you fancy one? I put them under a bowl on the kitchen table. Rosie only wanted the ones with pink and yellow icing so it's just chocolate and blue, I'm afraid.'

'I'll have one later,' Liz replied. 'Yum!'

Rosie was impatient to open the present which Liz produced from the carrier bag, wrapped in gold wrapping paper and with a tag attached saying: 'For you to have some fun with while you're recuperating. Don't make a mess for your mum! Love from "That Man" (Robert). PS The box you decorated for me is still proving very useful.'

Inside was a bamboo chest containing an array of watercolours, acrylics, chalk pastels, felt, glitter and fluorescent pens and brushes, plus coloured paper, wobbly eyes, white face masks, paper straws, lolly sticks, pom-poms, foam sheets and other materials for making collages. Rosie couldn't believe it.

'It's huge!' she said, holding up each pot and pen in turn so that she could see them properly before replacing them carefully in their original position. 'I've never seen such a big art set.'

She hadn't sounded as passionate about anything for a long time.

'Very nice of him,' Barbara commented. 'Funny sort of chap, difficult to read, but his heart's in the right place. He must be quite taken with you, Rosie.'

But she was too busy straining to read the leaflet with ideas for collage designs to pay attention.

On her way out, Barbara asked how Liz's afternoon had gone with her friend.

'I didn't see her,' Liz replied, sorry to be reminded. 'It's very sad, they've had to close their business. Her husband was there – and their son. The weird thing is, one of the removal men seemed to think they were moving to a big rented house near Looe before buying somewhere, but Jim didn't mention anything about it. He just said they'd come into a bit of money in the nick of time. He didn't make it sound like much.'

Barbara raised her eyebrows. 'People can be odd about things like that.'

She put on her coat which was hanging on a peg in the hall.

'I remember my Gareth, bless his soul, wouldn't even tell me at first how much his mum had left him in her will. I had to prise it out of him – and we were married thirty years!'

Liz frowned. 'It's not as if I'd tell anyone and besides, I'm pleased for them. It's got them out of a real fix. Iris was in such a state.'

'Ah well,' said Barbara, opening the door to let herself out, 'I wouldn't worry about it. She'll probably explain everything when she's good and ready and clear the air.

'Hopefully they'll have a great big housewarming in the new place with dancing and oodles of champers and invite you and Rosie along for the party. You can tell us all about it afterwards.'

Chapter Seventeen

PAT HAD A nasty dose of bronchitis and was stuck indoors. Liz didn't want to expose Rosie to infection, so although they'd been out together for short walks to the park and along the coast, she decided not to take her daughter shopping for the items that the old woman needed.

'I'll only be gone an hour,' she told Esme, who'd offered to hold the fort. Liz had become unexpectedly fond of her neighbour since Rosie's illness. 'I'll just pop to the supermarket and stay for a quick cup of tea,' she added, zipping up her anorak. 'Pat's a bit fed up on her own. Call me if there's a problem.'

'There won't be,' said Rosie, without looking up. She was sitting at the kitchen table which was covered with coloured paper, paint pots and glue, making a thank you card for Robert. It was a complicated affair, folded several times into a concertina shape with a different picture surrounded by an intricate border on each side, and she'd spent hours on it already. For once Esme, opposite, was quiet, obediently handing the artist her materials.

'Send her lots of love from me,' Rosie added.

Liz noticed with pleasure that her daughter's hair, though still closely cropped, was growing fast. It must have been getting on for an inch long now, the same dark blonde colour and thick, silky texture as before. She liked running her hands

236

through it when Rosie would let her, being careful not to touch the deep scar that was still tender, though healing nicely.

Rosie was embarrassed and only close friends were allowed to see her bareheaded, those she really trusted. She'd taken to wearing a scarf when she went out and Liz, who had abandoned colourful accessories while her daughter was ill, did the same to keep her company. They'd experiment with different styles to try to keep things interesting.

Rosie had more energy now and had put on weight, so that Liz was just beginning to allow herself to feel more optimistic than she'd been for a long time. Other than the fact that her vision had deteriorated, Rosie didn't seem to have suffered any after-effects from the operation and all being well, at the six-week check-up on Monday they'd say that she could return to school for a few hours.

Chemotherapy and radiotherapy had been discussed, but the view was that it was best to keep an eye first, with scans every three months. There was reason to hope that the small sliver of tumour that they hadn't been able to remove would stay dormant and cause no further problems, which was the best possible outcome, of course.

Pat was unusually grumpy, complaining about everything from her doctor to Nathan's habit of putting mail for next door in her own letter box.

'He doesn't read the envelope properly,' she said, adjusting the small, multicoloured crocheted blanket that Liz had made her and that was wrapped around her shoulders. 'I've told him about it time and again but he doesn't listen. I've a mind to write to the Post Office.'

'I'll have a word when I see him,' said Liz soothingly. She noticed that Pat's fridge was almost empty and felt bad for not having shopped yesterday. 'I heard his mum's been in hospital so he's probably got his mind on other things.'

They sat in Pat's small front room, a replica of Liz's, only filled with treasures that the old woman had bought or been given down the years: porcelain figurines of Victorian and Regency ladies in fancy hats and crinolines; an extensive collection of wooden and china owls of varying sizes which Liz and Rosie added to periodically, when they spotted something they knew she'd like at a fête or Christmas bazaar; various glass vases and ornaments; a grainy, black and white photo of Pat and her husband on their wedding day.

The room was boiling hot and Liz had to take off her sweater and push up the sleeves of her black cotton top. Pat started coughing, a painful, hollow sound.

'Don't know if I'll be able to live here on my own much longer,' she said gloomily. 'Stairs are a bother and if I can't get out—'

'Of course you will,' said Liz. 'Your cough will clear up with the antibiotics and you'll be right as rain again. And there's all sorts of ways you can adapt your house to make it easier if you need to. I can look into stair lifts, if you like?'

Pat muttered about 'the beginning of the end' and Liz went to fetch a plate of biscuits.

'Here, I've got some gossip,' Pat said when she returned, leaning forwards to reach for a chocolate digestive.

'Yes?'

She explained that her friend Elaine, who lived in Saltash, had heard via another friend that a couple in Plymouth had won the lottery.

'Two and a half million,' she said excitedly. 'Newsagents. It only happened a few weeks ago and they've closed down the business already. Couldn't wait to pack it in. Moving to some mansion on the coast. Seems they don't want publicity, which is why it hasn't been in the papers. It was their son who told Elaine's friend's grandson at college and word got round. I don't reckon I'd be able to keep it to myself, a win like that, do you?'

Liz was silent for a moment as the key slid smoothly into the lock. It all seemed to fit together perfectly: newsagents, mansion on the coast, college, Iris's silence and Jim's reticence. His admission that they'd 'come into some money'. But maybe it was just a coincidence. Surely he'd have told her, Liz, something, at least?

'Newsagents?' she said at last. Pat was twitching with impatience, waiting for a response.

'Yes,' she said eagerly, her aches and pains temporarily forgotten. 'From London way originally. Decent family, I hear, though the son's a bit of a tearaway. High spirits, you know, nothing really bad. Fancy winning that amount of money all in one go, though. You couldn't imagine it, could you? Like a dream come true.'

Liz thought of all the lottery tickets that she'd bought down the years and how she and Rosie, Rosie especially, had waited eagerly each Saturday evening for the draw. 'Better luck next time,' had been their mantra. Well, she was glad for her friends; it couldn't have happened to nicer folk. She just needed to sort things out with Iris, to explain that their friendship was more important than any amount of cash she might have won.

They changed the subject and Pat said that she missed her evenings with Rosie in front of the TV; she'd always looked forward to them. Liz felt almost guilty explaining that she didn't know if there'd even be a job for her at either Krystal Klear or A Winkle In Time now.

'Kasia and Robert both said I could go back whenever I'm ready but I don't know. It's been nearly six weeks.'

239

'Course they'll want you,' said Pat reassuringly. 'Who wouldn't? You cheer us all up.'

She gave Liz an update on her brother and his family, as well as each of her friends in turn.

'You've so many friends,' said Liz. She knew them all by name: Margaret, Bea, Winnie, Mo and the rest.

'Most of them dead now, of course,' Pat said, sliding back into moroseness. 'It'll be me next.'

'Nonsense, you've got years more,' Liz replied brightly. 'Anyway, you can't pop your clogs yet because Rosie and I need you.'

She rose to put the kettle on again and Pat's face fell when she said that she had to leave. 'Won't you stay for another cup of tea?'

Liz shook her head. It had been over an hour already.

'I'll come again soon,' she promised, when she returned from the kitchen with a refill for Pat and kissed her lightly on the cheek. 'You haven't been coughing as much – I think it's on its way out at last but you need to take care for a few more days.'

'It's worse at night,' Pat grumbled, summoning a token cough to demonstrate. 'I told that doctor I needed stronger antibiotics but she wasn't having any of it, wretched woman. I reckon she thinks we old things aren't worth bothering with. She'd probably like us all to put our heads in the oven and have done with it.'

While her daughter was watching a film, Liz took the phone into her bedroom and shut the door. She wasn't looking forward to the conversation and needed to prepare herself mentally. She had such peculiar, mixed feelings about Iris; she didn't know what to think. On the one hand, she was shocked by her friend's secrecy and, frankly, cold-heartedness for not having been in touch to ask about Rosie. Now that Liz knew – or strongly suspected – that some amazing good fortune had befallen the family, Iris's lack of communication seemed infinitely less excusable. In fact, Liz wouldn't have believed her capable of it. On the other hand, she wanted to give her the benefit of the doubt and find out what she had to say.

She took a few deep breaths before scrolling down for Iris's number. Eight long rings before a slight pause and the phone switched to voicemail. Liz's skin prickled slightly when she heard the older woman speak in her gravelly London accent: 'Sorry I'm not here to take your call...'

She hung up without leaving a message.

She tried again at about six. Again no reply, but Iris would surely see her number flash up and ring back. Liz remembered that she was never far from her smartphone; it was always somewhere within reach on the counter and she'd been addicted to online word games. Now that she wasn't working, you'd think that she might have more time to indulge her passion.

After supper she tried and failed to persuade Rosie to do some maths problems that her teacher had suggested she work on at home.

'I hate maths,' Rosie announced crossly, throwing the textbook across the floor. 'It's so boring.'

Liz decided that the sums could wait so they played cards instead and read their books side by side on her bed. She'd been to the library a few days before and stocked up on some with big letters for the visually impaired for her daughter. She was a good reader but the subject matter was a bit grown up for her which was a distinct advantage, as far as she was concerned. Liz thought that a few adult books wouldn't do her any harm until she could lay her hands on something more suitable.

After Rosie had gone to bed, Liz decided to have a bath and turn in herself. She was weary and besides, the prospect of yet another evening in front of the TV on her own seemed unappealing.

Since giving up the restaurant, early nights had become her new routine. She wasn't bored – there wasn't time, what with running around after the patient and trips to the doctor or hospital for blood tests, heart tests, eye examinations and so on – but there was a certain greyness to her days and nights, a uniformity that hadn't been there before that she found draining in quite a different way from cleaning and waitressing.

It seemed, if she stopped to think about it, that her life lacked colour, apart from the one bright flame that kept her going and that was her sole reason for being – Rosie.

After her bath, she checked her phone one more time to see if Iris had responded. Nothing. Perhaps she was abroad, Liz thought. Wasn't that what you'd do if you'd just won millions of pounds – go on a luxury holiday? The Maldives or something, wherever they were.

She remembered how Iris had pressed her, before Rosie's operation, to keep her updated on everything: 'Poor little mite. Tell her Spencer's been asking after her. He keeps saying: "WoWo, WoWo". That's what he calls her, "WoWo." He'll be so happy to see her again – we all will.'

Without stopping to ask herself if it was the right thing to do, she called Iris's number yet again. One, two, three rings, then an almost imperceptible pause, like a rapid inhalation.

She felt her stomach roll, as if she were on the point of launching off a diving board. Any moment now she'd hit the water...

'Hello, Liz.' Her voice sounded oddly flat. 'Look, I can't talk now. I'm that busy—'

'Why haven't you rung me?'

It was bald and to the point, but it was what she needed to know.

Iris was on the back foot, stumbling slightly. 'Like I said, I've had that much to do.'

Liz's hands felt clammy and her heart was pumping. She hated confrontation of any sort.

'Rosie had to have a life-saving operation and you had too much to do? What's going on, Iris?'

The other woman waited a moment before speaking.

'How is she?' she asked at last but her words seemed laced with formality, not genuine concern. 'Jim said she's on the mend.'

Liz couldn't bring herself to reply.

'I'm happy for you about the lottery,' she began, hoping that would clear the air.

Was there a sharp intake of breath? Perhaps she was imagining it.

'I don't know why it should come between us, if that's what the problem is. I mean, it's great for you and everything and I'm so glad, but it's only money.'

A nasty sound came from the back of Iris's throat, like a sneer, that made Liz shiver.

'That's what they all say.'

'What do you mean?' said Liz, shocked.

'Everyone's coming out of the woodwork now – long-lost relatives, "friends" we hadn't heard a squeak from for years,' Iris went on. 'Soon as they get wind of the cash they're on to us like a pack of vultures. It's disgusting.'

She spat out the final sentence like a piece of meaty gristle.

Liz's head reeled and she wondered for a moment if she'd got hold of the wrong Iris. Not kind, lovely, big-hearted Iris from Good Morning News, but some cold, hard person who'd stolen her identity and been transposed in her place.

'I don't want your money,' she said quietly. 'I can't believe you'd think that of me.'

Iris sniffed. 'Yeah, well, it's been difficult these past weeks.'

Was she asking Liz for sympathy? It sounded like it.

'What with all the excitement and shock,' she went on, 'I don't know if I'm on my head or my heels, to be quite honest with you.'

Liz thought of Rosie, asleep now, her precious little wounded fair head resting on the pillow, the deep red scar that ran from one side to another.

'I've been worried sick,' she said truthfully. 'I thought Rosie was going to die.'

Maybe Iris had failed to grasp the gravity of the situation. Liz tried to disguise the catch in her voice by clearing her throat.

'Well, she's better now?' the other woman asked, as if Liz were complaining of a graze that had ceased to sting. A tiresome, whining child.

'No,' she started to say, wanting to put Iris right, wanting to say, 'She had a huge lump in her brain and they couldn't remove all of it because it might make her blind or paralysed or impair her growth', until she remembered that the other woman didn't really care. She wasn't Iris any more, she was someone else.

There was an awkward silence while Liz waited with rising dismay for what she guessed would be coming next.

'I really can't stop,' said Iris. 'Like I said, I've got that much—'

'To do. I know, you're busy,' Liz interrupted, feeling like the nuisance caller trying to flog personal accident insurance or persuade you to take part in a phone survey.

'I'll get in touch when things have quietened down a bit,' Iris continued.

'OK,' Liz replied, still thinking that her friend might soften and melt. Just a few little words, something, anything, by way of apology or genuine explanation. It wouldn't take much; Liz wasn't over-demanding and she needed Iris; she needed all her inner circle, the people she could trust and rely on. She hadn't realised quite how much until now.

'Bye then, love.'

Even the 'love' had a hollow ring; it was convention, not a term of endearment. Liz had once found it sweet and charming.

She remained on her bed for quite some time with her knees pulled up, head in her hands, feeling as if she'd entered a cave so dense and black that no light at all could penetrate.

'Soon as they get wind of the cash they're on to us like a pack of vultures,' she'd said. The mere suggestion that Liz was one of them made her want to throw up.

Far worse, though, than being suspected of greed, was Iris's dismissive and uncaring attitude towards Rosie. Liz was so hurt on her daughter's behalf that she thought even speaking about the older woman or any of her family now in Rosie's presence would somehow contaminate her.

Rosie had mentioned several times that she'd like to see them soon, especially Spencer and Darren – 'He's so funny, Mummy, he makes me laugh so much.'

Liz swallowed, thinking that she'd have to come up with a cast-iron excuse as to why that wouldn't be happening. She couldn't bear Rosie to be upset for a second; she'd suffered more than enough already.

The trouble was, Liz couldn't talk to anyone about this because none of her other friends knew Iris and besides, she wouldn't want to spread poison, no matter how sad and aggrieved she felt.

At last she got up and threw her coat over her pyjamas,

tiptoeing past Rosie's bedroom into the backyard where she lit a cigarette and took a few puffs before stubbing it out. Tony's house was in darkness. He and Felipe were still an item, she'd seen them at the weekend, strolling past her bedroom window, but they were probably in London now.

Liz had hoped that some fresh air and a change of scenery would help her forget about Iris, but it didn't work. The older woman's face, her voice, kept worming their way back into her consciousness and there was a gnawing anxiety in her stomach that she couldn't explain.

It occurred to her that in all her confusion, she'd failed to ask Iris about the uncollected lottery ticket. Liz kicked herself, wishing that she could wind back the clock and find out what had happened to it.

She was being silly, she knew. Iris would have checked the ticket for her then thrown it away. Or it would have sat on the shop shelf behind her for weeks before being chucked out with the rest of the rubbish in the big clear-out.

But everyone knew that you should never give your ticket to anyone, however trusted. It was common sense. Liz shivered, suddenly cold. She should have been more careful.

She hadn't bought another ticket for weeks, she thought, putting the virtually unsmoked cigarette stub in the bin and heading back to the warmth indoors. Locking the door behind her, she resolved now that she never would again, not after she'd witnessed at first-hand what winning could do to you.

Like Frodo with the Ring of Sauron, the money seemed to have changed and corrupted Iris in ways that she never would have imagined and Liz wanted none of it. Quite frankly, if getting rich quick did that to you, she'd rather stay poor.

Chapter Eighteen

THE FOLLOWING MORNING was windy but mild and dry. Liz poked her head out of the back door while Rosie was still asleep and decided that they'd go for a short walk down to the harbour. She wanted some fresh air herself; she was still very upset about Iris and hoped that a bit of exercise and a change of scenery would take her mind off their conversation and the strange nagging in her stomach that wouldn't go.

'Have you finished your thank you card for Robert?' she asked her daughter over breakfast. 'We should drop it in today.'

Rosie went into her bedroom to fetch it and gave it to her mother who was sitting opposite, sipping a mug of tea. Liz took the work of art in her hands carefully, not wishing to crumple or make a mark. It was about the size of a normal greeting card but thicker, because of the extra pages.

On the front she could see three smiling people painted in delicate watercolours: a tall thin man in blue trousers with tousled brown hair, a much smaller woman with shoulder-length dark hair decorated with a big pink flower, and in between, a child with very long fair hair that reached all the way to her knees. The lines weren't as carefully drawn as they might once have been because of Rosie's poor eyesight, but it didn't matter, you could still make out who they were.

'That's me,' she said, leaning across the table and pointing to the girl in the middle, tracing a forefinger down the blonde tresses. 'I wish I still had long hair,' she added in small voice.

Liz glanced at her daughter's poor, shorn head that had been brutalised by the surgeon's knife, and touched her hand.

'It'll grow back soon,' she promised, wishing that she had a wand to magic a Rapunzel-like mane. 'And when it does I'll buy you some new hair accessories. We'll go into Plymouth together, shall we?'

Rosie, brightening a little, gave a small smile.

Liz hadn't looked properly at the card that she was still holding but she did so now. The three figures, standing very close together, had their feet on brownish yellow pebbles and above them was watery blue sky. Behind them you could make out a row of sketchy, uneven-shaped houses in white, baby blue and pink, and in the foreground was the greeny-blue sea and a red fishing boat. It was quite clearly their harbour.

'It's beautiful!' Liz said, opening the card up like a concertina and admiring the inner pages one by one. On each side, Rosie had created a different scene from the village: the restaurant, with white lettering against a blue background painted across the front; The Lobster Pot decked with hanging baskets; the general stores with unidentifiable people standing outside chatting; the bakery and the small beach.

She'd used fabric and pipe cleaners in places, from the special box that Robert had given her, as well as blobs of cotton wool and lolly sticks: material flowers in Barbara's pots, curled brown pipe-cleaners in the bakery window to signify loaves of bread, lolly sticks for the pavement.

On the very back page, in big, messy gold letters, she'd written 'Thank you Robert for my art box! I love it!' and signed it 'Rosanna Broome. (Rosie)'

'You should think about going to art school when you're older,' Liz marvelled. 'You're so talented. You don't get it from me, that's for sure.'

Rosie smiled, lapping up the praise. 'Do you really like it?'

Liz turned back to the front page and looked in more detail this time. Rosie had managed to capture Robert's reed-like body and diffident stance. Her own left leg was slightly thinner than the other and the foot turned in, Liz noticed, though not enough that anyone else would spot it, probably. She'd even given them the right colour eyes: hazel for him, dark brown for Liz and greeny grey for herself.

Now, Liz's gaze dropped to the middle of the picture and she started.

'They're holding hands!'

It wasn't immediately clear because their arms were by their sides, but when you looked closely you could see that the hands were touching, Robert's with Rosie's and Rosie's with her mother's.

'You don't mind, do you?' Rosie sounded shy and anxious, afraid that she'd done the wrong thing.

Liz hesitated, torn between telling her daughter to alter the picture somehow and not wishing to upset.

'It's fine,' she said quickly, convincing herself that Robert wouldn't even see. After all, it wasn't obvious, only if you really looked for it.

Rosie's shoulders relaxed. 'Do we have a big enough envelope to put it in?'

They wrapped up warmly and walked slowly up the hill. Rosie seemed frailer away from the comfort and security of her own four walls and her limp was more pronounced. Liz decided that it was most likely because her muscles would have weakened in the past weeks through lack of exercise. In any case, she could ask the consultant about it after the follow-up scan on Monday.

Esme was coming in the opposite direction and stopped to talk. Her navy fisherman's smock was smeared with dried clay and there was a blob on her cheek and more in the wisps of greying hair that fell around her face.

'What a lovely hat!' she said, admiring the peacock-blue beret with a sparkling diamanté brooch on the front that Rosie had pulled down low over her forehead and ears to hide her tufty head. 'You look like Queen Scheherazade!'

A frown, like a pencil mark, appeared between Rosie's eyebrows. 'Who's she?'

'My dear!' Esme exclaimed. 'You don't know? She was the beautiful Persian queen and storyteller of One Thousand and One Nights. I've got a glorious book at home, I can read it to you if you like. I used to love it when I was a child and I often look at the Arabic pictures to get inspiration for my work.'

Charlotte Pennyfeather came by with two heavy-looking bags of shopping.

'Hi,' Liz said, as Charlotte drew to a halt, 'so sorry we can't stop, we're in a rush.' She didn't feel too bad as it was clear that that Charlotte and Esme were poised to continue the conversation without her.

'Why are we in a rush?' Rosie asked as they set off again, sounding a little out of breath.

'We're not,' Liz whispered once they were well out of earshot, 'but I was afraid we'd be there all day.'

In truth, Liz was keen to be quick as she wanted to drop off the card before Robert arrived to open up the restaurant. She knew that she'd have to see him again sometime, but she was feeling so sensitive about Iris that she didn't think she could cope with an awkward encounter today. It was important for Rosie to thank him properly for his kind gift, though.

As they reached the top of the hill and turned left into South Street, she realised that she had guilt pangs about him. She'd spent so much time feeling remorseful about her own silly, flirtatious behaviour that she hadn't given his emotions much thought. But now she supposed that he might have been a little hurt by her coolness and the fact that she didn't want a visit from him.

Thankfully all the lights were off at A Winkle In Time and the door was firmly closed. The big brass letter box was low down, almost on ground level.

'You have to push really hard,' Liz explained, crouching beside her daughter and holding back the heavy flap with two thumbs. 'Careful not to trap your fingers.'

They heard the card, in a big brown envelope, slap onto the mat before continuing their journey down South Street towards Tremarnock beach. They were walking slowly now but even so, Rosie was dragging.

'Would you like to go home?' Liz asked anxiously, not wanting to tire her, but Rosie shook her head.

'It's nice to be out. Look!' She was pointing at Jenny Lambert with her Jack Russell. 'Is that Sally?'

Of course they had to stroke the dog, then they saw Rick Kane through the window of Treasure Trove. He came out to say hello and popped something in the pocket of Rosie's coat.

'A sweet bite for later. Don't tell your mum,' he winked and Rosie grinned back.

Ruby Dodd must have seen them too because she bustled out of her cottage and threw her arms round the little girl.

'Good to see you up and about!' she said, cupping her face in both hands.

Before they knew it, they'd been joined by Barbara, too, on her way back from the bakery with two white paper bags.

'We've been waiting for this, haven't we Ruby?' she said and the other woman nodded.

Liz thought that Rosie must be feeling like royalty.

By the time they reached the harbour wall, she was quite exhausted.

'My cheeks hurt from all the smiling,' she complained, settling on a bench, and Liz laughed, pleased to see that some colour had returned to her daughter's pale features.

The sea was murky grey and they enjoyed watching the waves slapping against the rocks sheltering the bay and flying up into spiky white pinnacles before subsiding. Listening to the swish and rattle of water dragging the pebbles as it withdrew was strangely hypnotic.

'I hope we don't have a storm like last year,' Liz commented, remembering how the lower roads and houses had been flooded, the bench that they were now sitting on torn from its metal brackets and hurled into the side of a building. It was lucky that no one had been hurt.

'Liz! Rosie!'

They turned to see the tall figure of Robert striding round the corner towards them. He was wearing a thick blue and white flecked sweater and the wind was making his hair fly in all directions.

'Thank you for the card!' he said, coming alongside, panting slightly, and looking straight at Rosie. 'I'll put it on my mantelpiece.'

Rosie got up and smiled shyly. 'I hope you like it, it's scenes from Tremarnock.'

'I can see that,' said Robert gently. 'The restaurant, the pub, the three of us on the beach...'

He glanced at Liz before looking away quickly. 'It's very lifelike.'

She felt her face heat up as he cleared his throat loudly and she was relieved when his gaze fell to his big brown lace-up shoes.

'It was very generous of you—' she started to say, meaning to thank him herself for the art box, but he interrupted her.

'How are you feeling?' he said, still looking at his feet.

Rosie, not quite sure whom he was addressing, eyed her mother who nodded.

'Much better, thank you,' the little girl replied. Her good hand shot up and she touched the top of her peacock-blue beret anxiously to check that it was still in place. 'My hair's started to grow back.'

'Good,' said Robert. 'Your hat's very pretty.'

Rosie, pleased, told him that she might be able to return to school next week after her scan. Her face fell as the reality sank in. 'I don't really want to though.'

Robert ran a hand through his windswept hair. 'It'll be nice to see your friends again though, won't it?'

She looked unsure.

'Oh come on,' Liz coaxed. 'It's only Kyle who's a problem and he won't be any trouble – I'll make sure Mrs Meakin watches him – and it'll be fun to see Mandy and Rachel and the other girls, won't it?'

Her daughter grudgingly agreed.

Liz was about to ask after Loveday and the rest – she felt that she owed it to Robert to show an interest even though really she wanted to be gone. Her previous life at the restaurant was so long ago now, it seemed as if it had nothing to do with her anymore.

'Liz?'

She turned her head and could see that Robert was struggling for words, rubbing his hands nervously down the sides of his trousers. She swallowed, wondering what was coming next.

'You know you're still welcome to come back to work whenever you want,' he mumbled.

She was aware that Rosie was listening intently, quiet as a mouse.

'Thank you but I can't,' she began. 'When Rosie goes back to school it'll only be for an hour or two each day and I'll have to pick her up if she's tired.'

Rosie interrupted with a small cry. 'Yes you can!' Liz looked at her, surprised.

'You can do evenings,' the little girl went on. 'I'm quite well enough to be left with Pat and she likes coming to the flat, you know she does. She says she misses seeing me.'

Liz frowned, racking her brains to think of an excuse. It was true about Pat but now that she, Liz, had crossed the Rubicon, she was virtually resigned to caring for Rosie full-time and living on benefits for ever.

'Anyway, it's boring for you being at home on your own when I'm asleep,' Rosie continued reasonably. 'It'll do you good to get out.'

Liz hesitated, stumped for words.

Robert looked up and drew his shoulders back.

'You could start a little later if you want, at seven, say? That way you'll have more time with Rosie before you leave.'

Liz shifted from one foot to another. It was tempting, certainly. She'd like to start earning again and it would be good to mix with adults. She hadn't realised until now quite how isolated she'd been feeling.

'Well—' she began to say.

Rosie clapped her hands. 'That's settled, then!' she said, flashing her funny, gappy smile. She looked up at Robert, who was staring out to sea. She had to crane her neck because he was so tall. 'Mum will call you after my scan to let you know when she's coming back, all right?'

He nodded obediently.

'OK, Mum?' Rosie asked, prodding her with a finger.

Liz was so taken aback at the turn of events that all she could manage was a mumbled 'Yes.'

After he'd left, Rosie practically skipped past the Pennyfeather's house and up Fore Street. She seemed to have acquired a second wind.

As they rounded the corner, they spotted Valerie Barrows, struggling to get an enormous suitcase into the boot of her car. They stopped to help and Valerie informed them that she was off on an extended holiday and Bag End would be empty.

'I can't wait to get some sun,' she said, straightening up once the job was done and slamming the boot shut. 'It's so *bleak* here.'

She went back in the house and Rosie nudged her mother. 'She never says anything nice about Tremarnock, does she?'

'I don't think she's terribly happy here,' Liz replied then she frowned, remembering the conversation with Robert.

'Won't you mind if I go back to work?' she asked, puzzled. 'I thought you preferred it when I'm home in the evenings?'

'No,' said Rosie brightly. 'I think you should have some stimulation.' She paused, pleased with her choice of vocabulary. 'Anyway,' she went on, 'I like it with Pat – and besides, Robert needs you.'

Chapter Nineteen

MONDAY ARRIVED AND Liz felt sick as she drove Rosie back
to the hospital. She'd been playing it down, of course, but her
daughter wasn't stupid.

'What if the tumour's grown?' she asked in a small voice
as they headed over the Tamar Bridge en route for Bristol. It
was 6 a.m. and it had been a struggle to wake her. Neither of
them was used to early mornings any more.

'It won't have,' Liz said, sounding far more confident than
she felt. 'But just supposing it had, they'd know what to do.
Doctors are so clever and there are all sorts of treatments.'

There was virtually no delay once they arrived and Liz felt
almost nostalgic for the times when they'd queued for hours
at Accident and Emergency for some minor injury that might
or might not require stitches; Rosie's brain tumour had cata-
pulted them into a different realm entirely, one where doctors
and nurses spoke in deferential tones and whisked you past
the rows of fed-up patients in corridors and waiting rooms
into the very heart of the hospital.

Once they'd checked Rosie over carefully and done the scan,
however, she and Liz did have to hang around for over an hour
to get the results. Liz's stomach was doing somersaults and she
had difficulty disguising her anxiety from her daughter.

'When can we go?' Rosie complained, kicking the leg of

her chair disconsolately until her mother had to tell her to stop. Perfect as she was in Liz's eyes, even she was capable of bad behaviour when cranky.

Please can it be all right, please don't let it be bad news.

'Not long now,' Liz replied, squeezing her daughter's hand before breathing in and out slowly in a bid to quieten her own thumping heart.

When at last she was called, the blood rushed to her head and she had to hold the nurse's arm to steady herself. The doctor smiled reassuringly as she sat down, but still she could scarcely process the words when the woman explained that the tumour was stable, it hadn't grown, and they could go away for the time being and start to rebuild their lives.

'We'll do a scan in three months and if it's fine, we don't need to see you again for six months,' she said, closing the brown file in her hands. 'The scar's healing nicely, her responses are good and I don't think there'll be any developmental delays. The surgeon did a great job.'

Liz heard a ringing in her ears and for a moment the world blurred over, until at last she was able to squeeze out a sigh of relief and manage a smile. 'Thank you so much.'

They stopped for a late lunch at the first service station they came to and sang for most of the remaining journey. Liz felt as if for the past six weeks she'd been trapped in a narrow underground cage and only now could she see the light, start to rustle her wings and learn once more to fly.

'Does that mean I'm cured?' Rosie asked in between songs. She'd caught her mother's mood and was gaiety itself.

Liz thought for a moment. Strictly speaking the answer was no because the tumour hadn't gone, but now that she'd finally received good news she wasn't prepared to let anything dampen her optimism.

'Very nearly,' she said, smiling at her daughter in the mirror and imagining that one day, perhaps, they'd be able to look back on this as a really bad dream.

It was after six by the time they arrived home and they were both happy but exhausted. Liz decided that it would be best to wait a couple of days before contacting the school to discuss Rosie's gradual return, but she seemed so bright the following morning that she rang the secretary and it was agreed that she would go in for a meeting with the head and class teacher on the Wednesday to discuss arrangements.

'Have you spoken to Robert yet?' Rosie asked when Liz told her that she'd be going back to classes for just an hour a day from Monday. 'If I'm well enough for school, you can definitely leave me with Nan in the evenings.'

Liz started. She'd been so preoccupied that she'd barely given him another thought all week and was inclined to think that it would be better to leave it till January to get in touch. But Rosie was having none of it.

'There are probably lots of customers at Christmas time and he'll want an extra pair of hands.' Was she ten – or forty-five? 'And think of all the tips! More presents for me!'

She grinned at Liz who was surprised, because her daughter didn't usually ask for much; she wasn't like other children, she knew they were hard up and was happy with a new jumper or some books as a gift. But it would be lovely to be able to treat her after all she'd been through.

'I'll ring him later,' she promised.

'Now,' Rosie ordered.

Liz sighed. 'All right. I'll send him a text.'

It was a business-like exchange and Liz found herself wondering, when she'd arranged to go in on Saturday evening, whether she'd remember what to do. On a busy night you had to move fast and keep your wits about you; she thought that she'd grown torpid since being home and mightn't be as efficient.

She needn't have worried, though, because Demi, the temporary waitress from Torpoint was still there, so with Loveday, too, that made three of them.

'When are you going, then?' Liz heard Loveday ask nastily when she was carrying in two plates of steaming food. 'We won't be needing you now Liz is back.'

Demi flicked her blonde hair and smiled, revealing big strong teeth.

'Robert has asked me to stay until after Christmas,' she said sweetly, 'then I'm going to move to London in the New Year. I've outgrown Tremarnock.'

Loveday scowled. 'Where would you live in London, though? It costs a fortune up there.'

Demi licked her lips; she wore pink gloss, she must have reapplied it ten times already. 'My aunty lives in East Sheen. Have you ever been to East Sheen? It's dead posh, lots of bars and restaurants and things.'

'It's not Chelsea or...' Loveday frowned, 'or Notting Hill, though, is it? If I was going to live in London I'd want to be in the trendy part.'

Demi opened her mouth to reply but Loveday had already sashayed over to one of her tables, swinging her ponytail as she went, leaving behind what Liz fancied to be a rather unpleasant smell.

Just as well those two wouldn't be working together for much longer, she thought, carefully lowering the plates in front of her customers. Still, she'd be grateful for the extra pair of hands while she reacclimatised to the job.

The Christmas decorations were up already in the restaurant, which looked very pretty and welcoming. White fairy lights were strung across the bar and around the wine bottles displayed behind, and there was a giant Christmas tree in the corner by the locked door leading to the flat above, which had been occupied for a few weeks, apparently, but was now empty again and probably would be until spring.

The tree was decorated with twinkling white lights, white, glass and red baubles and each wooden table had a fat red candle surrounded by a small garland of real holly and bits of spruce, which gave off a pine scent as the candles heated up. Mistletoe hung from the brass lampshades and there was an attractive display of fruit – oranges, lemons, walnuts and rosy red apples – in an exotic Chinese bowl at one end of the bar.

Liz hardly spoke to Robert. There seemed to be a problem in the kitchen with vegetables. Alex said Jesse hadn't cut the courgettes properly and had left stalks on the green beans and accused him of being 'cavalier'.

At one point she could hear raised voices and she noticed Robert stride into the kitchen to sort things out. When she went in to fetch some starters he was bending over the steel worktop, sleeves rolled up in a black and white checked apron, doing the beans himself. Alex, meanwhile, was glowering over the stove, Josh was lurking in the corner looking uncomfortable while Jesse had sloped into the backyard to cool off.

'There's a bit of an atmosphere going on in there,' she whispered to Loveday on her way out, which was the understatement of the year.

'It's been like that ever since SHE arrived,' she said, nodding at Demi who was sneaking into the Ladies to freshen her lip gloss again. 'She's a bad influence. The sooner she goes the better.'

'Why's she putting the boys in a bad mood?' Liz asked, puzzled.

Loveday pouted. 'For some reason,' she raised her eyes heavenward, 'they all fancy her, 'specially Alex and Jesse. I can't imagine why. The funny thing is, she's not interested in any of them and they just don't realise.' She'd turned rather red in the face. 'Stupid cow thinks she's too good for them.'

She glanced down at her very tight white blouse and did up a button, which was straining at her tummy and had popped undone. 'Just because she's thin and pretty…' she went on, sounding mournful. 'I don't know why they can't see through her, she's so *shallow*.'

'Well I don't think she's that good-looking,' Liz said soothingly. 'Too thin and horsey for my liking. You're much prettier.' Loveday brightened. 'Anyway, how's Ryan?'

'Dumped him last week,' said the younger girl. 'His eyebrows are like caterpillars – and he smells of fish.'

'That didn't put you off before,' Liz replied reasonably, remembering the girl's earlier enthusiasm.

Loveday shrugged. 'And he wears horrible shoes.'

Liz laughed, she couldn't help herself. 'Poor boy, what on earth's wrong with his shoes?'

'Cheap trainers,' Loveday replied, wrinkling her nose. 'Says he won't pay extra for designer cos it's a waste of money when they look the same anyway.' She shook her head. 'So wrong.'

'Hmm,' said Liz, glancing guiltily at her own discount footwear; Loveday wouldn't even have them in the house. 'Maybe the cheap ones are comfier?'

Loveday, noticing Liz's plastic pumps, smiled sympathetically. 'Well, your kind of shoes are all right. I don't s'pose I'll care what I wear either when I get *old*.'

By about ten o'clock, when some of the customers were still eating their main courses, Liz found that, discount shoes or not, her feet were killing her. She was out of practice, she realised, and it would probably take a week or two to get back up to speed. As she carried a pile of dishes into the kitchen she managed a quick chat with Jesse, who seemed to have recovered his composure and was rinsing plates and stacking them in the dishwasher. Josh, meanwhile, was stirring something sweet-smelling on the hob while Alex stood watching.

'How are things?' she asked Jesse quietly, placing the dishes on the draining board.

'Quite good actually,' he said, rising then lowering his eyes and nodding in Alex's direction. 'When he's not being an arsehole, that is.'

Liz ignored the last remark, concentrating instead on the 'good'. 'Anything interesting to report since I've been away?' she asked brightly.

Jesse wiped his brow with the back of an arm. 'Yeah, well, Robert's offered me the job of trainee chef. Things are going well and he says we're short-staffed. He's going to get someone in to do my job as soon as he can. Might not be till after Christmas now, though.'

Liz clapped her hands. 'That's fantastic news! Well done! So you're going to become a fully fledged chef. The next Jamie Oliver, maybe!'

Jesse, pleased, pulled back his shoulders and flicked his blond curls out of his eyes.

'Dunno about that, but it'll be good to get started on a real career. If I do OK, Robert says he'll help me get proper college qualifications, too. My mum's dead pleased.' He flashed a wide, white grin.

262

'I bet she is,' said Liz warmly. 'And you should be, too.'

She went back to the table to collect more dishes and when she returned, she asked nonchalantly, 'How's the love life, by the way?'

Jesse shook his curls. 'Nothing doing. I'm sick of one-night stands, getting too old for them. I'm looking for a meaningful relationship now.'

He sounded uncharacteristically mature. Liz, disguising her smile, glanced down at his feet and clocked the sleek black trainers with a white Nike tick on the side. 'Demi's off to London soon,' she said innocently, smoothing her apron. 'She's had enough of Tremarnock. And Loveday's split up with Ryan.'

She noticed Jesse's eyebrows rise, but vanished back into the restaurant before he had time to reply.

Later, while she and Loveday were stooping behind the bar fetching fresh glasses, she looked at the girl slyly.

'Jesse's going to train as a proper chef. Robert's promoting him.'

'Is he?' said Loveday haughtily. 'I wouldn't know.'

Liz cleared her throat. 'He's single at the moment, says he's had enough of one-night stands and wants a meaningful relationship.'

She stood up and one of the customers signalled to her for the bill.

'I don't believe it for a minute,' Loveday scoffed. 'He's such a tart.'

Liz nodded at the customer to say that she was coming. 'I think he means it, he's definitely more sensible now and thinking about his future.'

She picked up the bill in a black wallet that Robert had prepared earlier.

'He's awfully handsome,' she slipped in quickly. 'Best-looking boy in Tremarnock.'

'D'you think so?' Loveday said, as if it were a revelation.

'Oh yes,' said Liz over her shoulder as she made for the table. 'Good prospects – and nice Nike trainers, too.'

When the last customers left at nearly midnight, she was exhausted. How had she ever coped with cleaning in the mornings as well? She must have lost her stamina because she didn't think that she could do it now.

She fetched a wooden tray to carry the final plates and glasses into the kitchen and noticed that there was a large slice of leftover treacle tart in a baking tray on the counter.

'Is this going begging?' she asked Alex, who was hanging his white overall on a peg in the side room, ready to be cleaned.

'Take it,' he said, smoothing the dark hair off his face, which was grey and sweaty after a long night in the kitchen, 'before someone else does. It should be warm still. There's some custard in a jug in the fridge if you want to heat it up.'

Liz fetched a silver spoon and fork, napkin, and a china plate from the cupboard and popped the jug of custard in the microwave for a few minutes. Then she poured it over the tart and carried it to Robert, who was cashing up.

'I thought you might like this,' she said shyly, placing the plate beside him and being careful not to look at him.

'Mmm,' he said, eyeing the pudding hungrily and pausing from his work for a moment to take a bite. 'It's good.' He took another spoonful. 'Delicious.'

She hesitated for a moment, mustering courage.

'Robert?'

He put down the spoon, picked up a handful of pound coins and slid them into a see-through cash bag. 'Yes?'

'I – I wanted to say thank you.' She felt herself reddening and stared furiously at the next handful of coins as they slithered down to join the others.

He didn't reply but jotted something down on his cash sheet.

'For everything you've done for me and Rosie,' she went on, feeling like a stupid nuisance, but when was it ever the right time for a conversation like this?

He paused, but still said nothing.

'You've been so kind,' she ploughed on, 'and I feel like I must have seemed very ungrateful, not wanting you to visit and things. I wasn't, ungrateful I mean – not one bit – it's just that I was so worried—'

Robert crossed his arms tightly over his chest and made a nervous whistling sound; she didn't dare check his face.

'Don't,' he interrupted. 'You've been through hell. I quite understand.'

She swallowed. 'It's good to be back.' Her voice came out very small.

'It's good to have you back.'

To her surprise, he suddenly brushed past her, strode over to the heavy wooden sideboard near the entrance and pulled open a drawer. Peeping at him out of the corner of an eye, she saw him come back brandishing a teaspoon, which he thrust clumsily in her hand.

'D'you want to try some?' He nodded at the treacle tart which was still on the bar and nudged the plate towards her.

She hesitated for a moment, before severing a small piece with the edge of the spoon and popping it in her mouth.

The golden treacle spread over her tongue and trickled down the back of her throat. She closed her eyes for a second to savour the sticky sweetness, and when she opened them she saw that he, too, had taken a bite from the other side of the plate and was studying her while he chewed.

For a second she met his gaze, noticing again the amber flecks in his hazel irises, and instead of looking away, embarrassed, they both smiled.

'Yummy,' he said, the corners of his mouth twitching slightly.

'Yes,' she replied, 'completely yummy.'

'Want some more?' he whispered softly.

She would have taken him up on the offer, except that Jesse and Josh walked past, laughing. They stopped short when they saw Robert and Liz and she fancied Jesse's mouth dropped open before he gathered himself and closed it again quickly. But they weren't doing anything, were they? Only sharing a piece of treacle tart. There again, she supposed that they had been standing very close together...

Robert cleared his throat loudly. 'See you tomorrow, lads.'

'All right, guv, Liz,' Josh said with slight amusement in his voice, Liz thought hotly.

She made a point of moving away to fetch her coat before they left the building and followed after them with a quick 'Bye, Robert, see you on Tuesday.' She didn't want to cause him any awkwardness in front of his staff.

As she rounded the corner of her darkened street, she noticed a sleek red sports car just in front of her, going down the hill. You could hardly miss it; there were no other vehicles on the road at this time and no one she knew drove anything like as smart or expensive.

It slowed right down before stopping outside Bag End and the lights went off. She was intrigued and a little suspicious, too. Who on earth could be visiting at such an ungodly hour – and why?

Valerie Barrows was still away, Liz knew, but a few days ago she'd spotted Marcus, her son, strutting past Dove Cottage wearing a back-to-front baseball cap, bomber jacket, slouchy grey track pants and white trainers with the laces carefully undone at the top. He was carrying a smart, black leather suitcase and Liz guessed that he was here to stay for a while, worst luck.

She didn't know if it was what Valerie wanted but as Marcus had the key to Bag End, there wasn't a lot to be done. Besides, Valerie hadn't given Liz an address or phone number to contact her on.

She hung back and waited for the driver of the car to get out. She wouldn't have been able to tell who it was, except that there was a light on in the house's front bedroom upstairs, and she watched the car door swing open and a young man step out.

At first all she could see was his back view – tall and slim, in a dark jacket and jeans. But when he stood at the doorway and rapped softly, the bedroom light went off and another appeared in the hallway, illuminating the approach to the cottage.

The young man was wearing a baseball cap – the right way round. Liz took a step to the side so that she was hovering in a darkened doorway, and watched him pull the brim down, so that it partially obscured his face, and pull up the collar of his jacket. While he waited for the door to be opened he glanced this way and that, to check if anyone was watching, and now she could see quite clearly who it was: Darren.

She let out a small gasp, perceptible to no one but herself, then the door opened and Marcus appeared. The two men spoke quickly in lowered voices and Darren put a foot on the doorstep. She thought that he was about to go in and stepped out herself from the shadows. Before he did so, however, he looked once more to his left and this time spotted her. His eyes flashed in surprise and recognition but he made no acknowledgement.

Feeling like a child caught out in some misdemeanour, she put her head down and rootled in her bag for her key as if she'd been searching for them. By the time she looked up, he was gone.

Her heart was beating quite fast as she walked the last few steps to her cottage and she realised with some certainty that Darren – and Marcus, for that matter – were up to no good. She could only take a guess at what they might be doing, but she was quite sure that it was against the law. Why else would Darren be visiting at this time? As far as she knew, he and Marcus weren't friends. And what other explanation could there be for his furtiveness?

As she tiptoed inside, taking care not to wake Rosie, she thought sadly that in other circumstances she'd have found a way to tell Iris what she'd seen. That would be the kindest thing to do, so that Iris and Jim could be on the lookout and might perhaps be able to help their son before he did something foolish and got into real trouble.

In other circumstances... before their lottery win. A niggle of doubt sent shivers racing up and down her spine again. It was a Tuesday in October when Liz had bought her ticket – the one that she'd never collected. The Tuesday before Saturday's big draw. And it was straight after that draw that Iris had cut off contact.

Frightened by the path down which her thoughts were leading her, Liz tried to veer off in a different direction. The dates were just coincidence and she was being fanciful, leaping at dangerous, outlandish conclusions.

But despite her exhaustion, she found that she slept badly,

tossing and turning, her brain on overdrive, aching with fatigue yet unable to switch off. In the end she turned on the light and read till daybreak, finding that it was the only way to block out the darkness invading her unsettled mind.

Chapter Twenty

ROSIE'S RETURN TO school went better than Liz could have dared hope. Staff had prepared the other children well and they all knew why the little girl was wearing a headscarf, that she had to hold things up close to see them properly and what had happened to her, so there were no awkward questions.

In fact, when Liz came to pick her up after an hour, Rosie wanted to stay, so that by Wednesday she was already doing two hours and the following week, she was up to whole mornings.

She was exhausted when she got home and had to rest for a couple of hours, but Liz was delighted that she seemed a little stronger every day and was glad to be back with other children having lessons and feeling more normal.

On the second Friday in December, the Christmas lights went up around the village, making the streets and cottages, shops and harbour twinkle. Paid for through fundraising, the lights were owned by the villagers themselves and it was always a merry event that hundreds turned out for.

Liz was working at the restaurant, but Robert allowed the staff out to watch the grand switching on at 7 p.m. Most of the customers came, too, along with Pat and Rosie. There must have been a good five hundred people gathered in front of the brightly coloured Christmas tree in the small market square, made up predominantly of schoolchildren, pensioners and members of the nearby Methodist church choir, along with a brass band playing carols.

Meanwhile Robert, along with Barbara from The Lobster Pot, had donated free mulled wine and mince pies which were doing the rounds on wooden trays, served by some of Barbara's staff with tinsel in their hair, as well as local teenagers keen to sample any alcohol they could lay their hands on without being noticed.

Reg Carter, leader of the parish council, gave a brief speech and everyone oohed and aahed as the spectacular display, based on old Tremarnock stories of boats and fishermen, pasties and puddings, as well as Christmas themes, lit up against the night sky.

'Isn't it beautiful?' Rosie sighed, holding her mother's hand tight, her eyes sparkling as she gazed in wonder all around.

'It certainly is.'

Liz, recognising the deep voice, swivelled her head to find Robert standing close behind them. One of his hands came to rest lightly on her right shoulder, the other on Rosie's left.

She smiled and turned back to the lights, standing stock-still, not daring to move in case he became self-conscious and backed away. She closed her eyes for a second, feeling a warm glow spread through her. It felt so natural, so right, and she didn't want the moment ever to end.

At last the crowd started to move off, some heading for the pub, no doubt, others preparing to continue the party at home.

Robert's arms dropped and Liz felt a cold patch on her shoulder where his hand had been. She said goodbye to Rosie and Pat and headed reluctantly back to the restaurant, wondering if that sense of wholeness, of completeness that she'd experienced for those few delicious fleeting moments, had been merely an illusion.

But she fancied that Robert looked different, somehow, that evening. His cheeks were slightly flushed, his eyes bright, and although they scarcely spoke again, she was acutely aware of his physical presence. Whenever she brushed past him, the air between them seemed to fizz and crackle. She couldn't be imagining it.

She'd kept in touch with Hannah from the office by text, though they hadn't actually met since that day in the hospital when Hannah had so kindly driven Eeyore to Bristol for her and described her as 'vintage'. Now, Liz found that suddenly she had a few free hours each morning to herself, so she gave Hannah a ring.

'I'm coming to Plymouth tomorrow to do some shopping,' she said. 'Have you got time to meet for coffee?'

'You bet!' said Hannah cheerily. 'Make mine a double espresso. I might need a drop of whisky too. Hair of the dog. I'm out with some particularly thirsty clients tonight.'

They arranged to meet at Starbucks and, as Liz arrived first, she was able to get the drinks in and bag the last free table near the door. She watched all eyes turn as Hannah walked in, wearing a dramatic black, ankle-length, fluffy mohair coat and sky-high red heels.

'Darling!' she cried, flinging her arms around Liz, who staggered a few steps under the weight of the bear-like embrace before righting herself. 'It's so good to see you!'

Hannah, who said she'd had four hours' sleep, draped the coat over a chair and sat down. Underneath she was wearing her trademark crisp white blouse and she looked a million dollars as usual, fresh as a daisy.

'Got a bit out of hand last night,' she confessed, sighing. 'One of the chaps wanted to go on to a club in Union Street.

272

I was ready for bed but I could hardly bale out when I was the one who was supposed to be hosting and before I knew it, it was three a.m.'

'Blimey!' said Liz. 'Where did you sleep? Not under your desk again, I hope?'

Hannah laughed. 'No chance. Too cramped. Learned my lesson last time. Luckily there was a sofa in his hotel suite so he slept on that while I took the bed.'

Liz thought it wise not to probe further, so she switched subject and asked her friend what she was doing for Christmas.

It seemed that she was stopping off at a mate's in Exeter for 'a bit of a knees-up' on Christmas Eve, en route for her parents in Surrey on 25 December.

'It's always a massive to-do at Mummy's and Daddy's,' she said ruefully. 'Vast numbers of rellies and friends, too much food, too much champagne, you know the drill?'

Liz nodded as if she had too much champagne every day of the week.

'Then we're all forced to sit and watch the queen, before the grand present-opening ceremony when we have to drink more champagne and eat endless chocolate truffles. Ghastly.'

Liz laughed, she couldn't help herself. 'Poor you, what a nightmare!'

'Don't tease,' said Hannah, sticking out her lower lip. 'If you met Mummy and Daddy you'd know what I was talking about.'

Soon they got on to Rosie. Hannah wanted a full update and was delighted to hear that she was progressing so well.

'You're an absolute hero,' she said when Liz had finished.

'Me?' said Liz, surprised. 'Why? Rosie's the hero. She's been so brave.'

Hannah leaned forwards and touched her lightly on the cheek with a soft, manicured hand. 'Because you've been through the most terrible time, too, unimaginable, but you've held it all together, kept yourself and Rosie going and look at you! You're more gorgeous than ever!'

Liz, embarrassed, studied her fingernails.

'It's true!' Hannah said, pushing her friend's hands away so that she had to look up. 'Anyone else in your position would have aged twenty years, but you seem younger than ever. What have you done to yourself?'

Now Liz smiled. It was nonsense, of course, but she supposed that she was feeling a lot more cheerful and optimistic now that Rosie was out of the woods. And curiously, being back at A Winkle In Time had helped, too.

Hannah peered at her through narrowed eyes. 'Liz?' she asked suspiciously. 'Is there something you're not telling me?'

Liz blushed and shook her head.

'I knew it!' Hannah cried, thrilled. 'There's a man, isn't there? It's written all over your face. I can't believe I didn't twig sooner. Go on, who's the lucky chap?'

Liz was appalled at her own transparency, but realised that it would be good to talk about Robert to someone. Now that Iris was gone from her life, there seemed to be no one to confide in other than Tremarnock folk who knew him, and the prospect of one of them saying something about her to him was too horrific to contemplate.

The advantage of Hannah was that she was never likely to meet him, plus she did seem to know quite a lot about men, which could be useful. Perhaps she'd encountered nervous types before? Maybe if Liz told her what had happened up to now, she'd be able to interpret the signs and figure out whether he really was keen on her or not.

'There is this person...' she began, before going on to explain about the long hours he worked, his awkwardness, his generosity towards her and Rosie, the kiss, the hand on her shoulder.

'I'd completely ruled out any kind of romance after Rosie fell ill,' she continued, 'but seeing him again, well, I suppose it did make me realise how much I like him – but I'm not sure if he really likes me or if he's just being kind.'

'Of *course* he likes you,' Hannah said rolling her eyes, 'he's just too shy to make another move.'

Liz stared into her cappuccino. 'Do you really think so?'

Liz nodded. 'Absolutely.' She took a sip of espresso and tipped her head on one side. 'How old is he, by the way?'

'Forty,' said Liz, 'but he doesn't really look it.'

'Hmm,' said Hannah, mentally weighing up the information. 'Has he ever been married?'

When Liz said no and explained about the fiancée who'd dumped him just before the wedding, Hannah's eyes clouded over.

'Bad,' she said ominously, shaking her head, 'I don't like it.'

'What do you mean?' Liz asked, alarmed.

According to Hannah, a man of forty and above who'd never married wasn't to be trusted. By her logic, if some wily woman hadn't bagged him already then there must be something wrong with him.

'And why did the fiancée dump him? That's what I want to know,' she said, drumming her fingernails on the table. 'He must have done something pretty terrible for her to pull out at such short notice, but what? We need to find out before this goes any further.'

Liz felt her shoulders droop. It was true that she'd never thought to question why the ex-girlfriend had left him in such a rush. If anything, she'd assumed that the woman was to blame, rather than that there had been any wrongdoing on Robert's part, and she'd felt sorry for him.

'Besides,' Hannah went on, sucking reflectively on her spoon like Sherlock with his pipe. Tears sprang in Liz's eyes and she hung her head to disguise them. 'I think you should be very wary of a man who was engaged once and who apparently, as far as you know, has never been out with anyone else. It suggests to me that he's never got over this woman, whoever she is. Probably never will.'

'I guess you're right,' Liz said despondently. 'The thought had crossed my mind more than once. It's just that I wondered whether maybe with me it was different. When he said he really liked me...'

She sniffed and wiped her eyes with the back of her sleeve.

Hannah leaned across the table and took a hand in hers.

'Oh hun,' she whispered. 'I'm sorry, I didn't mean to upset you. I might be completely wrong about him. I probably am.'

She pulled her seat closer before resuming. 'I feel such a heel. I didn't mean to make you cry. It's just that I don't want you to get hurt, you see. You've suffered enough.'

Liz took a deep breath. 'No, you're right,' she replied, straightening her back and pushing the fringe out of her eyes. 'The last thing I need right now is an unrequited love affair. Best to leave things as they are, as boss and employee. Friendly and polite but nothing more.'

Hannah smiled, relieved that her friend had rallied.

'So when are you coming back to good ole Dolphin House?' she said suddenly, pushing back her chair to mark a change of subject. 'The new girl's not nearly as nice as you. No lovely early bird chats – and she smells of BO.' She wrinkled her nose. 'And that boss of yours – Kasia? – she's such a dragon, worse since you've gone. You must miss it,' she whee- dled. 'Come back, pretty please?' She cocked her head on one side and gazed imploringly.

Liz frowned. 'To be honest, I don't know. I mean, I suppose I could once Rosie's at school full-time, but I feel I need to be around if she gets tired during the day and wants to come home.'

'I'm joking, silly,' Hannah said gently. 'Of course you mustn't come back yet, if ever. Give yourself a break, girl, you've got quite enough on your plate.'

They'd been talking for nearly an hour and Hannah apolo- gised, saying that she'd have to fly. 'Keep in touch, though, won't you? We'll have a bite to eat next time, one evening when you're not working.' She winked. 'There's a dishy mar- keting friend of mine I'd like you to meet. He's got a lovely pad on the Barbican and a boat in the marina. I might bring him along for a drink. Handsome marketing types do exist, you know,' she added, noticing Liz's expression.

Privately Liz thought that she had absolutely no interest in meeting a marketing man, dishy or no, but she didn't say. She made a mental note, though, to be working every night for the foreseeable future if Hannah ever raised the subject again.

She made to rise before Hannah appeared to remember something and gave a little cry. 'I almost forgot, I've a present for you!'

She reached into her capacious white leather handbag and pulled out a parcel wrapped in gold paper. Liz was appalled because she had nothing in return and would have promised to reciprocate, had not Hannah pre-empted her.

'I don't normally do Christmas presents for girlfriends but I just thought this was so *you*,' she said, thrusting the parcel into Liz's hands. 'Go on, open it.'

Liz would have preferred to wait, but she could see that Hannah was dying to watch her unwrap. Whatever it was didn't weigh much, so she slipped a finger under the sticky tape that held the two sides of paper together and shook the parcel open.

Out fell a hairband the like of which she'd never seen before. It resembled a glamorous necklace, strung with red and white gemstone embellishments shaped liked little fans with a large pink, white and gold decoration in the middle and an oval crystal at the very centre. It looked delicate, beautiful and terribly expensive.

'I couldn't possibly—' she began to say before Hannah stopped her.

'I saw it in Liberty when I was last in London,' she said quickly. 'It wasn't expensive at all and I could just see you in it. You do like it, don't you?'

She looked so hopeful that Liz couldn't possibly do anything but agree.

'I love it!' she said, which was true, it's just that she'd never owned anything quite so gorgeous. 'I can't wait to show Rosie!'

Hannah's eyes lit up. 'Go on then, try it on!'

Liz wasn't in the mood but it would be churlish to refuse, so she swiftly took off the black and white spotty scarf that kept her ponytail in place, shaking out her dark hair and placing the band around her head.

'How do I look?' she smiled, glancing this way and that so that Hannah could view it from all angles.

'Lovely!' Hannah said, clapping her hands. She rootled in her bag and pulled out a compact mirror, which she opened so that Liz could see herself. 'Look!'

Liz had a peek and was surprised at how the jewels seemed

to make her pale face and huge brown eyes sparkle. 'It's so pretty, like a tiara!'

Rosie, at least, would appreciate it. She looked away quickly, not wishing to appear vain.

'It's ideal for Christmas parties,' Hannah said, delighted. 'You'll be the belle of the ball!'

Liz didn't like to mention that her diary wasn't exactly bulging with Christmas party invitations. No matter, she'd wear it on Christmas Day while she and Rosie were unwrapping their presents round the tree.

She followed Hannah from the café and they embraced once more outside the entrance.

'Happy Christmas, darling!' Hannah said, planting a slurpy kiss on Liz's cheek. 'I hope it's a good one.'

Liz watched her friend clip-clop expertly down the street on her high heels, all heads turning to watch as she sashayed by.

It was already gone eleven and there was scarcely time for shopping now, but it didn't really matter and she'd gone off the idea anyway. All she needed was a few stocking presents for Rosie and a little something for Pat. There was still plenty of time; she could come again another day.

She was heading towards the car park, still in her beautiful hairband which, she realised, must look ludicrously over-dressy on a grey Thursday morning, when she heard shouting on the other side of the street.

She glanced across the road and stopped in her tracks. There, on the same side as the Theatre Royal, was a woman in an expensive-looking long white fur coat, jabbing a finger at a plump, shortish, middle-aged man in a smart tweed jacket and brown brogues, and yelling at the top of her voice.

Quite a crowd was starting to gather around the two but they didn't seem to notice or care. Although she was some distance away, Liz quickly realised that the woman, with her mop of auburn hair, was Iris, dressed up to the nines and looking like a fifties movie star. The object of her rage was Jim.

Even if you hadn't heard shouting, you could tell from Iris's body language that she was very upset. She towered over Jim in her high black heels and the gold bangles on her arms flashed in the morning light as she waggled her finger at him. He, meanwhile, was a few paces back, leaning away from her as if afraid that at any moment she'd spring forward and strike like a panther.

'What's going on?'

A woman with a pushchair had stopped beside Liz, who shrugged. 'No idea.'

She'd never seen Jim and Iris disagree, let alone fight like this. They'd seemed to have such a loving, caring relationship. It was quite out of character and something must be terribly wrong.

At that moment a policeman seemed to appear from nowhere and march across the road, holding up a hand to stop the traffic as he went.

Instinctively Liz followed; she didn't even think about it, aware only that her friend was in distress, forgetting completely that they weren't friends any more...

'Move along now, let me deal with this please,' said the policeman, gesturing to the crowd which parted to make way for him but continued to gawp from a distance. Some people were giggling and nudging, others shaking their heads and muttering: 'Fancy behaving like that in public', and, 'They should know better.'

Liz heard one girl whisper to her friend, 'Hey, I reckon it's that couple who won the lottery.'

She hovered for a second while the policeman pushed

between Iris and Jim, speaking quietly to Iris, who was clearly the more disturbed of the two. Iris put her face in her hands and burst into tears and a large gold ring, with big sparkling diamonds in the centre, flashed on her third finger. Jim, meanwhile, was staring at the ground, hands behind his back, his mouth set in a grim line.

'Iris!' Liz called. It just came out. She wanted to run over and give her a hug, tell the policeman that it was all right, that she'd take care of her friend.

Hearing her voice, Iris dropped her hands and looked up, her nose running, her cheeks streaked with black mascara and tears.

Her eyes opened wide when she spotted Liz, but instead of relief and gratitude at the sight of a friendly face, Liz spotted something quite different: fear, horror, even.

She took a step back, shocked and winded, her heart hammering in her chest, feeling as if she'd been punched in the stomach.

'Move right off now,' the policeman said angrily, gesturing to Liz to leave the scene, an unwelcome intruder. 'It's not helping this lady having people crowding round.'

Liz stumbled away from the gathering, feeling like a monster. Never in her life had she provoked such a reaction in anyone. Iris looked aghast. If a madman had approached her with an axe she couldn't have seemed more terrified, yet Liz had only wanted to help. How on earth had she turned into this pariah? It was more than unsettling; she was devastated.

She felt as if people were staring at her as she staggered down the road towards the car park, wondering about the dreadful, interfering woman who'd only made matters worse. Her hands trembled as she put money into the pay machine and when she reached the car she had to sit still for a few moments, clutching the wheel and taking deep breaths to calm herself.

She tried to put Iris – and Hannah's earlier warnings about Robert – out of her mind and think of all the happy things that had occurred recently: Rosie's recovery, above all else; the unexpected present which she didn't want but that was such a kind gesture. So many blessings.

Other people seemed to like her, so what was it about her now that Iris so detested? It made no sense. Unless...

As she drove back along the windy country lanes towards Rosie's school, she couldn't help going over every encounter that she'd had with Iris in the past six months. Her visits to the shop to buy cigarettes and lottery tickets, chats about Rosie and Iris's children and about Gran and Spencer, the Easter lunch and Iris's confidences about Jim's failed business venture.

The picnic at Tintagel, too, that had been such a success all round. That uncollected ticket, sitting on the shop shelf beneath the cigarette lighter...

Where was it? Liz needed to know. All of a sudden it seemed like a matter of great urgency. But how could she ask now without sounding jealous or appearing to accuse Iris of stealing? The moment when she could slip the question easily into a conversation had well and truly passed. Moreover, if she tried to get in touch with her former friend again, she wasn't at all sure that she'd even agree to speak.

The sight of a smiling Rosie, hand in hand with the classroom assistant, making her way lopsidedly across the playground towards her mother, went some way towards cheering Liz up, but there was no doubt that the world seemed a bleaker, more confusing place.

One way and another it had been a bad morning, she thought, touching Hannah's hairband to make sure that it was still in place, ready for Rosie's inspection.

Anyone would think, back there in Plymouth city centre, that Iris had come face to face with the devil himself.

Chapter Twenty-One

THE SOUND OF letters plopping onto the mat once filled Liz with excitement, but that was a long time ago. Now, it was usually bills and needless to say, she was in no rush to open them.

She peered over the top of the café curtain in her bedroom and waved at Nathan, who was wearing a red Santa hat. It was grey and drizzling, though not cold, and he and the hat were somewhat bedraggled. Even so, he managed a cheery wave back before putting something in Pat's next door. His bike was parked on the opposite side of the road, leaning against the wall.

Liz was dressed already, having returned from dropping Rosie at school some half an hour earlier. There was a small pile of mail. She flicked quickly through and was relieved to find no brown envelopes, just what looked and felt like Christmas cards. People were sending fewer these days but she still wrote – and received – some. Villagers, of course, delivered by hand.

There was one from the hospital inviting Rosie for an eye appointment on 4 January. Liz had put off raising the issue of glasses with her daughter, but she knew that she would have to sometime. Teachers had been pointing out that it must be tiring for her, having to strain so hard, and Liz had only delayed because she knew how Rosie felt about the matter.

Luckily, however, one of her classmates, Imogen, had recently come to school in a pair of bright red ones which everyone had admired, so hopefully she'd smoothed the path.

Liz recognised Kasia's big heavy black handwriting on one envelope and her father's small neat scrawl, addressed to them both, on another. The third, she knew, was from Greg, with a second class stamp attached. Typical. Good job it had arrived in time. She popped them all on the kitchen table ready for Rosie to open when she arrived home.

It was the last day of term and Liz knew that she'd come armed with plastic bags containing drawings, crumpled pieces of work and the inevitable models made from painted egg cartons, cereal packets and toilet rolls all cobbled together with reams of sticky tape. Plus more cards from her class-mates and teacher, and exercise books to go through, sign and return in the New Year. It was amazing how much stuff the children managed to accumulate.

She was about to start preparing a creamy chicken dish that Rosie liked for supper when she heard a rap on the door and someone called through the letter box: 'Cooeee!'

She opened up to find a very soggy Esme on her doorstep, flapping a broken umbrella that had blown inside out.

'Come in!' cried Liz. 'You're soaking!'

When Liz had taken Esme's long purple velvet coat and put it on a hanger in the kitchen to dry, the two women took cups of coffee into the front room, where the beige table lamp was casting a warm glow.

Poor Esme's long grey hair had mostly escaped from its bun and was dangling wetly round her face.

'Would you like a towel – or the hairdryer?' Liz asked, concerned, but the older woman shook her head, spraying droplets of water all around like confetti.

'I shall have a hot bath when I get upstairs,' she announced grandly, 'and change my vestments. Even my smalls are damp.' She wrinkled her long thin nose.

It sounded like a foreign language to Liz, but she got the gist and nodded. 'Filthy weather. I hope it clears up for Christmas.'

'Speaking of which,' said Esme, leaning forward in the armchair, cupping the mug of coffee in both hands, 'I have a proposal to make. It's my turn to have the aged pa this year.' She rolled her eyes. 'My brother Gerald has decided to get as far away as possible – Tanzania, to be precise. So it'll be just me and the pater, bless him.

'I wondered if you and Rosie would care to join us? I thought I'd do goose rather than turkey, which is so dry, don't you think? It would be delightful to have you,' she continued, before Liz had time to answer, 'unless you're otherwise engaged, of course?'

'That's a wonderful invitation,' Liz said, meaning every word, 'but Rosie has already told me that she'd rather it was just the two of us. She still gets so tired and I don't want her to overdo it. I hope you understand?'

Esme nodded sagely. 'Of course, I suspected you might say that.'

'But let me treat you and your father to a drink at The Lobster Pot in the morning,' Liz went on. 'Pat said she'd like to come, too, before her niece picks her up.'

And so it was agreed.

Later, when Rosie came home, she opened Kasia's card first, then Granddad's, then her father's, saving the most precious till last. From Granddad there was a cheque for twenty pounds and the same amount for Liz.

'Wowee!' said Rosie, wide-eyed. 'That's more than usual, isn't it?'

Liz nodded. 'I expect it's because you've been ill. We'll put it in your bank account and you can choose something in the sales.'

Inside the card, he'd written a note to them both:

Hope you have a lovely day. Tonya, Davina and I are going to Tonya's cousin Lindy in Northampton for lunch. Davina has a new boyfriend, Stefano, who's coming too.

'Stefano?' said Rosie. 'That's a funny name, isn't it?'

Liz nodded. 'I think it might be Italian.'

'I wonder if he and Davina will get married,' Rosie wondered. Her eyes lit up. 'Maybe they'll ask me to be bridesmaid!'

'Oh, I don't think people have bridesmaids much these days,' Liz said quickly, thinking that there would undoubtedly be countless other children Davina would invite first, were Stefano brave enough to pop the question.

They put the cards on the bookshelf in the front room along with the others they'd received, then Rosie opened the one from her father.

'Look, there's a picture of a baby,' she said, as a four by six inch coloured photograph fluttered out along with a ten pound note.

She picked the picture up and held it close to her face, so that she could see properly.

'I think it's a girl,' she said, puzzled. 'She's wearing pink. Who is she?'

Liz's heart pitter-pattered. 'You'd better read the card to find out.'

'You read it,' said Rosie, still examining the picture, so Liz took the card from her.

'Dear Rosie, I'm glad you're feeling better.'

At his request, Liz had emailed twice to give brief progress reports, after the operation and before Rosie returned to school, and his replies had been equally succinct.

'This is your baby sister,' she continued, scanning his words. 'She's called Scarlett Grace.'

Liz glanced at her daughter and swallowed. Rosie's greeny-grey eyes had opened very wide. 'My sister?' she said slowly, as if savouring the words on her lips.

Grace was one of the names that Liz and Greg had considered for Rosie.

'She was born on 3rd December and weighed 6 lbs 13 oz,' Liz went on. 'Love from Dad.'

Rosie let out a small cry of excitement. 'I can't believe it! I never thought I'd have a real sister.' She paused, something having occurred to her, and looked at her mother anxiously. 'You don't mind, do you?'

At that moment Liz thought that she loved her daughter even more than before, if that were humanly possible.

'No, darling.' She cupped Rosie's face in her hands and kissed her smooth brow. 'What a sweet little thing she is! Fancy that!'

Rosie, reassured, wanted to know if the little girl had green eyes like her, but Liz said you couldn't tell with babies until they were three or four months old.

'I wonder if she'll like painting and drawing too?' Rosie asked. 'And cats – and hair accessories.'

Liz smiled. 'I wonder.'

'She's got a funny button nose,' Rosie commented, prodding it gently as if she'd be able to feel its softness beneath her fingers.

'Most babies have button noses,' Liz replied. 'They don't grow till you're bigger.'

Rosie sighed, suddenly sad. 'I wish I could meet her.'

Liz took a deep breath; she'd known this would come the moment she saw the photograph. 'I'm sure you will one day.' She straightened up. 'Now, I've got a surprise for you.'

Rosie brightened instantly; it didn't take much to cheer her up. 'What?'

'I've decided that we should have a real Christmas tree this year,' her mother smiled. 'Put your coat on again. We're going out to buy one now.'

She was woken on Christmas morning by the sound of Rosie shouting in her ear with a toy synthesiser from her stocking that she'd set to Dalek mode: 'Attention, attention! You are no longer permitted to sleep. You must report to me immediately or you will be exterminated.'

The last word was delivered in a tinny, robotic crescendo that made Liz wince.

She opened one eye tentatively and there was Rosie with her funny short hair, about an inch and a half long now, sticking out at right angles to her head on the side where she'd been sleeping. She lowered the synthesiser and there were brown marks around her mouth; evidence, no doubt, of the chocolate money she'd been scoffing.

Liz groaned. 'What time it is?' She felt as if she'd only just gone to sleep.

'Seven fifteen,' came the Dalek voice. 'You are permitted to drink your tea before rising.'

Liz started to sit up, reaching gratefully for the mug of tea that Rosie had placed beside her on the table.

'Lovely,' she said, taking a sip. 'A life-saver.'

A few more sips and she had come to enough to ask her daughter to hop in beside her. Rosie ran to fetch her stocking and proceeded to show Liz all the little items inside – a silly wind-up mouse, some stripy fingerless gloves, a chocolate reindeer – as if Liz had never seen them before. It was an annual ritual.

They ate breakfast in their pyjamas before showering and putting on warm clothes. It was cold and clear outside and there was even a hint of sunshine.

'You have to wear your beautiful diamond hairband,' Rosie announced, as her mother ran a comb through her shoulder-length dark hair and fluffed the fringe out of her face.

As far as Rosie was concerned, the band was incredibly precious, the most valuable item she'd ever seen. Diamonds or diamanté, it was all the same to her.

They knocked on Pat as arranged, and Rosie gave her a rousing rendition of 'We Wish You a Merry Christmas' when she came to the door. Then, arm in arm, they walked slowly downhill towards the beach and harbour, stopping every now and again to say hello to neighbours emerging from their cottages. There was no sign of Marcus or his mother, though. Liz assumed that Valerie, at least, must be in Bath.

There was a very jolly crowd gathered at the sea wall, some wrapped up like Liz and Rosie, others in swimsuits and silly costumes, stamping their feet and jogging on the spot to keep warm.

In previous years, Rosie would have insisted that she and her mother swim, too, although the sight of her daughter's thin little body, blue with cold even before she'd been in the water, always unnerved Liz. She didn't believe that Rosie could possibly enjoy it, but she couldn't bear to be left out. This year, though, even she had had to agree that swimming was a bad idea.

'Gracious, look at that one!' Pat exclaimed, pointing at a large man in a Wonder Woman costume, complete with conical breasts and a long black wig. 'Who's that then?'

'It's Rick,' Rosie whisper-shouted, giggling. 'You can tell by the beard and fat belly. I think he eats too much of his own fudge.'

There were quite a few folk whom Liz didn't recognise – some friends of Charlotte and Todd Pennyfeather, who always came as Batman and Robin, while the Lamberts – mum, dad and their two teenage children, plus extended family – were in a motley selection of Disney outfits – Snow White, the Little Mermaid and so on.

Jean and Tom were Mother and Father Christmas, cheered on by a gaggle of grandchildren, their mums and dads and assorted cousins. Jean had an enormous, extended family and was always forgetting their names. Rosie ticked her off about it.

Tony Cutt, meanwhile, was in a gorgeous purple and green genie costume, or he could have been Aladdin, while Felipe, shivering despite his thick tan shearling coat, woolly hat and gloves, looked on, horrified.

The parts of the swimmers' flesh that were exposed were a strange shade of blue and purple with unsightly goose bumps, but no one cared.

'Hurry up!' someone shouted, and at last the whistle blew and the gang of fifty or so brave souls hopped gingerly across the pebbles before reaching the sand, where their speed picked up.

Within minutes, the water was a seething mass of screaming bodies, kicking the waves, flapping their arms in the air and sending white columns and spirals into the sky as they dived in, churning the freezing sea as they struggled to catch their breath and swim. Those huddling by the sea wall in coats, hats and gloves, cheered and laughed: 'Well done!', 'Bravo!', and after a few more minutes, the first contingent came hurtling back, reaching out and clamouring for their colourful towels hanging on the wall or thrown to them by friends or relatives.

A few hardy souls managed more than a couple of strokes; Wonder Woman demonstrated her butterfly while Batman and Robin tried to do handstands underwater but the current was too strong and neither could stay up.

Soon, though, all the swimmers had departed for an assortment of prearranged neighbouring houses, with doors left open so that they could use the showers and get changed. The non-swimmers, meanwhile, stepped across the road to The Lobster Pot.

'Every year, I don't know how they do it,' Pat muttered, pulling up the collar of her coat with a knobbly hand. 'You'd think they'd die of cold.'

Inside, the low-ceilinged pub, which dated back to the seventeenth century, was deliciously warm, thanks to the open fire roaring in the big stone fireplace. There was a scent of pine cones, cinnamon and nutmeg, and soon coats and hats were being removed and cheeks were turning rosy red.

Ruby's husband, Victor, bought a glass of red wine for Liz, sweet sherry for Pat and a lemonade for Rosie, served by Barbara's son Aidan at the bar. It wasn't long, though, before Barbara herself appeared beside him, having shed her bathing suit and Fairy Godmother outfit, had a hot shower and changed into a figure-hugging crimson dress.

'Wow! That was quick!' Liz said admiringly. She'd even put on make-up, pearl earrings and a necklace, though her dark-blonde hair was still damp.

'No flies on me,' Barbara joked. 'I could do with a hot toddy now, though, I tell you. That water never gets any warmer.'

'Festive tidings and all that.'

Liz twisted round to find Esme close behind her. The room had filled up and she had to lift her glass high in the air above her head because there was such a crush.

'Come and meet my old pa,' Esme shouted.

Poor Rosie, still in her peacock-blue beret, was practically squashed.

'I'll get your drinks and meet you outside,' Liz mouthed. 'It's too packed in here.'

Esme nodded. 'Come along, Rosie, let's find a quiet spot. I can't hear myself think.'

It was a relief to be outside again, despite the cold, and they settled round a wooden table, coats reinstated.

Liz had met Esme's elderly father, Leonard, before, but not for some years, and he had to be introduced to Pat. After a few sips of sherry, Liz noticed with amusement, she turned quite giggly and flirtatious. Leonard was just her sort – attentive and debonair, in a tweed jacket and racy pink corduroy trousers. He must have been at least eighty.

'You remind me of David Niven,' she told him, twinkling. 'I think it's the moustache. He was one of my heroes.'

'And you, my dear lady,' said Leonard, leaning forward and patting her rather suggestively on the knee, 'remind me of Vivien Leigh.'

Pat blushed. 'Oh nonsense. I'm nothing like her. But I was quite a looker in my day, you know.'

Leonard winked. 'I can see that – and you still are, if I may say so.'

They were joined by Rick, now out of his Wonder Woman costume, and his latest lady friend, Nicole, wearing a rather

293

startling, straw-coloured wig. Perhaps she'd been unwell, or just liked big hair. Whatever the reason, Liz hoped that Rosie wouldn't comment.

She was just beginning to look a little bored, kicking her feet against Liz's chair until she had to tell her stop, when Robert came striding towards them, wrapped up in a navy polo neck and Barbour jacket. On his feet were big muddy walking boots.

His face had a healthy glow, as if his cheeks had been whipped by the Cornish wind, and his wavy brown hair was tousled. There was a hint of dark stubble on his chin where he hadn't yet shaved, and the whites of his hazel eyes were very bright.

He stopped short at the entrance to the pub and glanced at the watching crowd, gazing nervously this way and that.

'Where've you been on this fine, festive morning?' said Rick, rising and slapping him on the arm.

Robert took a step back and cleared his throat noisily. A Winkle In Time was closed today and tomorrow, but it was open for business over the new year period. Liz had no idea what her boss's Christmas plans were.

'Been along the cliffs,' he replied, playing with the zip of his coat, 'up to Hermitage Point.'

'Beautiful day for it,' Rick said, stroking his impressive grey beard. 'What can I get you to drink?'

Robert shook his head. 'I was just—'

'He likes wine, don't you, Robert?'

Rosie jumped up noisily and everyone turned to look at her as Leonard laughed loudly. She blushed furiously at being suddenly the focus of so much attention.

Liz would have come to her rescue but Robert got in first, his face breaking into a smile.

'I certainly do, Rosie,' he said, and, turning to Rick, 'I'll have a glass of red, thanks. A Merlot or something similar.'

Someone had just left the table next door and he pulled the vacant chair up and sat next to Rosie, stretching his long legs out in front of him across the path.

Liz found herself staring furiously into her half-empty wineglass, unable suddenly to think of a single thing to say to anyone. He, too, seemed dumbstruck, but then he was hardly a talker at the best of times.

Luckily, Rosie had recovered from her momentary embarrassment.

'You should have gone for a swim,' she told Robert. 'The costumes were so funny. Rick was wearing a black girl's wig and a gold bra. I couldn't tell who it was for a minute.'

Robert, who'd leaned in closer to her so that he could hear properly against the hubbub of chatter and waves swooshing up the beach, rattling pebbles, shuddered dramatically.

'Shall I let you into a secret?' he said, lowering his voice and leaning in even further.

Rosie nodded gravely.

'I can't swim very well.'

Rosie's mouth dropped open. She knew old people like Pat who didn't like swimming, but she'd never heard of a still youngish adult who actually couldn't.

'Didn't you learn when you were little?'

He nodded. 'I had lessons at school, but I always hated it when the water got up my nose.'

He wrinkled his nose and pulled a face, making Rosie laugh.

'You have to blow the water out,' she explained seriously, 'like a seal. It's easy, honest. I could teach you.'

He shook his head and shrugged. 'I'm afraid I'm a lost cause.'

Then he glanced at Liz. 'You and your mum are excellent swimmers, though. I've seen you.' He paused. 'Lovely hair-band, by the way, Liz.'

She examined her knees, as if conducting an important scientific observation, and mumbled a cursory 'Thanks'.

'Who are you opening your presents with?' Rosie suddenly chirped up. 'We're going home to open ours in a minute.'

Robert smiled. 'Ahh, presents. Yes. Very important. Actually, I'm not going to open mine with anybody. I'm more excited about my Christmas dinner, to be honest.'

Rosie frowned. 'Oh no,' she said gravely. 'Presents are much more exciting than food.' She grimaced. 'Especially stuffing. I hate stuffing.'

This time Robert laughed. 'I suppose it is an acquired taste. I don't think I liked it much when I was your age, but I make mine with a bit of bacon and some chestnuts and it's delicious.'

Rosie's eyes opened very wide. 'Are you cooking it for yourself? Just you? You're not going to anyone's house?'

'No,' said Robert. 'It might sound strange to you, but I don't mind being on my own. I'm used to it.'

Rosie cocked her head on one side, examining Robert slyly. Liz, who'd been peeping at them out of the corner of an eye, felt her heart miss a beat. She knew that look all too well.

'You can come to us,' said her daughter innocently. 'There's lots of food. We'd like that, wouldn't we, Mum?'

Liz thought that she could sense Robert stiffen. Feeling like a rabbit in the headlights, quick as a flash she blurted, 'Oh no!' She checked herself. 'I mean, I'm sure he wouldn't want to.'

Did his eyebrows rise hopefully, just a fraction?

She thought rapidly. 'I only bought a small turkey breast. If I'd known—'

'It's all right,' he said quickly. 'My sister asked me but I said no. She'd be furious if she heard I'd gone somewhere else.'

Liz tried to extract a few drops from her empty wineglass without success. She felt so mean. Something told her that he would have accepted, had she urged him, but she'd resolved to stay away, hadn't she?

'We should go,' she told Rosie, rising abruptly.

Rosie, defeated, followed suit obediently.

'Bye, all,' Liz said, pinning a cheery smile to her face. 'Happy Christmas!'

As she and Rosie walked away, she fancied that they were dragging an icy wind in their wake.

'I wish Robert was coming, too,' Rosie said petulantly. 'You should have asked him.'

'Don't be so silly,' Liz snapped back.

Chapter Twenty-Two

THE RESTAURANT WAS packed all over new year, but as soon as the country returned to work and the children to school, it went deathly quiet. Robert didn't seem worried though and nor was Liz; it was the same every January and they knew business would pick up again towards the end of the month when people grew bored with sitting at home and started to feel sociable again.

Rosie seemed to settle well into the new term and when it came to the appointment with the ophthalmologist, she accepted the need for glasses with good grace and chose a pale blue pair that Liz said went well with her eyes and hair.

'They make you look very intelligent,' Liz joked, 'like a university professor.'

'I *am* intelligent,' Rosie replied, pleased, despite everything, that she could now see people's faces more clearly and hold a book slightly further from the end of her nose.

In early February, Liz popped into Pat's with some shopping and they sat in her front room and had a cup of tea.

'I say,' said Pat, leaning forward conspiratorially. Liz recognised the signs; there was juicy gossip to follow. Pat explained that her friend Elaine had heard something via her friend from Devonport about the local newsagents who'd won the lottery.

Liz's stomach turned over, as it always did whenever she thought of them now.

'Elaine – you know, the one from Saltash?'

Liz nodded. She'd heard her mentioned often enough.

'Well,' said Pat, 'her friend in Devonport's grandson used to go to the same college as the boy whose parents won all that cash, see. They were quite chummy, as it happens.'

Liz didn't want to hear any more but when Pat was in full flow, it was hard to stop her.

'Anyway,' the old woman said, relishing her captive audience and failing to notice Liz's discomfort, 'that lottery boy, Darren I think he's called, he doesn't go to college any more. Gave it up the minute they won. Elaine's friend's grandson says he ditched all his old friends, too, and got in with a bad crowd. You know, drink and drugs, wacky baccy and worse, that sort of thing.' She shuddered.

'The girl – I can't remember her name – she's dating some ne'er-do-well in Plymouth. Property developer he calls himself, whatever that is, but Elaine says he's a crook and he's not nice to women either. Everybody knows it. And meanwhile...' Pat shuffled forwards even further; she was in her stride now, loving every minute. 'The newsagent hisself...' She always said hisself when she was excited. 'Well, Elaine's other friend, Bea, she moved to Looe where her husband's folks come from. Her husband Trevor, Bea's I mean...'

Liz was struggling to keep up.

'Anyway, Trevor, he's a nice chap. Solid. He says the newsagent chappie is always in the pub these days, knocking back the spirits. They're building a great big house on the cliff, swimming pool, tennis court, you name it, but the wife's tearing her hair out because the husband's drunk as a lord most of the time and she can't get him to look at the plans, nothing. Can't get any sense out of him. She's been down there a few times to drag him out. Of the pub, I mean. One time her old mum came, too, hobbling in with a stick and waving her fists at him.'

Pat pulled an angry face and waved her arm in the air to demonstrate.

'Apparently they were all shouting, making a right old commotion. Landlord didn't know what to do and ended up chucking the lot of them out in the street.'

Pat shook her head. 'Just goes to show, doesn't it? Money can't buy you happiness. Doesn't matter how much you have.'

Liz took a deep breath, thinking that Pat's account had probably become seriously embellished somewhere along the line. However, she had suspected that all wasn't well after spotting Darren going into Marcus's house, then seeing Iris and Jim rowing, and this latest piece of news only seemed to confirm it.

She felt no pleasure in Iris's misfortune, but she was aware of that nasty sensation in her intestines again, a dull pain that seemed to have no specific cause, and no treatment.

'I'm sure it's an exaggeration,' she found herself saying.

Pat harrumphed. 'True as eggs is eggs. Elaine's not one to spread rumours. Says her sources are copper-bottom.' She knocked twice on the table to prove her point. 'They always are.'

Liz felt gloomy when she went home and even the sight of a smiling Rosie at the school gates failed to cheer her up much. Her hair had grown fast and she was now sporting a pixie cut and had finally abandoned her headscarves.

'What's for tea?' she asked, clambering in the back seat of Eeyore and buckling up.

'Tuna pasta bake,' Liz said, wincing slightly and steeling herself. Rosie wasn't keen on fish but it was good for her.

'You know I hate tuna,' came the predictable reply. 'Can't I have pizza instead?'

By the time they reached the cottage, Rosie seemed resigned to her fate and settled down without a fuss at the little desk in her bedroom to do her homework.

She'd missed a lot of school and had needed catch-up lessons in maths, but her English didn't seem to have suffered, in fact she almost always got the top mark.

Liz had just filled a saucepan with water, ready to put it on the hob for the pasta, when she heard a crash. Leaving the gas ring burning, she hurtled next door to find Rosie slumped on the floor beside her overturned chair.

Blackness washed over Liz for a second or two, blind panic, until an inner voice screamed, *Pull yourself together.* Unaware of anything save the need to help her daughter, she swung into action, her thoughts chasing ahead of her like sailing boats whipped on the wind.

'Rosie?'

Where was the phone? In the front room behind the TV.

The little girl was rigid, her arms and legs outstretched, body and limbs twitching and jerking strangely. She didn't answer – but she was alive.

Was she having a fit? Put her in recovery mode. Make sure she doesn't hit her head.

Liz pushed the chair away and gently removed her daughter's broken glasses and turned her on her side, relieved that she was definitely breathing.

Call an ambulance, tell them to hurry.

She ran to get the phone, jabbing in the numbers as she returned to her daughter, noticing as she did so that there was sticky blood on her fingers. Glass from the broken spectacles? No, a wound on the back of her daughter's head.

She's injured. Oh God.

The operator's calm voice seemed to cut through the sickening swooping and swirling in her brain.

'It sounds like a seizure,' said the woman, patiently going through a list of instructions. 'You're doing the right thing. Don't try to move her.'

Liz had no idea how long it was before the ambulance arrived, but by the time the paramedics took over, comforting smiles, lights flashing, walkie-talkies chattering, Rosie was coming to, dazed and confused – but definitely still here.

As they left the cottage, Liz saw Pat on the pavement, wringing her hands and swaying anxiously, Esme's arm round her shoulder. Charlotte Pennyfeather – what was she doing here? Jean, shivering next to Tom. A dog was barking loudly, but she didn't know whose it was.

She climbed in the ambulance behind the stretcher, noticing that Rosie was starting to focus and her skin, scarily blue, was turning pink once more.

Liz smiled as reassuringly as she could. 'You're going to be all right.'

Inside, though, it felt as if someone were squeezing her heart and intestines, wringing them out like wet washing through a mangle.

Rosie couldn't ask questions because she was wearing an oxygen mask, but her eyes, full of fear, did the talking.

'It's the brain tumour, Mum,' she was saying. 'I know it. It's come back.'

Liz gripped her daughter's small cold hand – and waited, because there was nothing else that she could do.

Another night in hospital in Plymouth then back to Bristol for an MRI scan. This time she was more prepared, so that when they told her the tumour was growing again and Rosie would need urgent treatment, she had no desire to faint, she felt angry and raging.

'How are you going to stop it?' she demanded. She didn't want sympathetic looks or cups of tea, she wanted answers and solutions.

Rosie would have ten weeks of intensive chemotherapy first, they said, then radiotherapy. It was going to be a long haul, but there was a 70 per cent chance that she'd come through.

Liz's heart hurt, thinking of the suffering that her daughter was about to endure. She'd come across adults who'd had chemotherapy before and knew how bad it made you feel. She was cheered, however, by the positive prognosis and was just able to return to her daughter with a weak smile on her face.

'Look,' said Rosie, showing her mother the picture that she'd been drawing while Liz was in with the doctors.

It was a mermaid sitting on a rock, with long, wavy golden hair that reached below her waist.

Liz wouldn't tell Rosie just now that soon she'd be bald again. She thought that this, more than anything, would make her daughter sob. It was so cruel. Liz would have given anything for it to be her instead, but wallowing in self-pity would get them nowhere. Her role now was to support her daughter as best she could – and fight for her like a tigress if the need arose.

Rosie had recovered from her seizure and was allowed home after two nights, ready for treatment to begin the following Monday. She'd had six stitches in the back of her poor scarred head where she'd hit it on the corner of her bedroom door.

As soon as she was in the cottage once more, Liz rang Robert to tell him that she wouldn't be coming to the restaurant again.

'I'm sorry,' she said, 'but Rosie needs me. I hope you find someone else soon.'

Luckily, her daughter called at that moment so Liz could excuse herself and didn't have to hear the end of Robert's commiserations.

'Do get in touch when she's feeling better,' he said hurriedly, when he could hear that she was about to hang up.

'I will,' Liz replied, thinking that it wouldn't be anytime soon as the treatment would last for months.

Before long, they grew accustomed to the rhythm of chemotherapy one week, followed by a week off. It became the new norm. Every other Monday they'd be collected by taxi and taken to Bristol early in the morning for a day of treatment. Although administering the drugs only took about an hour and a half, they wouldn't usually get home until six or seven at night because there was always so much waiting around.

Liz would go armed with drawing pens and paper, books, toys and snacks, because Rosie said she didn't like the hospital food. That night, she'd often wake up with aches and pains in her arms, legs and tummy, and she'd feel exhausted, low and sick the following day and need to stay in bed. It wasn't long before her hair fell out and she couldn't bear to look at herself in the mirror.

'It's disgusting,' she said once, feeling her bald scalp, throwing the book that she'd been reading on the floor and bursting into hot tears. After that, she wouldn't let anyone except Liz see her without a headscarf, but she never mentioned her baldness again.

Quite often, though, when she was feeling particularly poorly, she would ask: 'Why does it have to be me?' Liz would struggle to find an answer and try to distract her instead.

Sometimes, Rosie would feel well enough again after che-motherapy to go to school on the Thursday or Friday for a few hours, but often Liz would get a call asking her to come and collect earlier than planned. Her eleventh birthday in March was a miserable affair because she wasn't up to doing anything special, though Liz did make a cake and buy some presents, as well as sweets to give to her classmates.

They watched a lot of TV, played games and read countless books together, but nothing seemed to dislodge the sadness that had settled on Rosie like damp fog. Just looking at her pale face and dull eyes made Liz want to cry.

At first she felt overwhelmed with the amount of informa-tion she was given about the type of brain tumour, the treatment and side-effects, but after a while she became an expert at understanding studies, interpreting statistics and badgering doctors with awkward questions.

Once again, friends and neighbours bent over backwards to help, offering lifts, house cleaning and babysitting, deliver-ing meals; at one point Liz had three cooked hams in her fridge that she didn't know what to do with.

Despite all the support and kindness, however, Rosie's tumour was the first thing that she thought about in the morning and the last thing at night. She stopped planning any-thing and tried to live in the moment because after so many setbacks, it was difficult to trust that the future was going to be OK.

When she bumped into neighbours and stopped for a chat, she'd feel jealous of their normal stresses and strains, wishing that she, too, was fretting about which secondary school to send Rosie to, or whether the water bills would rise again. But she didn't want to become hard and bitter and told herself to be thankful for the medicine on offer and grateful for people's compassion, which she could never hope to repay.

She allowed herself a brief celebration when the chemotherapy finally came to an end, but soon there was another bombshell: a further scan showed that the tumour had barely shrunk and intensive radiotherapy was now the best hope.

This was likely to be more effective than the chemotherapy, but the risk of severe, long-term damage was very high. Liz read the list of possible effects with mounting horror – blindness, poor memory, reduced intelligence, personality changes, behavioural problems, lack of growth, late puberty and inability to have children. She felt physically sick. They might just as well have said that Rosie would emerge from treatment a completely different human being, unrecognisable from the bright, cheerful little girl that she once was. A zombie.

Liz had heard the words 'proton beam therapy' – there had been stories about it in the papers and on the news – but the consultant had already said he thought that this wasn't suitable for Rosie's type of tumour. One evening, however, she sat up all night in the kitchen at the old laptop Barbara had passed on, and that usually lived in Rosie's room, and started to search the Web.

The treatment, she read, used beams of protons – or small parts of atoms – rather than high energy X-rays. The protons could be directed at a tumour more precisely than X-rays and stop once they hit the target, rather than carrying on through the body, causing less damage to surrounding tissues and reducing side-effects.

There was currently only one facility in the UK offering the expensive therapy, although the treatment would be offered to up to fifteen hundred patients in London and Manchester from 2018, following millions of pounds of investment. Until then, the NHS continued to fund only lucky, selected patients to be sent for treatments in other countries, including Switzerland, the Czech Republic and the US.

The following morning, after dropping Rosie at school for a few hours, Liz rang the consultant.

'Why did you say proton beam therapy isn't suitable for Rosie?' she wanted to know.

He explained that current research showed the treatment worked best only in rare instances, including on tumours affecting the base of the skull or spine.

'The truth is,' he said, when Liz pressed, 'I don't think you'll get the funding because of the nature of Rosie's tumour. Another patient in a very similar situation was turned down recently. They'll argue that, in this case, conventional radio-therapy will be just as effective.'

Liz, however, had long since ceased to accept what doctors recommended without asking a million questions. This was her daughter's life and if she didn't fight for her, who would?

Anger rose up. 'We've got to try.' So the consultant agreed that he would put Rosie's case forward for review by a clinical panel.

'I'll do my best, but don't get your hopes up,' he warned.

Liz mentioned none of this to anyone, not even Pat. The old woman would have had a million questions herself and Liz's head was already spinning with facts and figures, odds and outcomes. A permanent nausea kept her awake at night and she got through her days in a dreamlike half-state, focus-ing all her attention on keeping her daughter as comfortable and happy as possible.

Everyone told Liz that she was looking terribly thin and needed to eat, but food made her retch. It was the cups of tea and dry toast that kept her alive.

At last the consultant rang to tell her the news: Rosie had been turned down.

'I'm sorry,' he said. 'I feared this would happen. We need to start radiotherapy as soon as possible.'

But even as he was speaking the words, Liz's mind was spiralling off in another direction entirely. She'd already found out on the Internet that she'd need around £150,000 to get Rosie abroad for proton beam therapy and to pay for living costs while they were there. Other desperate parents had managed it somehow so she would, too.

She didn't have a house to sell or any savings, so she'd have to find the money some other way. It meant that there'd be a delay in treatment and time was of the essence, so she'd need to get started immediately. Her first stop: Greg.

She told the consultant her plans and he didn't argue with her. They'd had enough conversations for him to know that while Liz might seem small and fragile on the outside, inside she was pure steel.

'Good luck,' he said, after recommending various charities for her to approach.

'Thanks, I'm going to need it,' she replied.

Chapter Twenty-Three

GREG TOLD HER that she was mad and it couldn't be done; she'd guessed that he would so it didn't come as a surprise.

'How much can you give?' was all she wanted to know.

He ummed and aahed. 'It's difficult. Babies are so expensive and Louise isn't working at the moment...'

Liz assumed that Louise must be the girlfriend or wife. It was the first time that she'd heard her name.

'I understand,' she replied. 'I wouldn't ask for me, but for Rosie...'

He said that he'd do what he could but needed to think about it and get back to her. It was good enough for now.

Next stop was her father.

'Oh God,' he said, when she read out the list of possible side-effects from conventional radiotherapy. 'I need to talk to Tonya. Of course we'll do all we can.'

Liz imagined that she could picture her stepmother's face when he told her but she didn't care. The money – as much of it as possible – was all that mattered.

'Thanks, Dad,' she said before hanging up. 'Call back soon.'

He promised that he would and even mentioned a figure – five thousand pounds that he had in a savings account. It was a start, assuming that he could wrestle it from Tonya, of course.

Pat immediately offered two thousand pounds – her life's savings. 'You can't take it with you when you go, can you?' she said, when Liz baulked at the suggestion. 'And I can't think of a better use for it.' She also pledged to put aside as much as she could from her pension each week.

'What can *I* do?' Liz asked, frowning. 'Me personally, I mean? I don't have any savings and I need to do something.'

Pat scratched her snowy head then her eyes lit up.

'Hair accessories!' she cried. 'You make such lovely ones. You should sell them. I bet you'd have lots of takers.'

It had never occurred to Liz before and she wasn't sure. Where would she even begin? She'd never thought about setting up on her own and would there be any money in it?

However, she did still have lots of bits and bobs that she'd collected down the years for making her own hair accessories and she could always buy more from the market. It was worth looking into, anyway, when she got home.

'You should speak to Barbara as well,' Pat added. 'She'll get going with the fundraising, she's full of ideas and knows loads of people.'

Before Liz knew it, Barbara had indeed stepped in and taken it upon herself to become Chief Fundraiser. She called a meeting in the pub, for which practically the whole of Tremarnock turned out, and explained that it was all hands on deck and they'd have to move fast.

Tony Cutt offered his PR services and immediately set up a fundraising page through a well-known children's charity. Felipe, who was very artistic, designed posters and leaflets, and Jean and Tom, along with Jenny Lambert, her husband, two teenage children and a large group of their friends, went round neighbouring villages putting notices on cars, in letter boxes and asking people to stick posters in their windows.

Pat's friend Elaine from Saltash got her Plymouth friend to organise another large contingent to leaflet homes in the city, making sure that each street was covered, no house missed out. Meanwhile, Tony arranged interviews with local radio, TV stations and newspapers.

Liz, who hated being the centre of attention, would never have believed how familiar she'd become in a short space of time with speaking to journalists and was grateful for the acting skills, so long dormant, that she'd picked up from her mother all those years ago. She found, when the need arose, that she could disguise her shyness behind a mask of confidence and get her message across without stumbling. It was amazing what you could do when you had to.

The local Methodist vicar held an auction, which raised £1,000; Barbara had a rock night at the pub, which pulled in another £1,500; and Ruby and Victor Dodd, who were into classical music, arranged a series of concerts. Soon, donations were pouring in from complete strangers, including a professional footballer who read about Rosie and gave £2,000. He also tweeted a picture of her to his thousands of followers, with a message explaining how desperately ill she was. The response was incredible and soon Liz had forty thousand pounds in the bank. She couldn't believe it.

At the same time, Hannah got in touch to say that she, Kasia and Jo had been bullying everyone they knew at the office and elsewhere and they'd put their hands in their pockets to the tune of £2,500.

Charlotte Pennyfeather's husband, Todd, alerted all his City colleagues, who immediately signed up for a twenty-five-mile sponsored bike ride and between them raised an astonishing £30,000.

Rick Kane planned a 'walking on coals' event in the market

square, which pulled in another £900. Ryan and Nathan managed to put aside their differences and did a triathlon together, and Loveday set up a stall selling cakes that she'd made herself, which was remarkable given that Liz knew she mostly lived off takeaways and had probably never baked a cake in her entire life.

She handed over the £70 she'd made, in pounds and coppers, with a flourish. 'Ta da! Who'd have thought anyone would want to buy anything I'd cooked!'

Liz had tears in her eyes as she gave Loveday a huge hug.

'Aww,' said the girl, 'it was nothing.'

But it was.

In the meantime, Liz had discovered an international website, a bit like an online market, where you could sell handmade goods. She wasn't convinced that anyone would really want to buy her hair accessories but it was worth a try, so in every spare moment, especially the evenings after Rosie was asleep, she set about making batches of dolly-bow bands, butterfly clips, bandanas and wedding tiaras with little rhine-stone flowers, pearls or vintage-style roses.

Using the old laptop and following the instructions on the website carefully, she launched her own virtual 'stall' calling herself RosieCraft, and was amazed when the first orders started coming through from women all over the world who said they loved her unique style. Strangely, Japanese girls seemed especially keen. After two weeks, Liz felt confident enough to expand her repertoire to include seventies-style crocheted bands and scrunchies, and teeny versions of every-thing for babies and children.

The amounts that she was paid were small but anything was better than nothing. If only she had more time she thought that she could even turn it into quite a lucrative little business.

The next surprise came from Robert, along with Jesse, Josh and Alex, plus the new washer-upper and general jack of all trades, Callum. It was Barbara who tipped Liz off. At Robert's suggestion, apparently, they'd come up with a plan to do a sponsored skydive near Perranporth in July.

'I've always had a terror of heights,' Robert wrote in the publicity note that he emailed to every single person he knew, 'so please give generously.'

Liz remembered how he'd stood at the bottom of that ladder in the flat above the restaurant when the skylight was leaking, gripping the sides until his knuckles turned white. And how, embarrassed, he'd asked her not to tell the boys downstairs because they'd have made a mockery of him.

She hadn't seen or spoken to him since she'd phoned to say that she wouldn't be returning to A Winkle In Time, and now she felt ashamed of herself. She'd been so busy dwelling on her own problems that she hadn't given his feelings a thought, yet despite her rudeness, he'd seized on the very worst activity that he could think of in order to raise funds for her daughter. She decided that she was the most selfish person imaginable and he was the least. She didn't deserve his kindness.

Humbled, she left Rosie watching TV with Pat and set out immediately for the restaurant. It was after five and she imagined that she'd find him there as usual. It was now four and a half months since she'd handed in her notice, but little seemed to have changed as she pushed open the heavy wooden door and stepped into the main dining area.

The radio was on in the kitchen and she could hear bottles clanking in the backyard. She poked her head round the kitchen door to find the new boy, Callum, washing vegetables, while Jesse was up to his elbows in fish guts and Josh was putting something in the oven.

'Hey!' Jesse grinned when he spotted her. 'Long time no see!'

It was mid-June and the weather hadn't been particularly good, but still his tan was coming along nicely and his hair had turned from its customary winter dark blond to almost white.

Liz explained that she'd heard about their sponsored events and thanked them wholeheartedly. They wanted to know how Rosie was and she filled them in.

'What about you?' Jesse asked, frowning. Liz suspected that she must be looking pretty dreadful by the expression on his face.

'Quite tired,' she replied, which was an understatement. 'I'm just so overwhelmed by all the support, you know? It's incredible.'

Josh scratched his chin. 'Yeah, well, we all want Rosie to get better, don't we, Jess?'

Jesse nodded. 'Loveday's going to organise another cake sale when we do the skydive. She doesn't half make good brownies!'

Liz smiled. He sounded positively admiring; perhaps those two were talking again.

Just then Robert walked into the kitchen and stopped short when he saw Liz. 'Oh!'

He seemed to fill the room – she'd forgotten how tall he was – but his hazel eyes were wide open and uncertain, so that he looked very young, like a little boy almost. She had a peculiar urge to rush over and embrace him.

'I – I wanted to thank you,' she stumbled, feeling herself redden, 'for the fundraising. Words can't express how grateful I am.'

Robert swung his long arms backwards and forwards in a most peculiar fashion and rocked on his feet.

'Um...' he started to say.

Liz was aware of the others watching, which only made her more self-conscious.

She took a deep breath. 'I think you're very brave,' she blurted. 'I'm going to come and watch – that is, if you don't mind?' she added quickly.

It was the least she could do. It would be too far for Rosie to travel but Pat would help out. It would be the longest that Liz had left her daughter but she'd understand. She'd want her mother to go.

Robert's eyes lit up.

'Would you? Will you?'

He clamped his arms over his chest as if to stem the flow of words and stared hard at his feet. 'I mean, that would be nice.'

Jesse came to their rescue: 'Great idea, Liz.' Was he laughing at her? She didn't dare look at him. 'Robert could do with some support, couldn't you, guv?'

He mumbled something unintelligible.

'Can't say I'm scared of heights myself,' Jesse went on, 'but I'm crapping myself at the thought of landing. I'm gonna fall right into a big fat cowpat, I just know I am. Or a dog turd – that'd be even worse.'

Liz and Josh laughed, which eased the tension somewhat, and when she sneaked a peek at Robert she could see that even he had a small smile.

'See you in a couple of weeks then,' she said, wishing with all her heart that his incredibly brave effort was in aid of something else – a new village hall, perhaps, or social trips for the elderly – because then Rosie wouldn't be ill at all, she'd be cheering him on and coming up with her own ideas, no doubt, of how to raise money herself.

But that's why it was so amazing, wasn't it? That he'd dreamed up this whole scheme for Rosie because he really cared.

She remembered a poem her mother used to quote:

Life is mostly froth and bubbles,
Two things stand like stone,
Kindness in another's trouble,
Courage in your own.

Well, as far as Liz was concerned, Robert's fundraising skydive showed kindness and courage aplenty, and more than that, she thought, it proved that whatever anyone might think to the contrary, his heart was made of solid gold.

Rosie was getting weaker and Liz's anxiety grew as each day passed. She now accompanied her daughter wherever she went, even to the loo, walking one or two steps behind like a faithful dog because her daughter was liable to stumble and fall.

She was so weak and listless that sometimes Liz feared she'd go to bed and never wake up, so she'd taken to sleeping beside her at night, stroking her hair and singing to her until she dropped off.

Once she was sure that she'd gone, she'd tiptoe out to make hair accessories and return when she was too tired to do any more. Usually, despite exhaustion, she'd lie there for hours, listening to make sure that her daughter was still breathing, until at last she'd succumb to unconsciousness herself, so worn out that she couldn't struggle against it any longer.

Worry didn't come close to describing how she felt. It seemed as if she, too, were teetering on the brink, overlooking a precipice. If something happened to Rosie, she was sure that she couldn't go on. Her own heart would simply stop, which sounded in some ways like a welcome release. Then she'd pull herself up short, reminding herself that Rosie had a life-and-death battle on her hands and for her sake she must fight with every ounce of strength that she possessed.

Tests showed that although the tumour was stable for now, it was pressing on nerves and tissues causing numerous problems and Rosie was far too unwell to go to school. The consultant warned Liz that unless they started treatment soon, there was the possibility of irreversible damage.

'Just give me one more week,' Liz begged, 'then I'll make a decision, I promise.'

It was terrifying, but then so was the prospect of conventional radiotherapy. She felt caught between a rock and a hard place, her only hope the proton therapy that the NHS wouldn't pay for.

Rosie's fund now stood at an incredible £93,000, thanks to further huge efforts from the villagers, RosieCraft money, donations from charities and total strangers, plus a cheque for £5,000 from her father and £1,000 from Greg. Liz insisted on replying to every single letter that she received – including from the pensioners who sent cheques for £5.50 or £10, and the eight-year-old from Newquay who'd saved her pocket money for ten weeks on the trot and handed over a magnificent £50.

The overall figure was a major achievement, but it wasn't enough. There was still Robert's event to go, but it seemed unlikely that he and the boys would be able to raise more than a few hundred. Then Tony Cutt delivered another timely boost when he managed to get a piece in one of the national tabloids, with a link to Rosie's fundraising page. More cash poured in and Liz began to dare hope that the impossible might actually happen.

*

The morning of the grand skydiving event arrived and she left Rosie with Pat and wandered down early to the restaurant, where the boys were meeting, to see them off. Robert had put a poster in the window stating that they were closed for the whole of Saturday and giving the reason why. There was a photo of Rosie and information on how to donate, in case any passers-by were interested. No one wanted to miss a single opportunity to make a few extra pounds.

Jesse, Josh, Callum and Alex looked in fine spirits, laughing and joking with the onlookers gathered on the pavement in front of A Winkle In Time. Only Robert hung back, quietly putting supplies into the boot of his car which was parked right outside: water, sandwiches, protein bars, though he didn't look as if he could stomach anything.

Liz noticed that his face was very pale, almost green, and there was a tightness round his eyes and mouth and he was swallowing a lot – she could see his Adam's apple moving up and down.

'Let's hope the parachutes work!' Tony shouted.

'We'll be watching you two and a half miles up, freefalling at a hundred and twenty miles an hour,' Loveday joked, grinning at Jesse.

Liz would have liked to gag them both.

She noticed Jesse wink at the younger girl before her attention swung back to Robert, who looked as if he were about to bolt at any moment.

'You can do it,' she whispered when no one was watching, touching him lightly on the arm. 'I know you can.'

He gave a small, tense smile before telling the others that it was time to go.

'I'll see you there,' Liz added.

Robert opened the passenger door and the others

clambered in, wearing tracksuit bottoms, trainers and T-shirts – all the equipment would be provided on arrival. Then, without more ado, off they went to cries of 'Good luck!' and 'See you when you come back down to earth!'

Liz's heart fluttered as she thought of poor Robert standing by the open door of the plane, the noise of the engines and the wind raging in his ears, with only the outline of distant fields below. No doubt he'd be willing himself against all his better instincts to fall forwards into the clouds. She hoped that he wouldn't have a panic attack – or worse. She felt almost as frightened as if she were having to do it herself.

When she returned to the cottage, she found that she couldn't focus on anything. Rosie was moaning and uncomfortable, so Liz suggested a little outing in Eeyore to blow away the cobwebs.

It was about an hour and a quarter to Perranporth, where the boys were jumping, and Barbara had offered to drive Liz, Jean and Tom. The boys wouldn't actually go up in the plane until the afternoon when they'd completed their training session and been kitted up, and for this reason most of the spectators had agreed not to leave home until half past eleven, arriving just in time for a picnic lunch.

In truth, Liz hoped that a drive with Rosie first would take her own mind off things too, but no sooner had they left Tremarnock than the little girl started complaining of a headache and insisted on going home. Back they went, only for her to say that she wanted a hot chocolate at Peggy's Parlour, so they set off again. When they arrived, though, there wasn't a free table and Rosie, pale as a ghost, didn't feel up to waiting.

'I don't really want hot chocolate anyway,' she said miserably. 'I feel sick.'

Liz felt an increasingly familiar stab of fear. Even hot chocolate was no longer a treat, a sure sign that her daughter was deteriorating.

She trusted Pat not to leave Rosie unattended for a single moment and to call if she had the slightest worry, but still the prospect of several hours away was unnerving. When she finally said goodbye, she was in such a state of fretfulness, what with leaving her daughter and the prospect of Robert's skydive, that she nearly fell over the doorstep and landed flat on her face.

'Mind yourself,' Barbara said anxiously, standing by her car with the engine running. 'You're not the one who's supposed to go flying, you know.'

'I feel as if I am,' Liz muttered.

She tried to chat on the journey but her mind kept flitting from Robert to Rosie and back again. How was he feeling now? Would he be able to go through with it? What if he just couldn't? He'd feel so bad – ashamed and embarrassed. It would be hard, if not impossible, to try to convince him that no one would think less of him for it, least of all Liz.

It was a cheering sight, however, as they pulled into the airfield car park, to spot a sea of familiar faces camped out on the grass a little way off, some sitting on colourful rugs munching sandwiches, others standing nearby talking in groups and drinking from thermos flasks. It was like a village outing – there must have been fifty people there, including assorted dogs and a few strangers, friends and relatives, no doubt, who'd come along for the ride.

Loveday had brought a trestle table and set up a stall selling more home-made cakes and sweets, and Liz noticed that a few people were already buying. She thought of how much money there was still to raise and wished that Loveday could charge £50 a cake rather than the fifty pence or pound that she'd be asking.

Still, though, Liz was enormously grateful and ticked herself off for being negative. Everyone was doing their absolute best and she owed it to them to put aside her gnawing anxiety and make today as fun and festive as possible.

'Wine, anyone?' she asked, producing a bottle from her cooler bag, along with a stack of plastic cups. 'I've got some fizz for when the boys land. I think they'll deserve a toast.'

Luckily, she'd brought several bottles as there were quite a few takers.

'Cheers!' they all said.

'To the Tremarnock Daredevils!' Tony added.

'What is daredevil?' Felipe, beside him, asked. His English had greatly improved, but there was still a way to go.

'Brave person, risk-taker,' Tony explained. They had the same haircut, very short at the sides and long on top, and were now wearing gold bands on their third fingers, though they'd kept the wedding very quiet. 'Put it in your notebook, darling. I'll test you on it later.'

Felipe obediently produced a book and pen from his breast pocket and wrote it down.

'It's the only way he'll remember,' Tony whispered loudly to Liz, catching Felipe's gaze and smiling affectionately. He leaned in closer and cupped a hand around his mouth. 'He has many talents but learning new vocabulary isn't one of them.'

It was a beautiful day and Liz felt her body relaxing a little as she spread out on the rug, propped up on her elbows and allowing the sun to soak through her, warming her very bones. She hadn't sat out like this for a very long time.

Barbara, who'd done so much to organise the fundraising, knew that this event was pretty much the last. No doubt more donations would trickle in, but Liz had told her that time was running out and she'd have to make a decision in the next few days as to whether or not she had enough for proton therapy. Otherwise, Rosie would have to go down the conventional treatment route after all.

For once, though, Barbara didn't mention the looming deadline. Liz guessed that she, too, wanted this to be a special, happy day. After all, the village had come together in the most amazing way and achieved miracles. That alone was cause for celebration and every single person there deserved a big pat on the back.

At last Jean shouted: 'There they are!'

Liz sprang up and watched as five distant figures made their way from the main building to the small plane waiting for them on the tarmac.

They were dressed in dark jumpsuits and carrying helmets, but she knew instantly which one was Robert because he was so much taller than the rest. Jesse, Josh, Alex and Callum turned and waved at their supporters, who waved cheerily back, but Robert's focus remained firmly on the tiny, fragile-looking aircraft ahead, waiting to whisk them up into the clouds.

She felt quite sick as she watched them climb in then start to taxi slowly down the runway before picking up speed.

'It looks awfully wobbly and insubstantial,' Barbara commented, 'like a toy plane. I hope they'll be all right.'

Liz could imagine Robert thinking exactly the same thing and secretly crossed her fingers. She'd bet that he couldn't wait for the whole ordeal to be over; she couldn't wait either.

She watched the plane for as long as possible until it disappeared into the clouds before walking over to Loveday, who was serving a woman from a different, smaller group some way off. It seemed that she was waiting for her husband to jump.

'It's his fiftieth birthday present,' the woman explained, biting into a flapjack. 'He's always wanted to do it.'

Loveday, fiddling with one of her big gold hoop earrings and checking her reflection in the woman's black sunglasses, replied, 'Has he? My boy— er, my friend Jesse's always wanted to do it too. They're bonkers, aren't they?'

The woman wiped the crumbs off her chest and laughed. 'Totally mad. What's wrong with a nice spa day, that's what I want to know? It'd probably cost a lot less, too.'

There was a whoop and Liz swung round to see what was happening. There, high up in the sky, she spotted a brightly coloured, square-shaped parachute, floating gently down to earth with two tiny people dangling on the end like toy skittles.

Liz squinted but it was impossible to tell who it was until Loveday screamed, 'It's Jesse! I can tell by his trainers!'

Liz held her breath as Jesse and his instructor approached the ground, but to her surprise and pleasure, they landed daintily on their toes, still upright. She'd imagined a messy huddle of man and parachute tangled together.

Soon after, another parachute became visible through the clouds, then another and another. One by one, Jesse, Alex, Josh and Callum took off their helmets and, after shaking hands with their tandem instructor, made their way, grinning and doing thumbs up signs, to their excited supporters.

There was no sign of Robert and Liz feared that he'd lost his nerve and decided to return on the plane. She felt her shoulders droop and a painful lump lodged in her throat. This was such a big thing for him, he'd so wanted to do it but his phobia must have got the better of him. That bullying father who'd forced him to climb the tree as a small boy when he wasn't ready had a lot to answer for.

Suddenly, Felipe yelled beside her, 'Look! There!'

Liz started. She searched the sky and her heart was in her mouth as she spotted two more small figures bob gracefully this way and that, like leaves on the wind, before descending really rather elegantly into the drop zone. It was amazing how accurate the parachutes must be and how skilled the instructors at steering, because they were just a few feet from where the others had landed.

As the tall figure started to take off his helmet, Liz kicked off her sandals and found herself running, running towards him. She didn't care who was watching and she didn't care if he was still in love with his ex-girlfriend or what he'd done to make her call the wedding off. None of it seemed to matter.

Before long she was upon him, he'd put down his helmet, opened his arms wide and in she'd charged without a second's thought.

Tears sprang to her eyes and she found herself laughing as he staggered back under the force of her spring.

'Wooah!' he said, swinging her round and round until she was dizzy. He was laughing too. 'Guess what? It wasn't even that bad. I almost enjoyed it!'

When at last they came to a halt, she looked up at him and whispered, 'You're the bravest man in the world, I think you're a hero!' If he'd just returned from the Battle of Britain she couldn't have been more proud of him.

'No I'm not,' he whispered, brushing the hair out of her eyes. He was still holding her; she never wanted him to let go. 'Rosie's the hero. Thank you for coming. I don't think I could have done it without you.'

Arm in arm they walked slowly towards the assembled group and Jean thrust a plastic beaker of bubbly into their hands.

'I hope you don't mind but I took the liberty of opening it,' she said to Liz. 'You seemed to be rather busy.'

Liz blushed but nobody noticed, or if they did, they resisted saying anything.

'Congratulations, all!' Jean cried, holding up her cup. 'Just don't ever do that again because I don't think I could stand the anxiety!'

Reluctantly, Liz broke free from Robert's arm so they could all chink cups and swig their wine.

'Well done,' she murmured to Robert, when nobody was listening. 'I bet you're glad it's over – I am.'

Robert cleared his throat. 'I can't pretend it's my favourite pastime.' Surreptitiously he reached for her hand, knitting his warm fingers through hers. She didn't try to take her hand away.

'When it was my turn to jump,' he went on quietly, 'I closed my eyes and pictured you at the bottom. Don't tell the others, but I didn't open them once all the way down!'

Chapter Twenty-Four

IT WAS, DESPITE everything, an idyllic afternoon. Liz sat next to Robert on the tartan picnic rug, their bodies just an envelope's width apart, so that she could sense the rise and fall of his breathing, the warmth of his skin so tantalisingly close to hers.

Her head was buzzing pleasantly from the fizzy wine and she liked being able to examine him out of the corner of her eye when he was talking to someone else. His jaw was square and finely defined, his nose fairly small and straight, fullish lips and his hands were beautiful. How come she hadn't noticed them properly before? Smooth backs, slim, elegant fingers, with close-cut, square nails tipped with glossy white. They looked, to her, like the hands of an artist – sensitive yet strong, too. Hands that you could rely on.

She closed her eyes and breathed in deeply, catching the faintest whiff of his soap, skin and cedar-wood aftershave.

'Penny for your thoughts,' he asked quietly, hearing her sigh. He, too, seemed more relaxed than she'd ever known, his legs stretched out in front of him, mirroring her own position.

'I was just thinking that right now I feel really happy.'

Even as she spoke, a shadow passed over her and she sighed again. 'I wish it could last. I wish Rosie wasn't ill and things could be different.'

He squeezed her shoulder. 'I know you do. But she's going to get better. You wait and see.'

Liz smiled, glad that she hadn't told him. She didn't want him to know that in less than a week's time she was going to have to call the hospital and tell them whether or not she'd raised enough for Rosie to have her treatment abroad. After all the hard work and miraculous energy and goodwill, it seemed grotesque to imagine that they might fail, but it had always been a daunting target and no one could have tried any harder.

'I wish—' she began again but he shook his head.

'Shh. Just try to enjoy the moment, the right here and now. That's all that matters. Don't think about the future. Think about the warm sun on your face, being here surrounded by the people who love you...'

Her ears pricked but she didn't say anything.

Loveday, who was sitting beside Jesse, Josh, Alex and Callum a few feet away, suddenly got up, waving a phone in the air and laughing.

'Oi! Give me that,' cried Jesse, grinning and springing up too.

'Catch me if you can,' Loveday shouted, tearing off in bare feet in the direction of the car park.

Jesse raced after her and it wasn't long before he caught up, rugby tackling her to the ground and grabbing back his mobile from her outstretched arm. Soon they were a heap on the grass, giggling and throwing mock punches.

Liz smiled. 'Seems they've got over their differences.' She nodded in their direction. 'I always thought they were made for each other.'

Robert raised his eyebrows. 'He's a brave man.'

'She's a bit of a handful,' Liz agreed, 'but her heart's in the right place.'

'Not always her head, though.'

They were silent for a moment then he scratched his chin in a way that suggested he was about to speak again.

'I'm glad you came up to the flat that time and closed the skylight.'

'Me too,' she replied, 'otherwise the rain might have made an awful mess of the carpet and the ceiling downstairs.'

He smiled. 'No, I mean, yes it might have. But I'm glad *you* came because it was the first time you'd really spoken to me.'

She was amazed. 'I thought you didn't like talking to people much. That's why I deliberately kept away.'

'I don't,' he agreed, 'but I like talking to you.'

Savouring the sensation of warmth spreading through her, she lay back happily on the rug again and closed her eyes.

When the sun finally began to sink beyond the horizon, turning the sky a breathtaking red, orange and gold, she sat up and kissed him lightly on both cheeks.

'I have to go.'

Barbara had already risen and was shaking the grass off her skirt, while Jean was putting empty plastic cups into a black bin bag.

'Thank you again – for everything,' Liz whispered.

'Don't thank me – I should be the one thanking you.'

Liz was surprised. 'Whatever for?'

He smiled once more, making the corners of his eyes crinkle in a most appealing way. 'For being you, of course.'

On Wednesday, Barbara rang.

'Guess what?' she said. 'Robert and the gang have raised £5,390 and counting!'

'Wow!' said Liz. 'That's incredible. They've done brilliantly.'

'They have,' Barbara agreed. 'The fund now stands at nearly £115,000. Surely that's enough, isn't it? They can't turn you down when you've raised this much?'

She sounded so hopeful that Liz couldn't bear to disillusion her.

'I'm sure it'll be OK.'

In truth, though, she wasn't at all convinced. She'd read about other families in similar circumstances who'd managed to raise the full amount – but then they'd had longer to fundraise. If the treatment could only wait another few weeks... But Rosie's consultant had said in no uncertain terms that it was dangerous to delay any longer – he simply couldn't allow it.

'Friday's the cut-off,' he'd warned.

So Friday it had to be.

Liz came off the phone to Barbara and strolled into the sitting room to see Rosie curled up under the pink fleecy blanket in the comfy armchair, hugging a cat slipper.

The sight of her poor little bald head, ugly blue glasses and vacant, putty-coloured face made her heart bleed. An old James Bond movie was playing but her daughter didn't seem to be paying attention, she was staring into space, her greeny-grey eyes glazed, mouth slightly open.

'Rosie darling?' Liz whispered.

The little girl came out of her daydream and blinked a few times but didn't reply.

'Darling?' Liz asked again. 'Can I get you anything?'

Rosie shook her head slowly as if she hadn't the energy for anything more vigorous and pulled her knees closer to her chest. The short sleeves of her white T-shirt were much too wide for her thin arms and her chest in that position looked almost concave.

There was a drink of orange juice and a biscuit at her feet that she hadn't touched. She had no appetite any more. Even the drawing paper and pens on the small table by her side were just as Liz had left them. It seemed as if the sparky essence of Rosie had departed, leaving nothing but a hollow shell. This wasn't a life, Liz thought, wishing that she could rip the offending tumour from her daughter's precious head with her own bare hands and transplant it in her own. This was mere existence.

A wave of guilt washed over her. Had she done the wrong thing, telling doctors to postpone conventional radiotherapy? After all, if Rosie had gone ahead with the treatment straight after chemotherapy, she'd have finished by now and the hated tumour might be gone.

Perhaps the side-effects wouldn't have been as bad as feared and even if they were, Rosie couldn't be unhappier than she was now, staring listlessly into space, finding no pleasure in anything, all her joyfulness gone. It was cruel.

And yet… surely it hadn't been wrong to seek a better solution, to move heaven and earth to get the very best? But what good had it done, all this fighting, when in the end it seemed as if she'd have to have conventional radiotherapy after all?

Liz pulled up a chair beside her daughter and stroked her cold little hand. She was pretending to watch the film but really her mind was whirring. Had she explored every single avenue? Was no stone left unturned?

'She looks like Iris,' Rosie said suddenly, pulling Liz from her reverie. She glanced at the screen and there, indeed, was a curvy woman with thick dark eye make-up and a mass of auburn hair; she was much younger than Iris but the resemblance was unmistakable.

Liz's heart missed a beat. 'You're right,' she replied, hoping that Rosie wouldn't ask again why they never saw Iris now.

Liz had grown tired of explaining that the family had moved, that it was too far to visit and so on. Rosie wasn't fooled, she knew that something had happened, and the fact that her mother wouldn't let on had only made her more curious.

'Can't Spencer come here and visit?' she asked, but it wasn't really a question because she knew the answer already.

'No, darling,' Liz said patiently. 'It's too far to drive.'

'No it's not,' Rosie replied petulantly, but she left it at that.

Liz had been trying so hard not to think of Iris and co, preferring not to stir the seething waters of her mind, but now it came to her in a flash: as far as she knew they hadn't given a penny towards Rosie's treatment. Did they never read the papers or listen to the radio or watch TV? It seemed highly unlikely. Maybe they simply weren't aware of Rosie's plight, but surely with their millions, and despite whatever wrong they seemed to imagine that Liz had committed, they'd want to help a very sick little girl to whom they'd once been so close? It was worth a try, anyway.

She rose swiftly, kissing her daughter on the top of her sad, shorn head.

'I'm just popping next door to Pat's,' she said. 'I'll only be ten minutes.'

It didn't take Pat long to phone her friend in Saltash, who rang the Devonport chum who asked her grandson to find out from his college pals where the family were now living.

'I've got it!' said Pat triumphantly, having shuffled next door to Liz and Rosie brandishing a slip of paper with an address on it. 'It's not far out of Looe, see? They're still renting because the new house isn't finished yet. Apparently the rented one used to be owned by a famous actress.'

Pat lowered her voice. 'It's supposed to be ever so grand. There's even an indoor cinema and a pavilion thing in the garden. Fancy that!'

Liz thanked Pat, checked the location on the laptop in Rosie's room and printed out the instructions.

The following morning she rose early leaving Rosie still asleep, and, as arranged, knocked on Pat's door to ask her to pop in to keep the little girl company.

'Good luck,' said Pat, as Liz waved goodbye. 'Let's hope they give you a big fat cheque – they can certainly afford it.'

'We'll see,' Liz replied, feeling a mixture of hope, determination and fear.

She remembered Iris's hurtful words about gold-diggers sniffing round her since her win, and shivered. 'A pack of vultures,' she'd called them, rather implying that Liz ranked among their number.

Never in a million years would she have imagined a few months ago that one day she'd be begging her former friend for money – she'd rather have starved first. But there again, back when Rosie was well, she'd had no notion of just how far a desperate person would go to get what they needed.

It was only half an hour by car to Looe, but it took Liz longer to locate the house, which was north of the town, high up on the cliffs at the end of a winding road that ended with a big drop – and the sea.

Fortunately for her the electronically operated security gates were wide open. If she'd pressed the buzzer she wasn't sure that she'd have been allowed in.

Her heart was beating rapidly as she switched off Eeyore's

engine and stepped out on to the gravel driveway, noticing to her left an expensive-looking silver sports car, a bright yellow Porsche and a sleek black Bentley.

In front of her was an enormous, double-fronted, H-shaped house, painted cream and with two grand, ornately rounded gables that reminded her of pictures she'd seen of the houses in Amsterdam.

The central focus was the green front door, flanked on either side by pillars with a window above, encased in the same, ornate detail as the tall gables, and two more evenly spaced on either side.

Summoning every ounce of courage that she possessed, Liz stepped up to the door and rang the bell. She was half hoping that no one would be there, but soon enough she could hear footsteps and a young woman in a pale blue overall appeared, holding a yellow duster in her hand.

A little way behind her, further up the wooden hall floor, Liz spotted a plastic red bucket with a mop propped inside and caught the unmistakable scent of bleach.

'Can I help you?' asked the woman in a foreign accent – the cleaner, presumably – and Liz told her that she'd come to see Iris.

'She's having breakfast in the morning room,' the woman explained, as if this were the most normal activity in the world.

Liz didn't know what a morning room was but it sounded very grand. 'May I come in? She's expecting me,' she added quickly. The lie slipped out so easily that it took her by surprise.

The woman led her past several arched doorways down a long corridor into a vast, airy kitchen with soft lighting and a white marble island in the middle. To the right of that, she opened the door into a smaller room with a curved, floor-length window looking out onto a raised stone sun terrace.

Beyond it, a sloping, manicured lawn ran down to a stone wall and behind that were breathtaking views of the sea.

Liz scanned the interior quickly, noticing the marble fireplace, cream patterned rug and antique chairs before her eyes fell on Iris, sitting on her own at a round, mahogany table on which was an array of breakfast cereals, a jug of orange juice, a rack of toast and assorted jars of jam and honey.

There was the scent of toast and coffee in the air, mixed with lilies from the beautiful bouquet in the centre of the table.

'Oh!'

As Iris turned, her eyes widened and the knife in her hand clattered to the china plate.

'I need to speak to you,' Liz said quickly, before the other woman had a chance to object. 'It'll only take a minute.'

Iris nodded almost imperceptibly and the cleaner vanished discreetly, leaving the two alone.

Liz sat down unasked opposite her former friend, noticing that she was dressed in an oriental patterned orange and gold silk robe. Her red hair was messy and unbrushed, as if she hadn't long been out of bed, and her face looked different somehow, sort of tired and worn. Perhaps it was just that Liz had never seen her without make-up.

'Have you heard about Rosie?' she asked. There was no point in beating about the bush. Best to be direct.

Iris, who looked as shocked as if a long-dead relative had appeared before her, didn't say a word.

'She's very ill,' Liz went on boldly, before proceeding to explain about the little girl's prospects and the proton beam therapy that she couldn't get on the NHS.

'The deadline's Friday but we still haven't raised enough. Can you help? We need more.'

Iris's body, which had been tense and rigid, relaxed a little, as if this wasn't what she'd been expecting.

'You and five thousand others,' she muttered grimly. 'Money's all anyone ever wants from me these days.'

The corners of her mouth turned down and started to twitch and Liz could swear that her former friend's eyes were filling up.

'Are you all right?' she asked, thrown off balance. Despite everything, she couldn't bear to see anyone unhappy.

The older woman sniffed and a tear rolled down her cheek.

'Not really.' She wiped the tear away with the sleeve of her robe. 'Jim's never here. If he's not down the pub getting sloshed, he's at the bookies gambling it all away or hiding out with some tart who's only after him for his cash. Darren's God knows where getting stoned with his new so-called friends. And Christie won't speak to me since I told her what I thought of that good-for-nothing sponger and woman-hater she's shacked up with. She won't even let me see Spencer.'

Liz passed her a paper napkin from the table and she wiped away another tear.

'Even Mum's not herself. Keeps saying we were better off in the flat, and her chest's really bad.

'Look at us,' Iris continued, sweeping an arm around the room's grand interior. 'We've got everything we ever wanted and it's not enough. I reckon Mum's right. We *were* better off before.' She gave a humourless laugh. 'Ironic, eh?'

Liz swallowed, thinking that all the gossip from Pat had been true; they really were in a mess.

'I'm sorry,' she said, momentarily forgetting her mission and all that had passed between them.

Iris gave an odd look which Liz couldn't interpret. 'Oh, don't be sorry for *me*.'

Without more ado, she reached for her bag, which was on the seat beside her, produced a cheque from a book and rapidly filled it in. Liz, watching, scarcely dared breathe in case she changed her mind.

'Here,' she said at last, passing the cheque over, 'I hope Rosie gets better.'

Liz looked at the amount in her hand and gasped. 'Ten thousand pounds!'

Iris waved a hand in the air to stop any outpourings of gratitude. 'Thank Camelot.' No sooner had she spoken than her mouth clamped shut, as if she regretted the words.

Liz frowned. The lottery win wasn't exactly a secret. The whole of Devon and Cornwall must know about it by now. Her heart fluttered and that now familiar stab of doubt and anxiety poked again at her intestines.

She shook the doubt away, determined to focus on priorities. The cheque was on her lap, both hands on top to keep it quite safe, and she did a mental calculation. She had £125,000 but it still wasn't enough. So near and yet so far. Could she raid a bank or shop for the final £25,000? A newsagent, maybe? How would you go about that? She was going mad.

Her mind flipped back once more to the days when she was working at Dolphin House and she'd stop by at Good Morning News to buy her weekly ticket.

'What were your lucky numbers?' she asked suddenly. The words just slipped out; she hadn't planned them.

Iris made a small noise in the back of her throat, like a seagull's cry.

Startled, Liz glanced at her former friend and saw a flicker of something cross her tired countenance. It was so quick that she almost missed it but it was definitely there for a second or two, no more, that peculiar yet unmistakable look in her eye: guilt.

Liz's stomach turned over and her mouth went dry. The vacuum cleaner started up in the distance but she scarcely registered it. The whole world seemed to telescope into this one room, so that there were just these two women left on opposite sides of the table, focused entirely on each other.

'What happened to that lottery ticket I asked you to keep for me?' she said slowly, aware of the blood swooshing in her ears. 'You remember? I was late for work and I asked you to fill in my name and address on the back? I was planning to collect it later only Rosie was rushed to hospital in London and I forgot all about it. What did you do with it? Tell me. What did you do with that ticket?'

She looked steadily at Iris and watched the light in her eyes turn from silver to a hard, granite grey.

'Tore it up,' she said rapidly, 'after the draw. You didn't win anything.'

Liz found herself focusing again on the first part of that morning about nine months ago, now crystal-clear in her memory. She was dashing, late for work, after Robert had taken her out for dinner the night before and she couldn't sleep after that kiss. She was drunk and dizzy with silly girlish excitement. Discombobulated.

Iris taking the ticket and putting it on the shelf behind her under a red cigarette lighter. It was definitely red. Promising to look after it: 'It'll be quite safe there.'

The old man coming into the shop with a mongrel dog and inspecting the chocolate bars. Her standing at the door, asking Iris to scribble down her details...

'What date was it that you won?' she pressed, still staring at the older woman, unable quite to believe her daring.

The older woman's gaze slid from Liz to the uneaten toast on her plate. She attempted to pick up the knife that had fallen but her hands were trembling so that she had to tuck them under the table out of sight.

'Can't remember,' she growled, shrugging. Her tone was defiant and her mouth set hard, but was that sweat on her forehead and upper lip? Even the air around them seemed to vibrate with agitation. 'October time, that's all I know.'

Liz's heart drum-rolled in her chest as the penny dropped and she realised something with absolute certainty – that Iris was lying. It was there in her body language, her expression. Rosie used to look like that when Liz whipped off the bedcovers to find her reading with a torch beneath the sheets. Found out. Rumbled. Plus, Liz was sure that Iris *would* remember the date. Of course she would. It was the day her life changed. It would be etched in her mind for ever.

Iris rose abruptly, pushing back her chair which made a squeaking noise on the hard floor making Liz's teeth jangle.

'Now, if you don't mind...' She sounded very grand and imperious all of a sudden. 'I have an appointment to attend to.'

'Yes,' said Liz but she wasn't concentrating, she was thinking about that ticket underneath the red cigarette lighter, the look in her former friend's eye...

The phone rang, shattering the surface tension and sending frantic ripples round the room. Iris stepped over to an elegant little desk against the wall and picked up.

'What d'you mean it bounced?' she cried, temporarily forgetting Liz and losing her cool entirely. 'There was half a million in there last time I looked.'

She pulled her robe tighter across her chest with one hand. Liz, meanwhile, pretended to study a painting on the wall of an old-fashioned little girl with a dog while her thoughts whirled hither and thither. Then she heard the other woman whisper, 'You bloody idiot.

338

'All right,' she went on, lowering her voice even further. 'I'll do it now. Yes. I can't talk, I've got someone with me.'

When she'd finished, she turned to Liz and, attempting composure once more, gave a haughty flick of her auburn hair.

'This way please,' she said, as if Liz were a saleswoman who'd come to show her samples of curtain fabric or carpet for the living room. She followed meekly, still clutching the cheque for ten thousand pounds in her hand.

When they reached the door, Iris, whose expensive-looking tan suede handbag was dangling from one arm, stopped and rootled inside, pulling out a black leather purse. Liz, who had no idea what she was doing, watched her open the clasp and pull out a thick wad of bank notes.

'Here,' said the older woman, thrusting them on her. 'Take this. It's all I've got at the minute till I go to the bank.'

And with that, she almost pushed Liz outside, closing the door so fast that a gust of wind nearly blew the notes away.

For a moment Liz couldn't move, so shocked was she by what had passed between them. Then at last, still standing on the step, she glanced down at the wad of cash in her hand and counted out the fifty-pound notes, which amounted to a further one thousand pounds.

She stared at the notes and shivered, despite the fact that it was a warm summer's day. Acid rose in her throat and she was almost overcome with an urge to tear them up one by one and watch them flutter away.

They seemed to her to be contaminated, like hush money, given not so much to help Rosie as to shut Liz up. But why? Was she imagining things?

Or had Liz really scooped the prize and Iris stolen the winning ticket?

Now that she'd put her thoughts into words at last they couldn't be brushed away. The idea seemed so huge and portentous, with so many facets, traps and hidden angles that it made Liz's brain hurt and her throat and chest tightened so that she couldn't swallow, she could hardly even breathe.

'It's all I've got at the minute', Iris had said, almost as if she expected Liz to return for more cash, like some seedy little blackmailer.

Liz's head was pounding and she felt like throwing up. She could shove the cheque and cash through the letter box and drive off. That would seem to be the easiest option somehow. Get rid of the money and, with any luck, her suspicions with it – but that seemed impossible now and, more importantly, what good would it do Rosie?

Her heart was racing and her hands shook. So anxious was she to get away from the house that she put the car in reverse by mistake and almost crashed into the black Bentley, crushing both bonnet and gleaming number plate underneath that read: JIM 1.

As she accelerated down the winding street past two or three more grand, gated mansions, she felt the piercing of a dark, horrible and unfamiliar new emotion: hate. She realised that she'd never hated anyone in her life. She disliked Greg, she'd raged at him and found him hurtful and exasperating, but more than anything she pitied him because in the end he was the one who'd lost so much: Rosie.

Liz didn't care about the money for herself, but Iris knew that Rosie was desperately ill and would surely have heard about the villagers' massive fundraising efforts. It had been all over the local papers, radio and television for weeks, after all. Even if she'd lied about the winning ticket initially, how could she possibly keep it up, knowing that ordinary people were working so hard for a little girl, her friend's daughter, who needed that cash so desperately, far more than Iris or her family ever could?

Liz reeled, causing the car to swerve to the left, feeling as if she'd been punched. Despair seeped through her, turning the world black, and she was trembling so much that she feared she might crash and had to pull into a lay-by for a few moments to calm down.

Gripped with horrible loathing, she frightened herself with mental images of what she might do to the other woman to make the wrong right. Except that it wouldn't, it couldn't. Her former friend had betrayed her in a crueller, nastier way than Liz could ever have imagined. In fact it seemed, to her, as if Iris had viciously assaulted Rosie with her own bare hands.

She started up the car again, thinking that only the comfort and safety of her daughter and Tremarnock could calm her and with every mile that she put between herself and her former friend, she was relieved to find that she began to feel a little more in control.

As she whizzed along familiar country lanes, passing hedgerows teeming with wild flowers and fields bathed in the afternoon sun, she realised that in spite of all her fears and conflicting emotions she should be grateful for one thing at least – that she wasn't in Iris's position.

How would it feel to be her right now, weighed down by the knowledge of her treachery and drowning in deceit? If hell were terror, guilt, greed and self-loathing rolled into one, then she must surely be in it.

A vision of her former friend alone in her morning room, surrounded by opulence and fine furniture, flashed before her. It seemed to Liz as if Iris had traded not only her close, loving family but her personal integrity, her pride and self-worth, her very soul for a house crammed with antiques and a drive stuffed with flash cars.

Liz had only been with her for about twenty minutes, yet it had been enough to observe that the light had been sucked from her former friend's eyes and the spark from her personality. In fact, despite the luxury of her surroundings, the gleaming kitchen, lush furnishings and glorious views, Liz would go so far as to say that Iris, with all her wealth and defiance, seemed to her to be the saddest, loneliest woman in the world.

Chapter Twenty-Five

TWENTY-FOUR THOUSAND pounds. That was all she needed. Once, it would have seemed like an impossible sum but compared with the amount that they'd already raised, it was a drop in the ocean.

And yet...

On Friday morning Liz looked out of her bedroom window at the bright blue sky and wondered how the sun dared shine today. Pulling on her dressing gown, she tiptoed in to see her daughter, who was on her side sleeping peacefully, and brushed against a soft cheek with her lips.

Rosie mumbled something in her sleep and turned over.

'I love you,' Liz whispered, thinking that her heart might break. It was best that her daughter didn't know. She trusted her mother implicitly and she, Liz, had never done anything to shake that faith. Today, though, she wasn't going to be honest, she was going to lie and say that conventional radiotherapy was the preferable option.

Time had run out and what else could she do? Go back to Iris? Go to the police? Iris would deny what she'd done; effectively, she already had. How could she, Liz, prove that her former friend had stolen the ticket? And even if the police were prepared to get involved, it would take time, which she didn't have.

Liz had done her best but in the end she'd failed her daughter, it was as simple as that, and she was going to have to live with the knowledge for the rest of her life.

She walked into the front room and picked up the phone, noticing that her hand shook as she keyed in the numbers.

The consultant, Mr Horley, was firm: 'No more delays. We start on Monday.'

Liz, defeated, was too traumatised even to cry.

The weekend passed in a blur. She tried to put thoughts of Iris behind her because she wanted Rosie to have the best possible time. On Saturday they went on a trip to the aquarium in Plymouth, followed by a shopping spree.

Rosie, weary and confused, couldn't choose between pink, purple or navy leggings so Liz said that she should have all three, and a variety of colourful tops and pyjamas and a fluffy white cat that she spotted in a shop window. She'd never been given so much at once in all her life.

'Can we afford all this?' she asked, concerned, as they were queuing at the cash till.

'Oh yes,' Liz smiled, thinking that she didn't care if she spent the whole week's benefit money, so long as there was enough left for Rosie's needs. If necessary Liz would starve, or go next door to Pat for biscuits and tea.

After shopping they went to the cinema and the following day they drove to the zoo. Rosie was tired and needed a wheelchair to get around, but she enjoyed watching the animals as well as the other children's faces as they gazed in wonder at the baboons, tigers, crocodiles and giraffes.

Liz mooted tea at McDonald's after, but by then her daughter was worn out and wanted to go home instead.

'Will the radiotherapy hurt?' she asked on the drive back.

'No,' said Liz, omitting to mention that Rosie's poor hair,

just beginning to grow back once more after chemotherapy, would start to fall out again.

When they arrived home, she walked purposefully into her bedroom carrying a pair of scissors while Rosie was soaking in the bath. She'd made up her mind about her next course of action but didn't want her daughter to see, suspecting that she'd try to dissuade her.

Liz looked at herself in the little mirror on her chest of drawers. Beneath the heavy fringe, a pair of huge brown eyes, almost too big for the pale face in which they were set, stared back. She unloosened the tie that held her ponytail in place and a cascade of long dark shiny hair tumbled down.

Taking a chunk from one side in her hand, she lifted the scissors and lopped it off; the scissors were sharp so it wasn't difficult. She let the hair fall to the ground before taking about the same amount from the other side. Chop. Chop. Another wedge tumbled to the floor.

Once she'd shortened the length all round, she set about snipping the rest close to her head and above the ears, stopping only occasionally to make sure that the sides were fairly evenly balanced. It took longer than she'd imagined because there was such a lot of hair.

Finally, when there were just about two inches left all over, she laid the scissors down and allowed herself a proper glance. It was strange being able to see her eyebrows so clearly, and the smooth flat forehead, and her eyes seemed even larger now, like giant chocolate drops with a coal-black centre. She thought that she looked like a startled bushbaby.

She ran a hand over her head, trying to get used to the peculiar new feel. She'd never had short hair before, it had never occurred to her to get it shorn. It looked odd, certainly, because it hadn't been styled. No doubt people would stare, but that's what she wanted, wasn't it? To feel like Rosie? Now at least her daughter wouldn't be so alone.

Quickly, she swept up the pile of hair, as much as she could, with a dustpan and brush – she'd vacuum later – and walked slowly to the bathroom. It had crossed her mind that she could perhaps sell the hair, she might get a few pounds for it, but she'd soon dismissed the notion, reasoning that it would take too long for the money to come through.

'Rosie?' she said, lurking round the corner of the door. 'I've got a surprise.'

Rosie let out a cry when she saw her mother. 'Oh, what have you done to your hair?'

'I've cut it,' Liz explained, 'so we look the same, like twins.'

Rosie's little face crumpled and she burst into tears, as Liz knew she would. 'You shouldn't have done that, it's horrible.'

She was inconsolable for a while, but it was better by far that the tears should happen now, rather than when her own hair fell out in wispy clumps later on. Then she'd have a companion; they'd look odd together and wear scarves that covered their heads entirely. They could even laugh about it, two waifs and strays with funny, fluffy, sticky-out crops, like puppies or baby rabbits.

Much as Liz had prayed that it never would, Monday finally arrived and the pair headed in Eeyore to hospital in Plymouth, where the radiotherapy was scheduled. Liz tried to be cheerful, chatting about more of the fun things they'd do when the treatment finished, but Rosie was quiet, lost in her own thoughts, it seemed, and in the end Liz stopped talking, too.

'Here we are,' she said, when they finally pulled into the car park.

Somehow she still couldn't quite believe that after all her

prayers and so much fundraising, when the whole Tremarnock community had pulled together to achieve nothing short of a miracle, they'd reached this point after all.

She took a few deep breaths, swallowing down a lump in her throat that had been there all weekend, and turned to her daughter in the back.

'Come on then, miss, hop out,' she said, masking the tremble in her voice with a smile. 'Let's get this over and done with.'

Her feet seemed not to want to do as they were told as they headed towards the radiotherapy department. It was almost as if dead weights were strapped to her legs and she had to will herself to keep going.

'Won't be long,' the nurse said cheerily as they sat in the waiting room, giving Liz a slightly odd glance, probably because of the scarf wrapped like a turban round her head. The nurse smiled at Rosie, who was yawning with nerves and staring silently at her feet. 'Don't look so gloomy. It's not as bad as all that, you know.'

Yes it is, Liz thought, it's a nightmare come true. But she didn't say anything, taking Rosie's cold little hands instead and rubbing them between her own to make them warm.

She was rootling in her bag to find a book to read to Rosie when she heard a loud voice.

'Are they here?' someone asked. 'I must speak to them.'

Another person mumbled a reply that Liz couldn't catch.

'She mustn't have the treatment,' the loud voice insisted. Its owner had a distinctive, gravelly London accent, quite different from the soft, rounded West Country vowels common to this part of the world.

Liz's ears pricked. She'd recognise that voice anywhere and yet it couldn't be. Her mouth went dry.

'Iris!' Rosie cried, suddenly alert.

Before Liz had a chance to speak, her daughter had sprung up and was hurrying in her funny lopsided way around the corner of the waiting room towards the reception area.

'We're here!' Rosie shouted again, oblivious to the stares from other patients and their families.

Liz got up and followed her daughter, more anxious that she'd trip and hurt herself than of what might lie beyond.

'Wait,' she commanded, but Rosie paid no attention. She seemed to have a new lease of life.

Within a few short steps Liz had rounded the corner like her daughter and stopped short. There in front of her, talking to a flustered-looking nurse behind the reception desk, was Iris, waving her arms, her face almost as red as her mass of wavy hair.

On noticing the little girl limping towards her she opened her eyes wide. 'Thank God I've found you!'

'Do you know this woman?' the nurse asked Liz, who nodded, unable to prevent Rosie from hurling herself towards the older woman whom she'd once regarded almost as family, the one she didn't have.

'I haven't seen you for *ages*,' Rosie complained, as the older woman opened her arms to catch her. 'I've missed you, why haven't you come to visit us? How's Spencer – and Gran?' She was impatient; she wanted to know everything all at once. She needed information – and explanations, because she'd never believed Liz's.

'I've missed you too,' Iris said, wrapping the little girl in an embrace, then, collecting herself, 'I need to speak to your mum.'

Liz, who'd been hanging back a little, too nervous and confused to speak, now stepped forwards to within a few feet of her former friend. The proximity made her shudder, as if she were in the presence of an evil spirit. She reached out to Rosie and pulled her firmly back, perhaps fearing that contact with the other woman would taint her.

'What is it?' she demanded, finding her voice at last. 'Why are you here?'

Iris, ignoring the nurse who was watching the scene unfolding in front of her open-mouthed, thrust a white envelope into Liz's hands.

'Here,' she said roughly. 'It's for you.'

Liz's arms remained tightly clamped around her daughter, holding her close so that she couldn't break away again. She didn't trust the other woman or anything that she had to give. She'd hoped never to see her again.

'I met Barbara,' Iris went on rapidly. 'You haven't raised enough. Rosie can have that other therapy now. Tell the doctors you're not going ahead today.'

Liz didn't know what to think but she took the envelope just the same because Iris was forcing it on her, refusing to take no for an answer. Liz didn't want to open it, though. She thought it might bite.

'That'll cover it.' The older woman nodded at the envelope. 'It's the truth,' she added, sensing Liz's scepticism, 'I swear it.'

Liz's heart was racing and her thoughts were flying this way and that. Was it true? 'Why?' were the only words that she could summon.

She'd scarcely looked at Iris but now she could see that she was exhausted, pale, with dark circles under her eyes and heavy lines like fractures that cut into the side of her nose and tracked down the length of her cheeks to her chin. Her hair was dull and tangled and her mouth, like a fresh scar, was twisting in a strange way. From the redness of her eyes it seemed that she'd been crying.

Her gaze fell on Liz, who started, shocked into rigidity by the fear in the other woman's countenance. She quickly looked away again, however, as if the heat from Liz's glance was too much to bear.

Finally Iris shook her head, struggling, it seemed, for a reply.

'It's all that's left,' she said at last. 'The rest's gone. Jim's a drinker and a gambler, see, and Darren,' she sniffed, 'I never thought he'd...' Her voice trailed off and she swallowed, as if gulping down the tears. 'Even Christie,' she went on. She shook her head again. 'Bad business. It's little Spencer I feel sorry for. He's not done anything wrong, poor little soul.' She pressed a finger in the corner of her eye before taking a deep breath and straightening up. 'You'll have enough, though, with what's there.'

She paused, while Liz wondered what was coming next, then gave a rueful half-smile. 'None of us knew what to do with it, really. We just chucked it round. Shouldn't of ever had it, see...'

Liz's ears pricked again. Was this to be a confession? She waited with bated breath.

A frown crossed the older woman's face and she winced, almost as if she were in pain. She appeared to be struggling with something, some inner turmoil, a thought, perhaps, that seemed too big for the opening through which it would have to come.

Liz wanted to ask, 'Did you take it?' She needed to know for sure, to have it confirmed. She would have helped her former friend along but before she could speak, Iris's mouth had opened and there was a sound, like a muffled cry. 'I'm sorry.'

Liz was rooted to the spot, unable to move. Words crashed around her head, as yet unformed, but she didn't get the chance to say anything because without warning, Iris turned tail.

'Wait!' Liz cried, finding her voice at last, as Iris headed swiftly down the corridor away from her. 'We need to talk. What are you going to do? Where will you go?'

But Iris didn't stop, didn't even acknowledge the question, and before long she'd disappeared into the warren of corridors that led to different departments and wards, staircases, lifts, the exit, the car park – and whatever future that lay beyond.

For a moment or two Liz just stood, staring at the empty passageway down which her former friend had walked, still seeing her there, captured for ever in her mind's eye as clearly as a digital photograph.

'Well, what a strange thing!'

Liz was jolted out of her reverie. She'd forgotten all about the nurse behind the reception desk, even about Rosie who was still in front of her, pressing into her body, Liz's own arms wrapping around her tightly.

She realised that the white envelope was still in her hand and Rosie, as if reading her mind, pulled away, leaving an empty space between them.

'Open it, Mummy,' she said. 'What's inside?'

The nurse, unable to contain her curiosity and excitement any longer, scurried round from behind the desk to see.

Slowly, Liz slid a trembling finger under the seal at the back of the envelope and pulled out a slip of paper the size of a cheque. Hardly daring to look, she turned it over and her heart stopped.

'Oh!' she said, scarcely able to take it in. There, in front of her, written in thick black ink, was the figure £350,000 and beside it the words 'Three hundred and fifty thousand pounds only.'

She showed it first to Rosie, then to the nurse, because she couldn't speak.

'Gracious!' the nurse cried, almost lost for words too.

'Isn't she that woman who won the—'

Liz shook her head to shush her; she couldn't bear to speak about it, about Iris. She wouldn't even know where to begin. All that mattered at this moment was the here and now, the cheque like a promise in her grasp.

'Does that mean I won't have radiotherapy?' Rosie piped up.

Liz felt guilty. Her daughter was confused, of course, and had a right to know what was happening.

'Yes,' she said, managing a smile. It hadn't sunk in yet, it would take a while, but time was of the essence and she couldn't afford to ponder. She straightened up and, clearing her throat, turned to the nurse. 'I need to speak to Mr Horley as soon as possible.'

The woman bustled off, her body almost twitching with excitement, thrilled that she was the one who'd happened to be on duty that morning to witness the goings-on, delighted to be the bearer of such extraordinary news. No doubt she'd be talking about it for weeks to come, analysing every sentence, each gesture, perhaps reading into them extra meanings and significances that were never even there.

Liz, meanwhile, took her daughter's hand and walked slowly back to the waiting room, her heart still pumping in her ears, her mind a mass of conflicting colours and images.

She was thinking that if this were really true, life could throw up the most unexpected twists and turns. She was wondering if she and Rosie could truly be this fortunate – or was she in the middle of some weird, psychedelic dream? She felt the cheque, firmly in her hand, rubbing it between fingers and thumb to be certain. It was definitely there, tangible. No, she wasn't imagining it.

When they sat down, waiting for their summons, Rosie rested her head against her mother's chest and asked: 'Why did she do that? Why has Iris suddenly given us all that money?'

Liz frowned, wondering for a moment what to say.

'I don't know, darling,' she replied at last. 'I suppose she must have felt that it was the right thing to do.'

Rosie, seemingly content with this explanation for now, fell silent, leaving Liz to her own reflections once more.

So, she was thinking, despite all that's happened, good has won through. She didn't care about the money for herself, she'd never wanted big houses and fast cars, designer clothes and luxury holidays. They weren't her thing. But it mattered to Rosie and that was what counted. Rosie needed it.

Her daughter would go for proton beam therapy and she'd still be the same gorgeous, precious, bright little girl as before at the end. They'd target the tumour without destroying the tissue and nerves around it. Surely, now, everything would be all right?

She smiled to herself and a warm glow spread through her body, from the top of her head to the tips of her toes, like drinking a mug of thick, creamy hot chocolate on a freezing cold day.

Maybe, just maybe, she thought, hugging her daughter close, she hadn't been completely wrong about Iris after all.

Chapter Twenty-Six

AMERICA! LAND OF the free. Home to the Statue of Liberty, Abraham Lincoln, hamburgers, cowboys, cheerleaders, big cars, big buildings – and Oklahoma City's ProCure Proton Therapy Center.

Liz and Rosie stepped off the plane and started to descend the steps, blinking in the bright August sunshine and instinctively pushing up the sleeves of their sweatshirts as the wall of heat threatened to knock them sideways.

A shimmering haze hung over the tarmac, looking as if it would be wet and sticky beneath their feet. Thirty-two degrees Celsius, the captain had said it was out here; ninety degrees Fahrenheit. Back in Tremarnock they'd been accustomed to the mid-twenties; it was going to take some getting used to.

Two weeks ago Liz had put Iris's cheque safely in the bank. Mr Horley, who'd been so adamant about starting radiotherapy immediately, had grudgingly agreed that under the circumstances, a further short delay was acceptable.

Since then, instead of preparing Rosie for secondary school at the beginning of September, buying her uniform, worrying about homework, friendships and all those things that would have been so important and seemed so trivial now, Liz had sat anxiously by the phone waiting to hear where they'd be going

– Florida or Oklahoma, or maybe the Czech Republic? It all depended on what was available.

She completed the outstanding orders for RosieCraft and closed her site down somewhat reluctantly, in a way, because it had proved such a hit. In different circumstances she thought that she'd have really enjoyed it. She'd never seen herself as a businesswoman but it had made her hugely proud to think of women walking around in creations that she'd made. It gave her a tingle of excitement that she'd never experienced in any job she'd done before.

Finally, she'd received the call from a woman called Brandy who'd sounded so friendly and reassuring that she'd instantly put Liz's mind at rest. Oklahoma it was.

'You don't need to worry about a thing,' she'd said. You could hear the smile in her voice and Liz imagined that she'd have big white teeth and a tanned face; didn't everyone in America? 'We'll take care of it all.'

She hadn't really known what to pack so she'd thrown in just about everything: jeans, jumpers, shorts, a big bundle of scarves to cover their shorn heads, Rosie's enormous art box given to her by Robert, a bundle of books, the cat slippers and the toy cat. It was a good job that they were going to be taken by ambulance to the hotel because they'd never have managed to drag their suitcases around on public transport.

'It's so hot,' Rosie complained, stripping off her outer layer to reveal a pink T-shirt underneath. She looked so pale and thin beside the chunky, animated children going down the steps in front of them, a wisp of nothing. Liz shivered despite the temperature, hoping that the enormous American portions she'd heard so much about would fatten her daughter up a bit.

She took Rosie's hand. 'It'll be cool inside the airport.' Butterflies were fluttering uncomfortably in her stomach so she could imagine how nervous Rosie must be feeling. They'd never even been to France by ferry, let alone on a long-haul flight to the US. Everything felt strange and different, even the American voices, though at least they spoke English here. Liz felt as if she had the word 'FOREIGNER' emblazoned in big red letters on her forehead.

It was such a relief to spot the welcoming faces of ProCure staff that she could have kissed them. They asked so many questions as they drove to the hotel – 'How was your flight?'; 'What's the weather like in England?'; 'I've heard of Cornwall – where is it exactly?' – that she scarcely had time to look out of the window, but Rosie sat there, silent and wide-eyed, staring at the cars whizzing by and the massive buildings that dominated the skyline.

'I can't see any cowboys,' she piped up suddenly and everyone laughed.

'Don't worry, honey,' a woman called Roberta said pleasantly, 'there aren't too many live right here in the city but we'll take you to see some for sure. D'you like horses?'

Rosie nodded.

'You can have a ride on one, then, if that appeals.'

Liz couldn't imagine how they'd fit riding in with the treatment, but Rosie seemed pleased so she didn't ask. All would be revealed in good time, she supposed. She was in their hands now.

She could scarcely believe her eyes when they arrived at the hotel and staff showed her the suite that was to be their home for the next ten weeks. As well as two bedrooms, there was a sitting room with a sofa and chairs and a giant flat-screen TV, a vast window overlooking the busy street, plus a beautiful modern bathroom and fully equipped kitchen so that they could cook their own meals; it was like a flat rather than a hotel room. There was even a fitness centre and an outdoor pool in the basement, the woman who showed them round said, and complimentary guest laundry.

So they didn't even have to do their own washing? Liz was amazed. She didn't think she could possibly ask someone else to clean her clothes, but it would be something to tell her friends back home.

Pat would laugh; Liz could imagine her face. 'Lady Muck!' she'd say. 'You'd better not get a taste for it. Next thing I know, you'll be expecting me to do your washing when you come back!'

It was Saturday when they arrived and they wouldn't be going to the hospital until Monday. They were so tired and disorientated, though, that they were quite happy to spend most of their time in the hotel. There was a free hot breakfast served daily if they wanted it, but they had to make their own lunch and supper so they did venture out once in the heat to the shopping centre opposite to buy food.

Rosie wanted cereal in case they didn't like the breakfast and was astonished by the choice.

'There are so many, I can't decide,' she wailed, so she opted for cornflakes because at least she knew what they were.

Liz said that they should buy bagels because they were 'very American'. Rosie agreed, but she wasn't too keen on the idea of smoked salmon and cream cheese, so they found the 'foreign foods' aisle and bought Marmite instead.

She was fascinated by some of the different names for things.

'Do they really call crisps "chips"?' she asked. 'And why do they say eggplant for aubergine?'

They couldn't find any butter so Rosie went up to ask one of the staff who looked puzzled.

'Oh, you mean *budder*?' she said suddenly. 'It's over there.'

Liz and Rosie decided that they'd better try to adopt a transatlantic accent or they'd never be understood.

'Tom-ay-do,' Rosie said a few times under her breath, and 'parsta', because she'd heard a mother ask her child by the spaghetti and penne section if he wanted '*parsta* with meatballs' for dinner.

Even the TV in the hotel suite was a revelation.

'There are so many channels!' Rosie exclaimed, flicking from one to another until Liz's head spun. 'How can they ever find what they want?'

Soon, she learned to take the lift by herself down to the ground floor where there were drinks and chocolate machines; in truth, she didn't really want anything to eat or drink but liked chatting to the friendly staff who quickly came to know her.

'Here's Miss Daisy!' one of them, a big black man with gleaming white teeth, would say when she turned up.

'Rosie, not Daisy,' she'd correct him and he'd laugh.

'Well, I do apologise,' he'd reply, doing a mock bow from behind the desk, 'Miss Daffodil.'

Later, she'd come back and tell Liz about their conversations.

'He seems to think I know all about the queen, like we're related or something. He thinks everyone in England lives in a palace with butlers and maids and things. I keep telling him we don't but he doesn't believe me!'

When Monday arrived, they'd caught up on some sleep and were feeling a little more acclimatised. They arrived at the gleaming, state-of-the-art Therapy Center and were introduced to Dr Chinn, who explained about the treatment before Rosie had a number of scans and tests and a Hickman line put in. Then they made a special yellow face mask, carefully moulded to the size of the tumour, which she'd need for the radiation treatment.

They were also shown the giant machine that would be used to direct the beams to the correct part of her head, and showed how she'd be strapped to a bed with the mask on her face for thirty minutes a day. After four weeks, this would increase to forty-five minutes, with Saturdays and Sundays off. She'd be alone in the room but she'd be able to listen to CDs to make the time pass more quickly, and Liz would watch on a video screen outside.

It took a week to get organised, and in the meantime they were introduced to four other families from the UK who, it turned out, were staying at the same hotel.

Rosie quickly struck up a friendship with a girl the same age called Lottie, from Birmingham, and together they helped each other through.

The treatment itself didn't hurt but there were other side-effects. More of Rosie's hair fell out and she'd go to bed at night and wake up with her pillow covered. Liz made sure to keep her own hair trimmed close to her head, but her daughter didn't seem as sad this time about her own hair loss because it was happening to Lottie and the other children, too.

Her appetite, never good at the best of times, dropped further and she felt sick, so they gave her anti-nausea tablets which helped. Liz was so proud of the way she coped with it all. She'd watch Rosie on the video screen while she was alone in the treatment room and see that little foot tapping jauntily in time to the music that she was listening to and it made her heart bleed.

Despite all the drawbacks, though, Rosie did manage to enjoy herself because of her new-found friendships, the warmth of staff and the wonderful programme of activities that they put together for the children. Sometimes it almost felt more like a holiday than a nasty course of treatment.

There was a trip to the zoo, where Rosie sat on a giant turtle and fed stingrays, an aquarium, a science museum and a rodeo, where she rode on a longhorn bull. They also went to a basketball game and a theme park, visited a fire station, where they were allowed to slide down a pole and go on a fire truck, and Rosie fell in love with a horse named Buddy that she was allowed to ride when they went to some stables.

One day, staff laid on a girls' nail-pamper party and for the first time ever, Rosie had her nails painted. She chose yellow, with tiny flowers in different colours, while Lottie opted for pink with baby stars. They couldn't stop looking at them.

'Do you think they make me look older – like a teenager?' Rosie asked her mother seriously, admiring them for the hundredth time.

'They do,' Liz replied, smiling to herself. 'Very grown up.'

The staff were super-friendly and they got to know them all by name. They even gave the children dolls, with matching hair and eye colours. Rosie called hers her twin sister and named her Rowena. She went everywhere with her and was best friends, of course, with Lottie's doll, Lola. And each Friday the children were allowed to pick a toy from the toy chest which they'd keep with them for the weekend; they really couldn't have been better looked after.

Liz had been told in England that there was a 70 per cent chance radiotherapy would work. Dr Chinn, however, gave the proton beam therapy 90 per cent. He was so upbeat and reassuring that Liz was often swept along by his optimism. She threw herself into their new lifestyle with as much enthusiasm as she could and enjoyed seeing Rosie enjoying herself. She certainly deserved it.

Even so, there were occasions when a blackness seemed to settle on Liz that she found hard to shake off. What if they were being lulled into a false sense of security? It seemed so unreal, to be out here in this foreign land, surrounded by state-of-the-art equipment and unfamiliar, smiling faces. What if this were just a dreamlike interlude and the moment they returned to Cornwall, reality would strike and they would discover that Rosie's tumour hadn't gone at all?

Remembering Iris, too, upset Liz greatly, but sometimes she simply couldn't help it. Now that she'd had time to process what had happened, she found that every so often she'd become almost paralysed with anger and disbelief. She wanted to shout from the rooftops, to punish and humiliate her former friend for what she'd done. After all, she had cheated Liz – and Rosie – out of two and a half million pounds, a life-changing amount. Surely she deserved to pay for her crime?

But if Iris were to be believed, all the money had been squandered, except for the amount that she'd given Liz. She'd said sorry and in her own clumsy way, she *had* tried to right the wrong. Rosie had got her treatment and there was no doubt that Iris had suffered, and would continue to do so for the rest of her life. Did Liz need revenge? She wasn't sure, nor was she at all convinced, if she tried to pursue the family, that she would get justice anyway.

In short, she hadn't decided what to do about the theft or the remaining cash from the win, all £200,000 of it, which was sitting in Liz's bank account, a mind-boggling sum. She needed to think very carefully, when she was back home and could find the headspace to do so, to weigh everything up.

It was in her darkest moods that she'd find herself crossing her fingers that Robert would call. He'd been ringing most days to see how they were, usually in the evenings. Liz would be surprised and delighted to hear from him at eight or nine at night, even though it was two or three in the morning in England.

He'd always ask about their day and she'd forget about Iris and focus on Rosie again, giving him a detailed description of what they'd done. She'd try to sound upbeat – no one wanted to talk to a moaning Minnie – but sometimes her fears would slip out anyway.

'I'm scared they're going to say it hasn't worked,' she'd say. 'Rosie looks so frail. What if her little body can't cope with the treatment?'

He'd never try to whitewash over her fears with silly platitudes. There'd be a pause when she could almost hear him thinking, then he'd offer something like: 'She's in the best possible hands, Liz. They won't do anything that's too much for her, but we're just going to have to wait and see.'

Just hearing his voice seemed to calm her; he had a lovely voice, intelligent, deep and soothing, and he didn't seem so shy or awkward on the end of the line. In fact, he didn't sound shy at all. She thought that she could listen to him for ever.

'I'd better go,' one or other of them would say at last with a sigh, but it would take ages to hang up because neither seemed to want to leave.

'Bye,' he'd whisper.

'See you in a few weeks,' she'd reply.

'Yes. Is Rosie sleeping?'

'Mmm. Like a baby. You need to get some sleep too.'

'I will, but I don't feel tired now.'

'Nor do I.'

Then they'd set off on a new tangent and have to go through the whole farewell rigmarole again. Sometimes they'd be on the phone for hours.

For the last two weeks of treatment, Liz really pulled herself together and was determined to make the best of things, guessing that she wasn't likely to be in Oklahoma City again any time soon. The permanent blue skies certainly helped, and even though Rosie didn't put on a pound in weight, Liz could feel that her own jeans were getting tighter and her pale face seemed to have lost its pinched quality.

She hardly ever looked at herself in the mirror but she did notice that her cheeks were no longer hollow and the dark circles under her eyes had gone. She'd forgotten to cut her hair for a few weeks, too, and it had started to grow back slowly over her forehead and ears.

'Please don't cut it again,' Rosie begged one evening. 'I want you to have long pretty hair like before.'

Liz was touched. 'All right,' she promised, 'I won't.'

Although Rosie was the undoubted hero, Liz did allow herself a little pat on the back from time to time for adapting so well to their new lifestyle in a foreign country. She'd never have believed that one day she'd be able to navigate her way around an American mall, use dollars and cents instead of pounds and pennies, chat easily to people who, though English-speaking, nevertheless had different mannerisms and ways of doing things.

She'd also struck up quite a friendship with the other English mums at the Center, especially Lottie's mother Sam, a round, smiley woman with an infectious laugh and an anarchic streak, and it was a relief to be able to talk to someone who was going through the same thing.

One day, when they were accompanying the children on an outing, Sam whispered conspiratorially, 'I've had enough of museums and this one's dead boring. Let's go for a drink!'

It was late afternoon and, after telling the Proton staff that they'd be gone an hour or so, they slipped away to a bar. Liz, feeling naughty, was intending to drink just orange juice but Sam wouldn't hear of it and ordered cocktails for them both.

'C'mon, we deserve it!' she insisted.

They sipped margaritas and laughed about the vast quantities of food they'd been eating.

'I must have gained at least half a stone,' Sam said, grabbing a roll of flab from round her middle and squeezing. 'It's all the French fries and Dunkin' Donuts. I feel like a doughnut. No one will recognise me when I get home. They'll walk right past me.'

'Don't worry, the weight will drop off when you're back in England,' Liz reassured.

Sam looked doubtful. 'With Christmas round the corner? Mince pies and mulled wine? You've got to be joking.'

Up to this point they'd mostly chatted about the children, but now Sam revealed that she had a dress shop in Birmingham which a friend was running for her while she was away.

'It was going very well until Lottie fell ill,' she explained, suddenly serious. 'After that, I couldn't think about anything else. It was like our whole lives were put on hold and the shop definitely wasn't a priority any more. I couldn't get to any of the fashion shows and I'm afraid my stock's looking distinctly tired.' She shrugged her shoulders. 'Nothing's more important than our kids, though, is it? I'd give anything to have Lottie well again.'

Liz nodded, thinking how narrow her life had become in recent months, focused entirely on making Rosie better. She mentioned the huge fundraising effort that she and the villagers had mounted and also RosieCraft, which had taken off for a while in quite an astonishing way.

'Wow! You're incredible!' Sam said, whistling in admiration.

'Raising all that cash *and* setting up a successful business at the same time.'

Liz said that it had been a case of needs must, but Sam wasn't having any of it.

'Don't be so modest,' she chided. 'Any old person couldn't just launch a business like that and make a go of it. RosieCraft sounds great,' she added enthusiastically. 'You should deffo revive it when you get home. I'll stock your accessories and advertise them on my website. I'm sure the ladies of Birmingham will love 'em.'

Liz thought that Sam was exaggerating her achievements but she glowed with pleasure all the same. She hadn't thought of relaunching RosieCraft – she hadn't been able to look beyond the end of the proton beam therapy treatment – and said that she'd have to wait and see. Even so, a seed had been planted in her mind and she realised that the idea did appeal and perhaps it would be a mistake not to capitalise on her earlier success. Maybe, if Rosie became well again, she'd consider it. But it was a big maybe.

Sam ordered two more margaritas and when the waiter returned with the drinks, he handed Liz a silver platter with a note on it.

'The gentleman over there asked me to give you this,' he said seriously.

Surprised, Liz glanced over Sam's shoulder to see two attractive young men that she hadn't noticed before grinning at her from another table. The dark one nodded at her and waved, while the other one gave him a push.

'Open it,' said Sam excitedly as soon as the waiter walked away. 'What is it?'

Liz, alarmed, couldn't imagine what it was about. Was it a message from the Center about Rosie? Perhaps they'd been gone too long. She didn't recognise the men on the other table but maybe they knew something that she didn't. Perhaps they'd been asked to send her the message telling her to return to the museum straight away.

Anxiously, she opened the slip of paper and saw a line of writing – *Hi! I'm Michael. Call me* – followed by a telephone number.

Puzzled, she showed it to Sam who glanced over at the men furtively then whooped.

'Liz! You've only gone and pulled! They're not half bad-looking either. Maybe I can have the blond one!'

As the penny dropped, Liz blushed furiously and stared down at her drink, her face and neck on fire. The cheek of it, she thought, but she was secretly flattered, she couldn't help it, even if there was no way that she'd follow it up.

Maybe the change of scene, coupled with huge American portions, were doing her some good, she thought, studiously ignoring her admirer who was talking and laughing loudly with his friend in a bid to attract her attention. She certainly felt younger and less anxious here, though she knew that the feeling wouldn't last unless there was good news about Rosie's long-term prognosis, and until she'd resolved what to do about Iris and the £200,000.

Later in the week, staff at the Center threw an early Halloween party for the children because two of them, including Rosie, would be leaving before the real thing, and they made costumes and carved faces into pumpkins. They also put together a slideshow of their stay, with photographs and explanations of all the things they'd done and pictures of the people that they'd grown close to.

Rosie swapped addresses and phone numbers with the other children and there were promises to write and visit; in fact, Lottie begged her parents to agree to take her to Cornwall sometime over Christmas if she were well enough, because she'd never been. Liz said that she'd make a bed for herself in the front room while the girls could share Rosie's room and Sam and her husband Matt could have Liz's bed.

'You can meet all my friends in Tremarnock,' Rosie said excitedly and Liz smiled, thinking that Lottie might be a little surprised to meet Pat, Jean and Tom, Barbara, Esme, Ruby and Victor, Tony and Felipe, Rick and Robert. From the way her daughter was speaking, you'd think that they were contemporaries.

'You'll love our Cornish pasties,' Rosie insisted and, when Lottie pulled a face: 'No, honestly, they're not like those yucky ones you get in service stations, they're delicious.'

A return visit to Birmingham was also mooted sometime in the New Year.

'Matt can look after the girls one afternoon and we'll have a spa session,' Sam said happily. 'I know a great one nearby and maybe we can take in a film and dinner on the way back.' She winked at Liz. 'Because we're worth it!'

Liz, thinking of the expense, said that she wasn't sure, until she remembered Iris's cheque.

'We'd love to come,' she added hastily, smiling broadly.

She could take a little of Iris's cash for a trip to Birmingham, surely? It wouldn't cost that much and she and Rosie deserved some fun. There hadn't been enough of it in their lives pre-Oklahoma.

Of course there was sobbing when it was time to say goodbye to the ProCure staff and new-found friends and even Liz found herself dissolving into tears.

'Thank you for making us so welcome. We'll never ever forget your kindness,' she said, hugging the staff one by one.

She and Rosie had bought a little present for each from the mall the day before: a fluffy koala for Brandy who loved animals; a book about William and Kate for Noreen who adored the Royal Family; a bright yellow sports vest for Dr Chinn who was a keen runner.

The farewells were so emotionally draining that Liz and Rosie were on the plane home for a good few hours before they could speak. Lost in their thoughts, they stared out of the window or dozed until finally Rosie said, 'I can't wait to see Pat, and my room, and Jean and Barbara and Esme and every-one. And Robert.'

She looked at her mother inquisitively.

'Are you looking forward to seeing Robert again, Mum?'

Liz cleared her throat. 'Yes,' she said, 'and all the others. It's nice to go away but it'll be good to be home.'

Rosie wasn't satisfied.

'But have you missed him?' she persisted. 'Robert, I mean?' She wasn't letting go, she was like a terrier.

Liz knew what she was up to but didn't want to give her the wrong idea.

'I have,' she said slowly. 'He's been incredibly kind to us both and he's very fond of you.'

'He's very fond of *you*,' Rosie said crossly, 'if only you'd see it.' She frowned and raised her voice impatiently. 'Sometimes adults can be amazingly stupid.'

Liz looked around, hoping that no one had heard, but they were lost in their books or films, or fast asleep.

'Hush,' she chided. 'That's not a nice thing to say.'

Secretly, she was thinking, oh Lord, it wouldn't do for Rosie to go imagining that there was anything more to her and Robert than friendship. Children could so easily get the wrong end of the stick.

Rosie, who hated being ticked off, lowered her head and kicked her legs, enough to be noticed but not quite enough to hit the seat in front. Then she really would be in trouble.

'You've got the wrong end of the stick,' she whispered, glancing slyly at her mother from the corner of her eye.

Sometimes, Liz thought, that child really could read her mind. It was uncanny.

She buried her nose in the in-flight magazine and pretended that she hadn't heard.

Chapter Twenty-Seven

IT WAS A homecoming like no other. Tired and dirty as they were after their journey, Liz and Rosie couldn't help but be thrilled when, on walking into their flat and switching on the light, who should they find but practically the whole of the Tremarnock community, it seemed, plus a few extras, huddled behind chairs and curtains, lurking in bedrooms, bathroom or kitchen and generally making a not very good attempt at concealing themselves.

'Welcome back!' the well-wishers cried, jumping out from their very obvious hiding places. 'We've missed you!'

Before they knew it, Rick was waving a jeroboam in the air, popping it open, sloshing champagne into plastic cups and passing them round. Much to her delight, even Rosie got one, and for once Liz turned a blind eye.

'Tell us all about it,' said a pink-cheeked Pat, whose eyes were shining very brightly. She couldn't be squiffy, surely, after just a few sips? 'Every little detail. We want to hear it all.'

Liz didn't know where to begin.

'Well we, um, I...' she began, wondering whether to start with a description of the city or the hotel suite, the ProCure staff, the proton beam therapy machine, riding the longhorn bull, Lottie and Sam and their other new friends or Rosie's amazing yellow mask.

'Give the poor woman a chance!' someone cried. It was Barbara, squished between Esme, in an extraordinary pink and black kaftan on her left, and Jenny Lambert, clutching Sally the Jack Russell, on her right. 'She looks exhausted. She's only just got back.'

At that, space was quickly made for Liz on the comfy blue armchair and she flopped down gratefully, thinking that if she didn't sit she might just fall. Rosie, who seemed to have acquired a second wind, was moving round the assembled group and hugging them one by one.

Now, for the first time, Liz noticed Hannah from the office, standing at the back and looking a million dollars in a sharp navy suit and crisp white blouse. Beside her was Kasia and a blooming Jo, who had developed a large, round pregnant tummy since they last met.

Number five, Liz thought with astonishment, reminding herself to congratulate Jo in a moment. Goodness! She was going to have her hands full. She gave a thumbs up and Jo grinned back and blew a kiss. Liz was beginning to feel a bit like royalty and would have been embarrassed were it not for so many warm, smiling faces that dispelled any potential dis-comfort.

'So what's America like?'

She turned and spotted Loveday, crouched down beside her, her kohl-rimmed eyes wide with interest. 'Are they all obese?'

Liz took a swig of champagne and laughed. 'Not *all* of them. They do eat enormous portions, though.'

'What is portion please?' Felipe piped up.

He was scrunched on the floor behind Loveday, next to Tony. They looked very snug.

'Serving, darling,' Tony replied patiently, 'or helping, a helping of food. It's in your notebook, remember?'

'Ah,' said Felipe, producing the well-thumbed book from a breast pocket and quickly scanning the pages. 'Here it is. Portion,' he repeated, frowning at the word as if he'd never seen it before in his life. 'I know that, yes.'

Liz thought of something: 'Rosie, open my suitcase, would you, and get the *you-know-what*? It should be on the top.'

The little girl hurried off to find the bag, which was still blocking the hallway where Liz had plonked it down, and returned with a big plastic carrier tied in a knot at the top.

'Open it!' she said delightedly, handing it to Pat, who fumbled with the knot and had to pass it on to Jesse to undo.

He peered inside and frowned. 'What is it?'

'American sweets,' Rosie cried. 'There's Reese's Pieces and Jelly Belly jelly beans and Hershey's Kisses chocolate candy bars. They call it candy over there,' she explained, 'not sweets. And they eat peanut butter and jam, only they call it jelly not jam. It's weird.'

Nathan, standing by the window and sporting a rakish new goatee, pulled a face. 'Sounds disgusting!'

'It's not, it's really yummy!' Rosie replied, seeming quite the culinary adventuress. Liz didn't point out that in fact her daughter had been remarkably conservative and peanut butter and jelly was one of the few new things that she'd actually deigned to try.

'Oooh,' said Jean who, Liz noticed now, had brought her charges along. One toddler was in her arms and another clinging to her skirts, while a third sat at her feet. That would explain the double buggy by the TV, then. 'Go on, let's have a taste.'

The bag was passed around and the room went quiet as chatter was replaced with appreciative sucking noises. Liz, who couldn't face any of the sweets, having eaten so many in

Oklahoma, wanted to know what had happened in Tremarnock in their absence and, between munching, Loveday filled her in on some of the gossip.

'There was a right old row outside that Valerie's house between her son Marcus and some rough-looking blokes,' she said, unwrapping a Reese's Piece and popping it in. 'Esme went to see what was happening...' she glanced at Esme, who nodded gravely, 'and they called her a fat—'

'All right,' Jean said quickly. 'Liz doesn't need to know all the details.'

Loveday frowned. 'Anyway,' she continued, sticking the sweet in her cheek which bulged like a hamster's, 'they were shouting and swearing and two of the men started pushing each other around. Charlotte Pennyfeather was passing and called the police and the men were carted off in handcuffs.'

She grinned. 'It was a right old to-do. Charlotte said if the coppers hadn't of come there'd have been a proper fight. Most exciting thing that's happened in Tremarnock for years!'

'Gracious!' said Liz.

Pat tutted. 'That boy – Marcus – he's a nasty piece of work.'

'Has he been back here since?' Liz wanted to know.

Esme shook her head. 'Valerie's put Bag End up for sale. Good thing too. She's never here anyway, spends all her time in Bath.' She sniffed and the tip of her long thin nose twitched. 'Thinks she's too good for us but the truth is, we're too good for her!'

'Hear, hear!' said Rick, pouring himself another large slug of champagne.

Everyone wanted to know how Rosie was feeling and she told them that they wouldn't know for sure whether the proton beam therapy had worked until the next MRI scan.

'It won't have obliterated the tumour.' She said 'o-blit-erated' very slowly and seemed rather pleased with herself when she'd finished, looking around for signs of approval. 'But we hope it's dormant now. That means sleeping for a long long long long time, maybe for ever.'

This time it was Pat who made an 'ooh' sigh of admiration and delight. Rosie, noting, seemed to grow a couple of inches in height.

'Dr Chinn says he's very confident,' she added proudly, 'and he's brilliant. He knows everything there is to know about brain tumours. He's a world expert.'

'Well that's splendid news!' Esme said. 'Just what we'd all been hoping for.'

'Tip-top,' said Ryan the fishmonger whose presence, Liz realised, explained the fishy odour that she'd noticed when she walked in the front door.

When they'd quietened down again, Liz mentioned the money that they'd raised collectively for Rosie's treatment and that in the end hadn't been needed. She said that it would only be fair to ask which charity they'd like to donate it to. She, of course, would favour The Brain Tumour Charity which had given her so much support, but others might have different ideas and they should put it to the vote.

She'd been obliged to tell everyone about Iris's cheque for the treatment, because otherwise they'd have wondered where the mystery cash had come from. But she hadn't gone into why her former friend had suddenly come up trumps, or mentioned the £200,000 left over.

As far as her friends were concerned, Iris had decided to give some of her lottery win away out of the kindness of her heart. She could afford it, after all. This galled Liz, but she'd kept her mouth shut because she still wasn't sure what to do.

For now, at least, Iris would have to retain her saintly status in the eyes of the community.

'Give yourself time to recover from the jetlag before we discuss the cash,' Barbara said kindly. 'It's not going to run off anywhere now, is it?'

It was pitch black outside now and Liz rose to draw the curtains. As she did so, she noticed Loveday and Jesse standing side by side. They were very close to each other, framed by the doorway, and when she looked closely she could see that Jesse had his arm around the girl, his hand resting lightly on her shoulder. They looked very content, the perfect pair.

So it was still going strong then. Liz smiled, thinking what a handsome couple they made, him with his blond curls, surfer's muscles and gleaming white teeth, her with her black hair, teeny skirts and eye-popping bust.

It was only then, as she took a second to glance out of the window and sighed with relief at the sight of the dear, funny old uneven little whitewashed cottages opposite instead of mammoth concrete tower blocks, that she realised Robert wasn't here. She'd been so pleased to see the others, so busy chatting and sharing news, that it hadn't yet registered.

Her spirits sank slightly and she told herself not to be stupid. There was plenty of time to catch up with him some other day. It was after 6 p.m., for goodness sake, and he'd be at the restaurant now, far too busy to see her. In fact, he'd be missing Loveday and Jesse. Presumably Alex and Callum were with him to help. Aidan, Barbara's son, wasn't here either. Probably manning the pub for her. It was so kind of all the others to turn up like this.

She swung round quickly. 'Loveday, Jesse, Josh, shouldn't you be at A Winkle In Time?'

Jesse glanced at his mobile.

'A few more minutes,' he said. 'Boss told us to be back by six thirty.'

She went into the kitchen to make cups of tea for anyone who fancied one; she was gasping herself. As she popped her head round her own and Rosie's bedroom door, she was touched to notice a little spray of flowers on each of their pillows and she caught a whiff of furniture polish mingled with Ryan's fishy pong. Someone had given the place a spring clean in her absence.

There was a pile of letters waiting for her on the kitchen table including one, she noticed, in Greg's handwriting. She tucked it under what looked like a bill and filled the kettle. She'd heard nothing from him while they were away, not a single email, and it could certainly wait till morning.

It was good, she thought, putting mugs on a tray and plopping a tea bag into each, to be back in her own place. Humble as it might be, it was warm and cosy and felt like home.

The suite back in Oklahoma City might have been far grander and better equipped than Dove Cottage, but nothing could replace having your own things about you and, most importantly, your dearest friends next door, round the corner, up the road or, indeed, squashed like sardines into your front room.

Despite everything, she thought, she and Rosie were incredibly blessed. For the next few months, she must focus on making her stronger and fitter, and see her back to school and settled in. Surely a spot of Cornish air would put the bloom back in her cheeks?

The next MRI was scheduled for January when they'd discover if the tumour had, indeed, stopped growing. Then, and only then, Liz could start thinking about looking for work again and getting her own life back into some sort of order.

She doubted that she could ever again do the sort of hours that she'd put in before Rosie became ill, but she might be able to get a bit of cleaning in the village if Kasia had no space for her, and even the odd shift at A Winkle In Time if she were lucky...

Of course, the tumour could grow back in one, five, or fifteen years and Rosie would need scans for the rest of her life. But Liz had long since given up on certainties; it was the here and now that seemed to matter: today, tomorrow, next week, even next month, but not next year. The truth was that every moment with her daughter was precious. She couldn't imagine worrying about academic standards at her secondary school or whether she'd make it to university, when a walk on the beach beckoned, or tea and scones at Peggy's Parlour. These were the moments that made their world go round.

The kettle had boiled and she filled each mug and put a little jug of milk on the side before carrying the tray back to the front room.

'We wondered where you were!' Loveday commented, taking the tray from Liz and passing it from one to another. 'You were that long we thought you might have fallen asleep!'

Liz laughed. 'Sorry, I got distracted by a pile of letters. I feel like I've been away for years.'

Loveday handed her a mug, the blue one with the chip on the side. 'You look done in.'

Liz took a sip and felt the warmth trickle down the back of her throat and into her tummy.

'It's lovely to be home. I thought about you all so often, you wouldn't believe it.'

'Ditto,' said Loveday, twisting a giant gold hoop earring between her fingers. 'We've been dying for you to get back.'

At last Jesse said it was time to go and he grabbed his and

Loveday's coats from the peg in the hall. Josh followed behind while Liz went ahead to open the door.

'Thank you for coming,' she said, kissing them in turn and giving Loveday an extra squeeze.

'Good choice,' she whispered under her breath, winking at the younger girl when Jesse wasn't watching. 'I should hang on to this one if I were you.'

Loveday giggled. 'Thanks, Mrs Matchmaker. So long as he minds his p's and q's, you know, I think I might.'

The air felt cold and sharp, so different from the temperature in Oklahoma City, and Liz hugged her arms around her. She was looking forward to a bath, though she suspected that she and Rosie wouldn't sleep for hours due to the time difference.

She could hear noises behind her – Pat, Jean and Barbara, Jenny and Rick, who had the loudest voice of all – and guessed that they were planning to leave now, too.

'Come and see us in the restaurant,' Loveday said, 'when you're all unpacked and settled in and everything. I wish you'd come back to work.' She stuck out her bottom lip.

Liz smiled. 'We'll see.'

Just then she spotted a dark shape out of the corner of her eye, rounding the corner of South Street and striding down the hill on very long legs in the direction of the cottage. He was very tall, this person, and in the lamplight you could see that he had messy hair and a slightly distracted air. He seemed to be in a tremendous hurry.

'It's Robert!' Rosie shouted. Liz hadn't realised that her daughter was right behind her.

Before she had time to think, she found herself racing up the hill towards the shadowy figure, panting as she did so because the slope was quite steep and she hadn't had much exercise recently; in Oklahoma City they seemed to go everywhere by car.

She carried on until she was right up close, staring up at his surprised expression, then stopped short, suddenly overcome with confusion and embarrassment. She felt her face heat up, aware that her guests were watching on the pavement, wondering what on earth she was up to. And Rosie, too. What a fool she was making of herself. She wished that the ground would swallow her up.

She was about to mutter something, an apology, a formal hello, anything to ease the awkwardness, when she noticed that his arms had opened wide and he wasn't surprised and dismayed at all – he was smiling at her, a beautiful, uncomplicated, joyful, handsome smile.

Without further hesitation, in she hurtled, aware of his arms folding tight so that he was wrapped around her like honeysuckle round a tree. She breathed in deeply, soaking up the heady man-scent of his jacket, feeling the strength of his body beneath, aware of his heart beating loud and regular within.

'I've missed you so much,' she said.

What was the point in pretending? She remembered when she'd run into his arms once before. He'd just done the skydive so it was understandable, surely, because he'd been raising money for Rosie and she was deeply grateful and he was amused by her exuberance. But now there was no excuse, was there? She'd given her game away.

'Me too,' he mumbled into her funny, short hair, giving his game away, too. 'So much, you've no idea.'

They stayed in this position for what seemed like an age, her cheek resting on his chest, his lips brushing the top of her head. It felt so right, as if that place by his heart had always been there, just waiting for her. He was standing so still that he could have been a tree himself – an oak, she thought – or a rock. Immutable.

When at last she pulled away with a sigh, she slipped instinctively into his side, his arm around her shoulder, clasping tight with his hand, her arm around his waist. Neither seemed willing to let go, as if they needed this physical contact to reassure them that the other wouldn't vanish any moment in a puff of smoke.

She'd forgotten all about her friends, even about Rosie, but she remembered now and could see them waiting at the bottom of the hill just a little way off. Rosie was holding Pat's hand, watching them intently, and Liz could swear that there was a gleam in her greeny-grey eyes that seemed to sparkle in the lamplight.

Pat was pretending to talk to Rosie but really she was focused on Liz and Robert, while one of the heavy toddlers in Jean's arms was bouncing up and down impatiently but she seemed not to have noticed. Jesse and Loveday were pushing each other playfully and Jenny Lambert had tight hold of Sally who was yapping furiously – why hadn't Liz heard? – but appeared reluctant to put the dog down. Esme, meanwhile, was beaming furiously in a way that Liz had never seen before and Rick had an arm round her waist, which she was ignoring.

What did they make of it? What would Rosie make of it? Liz used not to be one for public displays of affection, it wasn't her style. She seemed to be making a habit of it now, though.

As they approached she could swear that she heard someone cry, 'Thank God for that!' And someone else might have said, 'At last!' But she could have imagined it, of course.

Suddenly, Rosie broke away from Pat and came running in her lopsided way up the hill towards her mother. It wasn't easy for her and Liz wasn't sure for a moment whether to wait or continue walking so that her daughter had less far to come.

She was speedy, though, and before Liz knew it, Robert was hoisting the little girl in the air.

'Rosanna Broome!' he said, swinging her round and round and making her squeal with delight. 'I thought you were never coming back!'

At last, he put her down carefully and she took her place between the adults, shyly and silently slipping a hand first in her mother's and then Robert's, linking all three together. It was like this that they took the final steps back to Dove Cottage where Hannah, Kasia, Jo and all the villagers parted without a word, allowing them to step into the house.

Liz scarcely had time to turn, say goodbye and thank everyone once more for coming before Robert closed the door softly behind them. Rosie raced down the corridor to her room, and he was about to take Liz in his arms again when she thought of something and froze.

'What about your ex-fiancée?' she cried, feeling a cold hand grip her intestines and squeeze.

Robert stopped in his tracks. 'Her?' he said, surprised. 'What about her?'

A lump appeared from nowhere in Liz's throat and tears sprang in her eyes. What was it that Hannah had said? That she should be very careful of a man who was engaged years ago and who'd never been out with anyone since. 'He's never got over this woman, whoever she is. Probably never will.'

'You're still in love with her, aren't you?'

Robert bent down and took her shorn head gently between his two big hands.

'You're joking,' he said, staring into her eyes, 'aren't you?'

He was gazing at her so intently that she imagined he could see into her very soul.

'Is that what you really think?' he said at last.

His hands dropped to his sides and he sighed, a great big sigh, so that Liz wondered what was coming next. Did she really want to hear? She had to, or the doubt would always be there.

'It's true,' he said slowly, 'it did take me years to get over her.'

She swallowed. Could she bear it?

'I tried to call the wedding off months before,' he went on, 'because I knew we weren't right for each other. But she threatened to kill herself and seemed so unstable that I really thought she might go through with it.

'I was at my wits' end, I didn't know what to do, then I found out she was seeing someone else – she was pregnant with his baby – but still she refused to go. It was only when I offered her money that she finally agreed. That's all she wanted, really, you see: cash. I don't believe she ever cared for me at all, it was my bank balance she was after.'

Liz gasped, she couldn't help herself. Could anyone be so devious, especially in matters of the heart?

'So why did Loveday say that she was the one who dumped you and you were devastated?'

Robert frowned. 'I've never told anyone this before.'

He grimaced, as if speaking caused him pain.

'It didn't seem fair on the child, to tell the truth, so I put it about that it was all her decision to go because she'd met someone else. Better for that poor baby to grow up thinking its parents loved each other – at least when it was conceived.'

He shook his head sorrowfully. 'She made me doubt my

own judgement, my capacity to recognise good from bad. I'd thought I loved her, you understand, but then, when I began to see through her, I wondered how I could ever have been so blind and stupid.'

He sighed again. 'Having made such a mess of that relationship, I swore I'd steer clear of them from then on because obviously I wasn't any good at them. And I kept to my word – until I met you...'

Liz was so busy digesting the information that she couldn't talk. She felt humbled by his generosity towards both the ex-girlfriend and her child. A lesser man would surely have wanted to drag their names through the mud.

'Does that answer your question?' he asked at last, still studying her intently, but before she had time to reply, he'd taken a step forwards and his big warm hands were encasing her own.

Instinctively she raised her face towards him and he bent down so that their lips were close, so close that they were almost touching.

She went up on tiptoes and closed her eyes and the strange yet familiar scent of his skin made the hairs on the back of her neck stand on end and her head spin. Her lips parted and his soft mouth met hers while his arms snaked around her back, pulling her tight.

'I love you, Eliza Broome,' he whispered, when at last they came up for air.

She smiled, thinking that life could go badly wrong but sometimes, just sometimes, it also went incredibly right.

'I love you too,' she replied, closing her eyes and losing herself once more.

Chapter Twenty-Eight

COMING HOME WAS a huge excitement in so many ways, but Rosie's mood dipped quickly and for the first few weeks she didn't have it easy. The after-effects of the therapy made her tired, clumsy and forgetful, as Dr Chinn had warned they would, and her bad left side seemed to be weaker still.

She managed to start at her new secondary school in the neighbouring village before the Christmas holidays, but often need to be picked up early and go to bed for a few hours. Even so, Liz felt cautiously optimistic because, while Rosie knew many of the pupils including Mandy and Rachel, Kyle had thankfully gone to a different comprehensive. Moreover, the head and Rosie's class tutor seemed very keen to make the settling-in process as smooth for her as possible and were bending over backwards to be kind and thoughtful.

Little by little, Rosie's symptoms did start to improve and Liz became more hopeful about the prognosis. Robert certainly helped, too. Since that memorable first night back in Tremarnock, it seemed that all their fears and reservations had evaporated and it was clear to them both that they were meant to be together.

They'd taken it tentatively at first, not wishing to do anything that would upset Rosie and aware that they couldn't make any firm plans until they knew the outcome of her next MRI scan. Even so, Robert had started spending increasing amounts of time at Dove Cottage and had even begun to stay over.

Wrapped, spoonlike, in his arms at night, feeling his warm breath against her shoulder as they drifted lazily off to sleep, Liz thought that she'd be the happiest woman in the world if it weren't for one thing – Rosie's health. But Rosie seemed to adore having him around and Liz knew that she was thrilled for her mother, too. She could see it in her daughter's eyes every time Robert touched Liz, or whispered that he loved her when he thought that no one else could hear.

The one change that they'd made to the flat since he'd virtually taken up residence was that, at his insistence, he and Liz had gone out one Monday when the restaurant was closed and bought a new sofa.

Now, the three of them could cuddle up together in their cosy front room to watch films. He was also very good at playing board games with Rosie and helping with her homework when she was feeling well, or reading books and talking gently with her when she was poorly. It made Liz realise, despite all the support from friends, how much she'd actually shouldered on her own; caring for someone was certainly easier when there were two of you.

On the Friday that Rosie broke up from school, Lottie and her parents came to stay for two nights. Neither of the girls were feeling one hundred per cent, but their spirits lifted on seeing each other and Rosie was thrilled to show her friend around the sights of Tremarnock and to introduce her to the locals.

It was a bit of a squash in the flat – Liz and Robert slept on his blow-up bed in the front room – and the restaurant was fully booked all over the Christmas period so that he was extremely busy. Even so, he managed to join them on a few outings and he and Matt got on very well.

On the Saturday evening he insisted on treating them all to a meal at A Winkle In Time. Liz, of course, had never eaten there as a customer and didn't know how she'd feel about being served by Loveday or the new waitress, Clare. Would she feel awkward and, more to the point, would the girls resent it?

In the event, however, they treated them all like royalty, Liz included. Loveday insisted they wear some silly paper hats that she'd bought especially and called Liz 'Madam' with a cheeky grin on her face, and curtsied once or twice. The boys in the kitchen put sparklers on their desserts and Robert, who was able to sit down with them from time to time, produced a bottle of his best champagne.

'To Rosie and Lottie,' he said as they raised their glasses. 'For being so brave and beautiful.'

'Rosie and Lottie!' they chorused, as the girls shyly sipped their sparkling apple juice.

'He's a bit of a catch, isn't he?' Sam commented, when Loveday told Robert that he was needed in the kitchen and he excused himself from the gathering for a few moments. 'Gorgeous amber eyes!'

Liz smiled, feeling her heart swell with pride, love and gratitude, that she'd managed to see past his clumsy awkwardness and he through her shy defensiveness, so that they'd found one another at last. Now, she could hardly bear to be apart from him for more than a few hours. How had she ever existed without him? Her life must have been so empty and yet, back then, she'd scarcely even realised it.

Liz asked Sam what they'd be doing on Christmas Day and she mentioned that her parents were coming to stay.

'My dad's not been too well,' she explained. 'Bit of heart trouble. They've got him on some new medication, though, and it seems to be under control. I'm looking forward to spoiling them both a little now that Lottie's on the mend.'

Liz felt sad suddenly, thinking of her own dad whom she hadn't seen for months and who'd seemed not too well himself when he'd come to Tremarnock. He'd emailed her when she was in Oklahoma and been kind enough to give all that money towards Rosie's fund, which she'd returned in full after she came home, along with Pat's savings, too, but he never sounded terribly happy. It was always 'Tonya says this' and 'Tonya doesn't like that'. Or 'I have to do so-and-so for Davina.'

'What about you?' Sam asked, and Liz replied that it would be just her, Robert and Rosie, though they'd go to watch the annual village swim on Christmas morning and have a drink in The Lobster Pot afterwards as usual.

No doubt her dad, Davina and Tonya would be off to Tonya's friends or relatives again, whether he wanted it or not, she thought, which made her sadder still. It didn't seem right, somehow, that he wouldn't be here to share in her new-found joy and toast the end of his granddaughter's treatment. She'd love him to meet Robert, too; she was sure that he'd approve.

After the meal, Robert took the unusual step of asking Jesse to shut up shop, saying he'd do the accounts in the morning, and he and Matt went for a drink while Sam and Liz returned to Dove Cottage with the girls.

Once Rosie and Lottie were in bed, the women settled side by side on the sofa in the front room, their legs curled up beneath them, glasses of wine in hand, and Liz asked her friend if she could let her into a secret.

'Of course,' Sam said, surprised. 'I won't breathe a word, promise,' and she made a zipping motion across her lips.

Liz swallowed, suddenly desperate after all this time to share her anger, worries and confusion about the lottery ticket and all that had happened between her and Iris.

She knew that she could have told Robert, of course, or any of the villagers, and it had been so hard not to. The truth, though, was that she was terrified of their reactions. She imagined that they'd be up in arms on her behalf and some of them, at least, swearing vengeance, trying to persuade her to a course of action that she wasn't at all sure she wanted to take. Sam, on the other hand, was likely to be cooler and more objective.

'I had this friend...' Liz began, before launching into the story. As she spoke, Sam, normally so chatty, sat silent, moving only occasionally to change position or sip her wine. She seemed stunned and Liz herself could scarcely believe what she was saying. She felt as if she were talking about someone else.

'So, the money's gone apart from two hundred thousand pounds which is sitting in my account,' she finished at last, setting her glass on the floor beside her and taking a deep breath. It was such a relief to have unburdened herself that she wondered, now, how on earth she'd managed to stay bottled up for so long.

'I don't know what to do with it,' she went on. 'I'm thinking I should maybe give it all away, give it to charity.'

Sam's mouth dropped open.

'But why?' she cried. They were the first words that she'd uttered for a good twenty minutes. 'It's your money, for heaven's sake! It was stolen from you.'

Liz frowned. This wasn't what she'd expected, but she

valued Sam's judgement and desperately needed a second opinion.

'To be honest, it terrifies me,' Liz explained, hugging her arms around her. 'It feels like dirty, tainted money and I can hardly bear to think about it. Look what it did to Iris – it brought her nothing but back luck. It broke up our friendship and tore that whole family apart. It ruined her.'

Sam was shaking her head and Liz eyed her friend intently, willing her to understand.

'What if it happened to me?' she whispered urgently. 'What if it changed *me* beyond recognition and wrecked my family, too? I've got everything I ever wanted now. Rosie's better and Robert and I are so happy. Why risk it?'

Sam leaned forward and took Liz's hand in hers.

'It won't change you,' she said gently. Her hands were soft, warm and strangely comforting. 'You're too nice. You're not like Iris. You never could be.'

Liz started to object but Sam interrupted.

'Anyway,' she urged, 'two hundred thousand sounds like a lot, but it doesn't go that far these days. It's not two and a half million, after all, and you must think of Rosie. God forbid, but she might need more treatment sometime. Or you could use the money for university fees or a house for her – or her wedding!'

Liz smiled, she couldn't help herself. Rosie married? It seemed such an absurd idea.

'Even if you don't want the money for yourself,' Sam went on, 'you must save it for her. We're not talking about ill-gotten gains, remember, you won it fair and square. Think about it,' she urged, giving Liz's hand one more squeeze before finally letting go. 'I can understand why you don't want to punish Iris, but don't do anything you might regret.'

Liz was still brooding on Sam's words after she, Matt and

Lottie left the following afternoon, with warm invitations to visit them in Birmingham soon.

'Penny for your thoughts,' Robert said when they'd finally closed the door and settled Rosie down in front of the TV; she was exhausted after her busy weekend but it had been worth it. Lottie had put a sparkle back in her eye and made her laugh out loud, which was worth a thousand early nights and restful days.

Liz sighed. 'Oh, nothing,' she said, but Robert was having none of it.

'I know that look. Something's bothering you.'

She couldn't lie to him so she decided to tell him about her father, who had also been on her mind since the conversation with Sam in the restaurant.

'It's so sad that Dad never comes here – for Rosie and for him,' she sighed, 'because he's missed out on so much as well. I know he loves Tonya and I'm so glad he found her, he'd have been miserable on his own. But I wish sometimes that he'd stick up for himself a bit and I'm not convinced she looks after him properly. Davina runs rings around him, too.'

Robert went silent for a while, knitting his brows and scratching his unruly brown hair.

She touched his arm, sorry that she'd mentioned it. 'It's not your problem, honestly.' She knew that he'd love to fix it for her, but this one wasn't fixable, not when there was the scary Tonya to deal with. It had always been her word above everyone else's and nothing would ever change that.

The restaurant was closed as usual on Monday and, uncharacteristically, Robert said that he had business to attend to and would be gone all day.

Liz, who'd scarcely bought any presents yet, decided that this would be the ideal opportunity to pop into Plymouth on her own, leaving Rosie with Pat next door. She'd never last a whole day jostling with the Christmas shopping crowds and besides, Liz needed to find a few things for her, too.

Without anyone else to worry about, she enjoyed picking out some new clothes for Rosie, plus a smart shirt and various edible items for the ever-ravenous Robert, a china figurine for Pat's expanding collection and a little something for Jean and Barbara. She saw an outrageously teeny, shiny black miniskirt in a shop window and couldn't resist that for Loveday, too, along with a pair of giant-sized, silver spangled hoop earrings and some black polka dot tights.

Robert called after her return at about 4 p.m. and said that he wouldn't be back till very late.

'Whatever are you doing?' she asked, munching on a piece of walnut cake that she'd picked up in a patisserie on her way home, one slice each for him, her, Rosie and Pat. 'You haven't even told me where you are.'

'Oh, just meetings about the restaurant, you know,' Robert said rather mysteriously, she thought. 'Going on longer than I expected. Awful bore.'

Just then Rosie interrupted, wanting some help with a crocheted collar that she was making for Jenny's Jack Russell, so Liz didn't press. She wasn't convinced that the collar was entirely practical, but it was the thought that counted.

'Don't wait up,' he insisted, before saying goodbye.

It was Christmas Eve the following day and Liz was so busy preparing the food and wrapping presents, while Robert was run off his feet at A Winkle In Time, that she forgot all about his expedition.

He popped home between the lunchtime and evening shifts and had a shower and changed, emerging in a fresh pale blue and white striped shirt, rolled up at the sleeves, and sand-coloured chinos.

'I haven't seen those before. You look gorgeous!' Liz commented. She was in her bedroom, sorting through a pile of ironed clothes, and stood back to admire him. His hair was damp from the shower and the slim-fitting shirt showed off his lean, fit body and broad shoulders.

'Bought them yesterday,' he replied shyly. 'D'you like them? I thought it called for something new – our first ever Christmas together.'

'Well I haven't got anything new,' Liz retorted, 'so you'll just have to put up with one of my boring old outfits, I'm afraid.'

'Oh, you don't need anything,' Robert replied. He lowered his voice and grinned cheekily. 'I prefer you without clothes anyway.'

Just then the doorbell rang and Liz heard Rosie emerge from the front room and hurry to open up.

'Who on earth can that be?' she frowned, praying for once that it wasn't one of the neighbours calling by for a cup of tea and a chat. The worst-case scenario right now would be Esme, who could never stop talking. Liz had been hoping to grab half an hour with Robert before he had to disappear again for the evening.

There was a pause and her ears pricked, then, quite distinctly, she heard Rosie's high-pitched voice: 'Granddad!'

What was she talking about? Liz, puzzled, glanced at Robert, whose face had broken into the widest smile that she thought she'd ever seen.

'What's going on—' she said, but before she had time to finish, Rosie had come hurtling into the bedroom followed by, of all people, Liz's father Paul, wearing a dark blue mac and carrying a heavy brown suitcase which he dumped unceremoniously on the floor.

'Hello, Eliza,' he said, glancing at her anxiously to gauge her reaction. 'I hope you don't mind, I know it's rather short notice...' He was sweating slightly and fished a handkerchief from his pocket and mopped his brow. 'I realise this might be a bit of a shock...'

She swallowed, looking so nervous that she couldn't imagine what was coming next. Had there been a disaster at home? Was he in trouble? Her thoughts whizzed round and round in ever widening circles.

'... but I've come for Christmas!'

Liz let out a gasp of surprise and delight and rushed round from the other side of the bed to fling herself into her father's arms.

He staggered slightly, unused to outward displays of affection, and patted her back awkwardly, but he was chuckling at the same time.

'Well, well,' he said. 'I think that's a yes, am I right?'

She kissed his cheek and stepped back slightly, just to make sure that this was really happening, that it wasn't an illusion and she hadn't misheard.

'All right?' she replied, seeing that he wasn't joking. 'It's fantastic!' Then she flung herself into his embrace once more and he hugged tightly back.

When at last she loosened her arms and drew away, a shadow passed through her mind. She'd been so busy rejoicing at the unexpected turn of events that she'd forgotten to ask the reasons behind it – and certainly hadn't considered the consequences.

'But what about Tonya?' she asked anxiously. 'And Davina? Won't they mind?'

The last thing she wanted was her stepmother on the phone, ranting and raving and pushing her father's blood pressure up to boiling point. Or, for that matter, to cause some permanent, terrible rift between husband and wife.

Paul shook his head and cleared his throat.

'Robert, here,' he nodded in Robert's direction as if Liz mightn't know to whom he was referring, 'he called me yesterday and took me out for a very nice lunch in Wandsworth. He put me right about a few things and said you and Rosie would like to see me and I just thought, you know – why not? I've never been here for Christmas before – we always go to Tonya's friends or relatives.

'I thought – it's about time I spent the festive season with my daughter and granddaughter for a change, especially after Rosie's treatment and all you've been through. Thank God we're out the other side of it now and everything's looking positive. It's important to be together this year. I'm sorry, I should have suggested it ages ago rather than springing it on you like this.'

He lowered his eyes. 'Tonya wasn't best pleased, as you can imagine, because we were supposed to be going to her friend Freda's along with Davina and Stefano. But when she started to argue I just told her what I was doing and packed my bag.'

And with that, he took off his coat purposefully and plonked it on Liz's bed.

'So,' he said, rubbing his hands together and, Liz thought, suddenly looking ten years younger and really rather pleased with himself, 'what can I do to help? Peel the spuds? Pour everyone a drink? I've got a bottle of rather nice wine in my suitcase, the one that Robert ordered for lunch. Hadn't had it before.' He smacked his lips. 'Found it in our local off-licence. Very good. I'm here till at least the twenty-eighth or twenty-ninth. That is, if you don't mind?'

'Mind? I'm absolutely thrilled!' Liz laughed, feeling as if

her heart might explode with happiness. 'You've made my day, you really have.'

She glanced at Robert, who was still smiling so much that she thought his cheeks might crack.

'Thank you,' she said, her eyes filling with tears of joy, not sadness. 'This really is the best present I could have wished for.'

The rest of the festive season passed in a blissful haze of laughter, hugs, silly games and quiet moments when Liz and Rosie would sit cuddling each other on the new sofa and talking quietly about the way their lives had changed in the past few months.

'We're a proper family now, aren't we, Mummy?' Rosie said a few times, as if needing confirmation that her dearest wish, the one that she'd dreamed about so many times in the past, had really come true. 'You, me, Robert, Granddad – and the others, too,' she added quickly, not wanting to exclude even absent members. 'We're not alone any more.'

Tears pricked in Liz's eyes for the umpteenth time and she squeezed her daughter tight.

'We are,' she said, 'a real, proper family – and, you know, I get the feeling that we might just be seeing a bit more of Granddad from now on, too.'

That night, when Robert slipped into bed beside her and wrapped his arms around her, she asked him what he'd said to her father to persuade him to come.

'It always seemed so impossible before because Tonya made all the plans,' she said, resting her head on his warm chest and breathing in the man-scent of his skin. 'There wasn't any room for negotiation.'

Robert stroked her hair, which was now just long enough to tuck behind her ears.

'I plied him with excellent food and wine, of course, then just told him straight that it wasn't good enough. You and Rosie needed him more than Davina and Tonya right now, as simple as that.'

Liz marvelled at his courage; she'd never have dared put it quite like that herself, but now that she and her dad were on closer terms than they had been for years, she thought that she wouldn't be afraid to stand up to Tonya any more. Perhaps, in a weird way, Tonya would even respect her for it and they could start to have a more equal relationship.

'Did you meet her?' Liz wanted to know, wondering what her stepmother would have made of this strange man turning up on her doorstep unannounced and whisking her husband away to an unknown destination.

Robert put a finger on her lips to shush her.

'Let's not bring her into it now,' he whispered, running a hand down her spine, which made her shiver with pleasure, and planting soft kisses on her forehead, her nose, her ears.

'All right,' she mumbled, rolling onto her back and closing her eyes, 'you can tell me about it tomorrow.'

'Mmm?' he said, pausing a second to look at her in the darkness. 'What did you say?' His eyes, framed by black lashes, looked very large and dreamy.

'I said you can tell me what happened with Tonya tomorrow,' she repeated.

But by then he was nuzzling her neck, her shoulders, the crooks of her elbows, her wrists and all the way back again... and she was pretty sure that he hadn't heard a word.

Chapter Twenty-Nine

'IT'S GRAPE-SIZED and it's stopped growing. It could stay like that for ever and cause no more problems.'

With these words ringing in their ears, Liz, Robert and Rosie stepped out of the hospital into the bleak January drizzle, feeling as if they were floating several feet above the ground on a cotton wool cloud made just for them.

'Does that mean I'm properly cured?' Rosie asked, eyes shining.

'As good as,' Liz replied, kissing her daughter's head, now covered in about three inches of soft, fluffy fair hair.

'Cured' was a big word and it wasn't entirely true, but she wasn't about to burst the bubble.

'My head's all better,' Rosie cried, grinning from ear to ear and hopping from one foot to another. 'I'm all well again.'

They jumped in Robert's car and drove to the main car park in the city centre, then he explained that he had something to do.

'You go for lunch,' he said, 'while I do a quick bit of shopping. I'll be about an hour.'

Rosie fancied pasta so she and Liz made their way to the Barbican, examining the menus in restaurant windows as they went. It was cold, damp and grey and folk with umbrellas were hurrying by in coats, hats, boots and scarves, no dawdling today, but the pair scarcely noticed. It was as if they inhabited their own personal, sun-soaked microcosm.

They picked a little place near the gin distillery where there was a table in the window and sat down. While Rosie perused the options, Liz sent a text to everyone she could think of to tell them the good news.

Scan EXCELLENT, she wrote. *Huge relief! Thanks for all good wishes XX*

'Mum,' said Rosie crossly, 'put your phone away! What are you going to have?'

Liz laid the mobile aside and examined the choices.

'Hmm. I think I fancy spaghetti Bolognese. What about you?'

Rosie chose lasagne then picked up her own phone, transferred it to her tricky hand and started playing a game on it, her good fingers working furiously.

'Hey,' said Liz, 'talk about double standards.'

She didn't really mind, though, she was happy to look out of the window, basking in a warm glow of contentment and reflecting that already this was turning out to be a pretty amazing New Year.

'When's the waiter coming? I'm hungry.'

Rosie's voice jogged Liz out of her daydream. She was about to signal for help, thinking that the service was rather slow, when she spotted someone rounding the corner on the opposite side of the street and heading in the direction of the harbour.

It was a young woman pushing a stroller with a little boy in it, aged about three. Liz noticed because although he was wearing a bright green waterproof coat and hood, the woman seemed inadequately dressed for the time of year in just a thin jumper and jeans. Her hair, plastered to her head, must have been soaking wet.

She was moving slowly, almost dragging her feet as if she hadn't noticed the rain, and her head was bowed, her bare fingers wrapped around the handles of the pushchair as if she needed it to hold her up. Liz felt a pang of sympathy. She looked as if she had the weight of the world on her shoulders.

It was only when they crossed the road and drew up close outside the restaurant that she could see the woman's face more clearly and she gave a start: Christie. And that must be Spencer, although the last time that Liz had seen him he hadn't been much more than a baby.

Without thinking, she jumped up and rapped on the window with her knuckles. The glass steamed up with her breath and she wiped it away. When the woman glanced up to see where the noise was coming from, her eyes opened wide with fright.

'Wait!' Liz mouthed, but Christie was already hurrying on, eager, it seemed, to get as far away as possible.

It took Liz no time to make up her mind. Recently, she'd found herself wanting news of Iris and family but, unusually, Pat had been unable to supply her with any information save that they'd gone from Looe, leaving behind a half-built house, a mass of unpaid bills and furious creditors.

'Rotten lot,' she'd muttered, shaking her snowy head. 'From down London, you know,' as if all vice stemmed from that part of the world and it wasn't at all surprising that they'd turned out bad.

'Stay here and order,' Liz commanded when Rosie started to rise with her. 'I won't be long.'

With that, she dashed from the restaurant and strode after Christie, who was now walking so fast in the middle of the road, head bowed, body pointing purposefully forwards, that Liz had to break into a jog to catch up.

'Christie!' she called several times at the top of her voice and at last Iris's daughter stopped abruptly in her tracks and turned around.

As Liz drew up alongside she gasped, because she could see now that the young woman was in a poor way. She had a black eye, which had turned a sickly shade of yellowy blue and was weeping slightly from one corner, and her upper lip was red and swollen, as if she'd been in a fight.

'What do you want?' she snapped, before Liz had time to ask how she'd hurt herself. 'I'm in a hurry, in case you hadn't noticed.'

It was a patent lie, given the slow and aimless way that she'd been walking earlier, as if she were just filling in time, disconsolate.

'I – I wanted to know how you are,' Liz stammered, knocked sideways more by Christie's appearance than by her abrupt manner. 'You, your mum and everyone. I haven't seen you.'

Christie shrugged. 'Yeah, well, not great, as you can probably see.'

Her eyes, including the bruised one, scanned this way and that as if she were checking for danger, looking for somewhere to bolt, and Spencer, cold and miserable in his pushchair, started to whine.

'If you want to gloat—'

'No!' Liz cried, horrified. 'You don't understand. Have you seen Iris?' she added quickly, sensing that she hadn't long because any second Christie might scarper, whatever Liz did to try to detain her.

The young woman shook her head slowly. 'She's in London. We don't speak any more.'

Liz felt a stab of sadness, thinking of that once close family now in tatters.

'You should go and see her,' she said gently, crossing her

400

fingers that her words wouldn't be misconstrued. 'She'll be missing you – and Spencer.'

Christie's face seemed to pucker into a thousand folds. 'Nah. She hates me, says I'm a fool for getting involved with Russell. He's my boyfriend.' She swallowed. 'Was.' She stared hard at her feet, as if to try to fix herself to the ground because otherwise the wind might blow her away. 'S'pose I am a fool.'

Liz reached out and touched her lightly on the arm but Christie flinched, as if she'd been stung, so she took a step back.

'She doesn't hate you,' she murmured, 'you're her daughter and she loves you very much. You should call her. It would make her so happy.'

Christie's eyes filled with tears which she wiped away with the corner of a grubby sleeve.

'It's too late,' she said. 'I've messed up big time, same as Darren and my dad. We all messed up.'

She frowned, suddenly angry. 'Not that you care. Why should you? I bet you're glad. Ha ha, they got their comeuppance in the end.'

Goose bumps ran up and down Liz's spine. She knew then, just as Darren and Jim must have known. Looking back, it had been written all over them that time she found them in the old flat, dismantling the exercise bike.

They all knew about the stolen ticket, even Gran, probably. It had been a family conspiracy. Whether they were aware of Iris's cheque for Rosie's treatment, though, was another matter. Perhaps not, as they weren't speaking. Maybe it was all her former friend's idea and she hadn't asked anyone for their opinion.

Liz took a deep breath. She could live her life hating them for what they'd done, but the rage and fury that she'd once experienced in great waves had subsided. What did it really matter now anyway? Rosie had received her treatment, Liz had found Robert and this was all she really cared about. Hadn't that family more than suffered for their wrongdoing?

'Can I have her address?' Liz asked suddenly. 'I want to write to her.'

Christie paused as if weighing up the words, before reaching in a black bag for an address book.

'S'pose so,' she said, riffling through the pages. 'She's at my aunt's in Croydon with Gran. Here.'

She passed over the book, open at the correct page, and Liz quickly fished a pen and a piece of paper out of her own bag and jotted down the details.

When she'd finished, Christie gripped the pushchair again and made to leave. Liz noticed that Spencer had stopped complaining and fallen asleep in the stroller and she thought how much Rosie would love to see him – and his mother, of course. She was still blissfully ignorant of all that had gone on between them. Better that way.

'Can't I buy you lunch?' she asked hopefully, but Christie said no, they had to get going. Quite where to was anybody's guess.

'Look after yourself, won't you?' Liz whispered, trying for one last time to catch the younger woman's eye. She wanted her to see the sincerity in her own, to know that she meant no harm, that she could even help, if Christie would allow it, but her gaze was fixed firmly elsewhere.

'See you around,' she said casually, as if they'd been chatting idly about the weather, or what kind of Christmases they'd had. And with that, she turned and set off again towards the harbour, leaving Liz to wonder if they'd ever meet again.

She walked slowly back to the restaurant, her mind filled with thoughts of their encounter and Christie's injuries, trying to imagine how Iris might feel, knowing that her daughter and grandson were in distress and feeling powerless to help them. It must be hellish.

Her food was already waiting on the table and Rosie ticked her off.

'Where *were* you?' she asked crossly. 'You took ages.'

Liz took her place opposite her daughter. 'Sorry.'

Fortunately, Rosie, soon tucking into a large plate of steaming lasagne, was too preoccupied to make further enquiries.

When she'd finished eating, Liz sat back and checked the time, realising that Robert had been gone well over an hour. She was about to order the bill and call him to suggest they meet back at the car park, when the door burst open and in he strolled.

'I've got something for you both,' he said with a wide smile. He was wearing a tatty waxed green jacket, he hadn't shaved, his messy hair was damp and Liz thought that he looked ridiculously handsome. He sat down next to her and she snuggled into his side while he dug something out of the opposite pocket and produced two small, exquisitely wrapped packets.

One he pushed across the table to Rosie and the other he gave to Liz. She, meanwhile, passed him the remains of her spaghetti to keep him going before he ordered his meal: 'Help yourself.' He picked up a fork and tucked in hungrily and she smiled, marvelling at how he was always ravenous, no matter how much he ate.

Rosie fingered her present, wrapped in shiny silver paper. 'What is it?' she asked, wide-eyed.

'Open it,' Robert grinned, before popping another forkful of food in his mouth. He was enjoying himself immensely.

Liz watched as her daughter undid the silky pink bow and carefully loosened the sticky tape that held the paper in place, until curiosity got the better of her and she started to rip.

She was all fingers and thumbs, quivering with excitement as the paper slid off and out dropped a sleek, navy blue box on the table. She glanced at Robert who was watching intently and he nodded, signalling to her to push the little silver clasp on the edge.

The lid sprang open and Rosie gasped. 'For me?' she asked incredulously, holding up a white-gold chain on the end of which was a tiny golden flower, just about to burst into bloom.

'A rosebud for a rose,' Robert explained, 'who'll be twelve years old soon.' Fancy that!

Now he motioned to Liz to open her parcel, which contained a white-gold heart studded with three tiny, sparkling diamonds on a delicate chain. Beside it was a pair of matching earrings.

'That's a diamond for each of us,' he said. 'Together for ever.'

'It's beautiful!' Liz gasped. 'You shouldn't have!'

But he was so delighted with his purchases and Liz's and Rosie's evident pleasure that he didn't seem to hear.

When they'd stopped admiring their gifts, he helped Liz to put her necklace on, then he leaned across the table and did the same for Rosie.

'My girls,' he said proudly, admiring them both in the jewellery that twinkled in the electric light. As warmth coursed through Liz's body, she hoped that if this were a dream, she'd never wake up. She couldn't remember ever feeling so happy.

They stayed in the restaurant for ages, while Robert ate a large portion of chicken parmigiana, then they all had pudding and coffee. Today was definitely a day to celebrate.

By the time they left, it was getting quite dark, and as soon as Robert had dropped Rosie and Liz at Dove Cottage, he had to leave for work.

'See you later,' said Liz. She hadn't yet decided what to do about the waitressing job, but when Sam, Matt and Lottie had visited at Christmas, Sam had talked to Robert and together they'd urged Liz to start RosieCraft again.

Spurred on by her friend's offer to buy a range of accessories for her shop, Liz had tentatively reopened for business on January 3rd. It was very early days but if it took off it would be a godsend, really, because she could work from home during the day and be around for Rosie in the evenings.

She thought that she'd still want to pop in to A Winkle In Time now and again, though, to catch up with the gang, and Robert had asked her to help him with an interior redesign he was planning, too. Business had been booming ever since Gretel, the restaurant critic's five-star review and money, it seemed, was no object.

'The place needs smartening up and you're so good with style and colour,' he'd said admiringly.

Liz, who'd always fancied having the time and cash to style her own home, was thrilled and she knew that Rosie would enjoy having an input, too.

'Hurry back,' she said, kissing him goodbye, reluctant to let him out of her arms. 'I get lonely without you.'

After closing the front door, she turned to Rosie.

'There's something I need to do,' she said mysteriously. 'It'll only take half an hour.'

'What?' Rosie asked, but she was dying to go next door to show Pat her new necklace and danced off without waiting for a reply.

Once she'd gone, Liz settled down at the kitchen table with a mug of tea by her side and bit the end of her pen. This wasn't going to be easy, but she'd already decided that the best solution was not to think about it too much, not to agonise. It didn't have to be perfect, after all, so long as it was from the heart.

She took a deep breath and stared for a moment at the blank sheet of white paper before commencing.

Dear Iris, she wrote,

I bumped into Christie in Plymouth today and asked for your address.

I want you to have this because I know you need it. I hope it helps and you can be happy again.

You'll be glad to know that Rosie's had her treatment in America and it seems to have been a great success. The tumour's much smaller and it's stopped growing. Doctors say it might never bother her again.

She'll have to have scans forever and we don't know exactly what the future holds, but she's so much better now and enjoying life to the max, which is the most important thing. You can imagine how much it means to me to see her well and smiling again.

I've got some other news, too. Remember Robert, my boss at the restaurant? We're getting married! He's gorgeous and Rosie loves him too.

We're in the process of buying Bag End, the cottage up the road, and the wedding's in July. Rosie can't wait because she's going to be a bridesmaid at long last! It's funny how things turn out. I never thought I'd meet anyone else, let alone get married. Just goes to show you never know what's round the corner.

Bag End is really sweet and pretty, perfect for the three of us. There's even an open fire and a spare bedroom for visitors. The great thing is that we'll only be a few doors further away from Pat, so she's delighted, and I've told Rosie that she can have a kitten as soon as we've settled in.

I'll sign off now but I wanted to say thank you for doing the right thing in the end. I know you had financial problems, you told me about them when I came to lunch that Easter Sunday, and I can imagine how tempting it must have been. I'm sure you regret what you did and there's no point beating yourself up forever. I'd like to draw a line under what happened and I hope you can too.

This might sound like a bad idea, but if you're ever in Tremarnock, Rosie and I would love to see you. We could have some laughs – just like old times – and I'd really like you to meet Robert.

Until then, look after yourself, Iris, and say hello to Gran for me.

From your friend,
Liz x

PS I told Christie to call you but she says you hate her. I said that's nonsense but I think you need to ring her first. She really wants it, she's missing you loads.
PPS Spencer's such a big handsome boy now. I can't believe how much he's grown!
PPPS Money enclosed – don't tear it up by mistake!
PPPPS I've put the rest in a special savings account for Rosie when she's older. I reckon she deserves it more than anyone.

And with that, Liz popped the letter and a cheque for twenty thousand pounds in the envelope – ten per cent of what was left of the lottery win – and sealed it firmly closed. Then she scooted down the hill with a spring in her step and a song in her heart to catch the last post before the morning.

Acknowledgments

With thanks to my very special agent, Heather Holden-Brown, and all at HHB Agency. I know how lucky I am. Also to the terrific team at Head of Zeus, especially Rosie de Courcy, who makes the editing process such a pleasure.

To the inspirational children and parents who were kind enough to share their stories with me, including Rowan Todd and Bethany Halliday, Lilly-May and Karen Anderson, Evie and Joanne Hayes and Vivi and Helen Gregory-Osborne. I learned so much from you all.

To Polly Newton and Beth Ryall, from The Brain Tumour Charity, Ginette Field, from The Pace Centre, Jackie Logue and Vicky Keeping at Scope and Dr Anna Galloway, from the paediatric and adolescent psychology department at UCLH. I couldn't have done without your invaluable contributions.

Also to my sister, Sarah Arikian, who has read all my novels in their early stages and made extremely helpful comments, to my friend, Yael Brown, for THAT chat on one of our Richmond Park runs, to Rachel Downer and Agnieszka Marchlewska from ServiceMaster, and to the inhabitants of a certain fishing village in South-East Cornwall who generously answered my questions and made me feel so welcome.